DANGER ON THE LOCH

OTHER BOOKS AND AUDIOBOOKS
BY PAIGE EDWARDS

Catherine's Intrigue

Deadly by Design

DANGER ON THE LOCH

A Pressley-Coombes Romantic Suspense

PAIGE EDWARDS

Covenant Communications, Inc.

Cover image: *Dominating the fog* © stock_colors, courtesy of istockphotography.com

Cover design by Natalie Brown

Published by Covenant Communications, Inc.
American Fork, Utah

Printed in the United States of America
First Printing: April 2021

28 27 26 25 24 23 22 21 10 9 8 7 6 5 4 3 2 1

ISBN: 978-1-52441-520-4

For
Ladd Edwards—you are my rock.
And for Traci Abramson and Ellie Whitney.

Praise for Paige Edwards

"*Danger on the Loch* grips your attention with its mix of romance and mystery to which any reader regardless of age can relate in terms of identity, family, and relationships. Castle Rannoch is a brilliant setting that breathes with a life of its own. With its stone walls, secret passages, and staircases, it exudes an air of mystery and foreboding that you want to unravel. Paige Edwards has created a mystery case worthy of someone like Sherlock Holmes to crack. The estate is a character in itself made only more haunting by the diverse characters within it. As part of the Pressley-Coombes Series, *Danger on the Loch* meets reader expectations in terms of offering high-tension suspense and feel-good romance."

—Vincent Dublado, *Readers' Favorite*

"Filled with vivid description, unique characters, and page-turning tension, *Danger on the Loch* is a perfect blend of suspense and romance. Paige Edwards's new release will thrill her many fans and garner her countless more."

—Sian Ann Bessey, award-winning author of *An Uncommon Earl*

"In *Danger on the Loch*, Paige Edwards has done a masterful job combining contemporary mystery and suspense with the United Kingdom's high society. DNA results, an unexpected meeting between father and daughter, and a blossoming romance are only a small piece of a story set in vividly-described Scotland. With stolen bank transfers, a possible traitor within the household, and a potential terrorist attack looming, expect to lose some sleep while racing to find out if James and Paisley will be able to survive long enough to find their happily ever after.

Paige Edwards just keeps getting better. *Danger on the Loch* is her best work yet."

—Traci Hunter Abramson, award-winning author of the Guardian series

"Paige Edwards delivers again. This book is the whole package: page-turning suspense, heart pounding romance, and an ending so satisfying you'll give an audible sigh as you read the last page."

—Heidi Kimball, author of *Where the Stars Meet the Sea*

"Edwards knows precisely how to blend suspense, romance, and depth of feeling in such a thrilling manner it will leave readers anxious for more."

—Esther Hatch, author of *A Proper Charade*

Acknowledgments

Special thanks to Dave Woodruff for his banking expertise. To Traci Hunter Abramson and Ellie Whitney for their encouragement during this last year when I wrestled for every word. For my critique group, Traci, Ellie, and Kyla—you ladies are such amazing writers. It's an honor to be a member of this group.

To my children, Angela, David & Carrie, and Ashley & Shawn. A mother couldn't ask for better children. To my mother- and father-in-law, Eddie and Katharine Edwards, for their constant love, support, and encouragement. And to the seventeen grands that call me Bock Bock: Connor, Nathanael, Hiram, Evie, Braden, Crew, Mariah, Cohen, Brighton, Jasmin, Zoey, Peyton, Emma, Hayden, Olive, James, and Finn.

To my editor, Ashley Gebert, who is always professional, makes my manuscripts shine, and is just a delightful human being. To Natalie Brown for the gorgeous cover that so perfectly captures both elements of this story, and to Amy Parker, my publicist and marketing guru extraordinaire. Your energy should be bottled and sold. To all the rest of the Covenant family, thank you for your dedication to clean and wholesome entertainment. I love you guys.

Most especially to my sweetheart, Ladd, who encourages and supports me on this crazy writing adventure, tromps the UK with me on a regular basis, and enjoys medieval castles almost as much as I do.

Lastly, I am forever thankful to my Heavenly Father and His Son, Jesus Christ. How I love them. They have encircled me in times of trial and raised me up on eagles' wings.

Scottish Vocabulary

4x4—SUV

Aye—Yes

Ah dinnae ken—I don't know

Awa' an bile yer heid—A term of exclamation if someone is doing something stupid and it's annoying to you

Bairn—Baby, or child

Bonnet—Hood of car

Boot—Car trunk

Burn—Stream

Cannae—Cannot

Ghillie brogues—Scottish dancing shoes

Hairy sporran—Part of male Scottish Highland dress; is a pouch that performs the same function as pockets on the pocketless kilt. Made of leather or fur

Highlands—Mountainous part of Scotland, north of Glasgow

Hillwalking—Americans' hike, New Zealanders' tromp, the British hillwalk

Ken—Know

Kissing gate—A type of gate that allows people, but not livestock, to pass through

Lad—Boy

Lass—Girl

Layby—An area at the side of a road where vehicles may pull off and stop

Lead—Leash

Loch—Lake

Mist—Fog

Munro—Mountain

Munro bagging—The activity of climbing all the listed Munros over 3,000 ft.

Och—Used to express surprise, or to emphasize agreement or disagreement with what has just been said

Primogeniture—The right of succession belonging to the firstborn child by which the whole real estate of an intestate is passed to the eldest son

Prince Charlie Jacket—A formal black-tie Highland dress jacket

Save your breath to cool your porridge—Look after your own affairs

Sgian-dubh—A short knife worn in the male stockings of traditional Scottish Highland dress

Scottish reel—Scottish country dances

Sett (Tartan)—The pattern of a tartan

Tae—To

Tartan—Plaid

Torch—Flashlight

Verges—Side shoulder of the road

Verra—Very

Wee—Small, little, young

Prologue

Sir Edmund Dalrymple, lead in Scotland's World Finance Bank investigation, tromped the overgrown path edging Loch Morar while his eyes scanned the empty shoreline for a good place to set up his fishing pole.

A sharp wind from the north stung his eyes, and he paused to readjust his scarf. The forested hills on both sides of the vast body of water showed tinges of scarlet and gold. This would likely be his last fishing expedition before winter descended on the Highlands.

Setting off again, he passed a dilapidated croft whose roof had gone, and only broken granite walls remained. Pebbles rattled on the path. Edmund turned sharply to discover the cause, but an empty trail stretched through the thicket of trees. Attributing the noise to the overpopulation of red deer that roamed the area, he moved on.

He had taken a much-needed break from the bank investigation and had driven to Mallaig to clear the cobwebs from his brain. The deeper he dug into the WFB inquest, the more he unearthed. Alarming discrepancies in account finances had come to light, reaching far beyond UK shores. He had an appointment with the First Minister of Scotland on Monday to report his findings.

After sighting a clearing along the shore, Edmund pushed through the undergrowth of saplings to reach the rocky scree beside the water's edge. Anticipation hummed through him as he set down his creel and tackle to bait his hook. He had every intention of catching his limit before he went home. The idea of frying fish for supper made his mouth water.

Another rattle of loose stones, this time much closer, accompanied by the ring of nailed boots on rock. Hair rose on Edmund's arms. He leaned to set down his pole. Before he could, a sting in his neck, like the jab of a needle, came from behind. Images blurred and spun. He flung out his arms to keep his balance, but his knees buckled, and his heart stopped before he hit the rocks.

Chapter 1

THE BUS DOORS WHOOSHED OPEN, and Paisley Clark clattered down the steps to the brick sidewalk. With a clang of gears and a puff of exhaust, the public transit vehicle lumbered toward its next stop, leaving her in the heart of the small riverfront city of Fredericksburg, Virginia.

Paisley slung her camera bag over her shoulder and started down the tree-lined street toward the restaurant where she worked. Gold and orange leaves fluttered in the late afternoon breeze and gathered in piles against the wrought-iron fence surrounding St. George's Episcopal Church and cemetery.

She slowed her steps and gazed up at the tall pointed steeple that towered above Old Town's other historic buildings. Unable to resist the green patina of the 18th-century spire, Paisley drew out her camera and attached her zoom lens.

Adjusting the aperture, Paisley then focused on the spire in an attempt to capture the glint of sunlight on the tip of the steeple. Not liking the angle, she backed into the road, her eyes set solely on her optical viewfinder.

A horn blared. Tires squealed. And a midsize SUV stopped five feet to her left.

The driver lowered his window. "Get out of the way, lady."

"Sorry." Paisley's face burned. She regained the curb and cringed when the driver shook his head at her and swerved back into traffic.

As she packed her camera away, her hand brushed against the small outdated model at the bottom of her bag. Without conscious thought, her fingers ran over the etched words on the housing, a message her father had sent to her so long ago . . . the only proof of his existence and love.

Paisley had quickly learned at a young age that the topic of her father was strictly taboo. Mom had refused to speak his name and had changed her and Paisley's surnames when Paisley was too young to remember her original one.

On her eighth birthday, a package had arrived by private courier. Since it was addressed to Paisley, she had opened it before her mother returned from work. Inside was a camera with a flash attachment and several lenses. There was no return address—not even a card.

Paisley was enchanted with her gift.

When her mother had arrived home from work and saw the present, she had been furious and had threatened to toss it out. Paisley had cried buckets and begged to keep the camera. Reluctantly, her mother had acquiesced.

Paisley found the message scratched into the plastic housing: *To Paisley. Love, Dad.* Some internal sensor had kept her from telling her mother about the message. Even at such a young age, Paisley had realized her mother had known the sender's identity, and that was what had precipitated Mom's fury.

Paisley had long since advanced to more sophisticated cameras, but that 35mm remained her most cherished possession.

By the time she reached middle school, Paisley had scoured her townhouse from basement to attic for a picture, a note, a name—anything associated with her father's identity. But not one shred of evidence had survived her parents' divorce.

Her mother had obliterated him from their lives.

The mystery of her father's identity had preyed on Paisley all her life. Who was he? And if her father loved her, why had he abandoned her?

Those questions and others had driven her to take a DNA test in the hope of connecting with someone in her father's family—someone who could give her the answers she sought.

Just this morning, the DNA bank had sent her a possible parental connection. Since Mom insisted DNA collecting was a scam to compile personal information, the DNA relationship could only be her father's. Paisley had opened the email with bated breath.

Cameron Douglas. Her father's name was Cameron Douglas, and he was from Scotland. That wasn't altogether surprising. Her DNA results had come back as 87 percent Scots, 8 percent Norwegian, and 5 percent Irish.

Her father had kept his family tree private. After a quick Google search of all Cameron Douglases in Scotland, she had given up. There were too many results to guess which one he was.

Rounding the corner, Paisley passed the rickety picnic table beside the graveled lot behind the restaurant where she and her coworkers took breaks. Her musings had occupied her all the way to the work.

Since the DNA site had linked her to her father, she had waited—vacillating between a desire to contact him and fear of what would happen if she did.

***

Paisley paused in the act of gathering the entrées off the restaurant's stainless-steel counter to double-check the meal tickets.

"Get a move on, Paisley," the sous-chef hollered above the clatter of crockery and sizzling steak.

She hoisted the tray of main courses onto her shoulder and straightened to her full five-foot-one height, then started for the dual swinging door, her four-inch heels clicking on the tile floor. If her photography business took off again, maybe she could drop a few shifts and get her own place—again.

As she entered the main dining room, her eyes drifted to the entrance, where a pair of newcomers conversed with the hostess. The tray of entrées wobbled in Paisley's hands. What was James Pressley-Coombes doing back in Virginia?

The soft glow from the wall sconces highlighted James's strong jaw and cheekbones as he and his companion followed the hostess to a linen-covered table. Paisley continued to her assigned area and set out her orders. "Here you go," she said.

Her eyes drifted across the room to James. He took a seat with his back to her, but she had a clear view of his date. Paisley started in surprise. Sidney Colby had pursued James since she and Paisley were freshmen in high school and he a celebrated senior.

She tore her eyes away from the couple and moved on to the next table in her section.

"Could I interest you in some coffee or dessert?" Paisley asked a young married pair.

"We'd like to split a banana pudding." The pretty blonde smiled up at Paisley, and the air around her fairly sparkled.

"Are you here for a special occasion?" Paisley glanced back and forth between the two. They hadn't ordered from the exclusive wine menu, yet they seemed in jubilant spirits. The blonde glanced at her partner, a short man with glasses and a besotted smile, as though asking for permission. He nodded slightly.

"We just found out we're expecting," the blonde said.

"Congratulations." Paisley's smile shone on both of them. "That's definitely something to celebrate."

"Thank you," the blonde said.

Straightening, Paisley wrote down their dessert choice and moved to her next table with only the smallest glance in James's direction. He raised a hand in greeting and mouthed something to her, but Paisley couldn't make it out.

Sidney tapped James on the shoulder to regain his attention, then flipped her hair several times. The woman was about as subtle as the rumble of a Mack truck's Jake brake. Paisley tossed James a brief smile to acknowledge his greeting on her way to the manager's office and rapped on the wood frame surrounding the door.

"Yes?" came the muffled response.

She poked her head inside the small office. "We've got a newly expecting couple at table fourteen. They're here to celebrate."

"Let me guess; you want their dessert on the house?" Her manager, a tall beanpole of a man, glanced up from his computer screen.

"They're so cute. C'mon. It's their first baby."

"Paisley, do you know how many free desserts I give out every time you're on shift?"

"It's just pudding. You aren't giving away the Taj Mahal. Besides, you know it's good PR." Paisley batted her eyes.

"Fine. But you take care of it. I'm up to my ears in food orders." He turned back to his calculations, then asked offhandedly, "By the way, have you figured out if you're going to reach out to your dad or not?"

"No."

"No, you aren't, or no, you haven't figured it out yet?" He glanced up from his computer screen again. "You're chasing a pipe dream if you do. A loser like that has nothing to offer. People make their own happiness, Paisley."

"Thanks for the pudding and the free advice." Her manager was entitled to his own opinion, but Paisley had no intention of labeling her father until she had all the facts.

She hustled to the kitchen. Typically, the manager presented on-the-house desserts, but Paisley didn't mind taking on that duty. Grabbing a ticket, she put her manager's name on it and snagged a banana pudding and two spoons off the dessert counter.

"I've got an on-the-house pudding," she called to the pastry chef. Crossing the tiled floor, Paisley placed her shoulder against the swinging door, backed out, pivoted on her heel, and rammed into a hard chest.

"Oomph."

Paisley made a wild grab as the pudding dish flew into the air and spilled yellow goop down the front of her uniform. Luckily, she caught the bowl before it hit the floor and shattered.

What kook stood in front of a kitchen door? Couldn't they see it swung both ways? Paisley gave the choreographer of this disaster a dirty look. James Pressley-Coombes's warm chocolate-brown eyes met hers. *Figures.*

"Thanks," she snapped.

"Sorry, Paise." James's twinkling eyes belied his apology.

His Brooks Brothers suit had escaped untouched while her white blouse dripped yellow pudding and whipped cream. She bolted back inside the kitchen.

James followed her.

"You aren't supposed to be in here," she said over her shoulder.

"Look, I'm really sorry. I came back here to see how you're doing."

"As you can see, I'm a little busy." Paisley grabbed a handful of paper towels. "You had better get back to your table. Sidney will be wondering where you are."

Paisley dabbed at the mess on her shirt, then headed to the sink to wash her hands and hunt for an apron to cover the stain.

"Sidney split." James tugged at his collar as if it were too tight.

Paisley looked up from tying the apron around her waist. For as long as Paisley had known Sidney, Sidney had been as focused on obtaining a Pressley-Coombes surname as the Washington Capitals were on winning another Stanley Cup. James must have done something spectacularly stupid for Sidney to walk out on him.

"What did you do?"

"I have no idea." James looked utterly baffled.

The Pressley-Coombes men were clueless when it came to women. Scratch that. Jack, the youngest brother, had recently married, proving that some of the men in their family were capable of figuring things out in that department.

As much as Paisley wanted to hear about James's derailed date, she had customers to serve. Grabbing a second pudding and two clean spoons, she said, "Stay here, and don't touch anything."

James held up both hands and gave her an innocent stare. She had to admit, he looked awfully cute, but her lifelong friendship with the Pressley-Coombes brothers had inoculated her against James's particular brand of charm. Paisley refused to join the endless string of female casualties left in his wake.

"Don't pull an innocent face, and stay out of the food." She marched out of the kitchen and delivered the pudding to the expectant couple.

"How kind. Please thank the manager for us," the blonde said as she dipped her spoon into the confection.

After two drink orders at an adjoining table, four entrée tickets, and a soda refill request, Paisley started toward the kitchen. When she had spoken to James over the summer, he'd told her that the hospital build he and his twin, Ben, were overseeing in the Midwest would take another year to complete. So what was James doing in Virginia?

James's father, Richard, had acted a little preoccupied Sunday at church, but he hadn't mentioned anything to her about the twins' impending arrival. For almost twenty years, Richard and his wife, Dana, had looked in on Paisley and her mother, making sure their townhouse was in working order and attending every major event in Paisley's life. When Dana died of cancer a few years ago, Richard had quietly doubled his workload and aged a decade overnight.

Paisley's heels clicked rhythmically on the plank floors as she passed the last table in her section and pushed open the dual swinging door to reenter the kitchen at the end of her shift.

She found James where she had left him. Sort of. He had peeled off his suit jacket, rolled up his sleeves, and donned an apron and was now busy swapping baseball stories with the sous-chef as he cut vegetables. The partially eaten steak on a platter beside him told its own story.

"You're still here?" Paisley breezed past James and glanced at the oversized clock above the sink station. Opening her locker, she eyed her bright-red cardigan hanging inside. If she buttoned it to the top, it would cover the pudding stain on her blouse. Hurriedly, she pulled on the sweater, did up the buttons, and grabbed her camera bag.

"So." James came up beside her. He removed the apron and shrugged into his suitcoat. "Where are you off to?"

"Baby shower. I've got to be across town in half an hour." She indicated her camera bag. "See you tomorrow," she called to the kitchen staff.

"Bye, Paisley."

"Take some good shots," the group chorused.

"I will."

"I heard you'd opened your own studio." James held the back door open and followed her outside the restaurant.

"Opened and closed. I think I set a world record." Her failure still stung, and Paisley was grateful the darkness hid her burning cheeks.

James looked at her in question.

"I left my day job too soon." She exhaled softly. "Your dad warned me to wait until I had six months of savings before I launched my studio. Two of my biggest clients canceled last minute. When I went back to the senior care center to get my activities director job back, they had already filled the position."

"Rotten luck."

"The worst. I moved in with Mom last month." She pulled out her cell phone. "Hang on. I've got to get an Uber."

"I'll give you a lift." His brown eyes were almost black in the dim light.

"Thanks."

Crickets chirped in the crisp night air as she and James walked to his car. She wondered yet again what had made Sidney leave him high and dry in the middle of dinner.

"How'd you manage to chase Sidney away?"

"She said I was ignoring her."

"Were you?"

"Maybe?" James pressed the fob in his hand. The silver Mercedes SUV lights flashed, and the doors unlocked. He opened the passenger side for her. "I lost my appetite watching her flip her hair. I started to worry that she had nits."

Paisley tried not to laugh as she slid onto the soft leather seat. Poor Sidney. James wouldn't understand a female signal if it bit him on the nose.

He climbed behind the wheel, punched the address she gave him into the GPS, and cranked up the heat. The burst of warm air ruffled her long dark hair. She angled the vents in James's direction as he eased onto Lafayette Street and waited for the signal to change.

Colorful leaves outside the passenger window fluttered to the pavement under the golden glow of old-time streetlamps. Giant spiders, witches, and ghosts filled storefront windows, and a cluster of pedestrians ambled down the brick-paved sidewalk.

The light turned green, and they started across the Rappahannock River with the harvest moon spinning a silvery pathway over the darkened water. Paisley leaned back in her seat and enjoyed the luxury of being driven by a competent driver in a car that didn't need weekly visits to the mechanic.

"What are you doing back in Virginia?" she asked at length.

He glanced in her direction, but Paisley couldn't make out his expression in the shadowy interior. "Good question. Dad called last week and said he wanted to meet with Ben and me. We've got a meeting with him tomorrow morning at the corporate offices. Stay tuned."

"Any idea what it's about?"

"Not a one."

He sounded nonchalant about the situation, but then, that was James—affable, laid-back, and incredibly talented. He had a lot going for him. Then she remembered Sidney and bit back a laugh. When it came to women, though, he was as obtuse as his twin.

Sidney. Paisley sighed and shifted uncomfortably; she would hear about Sidney's hurt feelings soon. That woman wasn't one to suffer in silence.

Being a close associate of the Pressley-Coombes family held one demerit; every single bruised heart the twins left in their wake found its way to her door. Did these women really think she could fix things for them? Paisley snorted. Anyone with half a brain could see that the twins were relationship dorks. At twenty-nine, neither had a girlfriend—never had.

"What happened to your car?" James interrupted her thoughts.

"The alternator went out. Phil, Mom's boyfriend, said he'd fix it, but he's been busy."

"Ben and I can look it over tomorrow."

"That's really nice of you. Thanks." With a dysfunctional vehicle, a quarter of her paycheck had funded Ubers for the last month.

"It's no big deal. Jack isn't the only Pressley-Coombes who enjoys tinkering under the hood of a car."

"And I thought you were offering to fix my car out of the goodness of your heart," Paisley teased.

"I'm desperate. Ben's driving me crazy."

Ben's restless energy was a tremendous asset in a corporate setting, but it didn't make for relaxing company.

Her cell phone beeped with an incoming email. Mildly curious, she opened the screen and read: *Message from your recent DNA connection.* She pressed the icon and landed on the genealogical website where a memo from her DNA match blinked.

Paisley's heart skittered inside her chest. After twenty-four years of radio silence, her father had tuned in to her frequency. He wanted to meet her.

Chapter 2

James turned off the main thoroughfare on Butler Road and entered a darkened neighborhood. Broken-down cars lined the avenue, and half the streetlamps were out. He frowned as they passed a group of teenagers clustered on the sidewalk.

Usually, Paisley was excellent company, but she had gone quiet a few minutes ago. Maybe this neighborhood was giving her the same uneasy vibe as it did him.

"You have arrived at your destination." The GPS audio voice broke the silence.

James pulled to the curb and turned off the engine. No porch light shone at the single-story rancher. If this was a baby shower, James would eat his keys. No way was he leaving Paisley in this neighborhood without a means of escape. Before she gathered her bag, James hopped out and circled the SUV to open her door.

"Thanks for the lift." Paisley slid out of the Mercedes, her short legs stretching for the step.

"Do you know these people?" James indicated the house for Paisley's photo shoot.

"They're friends of a friend," she said airily.

"That would be a *no*." He accompanied her up the uneven sidewalk to the front stoop.

"What are you doing?" Paisley hissed in a low voice.

"Making sure this is a legitimate shoot."

Paisley rolled her eyes and pressed the bell with enough energy to jam her finger. The chime signaled on the opposite side of the door. He waited beside her, his ears straining for typical party noise.

Footsteps sounded in the hall. The porch light flipped on. A burst of masculine laughter. The door opened a crack, and one bloodshot eye examined Paisley on the front porch.

James removed his hands from his pockets and closed the distance between himself and Paisley. His eyes bored into the man's.

Paisley gave the disembodied eyeball a bright smile. "I'm Paisley, the photographer you hired for the baby shower."

"Who's he?" The man indicated James. The door opened a fraction wider, revealing a man with a scraggly beard and a stained T-shirt that reeked of booze.

"I'm her assistant," James cut in before Paisley could respond.

The man slammed the door in their faces.

***

Paisley owed James big time. As annoyed as she was at his playing protector, she couldn't deny that anything could have happened to her if he hadn't accompanied her to that so-called baby shower. Paisley inserted the key into the lock and let herself inside her mother's townhouse.

The smell of pot roast and the swoosh of the dishwasher enveloped her as she kicked off her heels beside the door. The habitual clutter on the center of the kitchen table had been tidied away—a sure sign that Mom had company.

The murmur of voices and clink of glasses from the living room confirmed Paisley's deduction. Mom had been seeing Phil, a circuit court judge from a neighboring county, for the last few months. He was okay if you liked to discuss court cases or legalities twenty-four seven, which Mom, of course, did, being a district attorney.

Paisley padded to the built-in kitchen desk in her stockinged feet and laid her camera beside the computer. Despite the nixed "baby shower," she had pictures to download—random shots she had taken of the colonial buildings in Old Town. If they were good enough, she hoped to sell them at local galleries and add to her meager savings.

She connected her camera to the computer and started the download while her father's message swirled inside her mind.

Paisley,

You cannot imagine my happiness at making this connection. Doubtless you have many questions, all of which I shall answer. Before I do, however, I should like you to visit me here in Scotland. Much will become clear when you do.

I have attached a first-class airline ticket. The date is negotiable—to best fit your schedule.

Affectionately,
Your father, Cameron Douglas

Paisley's heart thumped at full throttle. Should she respond to him or just keep the status quo? Her boss was of the opinion that she should leave it alone. But her fingers hovered over the computer keyboard as the two-way emotions warred within her.

The tread of feet sounded in the hall. Paisley clicked off the computer screen guiltily and looked up as her mother and Phil entered the kitchen.

Mom had a highball glass in one hand. She was no longer a practicing member of their church, and it hurt to see her mother slipping further from the tenets of their faith. Mom's drinking had increased since she had started dating Phil.

Phil came up behind Mom, wrapped his arms around her, and nuzzled her cheek. Paisley shifted uneasily. Mom and Phil were never touchy-feely in front of her.

"Paisley, we have something to tell you," her mother said with a huge smile. Not, "Hi, honey. How was your day?"

After a second swift glance at the two of them, understanding dawned on her. Casually, Paisley peered at her mother's left hand. A big sparkly diamond glittered under the recessed lighting.

"Congratulations. When's the big day?" Paisley bared her teeth appropriately but didn't hug her mother. They didn't have that kind of a relationship.

"Phil and I signed on a waterfront house today at the Fredericksburg Country Club. It clears escrow in four weeks. We're planning our wedding around it." Mom took a sip of the amber liquid in her glass.

One month. Paisley's chest tightened, and she pressed her lips together. Mom's memo came through loud and clear: Paisley had thirty days to find her own place.

Dreams of reopening her photography studio in the next twelve months went up in flames. It didn't take a gifted IQ to do the mental math. If she sold her car and combined that with the cash in her bank account, she might have enough for a deposit on a studio apartment.

How like her mother to inform her this way. Mom's child-rearing skills were akin to vegetable gardening: plant a seed, apply water and fertilizer, pull weeds, and expect produce. No warmth. No cuddles. No giggles. Mom was like the law—fair, even-tempered, and detached.

During Paisley's childhood and early teens, she had observed the world through her camera lens, viewing but rarely participating. Because of it, she'd become an adept discerner of human nature. And a bit of a loner—only letting a handful of people penetrate her protective barriers.

Even though she didn't understand why Mom and Phil were getting married after only dating each other for a few months, she asked, "Would you like me to photograph your wedding?"

Mom and Phil exchanged glances.

"We're going to the courthouse for the ceremony. We've both been married before and don't want any fuss," Phil said.

"A few people at work are interested in the townhouse," Mom said matter-of-factly.

"No realtor?" The townhouse had been their home ever since Paisley could remember.

"We don't need one. Phil and I can handle the legalities."

Nice and neat. Just the way Mom liked things. It was too bad Paisley wasn't hardwired the same way. Mom and Phil looked expectantly at Paisley, neither saying a word.

Paisley interpreted the nonverbal question. "I'll be out in thirty days."

***

James shifted his grip on the container of Kansas City barbeque sauce while the security officer, a sturdy former Marine, let him and Ben inside the Coombes Enterprises corporate offices. Why Dad had insisted on a 7:00 a.m. meeting had James more than a little curious. And a little on edge.

That edgy sensation had gnawed at him during his morning workout, so he'd dressed with care: slacks and a fitted shirt. He had even snagged one of Dad's ties on the way out of Edgehill House, the family's white-pillared antebellum.

"Please sign in, Mr. Ben, Mr. James." The guard nudged the security book across the desk toward them.

Out of habit, Ben went first, then handed James the pen. He switched the barbeque container to his opposite arm and filled out the form. By the time he finished, the elevator had dinged. James sauntered inside. The door slid shut, and the elevator started up the brick-and-glass shaft.

Ben was slumming it today in a pair of jeans and an orange polo. Just a shade under six feet, James's brother's identical face with its chiseled jaw, angular lines, and chocolate-brown eyes stared back at him. The skin around Ben's eyes crinkled at the corners, letting James know he had spotted the barbeque sauce.

"Don't you think you've paid Miss Penny back for all the jelly beans we swiped?"

James shrugged. At age nine, he'd had a weakness for fruit-flavored jelly beans, and Miss Penny's colorful jar was a huge temptation he had rarely resisted. On one memorable occasion after baseball practice, James had snarfed down the entire contents of her jar. His stomach rebelled, and he had decorated the carpet in front of her desk.

Miss Penny had walked in on the chaos. Without a word, she'd gotten him a lemon-lime soda and cleaned up the mess. She'd never ratted him out to Dad either.

Over the years, James had discovered Dad's stern-faced secretary had a fondness for barbecue and ice hockey. Whenever he popped home for a visit, James brought her a container of barbeque sauce or a ticket to a Caps game.

"Do you have any idea what Dad has up his sleeve?" Ben asked when James refused to rise to the bait.

"No clue, but Dad wouldn't have sent for us if it wasn't important."

"You're right." Ben leaned against the wall and folded his arms across his chest. "Something's been eating at him for the last month. He's been grilling me about the hospital build and checking and double-checking every report. I don't know what his deal is. We were ahead of schedule until I got a phone call last night that our steel beam order has been delayed."

"That will set us back six weeks." James groaned. The beams were en route from Spain via shipping container. James folded his arms with his feet shoulder-width apart and mirrored his brother's stance. "What are you going to do about it?"

"Since this is Perez's fault, I'll make sure they give us a discounted rate." Ben straightened as the elevator car slowed.

The door slid open and revealed a frosted-glass wall with the corporate branding. Dad had built Coombes Enterprises from the ground up. Today, it was a thriving multi-million-dollar construction corporation.

Miss Penny sat at her desk, her clothes perfectly pressed and her teased and lacquered hair immovable. James wondered how many cans of hairspray she went through in a month. Miss Penny had been with Coombes Enterprises since Dad had launched the fledgling company. She must be pushing sixty-five now.

"Good to see you, Miss Penny." Ben acknowledged her with a nod.

"You too, Mr. Ben. How are things in Kansas City?"

"Can't complain. Their version of rush hour is a twenty-minute slowdown."

One side of James's mouth quirked up. Of all the things to enjoy about Kansas City, Ben would focus on the commute instead of on pro-ball, great barbeque, and friendly people.

"Go right in. Your father's expecting you." Miss Penny returned to her typing.

"Thanks." Ben nodded and entered Richard's office.

James hung back and waited for a private word with his father's secretary. He plunked the semi-thawed container of barbeque on the edge of her kidney-shaped desk. "I brought you a new flavor."

"Bone-sucking sauce?" Miss Penny read the label aloud and raised an eyebrow.

"Trust me; it's awesome. Once you've sampled that, you'll be booking a flight to Kansas City for more. I know you like their zinger sauce, but it never hurts to try something new."

"I hope you're a firm believer of that mantra." Miss Penny's glasses winked under the fluorescent lights.

James stirred, and the twinge of uneasiness he had experienced earlier came back with a vengeance. "Why is that?"

"I couldn't say, but just so you know, I think your father's right."

With her words jangling inside his head, James entered his father's office. A patterned reveal of gray waves covered one wall, and the three remaining walls were glass. Ben lounged on one of the two leather sofas on the far side of a granite coffee table. Above him, an ironwork chandelier, gifted by Richard's new son-in-law, the Earl of Rivendon, filled the space with incandescent light. Richard paced the end wall fronting the Rappahannock River.

James still didn't understand why Dad hadn't talked this out over breakfast. But for Richard, work stayed at work, unless he was holed up inside his home office after the ten o'clock news. The man ran his company like a well-oiled machine, and Ben was just like him. Work. Work. Work.

James worked hard, but he played hard too. Lately, Ben hadn't been as available for a game of ball after work or their Saturday morning kayaking trips, and it had left James scuffing his proverbial feet. He was bored professionally and socially. At some point, he'd like to utilize his marketing degree instead of crunching numbers for corporate proposals. Settling down wasn't entirely abhorrent to him either, not after he had witnessed his brother's and sister's newfound happiness with their respective spouses.

He shuddered when he remembered his disastrous date the previous evening. At the rate he was going, marriage wasn't in the cards.

James blamed his and Ben's romance issues on their mother's DNA. As far back as they had records, Mom's people flew solo until, or if, a unique individual entered their lives. Then bam. That was it—end game. A good number of her people never married but had poured their energies into successful careers instead. James wasn't too worried. At twenty-nine, he had lots of time before he settled down.

He lowered himself onto the sofa facing his twin.

"I'm glad you boys were so prompt." Richard unbuttoned his suit coat. "Let's get down to business. I've decided Ben will head the Midwest project until it wraps."

Ben nodded and crossed his ankle over his opposite knee. Nothing earth-shattering there. Ben enjoyed playing front man in the day-to-day operations while James kept a firm control of their profitability.

"However," Richard continued, "James's skills are needed elsewhere."

"What?" James's heart jolted in surprise. He and Ben worked in tandem, as a team—a prepackaged deal. The only time they had been separated was during their two-year stint as missionaries for their church.

"You're splitting us up?" Ben's face went white under his tan like someone had sucker-punched him.

"I need James's advertising and PR skills on an overseas project with a British developer I've partnered with in the past." Richard turned to James, his dark eyes direct. "You'll be stationed in the UK for the next eighteen months, possibly longer, if this goes well. We need a good marketing man on-site to help promote this venture, and others in Europe are in the works."

Marketing? Dad was giving him a chance to do something he loved—finally. Excitement fizzed like a bottle of shaken soda, spilling out into a full-blown grin. James looked at Ben to gauge his brother's response.

Ben's eyes had gone blank, his face completely devoid of expression. Twin was taking it hard. James reined himself in and rearranged his features into more sober lines.

"This isn't permanent. But it's time the two of you learn to do things on your own." Richard turned to James. "You remember Kinross, don't you?"

"Isn't he that Scottish guy who invested in our hospital build?" James asked.

"The same." Richard nodded briefly. "I met him decades ago at a black-tie event in New York. He's pushed to partner with Coombes Enterprises on other venues for some time."

"What's the venture?" James asked, his interest piqued.

"He wants to develop a resort in the Scottish Highlands but has little experience with this sort of thing. That's where we come in."

"As what? Does Kinross understand what running a business entails after the resort is completed?" Ben's mouth twisted into a nasty line, and he looked like he could spit nails.

"Kinross's holdings are extensive, and he runs over a dozen businesses: clean energy wind farms, forestry, sheep, auto dealerships, whiskey distilleries, stud farm, and a racetrack."

Richard's eyes slid to his oldest son's. "A large tract of land on his estate remains undeveloped. He'd like to make it pay. Coombes Enterprises will supply three-quarters of the finances while Kinross provides the property, startup fees, and maintenance."

"How well do you know this Kinross?" Ben folded his arms.

"Well enough to trust him," Richard said.

James didn't have an issue with it. If Dad had partnered with Kinross before, the man must be reliable. Caution was Dad's middle name.

A spurt of excitement shot through him as marketing ideas percolated inside his brain. James ran a hand over his jaw and encountered a patch of stubble he had missed that morning.

He made the mistake of glancing at Ben. His brother was barely holding it together. Guilt pummeled James as loyalty to his twin and enthusiasm for this new business venture warred inside.

To soften the blow, James said, "It's cold and wet in the UK."

Chapter 3

Paisley carried two steaming foam cups of hot chocolate outside. It was the least she could do since the twins had dropped by to work on her car. Leaves crunched under her four-inch heels as she crossed her mother's postage-stamp-sized lawn. She came up beside Ben, who stood at the curb.

James leaned under the hood of her Civic and poured pink liquid through a funnel into a plastic reservoir. The label on the container said *coolant*. Why she needed coolant when the weather might reach the low sixties, she had no idea.

She handed Ben one of the overwarm cups.

"Thanks." He took it from her absently, his face paler than normal.

"You feeling okay, Ben?"

"Yeah. Sure." The dark eyes that were so like his brother's flicked in her direction, then away.

Something was definitely wrong. Normally, the twins tossed good-natured insults at each other with an occasional one in her direction for good measure. But the dirgelike mood Ben exuded was more in keeping with a wake.

"So, how's the hot chocolate?" She attempted to draw Ben out.

"Hmmm." He obediently took a sip.

James poked his head out from under the hood and sealed the cap on the container of coolant. A smudge of grease marred his jawline. "Is that for me?"

"No, I always carry a spare cup of hot chocolate around on my way to work," Paisley said.

Apparently unconcerned by her sarcasm, James peeled off his latex gloves and relieved her of the steaming cup. After a tentative sip, he smiled at her. "That's pretty good. When did you learn how to cook?"

"If you call boiling water and dumping a couple scoops of mix into a cup cooking, we're in trouble," Ben rejoined, sounding more like his old self.

"Hey, don't knock her skills," James said. "You can't even stir cocoa properly. You get it all over the counter when you try."

Ben rolled his eyes and took another swallow.

"I hate to break up the party, boys, but are you two about done with my car?" Paisley stepped back onto the sidewalk when her heel started to sink into the grass.

"Yeah. We're done. We would have finished sooner, but genius here drained out your coolant. I had to go to the store and get more to replace it." James picked up a rag and wiped grease off his forearm.

"Why were you guys messing with my car fluids? All I needed was my alternator replaced."

"James had your alternator switched in an hour, then he got this bright idea that your system needed a flush," Ben said.

"That was only after you almost poured oil in the—" James sputtered.

"Okay." Paisley held up both hands. "I just want to know if my car is finished so I can get to work. I've got to be there in twenty minutes."

"Yeah, we're done," Ben said.

"I'm going to ride with you to make sure everything's running okay." James tossed his rag onto the pile of tools beside the curb.

"How will you get home?" Paisley asked.

"Ben will follow us."

Paisley glanced at Ben for confirmation.

He nodded. "We didn't get a chance to test-drive your car. For all we know, James still has a few screws loose."

Paisley rolled her eyes and took their empty cups, stacking them one inside the other. "Are you ready? I really need to go."

"Let's do it." James opened her door and waited for her to climb into the driver's seat while Ben picked up the tools.

She placed the stack of empty cups in a holder and fired up the engine. James helped his twin load their tools in the back of their SUV, then tossed the keys to Ben and climbed in the passenger seat of Paisley's car.

Paisley was quiet on the way into Old Town, barely taking notice of the scenery along River Road as she debated with herself. "James, can I bounce something off you?"

"Sure." He looked at her expectantly.

"I got a DNA kit for my birthday. The results came back a few weeks ago."

"And you found out you're from an aborigine tribe in New Guinea?"

"Very funny." Her skin was pale in the rearview mirror, a huge contrast to her dark hair and eyes.

"You never know. You are pretty small."

She ignored him. "I got a match."

"And?" He must have sensed this was serious because the teasing tone faded from his voice.

"The email said it was a possible parental relationship."

"Wow."

James was aware of her mother's adverse opinion on DNA testing. The match could only be to her father.

"Did you write to him?" he asked.

"He emailed and wants to meet. Now that he has, I'm really nervous about the whole thing."

"You aren't going to chicken out, are you? You've talked about wanting to meet him for half your life."

"What if he—?"

James touched her hand, a strangely intimate gesture that made her shiver. "One step at a time, Paise."

She drove over the Rappahannock bridge, not even glancing at the river. On the opposite side, she stopped at the light on William Street.

"DNA testing is pretty cool." James's knee bumped against the glove box. "My dad gave each of us a DNA kit for Christmas last year. I'm pretty sure he was just checking to see if Jack was really related."

The comment was so ludicrous that Paisley laughed. Save for his dimples and extra few inches, no one could mistake Jack's resemblance to the twins and Richard.

"I've been imagining all kinds of things," Paisley admitted, squeezing the steering wheel. "What kind of man abandons his wife and baby? Do you think he committed a heinous crime and was imprisoned all this time?"

"There's only one way to find out."

"I was afraid you'd say that," she muttered.

"Let me know how that goes, will you?"

"Sure." The light changed, and she stepped on the gas. "What happened at that meeting with your dad this morning?"

James rubbed his jaw, his fingers smearing the grease mark. "Dad signed a contract to partner on a resort build in the UK. He wants me on-site for the next eighteen months to head the marketing campaign."

"Oh." Paisley's stomach plunged, and dismay filled her at the thought of not seeing him for so long. "No wonder Ben's not himself."

"Yeah." James expelled a long breath.

"How do you feel about that kind of a move?" She fought against the sudden heaviness pervading her heart and made an effort to keep her tone light. She was used to having James pop in and out of her life. But for him to move across the ocean . . . It seemed so final.

"I don't want to leave Ben high and dry, but part of me is dying to do something different."

For the last few years, James had been spinning his wheels, going nowhere fast. When she thought about it, Richard's decision made perfect sense.

"That's a dilemma."

"I don't know why Dad is pushing for this right now. Ben and I could hop the pond after the hospital build wraps."

Her hand moved involuntarily on the steering wheel as if to object, but she hesitated to voice her thoughts.

"Spit it out," James said. "I can see it's killing you to hold back."

"Your dad's right. This is a good idea."

"You agree?" His voice went up a couple notes, his surprise evident.

"It's about time Richard split the two of you up."

"Why?"

"Come on, James. Think about it. If the two of you didn't have each other's backs, one or both of you might actually move on in life."

"I've tried." He turned his body toward her on the passenger seat.

"If you call dating girls like Sidney a concerted effort in that department, think again. You'll never fall for the women you date. They're after your money or don't have enough brain cells to challenge you."

"Don't sugarcoat it." A hint of resentment swirled in the depths of his eyes.

"How do you know I didn't?" She gave him a sassy smile.

"I don't like being psychoanalyzed by someone I babysat as a kid. Besides, you're a great one to talk. You're still single."

"I'm younger than you."

"Only by three years. Twenty-six is getting up there, Paisley."

"I'm not the one pushing thirty." She flipped on her blinker and turned into the parking lot behind the restaurant. Ben pulled into a spot beside her.

"When do you leave?" She set the parking brake and turned off the engine.

"Tonight. I'm taking a red-eye back to Kansas City to get my stuff. Dad wants me in the UK next week."

"That's fast." A sudden wave of homesickness for James swept over her. He and Ben, despite their teasing, had always been there for her. Today was a prime example. "I'll miss you."

"Yeah, me too, squirt." He reached over the middle console and gave her a hug.

She closed her eyes, her heart aching.

"You okay?"

"I hate goodbyes." She dropped her arms from around his shoulders and drew a shuddery breath. "I meant to tell you; Mom's getting married."

"She is? To whom?"

His surprise sounded almost as great as hers had been.

"A judge from Spotsylvania County. They've been dating for a couple months."

"That's a bit sudden."

"She and Phil bought a house on the river. They're getting married when it closes."

"And you're out on your ear." It wasn't a question. James knew her mother all too well.

She shrugged. "How much do you think this car is worth?"

"You need your car. Public transportation sucks here." A frown scored the area between his brows.

"I'll find a studio apartment in Old Town, then I can walk to everything."

"You can't make it to photo shoots without a car." He folded his arms across his chest.

She ground her molars and wished she hadn't told him.

"You need it for a down payment on a place, don't you?"

She refused to answer, knowing by long association where this was headed. She didn't want a handout. And he was going to insist on one.

Whenever she hung out with the Pressley-Coombes siblings, she was reminded of her inadequacies. Everything they touched turned to gold. While she was not so mean-spirited as to envy their achievements, she wished their successes didn't underscore her lack of financial acumen.

"I'm going to be late for my shift," she said, reaching for her door handle.

James had no option but to let himself out the passenger side.

She approached the parked SUV where Ben sat behind the wheel looking like someone had bested him on a multi-million-dollar merger.

"Thanks for fixing my car, Ben. I hope you guys have a safe flight."

"Our pleasure, Paisley." Ben slipped out from behind the wheel long enough to give her a quick hug. "Take care of yourself."

She stepped away from the car, and Ben hopped back into the driver's seat. She turned around, and James pulled her in for one last hug.

"Get a hold of me if you need anything. I mean it."

"That's very kind of you, James, but I can do this on my own. I'm a big girl."

"No, you aren't. Despite those silly heels, you'll always be a pipsqueak." He touched her nose, then climbed into the passenger seat beside Ben. The SUV tires crunched over the loose gravel in the unpaved lot as they pulled away.

A lump clogged Paisley's throat and made it difficult to swallow.

James waved one last time as they started down Sophia Street toward the bridge.

She waved back and smiled. Her face ached from the effort. When the SUV rounded a curve and disappeared from sight, a single tear slid down her cheek.

Chapter 4

Overhead speakers blared last-minute gate changes. Jet engines thundered outside the airport windows every few minutes as another flight took off from London Heathrow International. James readjusted his grip on both suitcase handles and continued down the wide concourse toward the terminal exit.

A man in a three-piece suit and turban bumped into him and apologized in a foreign tongue. People of all nationalities bustled around him, a beehive of moving bodies. An iron band wrapped itself around James's chest and squeezed. He tugged at his collar as the old panic began to rise. He had to get out.

It had been a while since his last panic attack. He had believed himself cured. Stupid. No one got over being locked inside a trunk for hours when they were four years old and emerged unscathed.

Spots danced in front of his eyes. He sucked in through his mouth and focused on the escalator moving toward the second level. Keeping his eyes on the moving stairs, he took short sips of air. The tight knot of travelers parted, and the band of iron loosened its grip, clearing his vision.

He moved on, looking neither to the right nor the left, passing duty-free shops displaying their wares. Heavily scented perfume wafted out an open door and tickled his nose. At last, a large exit sign appeared above a bank of glass doors. He burst outside the terminal, his lungs sucking in the heavy, moist air. For several seconds, he did nothing but breathe.

Slowly, he became aware of his surroundings: gray skies, cold weather, and drizzling rain. Nothing had changed much since his last trip to the UK. Why his younger siblings had married British citizens and relocated to such a miserable climate, he would never understand.

He zipped up his jacket and moved under the awning with his luggage to wait for his sister, Catherine. They had exchanged texts during his layover in Reykjavik when he had updated her with his delayed arrival.

Despite the dismal weather, his body hummed as he considered his new job. Dad had finally given him something that would challenge him professionally, and James intended to make the most of his solo experience.

A woman with a large suitcase and three little boys joined him under the awning. While she hailed a taxi, two of her sons shoved each other good-naturedly, obviously happy to escape the confines of a long flight. The smaller of the two tripped and fell, knocking over James's bags.

A taxi slid to the curb. Turning back toward her children, the mother took in the situation.

"Sorry, love." She gave James an apologetic stretch of lips as she picked up her son and straightened James's cases.

"No big deal," James said, wishing he wasn't a stranger and could help load her luggage inside the cab. In this day and age of suspicious behavior, he didn't dare.

The cab pulled away with one of the boys blowing a raspberry on the inside pane of glass. James smirked. That kid was going to give his mother a run for her money.

Overhead planes descended, floating like impossible-sized birds before they disappeared behind the terminal. After twenty minutes, James was sure something had happened to Catherine. Normally, the family could set their clocks by her punctuality.

Another group of travelers burst through the closest terminal door and headed out into the drippy afternoon. James pulled out his cell phone and started to text Catherine. As he typed, a classic green Jaguar shot across two lanes of traffic and angled nose-first toward the curb beside him, successfully blocking two lanes.

James recognized Gillian, his brother Jack's new wife, behind the wheel. A horn blasted, and a cab screeched to a halt behind her. With apparent unconcern, Gillian popped the Jag's trunk and came around the hood to greet him, a huge smile on her pretty face.

"James! Welcome to England!" The curvy dynamo gave him a warm hug. She was like an electric current of good cheer wrapped in stylish business attire. Gillian's pale-blonde hair was in some sort of updo that showed off her high cheekbones and sparkly blue eyes.

"How was your flight?" she asked.

"Can't complain." He deposited his two suitcases and duffel inside the trunk and slammed it shut. Gillian might be oblivious to the backed-up traffic, but he wasn't.

Once settled inside, she put Jack's sedan in gear and pulled out, gunning the engine. James gripped the hand pull and tried to keep a straight face.

When Gillian narrowly missed going up the tailpipe of a double-decker bus, the question burst from James. "I thought Catherine was going to pick me up."

"What's the matter, afraid of my driving?" Gillian's eyes gleamed.

"Nooooo," he said as she swerved between two cars and slammed on her brakes at the signal. How his Formula One designer brother could have married a woman who drove like a maniac left him scratching his head.

"Why not? Everyone else in the family is. Nick won't let me touch his motorcars."

"Why does Jack?"

"He doesn't know I borrowed it." Laugh lines crinkled the corners of her eyes. "When your plane was delayed, Catherine realized she wouldn't get back from the airport in time for her last committee meeting for Run Against Trafficking."

"When is the event?"

"Tomorrow. Are you going to join us?"

"I could. I don't have to leave until Sunday. Does Catherine need my support?"

"It always helps to have family involved, especially when BBC News is covering it."

"That sounds serious. Who's running?"

"Seems like half the UK signed up. Lots of celebrities and Nick's titled friends. He has a great deal of influence."

His brother-in-law, Nick, held the title of Earl of Rivendon and was kind of a big deal in England.

"So how are you going to return Jack's car without him realizing that you swiped it?"

"He'll be fine." She gave him a wide smile and added, "Eventually."

"How's Thierry putting up with having Jack for a father?"

Thierry was Gillian's eight-year-old daughter. Jack had adopted her when he and Gillian were married a few months ago.

"It's more like their two against my one." She swerved over the middle line, almost scraping paint off the car in the adjoining lane. "Jack would rather play with Thierry than watch a car chase."

Until Gillian had breezed into Jack's life, James's girl-stupid brother had barely given women a glance. Then Jack had taken one look at Gillian, and that was that. Formula One cars, his obsession since the age of five, had taken a back seat.

Gillian took an exit, and within minutes, they left the closely spaced houses for the rolling countryside. Hedgerows lined both sides of the highway. Now and again, the vista opened to rolling hills dotted with sheep. New crops of rapeseed covered the farmland. In the distance, ancient spires occasionally parted clusters of trees.

"Did you sleep on the plane?" Gillian asked.

"I did all right." He had dozed off a few times, but adrenaline and a fussy baby in the row behind him had kept him awake.

She overtook, then cut off a semitruck with a hair's breadth to spare. The trucker laid on his horn. Gillian waved and pressed down on the accelerator. After a few more close shaves, James determined she had more than one guardian angel; probably more like a legion of angels had been assigned to protect her.

Gillian cranked up the heater. The warm air combined with little sleep soon had him nodding off. Before James realized it, the Jag slowed as the wrought-iron gates swung open between two stone pillars.

"When did Nick get an electronic gate? I thought he left these open."

"He installed a new system a few months ago. This one puts Fort Knox's to shame."

James took note of the multiple cameras. "Is he paranoid?"

"Not at all, just cautious after what happened to Catherine last year."

The Jag entered the estate, and the gate closed automatically behind them. The narrow lane zigzagged up a steep hillside. It had been originally created for carriages, funneling between maturely planted lime trees and a rock wall carved from the hillside. James heaved a sigh of relief when the car nosed over the top of the incline, and the priory came into view.

Ashford Priory, a manor house of golden stone and mullioned windows, queened it over the valley below. Gillian took the left fork and followed the lane as it curved past a large pool and spraying fountain toward the semi-circular drive in front of the house. She parked beside a covered porch with massive stone pillars flanking a large wooden door.

Catherine waited for them at the top of the stone steps. Her wide smile flashed, and her aquamarine eyes twinkled when James stepped out of the car. She had never looked lovelier. He bounded up the steps and hugged his sister.

"James! I'm so glad you can spend the weekend with us."

"Hey, sis. You're looking good," he said and patted the apparent belly bump on her otherwise slight frame.

"Thanks. We just found out we're having twins." Catherine made a face. "Dad's elated. Apparently, they run on both sides of the family."

"Well, there's evidence," James said dryly. "At least there was the last time I looked in the mirror."

Catherine rolled her eyes theatrically. "Heaven help us if this set is anything like you and Ben were."

"I've been here a minute, and you're bashing me already?" James protested.

Catherine looped her arm through his. "From what I've been able to gather from the staff, Nick was no angel himself. I'm praying for girls."

Chapter 5

HUDDLED ON THE RICKETY PICNIC table behind the restaurant, Paisley silently prayed for direction. Her breath clouded the air while a fog of confusion swirled in her mind as she stared unseeing at the red and gold foliage around her.

She didn't know what to do.

With her mother's approaching nuptials, it was obvious she needed her own place. If she sold her car and got rid of the insurance, she might be able to swing it. But James had insisted she needed her car to up the amount of photography jobs. And she had to admit he had a point.

Paisley didn't have enough cash for a deposit and first month's rent on a studio apartment if she kept her Civic, which meant she had to either ask for a handout or accept her father's one-way ticket to Scotland.

A brown sparrow chirped in the tree overhead, his chest heaving with each note.

All her life she had longed to know her father. As a child, she had created fantasies about the day he would return with a perfectly logical explanation for his absence.

Mom's detached parenting style had made Paisley long for the easy affection that existed within the Pressley-Coombes family. Would she experience something similar with her father if she took him up on his invitation? Or was he merely curious to meet her?

She rubbed the rough edge of the picnic table with her fingers. If she flew to Scotland, how would her mother react? Paisley had no desire to damage the only parental relationship she had in order to chase a dream that might be as insubstantial as fog on the Rappahannock.

Her heart teetered on the precipice where fear of disappointment warred with her lifelong yearning.

Richard's words from a previous conversation came to mind. "You can't play it safe all your life, Paisley. You'll never get ahead if you don't take a few risks along the way. Weigh each of them, then go with what feels best."

Deciding to follow Richard's counsel, she brushed aside her worries and picked up her cell phone. For better or worse, she was going to Scotland. Now all she had to do was break the news to her mother.

***

Achmed Razool was a lucky man. Every morning when he drove his small Vauxhall through Castle Rannoch's gate, he wanted to punch the air. He parked at the former stable block the duke had converted into his corporate headquarters and waited at the door for the night guard to let him inside.

Few program analyst positions were available in the Highlands, and Achmed had bagged the biggest one of all only three years out of university. Kinross paid a generous salary, one which covered Achmed's expenditures and allowed him to assist his little sister, Padma, with her uni fees—as long as he stayed away from the ponies.

Today, he was celebrating! After months of overtime, he had finally returned the money he had "borrowed" from Kinross's coffers. He had learned his lesson with no one the wiser. He had no intention to venture near a racecourse again.

A creature of habit, he beelined it for the coffee machine and started a pot before he took off his coat, hat, and scarf. Armed with his first shot of caffeine, he situated himself at his workstation and booted up Kinross's financial analytics program. He had a report due at the end of the day.

Letters typed across his monitor, filling the screen in bold letters.

I know what you did.

He froze, and panic slithered across his skin. He glanced sharply over his shoulder to make sure no one had arrived in the office and was playing a joke on him. He was alone. Clicking off the screen, he switched to another task in a different program.

I know what you . . . started across his monitor.

Someone had accessed the company mainframe.

Achmed shut down his computer and stood, hands trembling. No one knew what he had done. He had been careful and covered his tracks.

This was a bizarre joke.

His eye landed on the calendar. Mid-October. Halloween. In the last decade, American imperialism had spread its tentacles across the pond, commercializing a lesser holiday. This entire incident was foolishness—a joke by British employees to mock the Persian man—racism at its finest.

Blimey, they'd had him for a sec. He expelled a breath, went back to his desk, and started his computer, determined to ignore the hoax.

Go to the car park in ten minutes or your sister will suffer.

Achmed clenched the mouse in his right hand while fury bubbled inside. No one knew what he had done. No one. Even if they suspected, they had nothing on him. He was that good.

Ignoring the message, he opened Kinross's financial spreadsheets but kept a wary eye on the lower right hand of his monitor to watch the minutes. A quarter hour passed, and no other messages appeared on his screen.

He closed his eyes and exhaled slowly. It was a joke. That's all it was, a filthy joke.

***

Paisley picked at her casserole and glanced across the kitchen table at her mother for the third time. Per usual, Mom was buried in a legal brief, the open file beside her dinner plate.

"Big day in court tomorrow, Mom?"

"Mmmm."

"I . . ." Paisley struggled for words that wouldn't antagonize her mother.

If she didn't tell her mother, how else would she explain her trip to Scotland? Mom knew she was broke.

Her mother glanced at her briefly over the top of her glasses.

Paisley inhaled deeply, then blurted, "I got a DNA kit for my birthday."

"Why? I've told you that process is highly suspect."

"I was curious to find out what countries I'm from." Paisley toyed with her fork.

"What did you learn?" Slowly, her mother laid down her file and gave Paisley her full attention.

"I'm 87 percent Scots."

Mom didn't look the least bit surprised.

"But you knew that already, didn't you?" Paisley asked.

Mom nodded slightly, her red bob swinging about her chin.

"When you take a DNA test, it links you to other family members who have taken the test. I had a hit—a parental connection . . ." Paisley trailed off. Mom's stony expression wasn't making this easy.

"I see." Her mother took a sip of white wine, then asked, "I suppose you've spoken to your father?"

"He wants me to visit him."

Her mother appeared to absorb the information with equanimity.

"You aren't angry?" Butterflies churned in Paisley's stomach.

Her mother toyed with the edge of the file. "You're old enough to know your own mind."

"I assumed you'd be upset. You refused to talk about him when I was a child."

"You can't begin to comprehend the pain I suffered." Her mother lifted her glass and took another swallow. This one was more of a gulp.

Paisley tensed. "What did he do?" she asked, almost afraid of the answer. If her father was that horrible, maybe she shouldn't have agreed to go to Scotland.

"He derailed the plans we made as a couple. We were to live in the United States after grad school so I could practice law for a decade before we moved to Scotland. But he retracted everything just before my last year of law school."

People generally had a reason for changing their plans. Paisley's photography studio was a prime example. "Why?" Paisley asked. "What happened?"

"We were in grad school when you were a toddler. One afternoon, your father didn't show up when it was his turn to watch you. I missed my class. He came back to the apartment later that afternoon. He looked horrible. His father had a stroke and wasn't doing well.

"Cam had to return to Scotland immediately after his graduation to handle the family businesses until his father recovered. He informed me he had booked flights for all of us." Her mother tucked a strand of hair behind her ear. "It was only two weeks until your father received his MBA, but I had another year of law school."

The casserole had congealed on Paisley's plate. She put down her fork and pushed it aside. Her mother's first love was the law—always had been. It didn't have messy feelings.

"When I expressed my frustration at having to start my law degree all over again in Scotland, Cam blew it off. He knew how much becoming an attorney meant to me, but his father was more important than our plans as husband and wife."

Mom drained her wine glass and refilled it. "I told him I was staying in the US until I completed my degree and was going to practice law as we had planned. He could visit us periodically until his family matters were squared away and then rejoin us in the States. That way I wouldn't have to leave school."

"That sounds like you." Being flexible and sympathetic had never been Mom's strong suit. Paisley could only imagine the uproar when her number one passion was threatened.

"What do you mean? *Your* father insisted my idea was impossible and refused to explain why he couldn't return to the U.S. He begged me to come with him and said I would understand why when we arrived. I told him that if he didn't have the decency to support me until I graduated, we were through."

"Maybe if you had gone with him for a few weeks to see what he meant—"

"How could he expect me to give up my life's dream just like that?" Her mother snapped her fingers. "I never would have married him if I'd known he was so inflexible."

"Why didn't he tell you why he needed to return to Scotland?"

"I have no idea. Cam was always secretive about his past."

"Didn't you want to find out?" Paisley asked.

"Why? I had everything I wanted."

Mom might be a DA, but she had a narrow mind toward anything and everything except the law.

"How did the two of you even get together?" Paisley couldn't resist the opportunity to learn more about her parents' relationship.

Her mother's face softened and took on a reminiscent half smile. "Cam had a cute accent and a quick mind. We met during my first semester of law school. I could tell he came from money; but not once in all the time I knew him did he ever mention his family. He spoiled me rotten: skiing in the Rockies and yachting on the Caribbean."

Paisley opened her mouth, then hesitated before she asked quietly, "Did he know about me?"

"Of course he knew about you," her mother snapped and eyed her as though she had asked something incredibly stupid. "When you came along, I never saw such a devoted father. He rocked you night after night for hours so I could sleep. Our life was perfect."

Paisley's heartbeat quickened. Her mother had actually loved her father. She didn't know why, but that came as a huge surprise.

"If you loved him, why didn't you try to patch things up?"

"Why? Cam ruined everything."

"His father was sick. His family needed his help," Paisley protested.

"Paisley, I wasn't a fool. I knew he wasn't coming back. We fought constantly after that, mostly about you. I insisted that you belonged with your mother, not with foreign nannies."

Paisley pressed her hands together and stared at her plate. Her father had wanted her? That meant the message on her camera was real, not just the yearnings of her heart. Her father really had loved her.

"After he left, I filed for full custody and requested no further contact." Mom shook her head. "In the middle of all this, your grandfather died. Back in those days, there wasn't joint parenting, and courts generally ruled in favor of the mother."

"Have you heard from him since the divorce?" Paisley's voice was the barest whisper.

"He left a message the following year, but it came while I was taking my bar exam. When I called him back, he didn't respond. All communications after that were through attorneys." Mom picked up her pen, obviously ready to get back to work.

"Why didn't you tell me about him sooner?"

"After your tenth birthday, you quit asking. I assumed you'd gotten over that childish fantasy of yours—thinking he'd return to us."

"Well, I didn't," Paisley said.

"Any man who walks out on his family doesn't deserve them."

"He wanted us to go with him," Paisley defended.

Her mother sighed and looked out the window. "Yes, he did."

"Years ago you told me that he abandoned us. But he didn't, did he." Paisley shook her head. Her mother was just as guilty as her father for the divorce, probably more so.

"That happened so long ago. It doesn't matter anymore." Mom reopened her file.

But it did matter to Paisley. It really did. She needed to meet him and spend time with him. Because more than anything, she wanted a father. One who loved and valued her.

***

Achmed shuffled his file folder and glanced at the clock. 10:07 a.m. He bit back a sigh. The monthly board meetings would last until noon.

Ward MacKenzie, Kinross's chief operating officer, a tall man with thinning hair and bad teeth, droned on about the success of the clean energy farm on the north end of the estate's granite flats. Of course it had done well. Scotland's gales were famous. Wind power, if one could afford the massively priced turbines, had provided easy profit a decade past. Nowadays, Scotland had an overabundance of energy, and future wind farm development had been placed on hold.

MacKenzie picked up the top file of quarterly reports. Achmed's stomach tightened, and he forced himself to breathe normally.

"Our first-quarter numbers for this fiscal year are in." MacKenzie frowned as his eyes swept over the charts. "We have a bit of a conundrum. A discrepancy between his lordship's profits and bank records has arisen. I'm sure it's a simple bank error, but I'd like accounting to review this more thoroughly on our end. Our numbers show a modest profit, yet according to WFB, we've suffered a slight loss."

Despite MacKenzie's bonhomie, Achmed's palms began to sweat, and he loosened his green checkered tie. No one would link the siphoning to him. Not even Kinross's accounting department was clever enough to trace that money. The trail led in another direction entirely. He had made sure of it.

His mobile vibrated inside his pocket. Achmed slipped it out far enough to check the screen. Not recognizing the number, he touched the red icon and disconnected.

"As you know," MacKenzie blathered on, "WFB's UK offices are under investigation. The allegations against their London-based headquarters are distressing indeed."

Kinross owned numerous lucrative businesses all financed through WFB, the globe's largest world bank.

"His Grace has considered transferring to another financial institution," Ward continued. "Unfortunately, due to his overseas investments, WFB is still his best option, especially since his latest venture is with a foreign investor."

Achmed's phone vibrated again. Again, he ignored it while he caught the last of Ward's brief.

Evidently, Kinross's newest project, a holiday resort build on the southern end of the estate was a joint venture with an American corporation. The son of said American business owner would be on-site the next day to take over the international marketing campaign. Kinross's staff were expected to lay out a warm welcome.

Hannah, Ward MacKenzie's secretary, knocked on the boardroom door and poked her head inside. "Sorry to disturb your meeting, sir, but this is rather urgent."

MacKenzie moved out of the way as Hannah carried the note across the room and handed it to Achmed. Her eyes were sympathetic. "You're needed at Perth Royal Infirmary."

In stunned silence, Achmed rose from his chair. "If you'll excuse me."

"Of course," MacKenzie said.

Achmed exited the meeting, his legs moving mechanically. When he reached the corridor, he asked Hannah, "What's happened?"

"Your sister, Padma, has been in a car crash outside Perth. They're preparing her for surgery."

Not Padma. He couldn't be hearing right. Fear lumped into a knot inside his throat. This was all his fault. Those messages on his computer screen weren't someone's idea of a sick joke after all. Someone had found out what he had done. Because he had not listened, Padma had paid the price.

Achmed's stomach roiled, and he fought down the bile which threatened to come up. Padma had been on her way from the University of Edinburgh to meet him tonight for his birthday celebration.

Trembling, he bypassed his desk and left the building for the car park just outside. His mobile rang as he switched on the engine. Thinking it was the hospital, he answered.

"Hullo."

"Next time she dies if you don't do what we ask," an electronically altered voice said through the speaker. "Instructions will be forthcoming."

"Who is this?" Achmed demanded.

But the line had already gone dead.

Chapter 6

After saying his goodbyes, James retrieved his coat from his sister's butler and descended Ashford Priory's pillared steps. He stowed his luggage behind the seats of the two-seater, red MGB Catherine had loaned him and was anxious to be on his way.

Nick rounded the side of the priory dressed in business attire, his tie partially dangling out of the top of his briefcase. The man flew all over Europe conducting and promoting businesses. He had left directly after the trafficking run yesterday to attend a meeting in Bruges.

"Where are you off to?" Nick stopped beside a tall Doric column on the porch.

"Castle Rannoch. According to my satnav, it's in Perth and Kinross."

The yellow mums in the urn behind Nick stirred in the gentle breeze. Nick didn't shift position, but something came and went in his eyes that made James pause.

"Do you know the place?" James asked. His father had been unusually taciturn on the subject of this Coombes Enterprises joint venture before James had departed for the UK.

"I installed several electronic gates for the duke a few years ago."

"My father never mentioned Kinross was a duke."

"Kinross doesn't use his title outside the UK. From what I've gathered, he holds tight rein on the family corporation and is rather a lone wolf when it comes to joint ventures. How did your father manage to form an alliance with him?"

"They hit it off at a black-tie event almost twenty years ago. They've partnered on several projects since then."

Nick rubbed the back of his neck. "Well, have a safe trip. Just so you know, the secondary roads narrow to single lanes north of Perth. Watch out for laybys, or a lorry is liable to run you down."

"Good to know." James climbed into the driver's seat and fired up the shiny red MGB. The engine roared to life, then settled, purring like a well-contented cat. James put the sports car in gear and started down the long sweeping drive toward the switchbacks.

In the rearview mirror, Nick stood watching.

James honked twice.

Nick raised his hand in farewell, then disappeared from view.

Downshifting, James nosed the car onto the first switchback. The overarching lime trees blocked the sky, and the sudden gloom darkened his spirits. He flexed his hands on the steering wheel. For better or worse, he was flying solo for the first time in his life, and he wasn't so sure he liked it.

***

James stifled a yawn as he turned the MGB off the A-85 onto a narrow, one-lane road. Stars sparkled overhead in the midnight sky, then vanished behind patches of cloud. According to the satnav, his estimated time of arrival at Castle Rannoch was thirty-eight minutes away.

Positive his satnav had miscalculated, James double-checked the information. How could it take thirty-eight minutes to go twelve miles?

Thick trees and sporadic boulders lined the side of the road. He downshifted around a tight curve, but before he could straighten the MGB out, oncoming high beams blinded him. James pulled into the nearest turnout and let the vehicle pass.

Another set of headlights approached. Instead of regaining the road, James let the car idle while he waited, tapping his index finger on the dashboard. If this kept up, it would take him more than the allotted thirty-eight minutes to reach his destination.

James shifted to first and regained the road once the way was clear. Nick had warned him about the secondary roads in the Highlands, but James hadn't realized these one-lane affairs with their small turnouts, which the road signs called laybys, for passing oncoming traffic would be so narrow.

A loch shimmered in the moonlight through the trees, then went dark as clouds obscured the night sky. The glow of Perth had long since dissipated in the rearview mirror as the heavily forested hills of Perth and Kinross closed in on either side of the glen. He had read somewhere that this area was referred to as Big Tree Country. James would have to take the travel blogger's word on it. Without the moon, James could barely see past the end of his headlights.

The outside temperature continued to drop. James cranked up the heat. Ben would have plenty to say about this sparsely populated area of the world. Personally, James breathed easier in less-crowded locales, but not having his twin around to share this experience was starting to wear thin.

He turned on his Bluetooth. "Call Ben."

Silence.

James took his eyes off the road and checked the cell phone. No connectivity.

The inky night and subsequent silence enveloped him. He turned on the radio, but static filled his ears as he scrolled through all the stations before he finally gave up. If this was a taste of things to come, James doubted he'd last two weeks in such an environment.

He hummed to keep himself awake while he kept an eye out for deer until, at last, he arrived at the castle gates. Edging to the side of the road, his headlights picked out a large central crest emblazoned in gold at their center, topped with golden spikes and acanthus leaves. James let out a low whistle as he set the parking brake.

Leaving the engine running, he hopped out and jogged to the gate. Cold air pierced through his clothes like icy needles, the wind penetrating his very bones. James blew on his hands before he punched in the code Kinross had texted him, then beat a hasty retreat to the car and waited for the gates to swing wide.

Shifting to low gear, he followed the winding lane through miles of woodland. The MGB rumbled over several stone bridges before the trees petered out. A dramatically lit medieval castle stood on a rocky headland above the dark waters of Loch Rannoch.

James expelled a heavy breath. His father had been close-lipped about his business partner. Due to the prior connection, James hadn't done his usual research when embarking on this new venture. Richard could have warned him that Kinross had enough gold to fill a Scottish loch.

Too tired to dawdle, he parked beside the front steps and climbed out, zipping his jacket against the wind's arctic embrace. Hastily, he grabbed the luggage from the cubby behind the seats and dashed up the granite steps to the massive iron-studded door.

Before he could knock, porch lights flickered on, and a dignified man in his late fifties, dressed in a three-piece suit, opened the door.

"Mr. Pressley-Coombes, welcome to Castle Rannoch. I am Henderson, the duke's butler. Won't you come inside?" Without waiting for James's reply, Henderson relieved him of one of his suitcases and led the way into the multi-storied receiving hall.

Crossing the threshold, James tried not to gawk at the paneled walls covered in battle-scarred weaponry arranged in starburst patterns up to the ceiling.

"It's a bit much for those not used tae such things," Henderson said, catching his unblinking stare. "I'll show you tae your room and send up a tray from the kitchen in a quarter hour. The duke will wish tae welcome you personally in the morning before he leaves for Edinburgh."

"Sounds good." James followed the spry butler up a curved staircase, the posts of which were carved in the image of stag heads.

On the landing, two life-sized oils caught his attention. In the first, a young boy with luminous dark eyes had his arm wrapped about the English foxhound at his side. James shifted his gaze to the second portrait, inhaled sharply through his nose, and gaped like an idiot.

It was Paisley Clark. But that was impossible.

The subject in question wore a floor-length white gown. Masses of long dark hair were piled on top of her head. The same luminous dark eyes as Paisley's stared wistfully into the middle distance. The model was attractive, beautiful even, with delicate features, a slender figure, and a pale complexion.

James shook his head slowly. The likeness to Paisley was uncanny. Everyone had a doppelgänger, he supposed, but what were the chances? Tomorrow he'd text Paisley the picture and see what she had to say.

Rounding the landing, James glanced over his shoulder at the portrait one last time before he started up the stairs after Henderson. The brass plaque beneath the painting said, *Lady Margaret Douglas.*

***

Due to the duke's early morning departure, James once more found himself following Henderson down a series of dimly lit corridors to meet with Kinross. James stifled a yawn and admitted that if Henderson weren't here, he'd be completely lost. He needed a map to find his way around the castle.

Henderson stopped in front of a door and rapped on the wooden panel.

"Come," a muffled voice called from within.

Turning the handle, Henderson announced, "Mr. Pressley-Coombes, Your Grace."

"Thank you, Henderson."

Henderson bowed and left, his retreating footsteps echoing down the flagged hallway.

In comparison to the rest of the castle, the vast, modern space, complete with chrome and glass tables, jarred the senses. The occupant sat partially hidden behind three computer monitors and an enormous glass-and-mahogany desk.

The duke pocketed a pair of glasses and came around the desk to greet James. Pushing sixty, Kinross stood half a head shorter than James and possessed a dark, penetrating gaze.

James self-consciously straightened and cleared his throat before he shook the duke's hand. The firm clasp and calluses reassured James that despite the duke's obvious wealth, this was not a man used to soft living.

"James. You don't mind if I call you that?" Kinross's lilted burr was evident but not overpowering.

"Not at all."

"I'm Cameron, or Kinross, if you must." The duke's manner held the deep-seated appeal of a capable man who understood the ramifications of his title.

Never one to call his father's contemporaries by their first names, James hesitated.

"Kinross, then." The duke correctly read James's disinclination to comply with a first-name label. "May I offer you some refreshment?"

James held up a splayed hand. "I'm good. Henderson made sure I had a hearty breakfast."

"Sorry, I'm running a bit late. Have a look around while you wait." Kinross returned to his desk.

James gravitated toward the bookshelves. An entire section on wind farms held his attention for ten seconds flat before a framed snapshot caught his eye.

His breath suspended. Paisley Clark and his sister, Catherine, sat playing with a litter of kittens. *Doppelgänger, my eye.* James snagged the small silver frame, the metal digging into his skin. The girls couldn't have been older than seven in the photo.

He set the picture back on the shelf and glanced about the room. Dozens of small, framed photos lay scattered on every conceivable surface. On a glass-and-chrome table holding a huge amethyst geode, a triptych of small paintings drew him. He recognized the small boy from the oil on the staircase landing. The child's expression was solemn as he stood beside a striking Persian woman.

In the second photo, Paisley again was the subject. She couldn't have been more than eight. Oversized glasses dwarfed her face while she examined a camera with an absorbed expression.

Awkwardly, James returned the picture to the glass surface, heedless of the other objects on the table. He glanced up and met Kinross's eyes over the top of one of the monitors.

"Has something upset you?" Kinross rose to his feet and came around from behind the desk.

"Why do you have pictures of Paisley?"

"To be precise, her name is Lady Margaret Douglas. Her mother and I divorced when she was a wee bairn."

"She goes by Paisley Clark."

Anger bubbled just under the surface, and James made an effort to tamp it down. What kind of game was Kinross playing? And how deep was his own father involved? James had no idea how Paisley would respond to this when she found out. He needed to call to check on her and make sure she was okay.

"It's obvious by all these pictures that you knew where Paisley was. Why were you absent from her life?" James demanded. "Were you aware she was practically a cipher in her own home? If my parents hadn't taken an interest in her, I hate to think what would have happened to her."

"I attended her milestone events," Kinross said quietly, his fingers grazing the top of his desk.

"That's crock." James's indignation blossomed into full-blown anger. He didn't care if his attitude blew their resort contract to smithereens. Kinross had a lot to answer for. The wistful expression the artist had captured in Paisley's oil painting had perfectly represented the lonely girl when she thought no one was looking. James had an affinity toward hurt things, be they animals, children, or adults. At a young age, Paisley had fallen under his protective sphere and, by association, Ben's as well.

"My divorce is not up for discussion, nor is my relationship with my daughter. Suffice it to say, when I met your father, we stumbled upon our mutual connection."

Always quick to give a person the benefit of the doubt, James floundered for words. "I apologize," he said stiffly. "Does Paisley know who you are?"

"She knows nothing about my title—or hers, for that matter."

"You contacted her through that DNA test. Why? You knew where she lived. Why didn't you call her or visit?"

Kinross raised an elegant brow.

"I'm a little protective where Paisley's concerned," James said by way of explanation for his bad show of manners.

"No offense taken." Kinross actually smiled. "I would think less of you if you weren't. To answer your question, yes, I contacted her through a DNA test. She's coming here, you know."

James's heart somersaulted at Kinross's words. "No, I didn't." How would meeting her father affect Paisley? Thankfully, he'd be here for her, no matter what happened.

"I'd appreciate you not telling her about me." Kinross motioned toward the room, indicating the castle at large. "I want to break this to her myself—after we meet. I believe it will be easier to explain to her in person."

"Of course. Does Paisley really not know about your title?"

"No. For that matter, neither does her mother. It's a long story meant for another time." The phone rang. Kinross glanced at the caller ID. "If you'll excuse me, I need to take this."

"No problem." James loosened his tie and wandered back to the bookcase. Randomly, he selected a large hardback on the dental anatomy of ruminants. Flipping open the book, he stared blankly at the colored drawings.

Obviously, Paisley's parents' divorce had been an unpleasant one. James was grateful for the deep-seated affection his own parents had shared and the devotion to God that had cemented their relationship. It had provided a stable environment for him and his siblings.

Since his mother's passing, James worried that his parents' marital success had something to do with Mom's funky gene pool. Most everyone up her family tree fell in love once and only once. The phenomenon had been documented all the way back to the seventeenth century. But many of her family members had never married as well. From time to time, he wondered which camp he'd fall into.

Though James had been attracted to women since his early teens, he hadn't been interested in settling down through most of his twenties. Lately, however, dating had lost its appeal, and he found himself longing for what his younger brother and sister had found in their respective marriages.

But he had never been in love. In *like*, yes—dozens of times. Unfortunately, he always lost interest within a day or two and ditched his dates for a ballgame with his siblings or a drop-in at Paisley's. With that kind of track record, he was fairly certain he hadn't inherited Mom's ridiculous love gene. Perhaps her DNA had mutated or skipped him altogether.

"Aye. I'll see you this afternoon." Kinross concluded his phone call and hung up.

James returned the scintillating book on bovine dentistry to the shelf and shifted to face Kinross.

"While I'm in Edinburgh, I'd like you to visit the job site with my CEO, Ward MacKenzie, and become familiar with the resort plans your father and I put together." Kinross picked up a binder and thumb drive off his desk and handed them to James. "These will provide perspective for the size and scope of the project."

James flipped through the pages. "Thank you. This should trigger a few ideas for our marketing campaign."

For the next eighteen months, James was here to do a job. Starting this project without his twin was a definite handicap. A hollow feeling started in the pit of his stomach, and the initial excitement he had experienced in Virginia, when his father had given him this assignment, had fizzled. Working without his twin didn't hold much appeal right now. Ben always kept him grounded. Who would clip his wings and tell him he was off course if he pursued a wild idea?

On the other hand, if he was ever to climb out from behind Ben's professional shadow, this was his chance. James had a lot to prove to his father, to Kinross, and to the corporation, but mostly to himself.

Then there was Kinross. James didn't care for the way the man had dealt with Paisley. Good thing he was here to keep an eye on him. And on her.

Chapter 7

ACHMED DIDN'T LIKE LEAVING HIS car at the park and ride, but he liked driving in the city even less.

He climbed aboard the Lothian bus bound for the heart of Edinburgh. The public transit bus was filled with early morning passengers, packed like tinned sardines, on the way to work. He grabbed a hand strap near the front, jostling against fellow travelers with every bump. At his stop, he stepped off and walked the last half block to the World Financial Bank's Scottish headquarters, his steps slowing the closer he drew.

He wouldn't be in this mess today if he hadn't siphoned funds from Kinross's business account to cover his gambling losses. Even though he had returned the money, someone had discovered his perfidy and coerced him to help rob the duke. Not only had he robbed a man he respected, but his actions had inadvertently placed his sister in the hospital. The only relief in this horrid disaster was that Bancroft's family was safe, whereas Padma would suffer long-term injuries because of his compulsive behavior.

His palms slipped on his briefcase handle, and his shirt plastered itself to his back under his sport coat. He stopped on the pavement outside the bank, pulled his hat low to obscure his features, and glanced at the WFB sign, positive the security cameras could detect his accelerated heart rate.

If he didn't do as directed, his sister, Padma, would die. He had no other option. Instructions had arrived by express mail early that morning. He had until noon to complete them.

Taking a deep breath, he entered the building and hesitated in the foyer. The red and white utilitarian decor struck a discordant note. For some reason, he had expected opulence for a bank with a global presence.

"Is there something I can do for you?" a woman asked.

Had his expression flagged an employee's attention?

Not good.

He gave her a polite smile. “I have an appointment with Mr. Bancroft.”

“This way, please.” She led him down a corridor and past several glass-walled offices and laminate-clad doors to a small private lobby. “Would you like a coffee or tea while you wait?”

“No, thank you.”

He took a seat on the black sofa beside a potted ficus. The weeping fig’s drooping branches mirrored the heaviness in his shoulders from holding up his head. He wanted nothing more than to melt into the carpet and disappear. If he hadn’t bet against one of the duke’s horses and lost, he wouldn’t be in this position. Now he was a pawn in a deadly game with no foreseeable way out.

The employee returned. “Mr. Bancroft will see you.”

He rose to his feet and followed her to Mr. Bancroft’s office.

“I understand you’d like to open a business account,” Mr. Bancroft, a middle-aged man with a soft Scottish burr said, shaking his hand.

“Yes. I . . .” Padma’s battered face swam before his mind’s eye, and Achmed stiffened with resolve.

After opening his briefcase, he removed a file folder. Bile churned inside his stomach as his fingers closed over the high-gloss photos. One by one, he laid them out on the desktop.

Mr. Bancroft’s eyes widened and met his.

“You are going to open a business account that will allow me to scatter funds to multiple accounts simultaneously. When that is completed, you are going to transfer the money the Duke of Perth and Kinross set up for this morning’s wire transmission into my account. Everything you need to start up that account is right here.” Achmed scooted the folder across the desk to the banker.

Mr. Bancroft’s tongue darted out and wet his lips.

“If you attempt to call the police, you will never see your family again.”

Achmed nudged the picture of Bancroft’s two daughters playing in a pile of autumn leaves in Bancroft’s back garden. The photo had been taken last week. The other was of Bancroft’s wife in nurse’s uniform, getting out of her car at the Perth Royal Infirmary.

“If you try anything, your family will disappear before the police arrive.”

Bancroft swallowed noisily, and beads of sweat broke out on his forehead.

Achmed steeled himself against the man’s obvious terror and kept an eye on the silent alarm beside Bancroft’s desk.

“How can I do that?” Bancroft asked and wiped his brow. “The duke has an appointment to complete the transaction.”

“The duke will call at the set time of transfer. Make sure you take that call.”

Bancroft nodded, his eyes enormous. He opened a program on his computer and attempted to type with shaky fingers.

Achmed ground his teeth and checked his watch. "May I suggest you hurry?"

If Bancroft did not complete this task in time for those manipulating the voiceover to transfer Kinross's funds, his blackmailers would kill Padma. Achmed wiped his palms on his trousers.

"I have prepared the account to automatically move the funds when the duke calls to verify his transfer." Bancroft's eyes fairly bulged.

"No holdups or time constraints on the wire?" Achmed had to make sure.

"No. I've used my manager override. I will need the duke's security code for this to work."

Achmed rattled off the required numerical sequence. He had memorized it on the drive from Castle Rannoch. His blackmailer had choreographed the transfer's timing to occur before Kinross reached the bank, emphasizing the fact that he didn't have time for sloppy mistakes.

Even with the stalled tactics, nothing would keep Kinross from making his appointment before he collected his daughter at the airport. Achmed glanced at the clock again. Kinross's daughter was due to land in less than an hour. This was going to be tight.

Refusing to meet Achmed's eyes, Bancroft entered the information, typing a lengthy string of instructions. Achmed sighed and rotated the monitor to ensure Bancroft wasn't sending a private SOS to another employee.

The transfer form blinked on the screen, and the tension in Achmed's neck eased marginally. He leaned forward in his chair and checked the amount, counting the six zeroes after the one. £1,000,000.00. He nodded, then noticed the discrepancy between the computer time and the wall clock.

"I thought your clock was on time." Achmed sucked in and nodded toward the wall clock.

"All of our clocks are set ten minutes behind schedule to allow for evening stragglers. It's our way of accommodating patrons who arrive last minute to do their banking."

A buzzing started in Achmed's ears. He closed his eyes and took a deep breath before he opened them once more. He was late—behind schedule. If Kinross showed up before the call came through to transfer funds, he would be caught.

"Hurry, man. More lives are at stake here than you realize," Achmed said, unable to suppress the near panic inside him.

Evidently, his behavior spurred Bancroft to finish setting up the account.

"It's ready."

Achmed texted his contact. *Ready.*

The intercom buzzed. Achmed nodded for Bancroft to answer.

Bancroft pressed the button. "Yes?"

A woman's voice crackled through the speaker. "The Duke of Perth and Kinross is on the line to verify his transfer."

"Patch him through to the voice imaging system," Bancroft said and hung up.

The call came through not a moment too soon by Achmed's way of thinking. He rose to his feet, pulled his hat low over his forehead, and gathered the glossy pictures off Bancroft's desk. "Your family will benefit from your cooperation."

Achmed left Bancroft's office and paused in the hallway. He couldn't leave the building yet, not with the possibility of running into Kinross on the way out. The office adjoining Bancroft's was dark. He slipped inside and took a seat against the thinly partitioned wall so no one could see him from the corridor.

The clock above his head ticked away the minutes. Ten minutes. Twenty. Achmed sighed. How much had his blackmailer delayed Kinross's appointment by? The clock ticked on. Thirty minutes. Achmed crossed his leg and jiggled his foot.

Bancroft's intercom buzzed.

"Sir, the Duke of Perth and Kinross is here to see you."

"Send him in." Bancroft's voice carried through the thin partition of the adjoining office.

Achmed leaned closer to the divider.

"Your Grace. How nice to see you again."

"Sorry I'm late."

Kinross's low-pitched voice carried through the wall. The slap of a handshake and the creak of an office chair sounded a few seconds later.

"What brings you to our office today?"

Achmed heard the groan of a desk chair.

Bancroft sounded a trifle nervous. He had reason to be.

"I had an appointment with you thirty minutes ago," Kinross said.

"There must be some confusion. We had you slated for a money transfer, which you will be happy to note took place at the prescribed time." Bancroft emphasized this with a little too much geniality for Achmed's taste. But he had to give the man points for effort.

"How is that possible? I came to oversee that transfer myself."

"There must be some mistake. We took care of the transfer this morning as scheduled," Bancroft said.

Achmed held his breath, not fully trusting Bancroft to keep quiet about their recent encounter.

"How much was transferred from my account?" Kinross asked.

There was a sound of faint typing.

"All but five thousand pounds," Bancroft replied.

Hands slammed down on something hard. "Where is my money? The bank can trace my transfer. I want to know where it went."

Achmed flinched.

"When was the account emptied?" Kinross demanded.

More clicking of computer keys, as if Bancroft didn't know. Achmed shook his head in reluctant admiration. The man was a born actor.

"Thirty-four minutes ago."

"I don't understand how your employees could transfer those funds without my permission." Something drummed rapidly on a solid surface.

Bancroft cleared his throat. "I assure you our system would have notified us if everything was not aboveboard for that transfer. You called at the appointed time to grant authorization. Since you had visited earlier in the week in regard to the transfer and your voice matched on our state-of-the-art recognition system, the transfer took place."

Dead silence.

Achmed squirmed in his chair.

"Mr. Bancroft, I did *not* authorize that transfer."

"Your Grace, no matter how good a mimic, our technology would catch an impersonator. No one can copy another's vocal inflections perfectly. They are like a fingerprint on our voice recognition system."

"Then the thief must have spliced sound bites together to create a recording that would pass your system. Let me be plain: I did not authorize the removal of those funds. Someone has masqueraded as me."

"Again, I assure you everything was in order for that transfer."

"I was scheduled for an in-person transfer of funds, was I not?"

"Yes, Your Grace." Bancroft's voice heightened in volume. "But when the call came, we assumed you must have changed it to a call."

"Have I ever wire transferred such a large amount?"

"No, Your Grace."

"Then that phone request was out of the ordinary. Correct?"

"Yes, Your Grace."

"Find my money." Kinross's tightly clipped words carried through the thin wall as though he clenched his teeth.

"Yes, Your Grace," Bancroft said.

The sound of furious typing. "The funds were wired to a numbered account within the branch."

"Whose account?"

"It is against bank procedure to share personal information with our other clients."

Kinross laughed, a bitter sound. "You dare say that to me after what has occurred? I shall speak in simple terms. As both accounts belong to this branch, the funds should be easy enough to return. Just do it, and I won't report your institution." Kinross expelled a pent-up breath.

"That isn't possible."

"Whyever not? Transferring missing funds back into my account should be simple."

"No holds were placed on the funds because it was an in-house transfer." Bancroft's fingers typed furiously, clicking away on the keyboard. "The other account is empty. The money scattered almost immediately to over thirty separate accounts," Bancroft said faintly. "Most of those accounts are located in the Middle East. All I can do is contact SWIFT to trace them."

Achmed's temples throbbed as he struggled with the information he had overheard. Having grown up in the Middle East, he was well aware that funding for terrorist organizations came through outside sources. Kinross's business account had almost surely just gone to assist a terrorist regime. Achmed's mouth went dry, and he rubbed his pounding temples. As a refugee, he had come to the UK to leave that world behind.

"Unfortunately, SWIFT has no jurisdiction in the Middle East," Bancroft said.

"You are telling me my funds are lost?" Kinross enunciated his words with clipped precision. "This matter will be handed to the Office of Financial Sanctions Implementation. You may be assured I will join the patron lawsuit that is in progress against your bank."

"I understand." Bancroft sounded subdued, resigned to the inevitable.

"My accounts will close within the week," Kinross said. Something dragged across the carpet—most likely Kinross's chair. "During the interim, you will ensure no other funds go missing. I will hold you personally responsible if they do, and measures will be taken against you."

"Yes, Your Grace."

The door to Bancroft's office opened, and Achmed flattened himself against the wall, praying to Allah that Kinross did not see him through the glass-fronted office. He needn't have worried; Kinross stormed down the corridor.

Achmed rose to his feet and went to the door.

The secretary's voice magnified over Bancroft's intercom and filtered through the thin wall. "Yes, Mr. Bancroft?"

"Please cancel my appointments for the remainder of the day. I'm going home."

Chapter 8

SCOTLAND DID NOT LAY OUT a warm welcome for Paisley. For a minute or two, she was convinced they were going to kick her out of the country. First, passport control didn't like her photo ID. The photo was taken when she had put a rinse in her hair, and the color had thrown off the electronic reader. Afterward, immigration officials had taken her aside for questioning.

Moving on to customs, her bad luck continued. She was randomly selected for a bag search. The male agent unzipped her suitcase and pawed through every item, even holding up her turquoise, lace underthings for inspection. She had turned bright red.

By the time Paisley received the green light to enter Scotland, she had blisters on her fingers from twisting her camera bag strap and was seriously considering booking the next flight back to the US of A.

Loudspeakers blared overhead, announcing a flight change. Disoriented, she glanced about, trying to figure out where her father was in the melee of moving bodies.

A kilted man in hiking boots kept pace with her while he spoke to his companion. Their lilted commentary was almost incomprehensible. Why hadn't someone warned her that Scots English resembled something from Middle-earth?

Just then, the wheel of her bright vermillion suitcase caught on a fry container and tipped. Paisley started to right the heavy case, but a well-dressed gentleman beat her to it, easily placing all four wheels back on the polished beige tiles. Paisley opened her mouth to thank him, but the words died on her lips.

He was shorter than she had expected, with the same dark eyes and pale skin that greeted her reflection every morning in the bathroom mirror. Though his brown hair was sprinkled with gray, it had the same bright sheen and hint of wave as hers. A heavy gold signet ring stood out on one hand, and a wedding band with an inlaid emerald adorned the other. He was dressed casually in an open jacket over a collared shirt and wool sweater. Despite their simplicity, his clothes were of the finest quality.

She fought a rising self-consciousness as she stood before her father in her thrift-store duds. Absently, she ran a hand over her tangled hair and wished she had stopped to brush it in the bathroom after the overnight flight. Tentatively, she met his eyes, and an overwhelming sense of familiarity enveloped her.

"Hello, Paisley." Her father smiled at her.

She attempted to return the greeting but misted up instead and bit the inside of her bottom lip to keep from making a fool of herself. Unsure who moved first, suddenly she was wrapped in a fierce hug that was the epitome of every childhood dream. She soaked up the sensation and stored it away to revisit later.

Her father stepped back and motioned toward a side exit. "Shall we?"

Paisley nodded, not trusting her voice.

He clasped the handle of her battered suitcase in one hand and her upper arm with the other as though afraid to lose their physical connection. As they walked toward the exit, a few travelers nodded to him. Others held up cell phones and took pictures.

"We've been spotted," Kinross said, his voice pitched low so no one could overhear. "When we go outside, keep your head down. Things might get a wee bit dicey."

He whisked her out the side entrance to a waiting SUV with tinted windows. The driver, a stocky, ginger-haired man, took Paisley's suitcase and stored it in the back. A half dozen photojournalists caught sight of them and charged en masse.

The driver waved them off and shouted in thick Scots, "Awa' and bile yer heid."

Kinross opened the back door and waited for Paisley to climb inside, which she did to the click and flash of cameras.

"Keep your head down and buckle up," Kinross instructed as he joined her.

Paisley did as she was told and slouched in her seat. "Why are they taking pictures?"

"All in good time." Kinross pronounced it "goot" with the hint of a lilt.

The driver took the wheel and stepped on the gas. The SUV shot toward the airport exit. Thickets of scrubby trees lined both sides of the dual highway;

their gold-and-orange plumage made it impossible for Paisley to see what lay beyond.

They entered a roundabout with roadways that peeled off in multiple directions.

"The Balmoral?" the driver asked.

"We're booked in Fife at the Donnistair on Margety Bay. They've a private entrance and a restaurant on-site. But I'd like to run an errand in Edinburgh before we leave the city."

"Very good, Your—"

"Hamish, I'm going to roll up the privacy window," Kinross interrupted before Hamish completed his sentence.

"Aye."

Kinross pressed a button beside him, and a soundproof divider rose between the front and back seat. "Hamish is a first-rate fellow, but he's prone to gossip. We don't need our reunion shared with the entire estate. What I have to say to you cannae wait."

"You aren't a Scottish rock star or something, are you?"

"I'm afraid it's much worse than that," Kinross said, apology lacing his tone.

An odd disquiet filled her, and Paisley crossed her legs and fiddled with the electronic buttons on the leather arm rest beside her.

"How much do you know about the British aristocracy?" Kinross asked.

Evidently, her father wasn't one for idle chitchat. Paisley directed her thoughts to the few tabloids she had seen of the royal family on her daily newsfeed.

"They go by funny titles instead of using their real names, wear absurd-looking hats, and live in large, drafty houses?"

A rusty sound escaped her father's throat and reminded her of an old handsaw. It took Paisley off guard. Did her father not laugh very often?

"Am I close?" she asked.

"Not bad." He beamed at her, then sobered almost immediately. "When I went to the States, I purposely dropped my title. I wanted acceptance on my own merits."

"Title?" Paisley's heart skipped a beat. "You aren't the secret heir to the British throne, are you?" She tried to laugh it off.

"I'm thirty-seventh in line to the British crown."

"What are you exactly?"

"First and foremost, I am your father. That is what matters most. I am also Cameron Archibald Andrew Douglas." He hesitated before adding, "And I'm a duke."

"You're a *duke*?" Paisley's eyes bulged. Even she, with her limited knowledge, knew that dukes were top-ranking aristocrats just after royals.

He nodded. "And you are my daughter, Lady Margaret Iona Paisley Douglas."

Paisley's pulse took off like a racehorse out of the starting gate. *A lady?* She glanced down at her secondhand clothes. All her life, she had been plain old Paisley Clark. She liked hiding in the background and observing the world from behind her camera lens. Did her father expect her to wear floral dresses, eat nasty cucumber sandwiches, and drink herbal tea with a curled pinkie finger?

"You don't live in a big, drafty house, do you?" she asked suspiciously.

"Several of them, actually."

"I don't envy your utility bills," Paisley muttered under her breath, hearkening back to the one-bedroom apartment she had struggled to heat last winter before she lost her business. "Does my mom know?"

Her father cleared his throat. "I had planned to tell her when she visited Scotland after she concluded her graduate studies."

"But Mom never went to Scotland. You were divorced before she graduated," Paisley filled in for him. "Were you a duke when you married her?"

"I was the Marquess of Crieffmore in those days." He shifted slightly in his seat.

"Oh, *only* a marquess." Paisley tried not to roll her eyes. How could her father have kept something like that from her mom? "Why didn't you tell her?"

"Your mother expects the absolute truth. When I went to America, I enrolled in graduate studies as Cameron Douglas. If she had known about my background and what was expected of me, I doubt she would have accepted a single date." Her father's fingers twitched in his lap, and he glanced out the window. "And I wanted to date her verra much."

As a child, Paisley had learned it was always best to be candid with her mother. Even little white lies had ended with lengthy groundings. If her mother had realized her father's evasion of the truth, her reaction would have been akin to Chernobyl's nuclear blast.

"Did you honestly believe that if she'd gone to Scotland you could have swayed her to leave the US?"

"I fooled myself into thinking if she loved me, it wouldn't matter." His voice throbbed with emotion. "When my father's stroke demanded my immediate return to Scotland, your mother refused to accompany me. She had one year left of law school. When we married, I had foolishly promised she could practice for a decade before we moved to the UK. Even with my father so sick, she insisted I keep my word. At first, I thought I could fly back and forth between the two countries, but my father's condition worsened. Visits to the States were impossible, and your mother refused to compromise." Her father looked out the window and said no more.

Paisley wanted to defend her mother, but her father's voice rang with truth. Mom's one and only passion was the law. Family always took a back seat.

She glanced at her father. Did he still harbor ill feelings about the divorce? If he did, it hadn't kept him from moving on. Paisley hadn't missed the wedding band on his finger. Why hadn't his wife come with him to the airport? And why hadn't he mentioned her?

***

Twenty minutes later, Paisley was still mulling over the fact that her father had called her a lady with a capital *L* as Hamish wove through Edinburgh's heavy traffic. Did that mean she had to attend garden parties and curtsy to the queen? Paisley didn't want to meet any of the royals. With her luck, she would probably trip and fall flat on her face.

Her eyes darted to her father, then quickly away. Why, oh why, couldn't her father have been a simple rock star? Athletes' and musicians' families didn't live in the spotlight. She *hated* the spotlight.

Her father lowered the soundproof glass between the front and back seats. "Hamish, Lady Margaret's suitcase is sticking. I'd like to replace it. Could you stop at Mulberry in Multrees Walk and get her a new one before we leave the city?"

"Really. I'm fine," she protested. Paisley had no idea how to address her father. Dad was too familiar and Cameron too disrespectful, so she avoided addressing him by name altogether.

"Let me spoil you a little."

Paisley leaned back in her seat and fought the urge to argue. She had been kind of proud of that stylish, albeit battered, red suitcase, having bought it for five bucks at a garage sale. The case had at least another half dozen flights of wear in it before it went to suitcase heaven.

Following the duke's instructions, Hamish came to a stop in front of a luxury leather-goods store. Taking her father's credit card, Hamish left the four-wheel drive running in a no-park zone and went inside.

Paisley leaned back in her seat and closed her eyes. Sleep had been scarce the last few nights due to the anticipation of meeting her father. Now her body screamed for relief.

Before she drifted off, a feather-light kiss touched her brow. It startled her enough to rouse her sleep-deprived brain. Not used to physical contact by her mother, she didn't know how to respond. She opened her eyes and looked at her father.

"I'm sorry I woke you." Regret showed in her father's expression.

"It's all right." She rotated her neck and glanced out the window just as Hamish exited the store with a large Louis Vuitton suitcase.

Paisley had admired knock-off versions of that same case when she had taken the Chinatown bus to New York City. Afterward, she had Googled authentic LV handcrafted trunks on spinners—talk about a hefty price tag. But neither man seemed concerned that her father had just forked out £3250.00.

That suitcase represented two months' rent for a studio apartment. Paisley pinched herself, positive she had entered a virtual reality. Only the very wealthy or foolish would purchase something that extravagant. She was neither.

***

The change in road surfaces woke Paisley. Bleary-eyed and drugged from sleep, she watched two large gates swing open under a stone arch. The SUV's tires hummed as the vehicle entered the cobbled courtyard of a spacious, two-story building.

"Where are we?" Paisley asked, pushing hair out of her eyes.

"The Donnistair on Margety Bay in the Kingdom of Fife," Hamish said, setting the handbrake, before he let her and her father out beside the waiting bellhop.

"It's good to see you again, Your Grace. If you and your party would be so kind as to follow me." The bellhop escorted them through a discreet side entrance and down a hall lit with antique lanterns to their suite of rooms.

"If you should need anything, there is a buzzer on your bedside table. Your driver's room is next door but one." The bellhop handed Hamish two sets of keys. "Have a pleasant stay."

"Thank you," her father said and waited until the bellhop closed the door.

Paisley found the entire experience a little odd. Was it considered bad manners for her father to purchase items or carry keys? She had no idea and turned her attention to the suite.

Plush sofas, a flat screen, and walnut occasional tables filled the sitting area. Paisley crossed to the window and tugged open the draperies. The Donnistair sat on the rocky shoreline of the Forth estuary where it joined the North Sea.

A stiff breeze tore at the tufted grass outside the picture window in the sitting room, and white caps dotted the turbulent blue-gray water under a gloaming sky. In the distance, the iconic Forth Bridge, a red cantilevered rail bridge connected Fife to the opposite shore.

Paisley snatched up her photo bag and started for the door.

"Where are you going?" her father asked.

"The view is incredible. I want to take a few shots before the light changes."

Her father's lips curved ever so slightly. "Before you do, there are a few items I wish to discuss with you."

Paisley set her camera bag down. "Such as?"

"If you are amendable, I'd like you to stay for an extended period so we can get to know one another."

"How long were you thinking?"

"Six months."

Paisley, never good at hiding her emotions, almost choked. "That's a long visit."

Her father shrugged, but his dark eyes, so like her own, implored her to stay.

When he had sent her the airline ticket, she hadn't considered the duration of her stay. Six months seemed excessive even when she didn't have anything to return to in the States, having taken indefinite leave from her waitressing job before she left. She bit the inside of her lip as worries swirled inside. What if she and her father didn't get along? Then what?

"How about three months with the opportunity to extend?" she countered.

A smirk came and went about his mouth. "Och, lassie, you drive a hard bargain—like any true Scot. Aye. We'll revisit your demands in three months. Deal?"

"Deal," she agreed and picked up her camera bag once more.

"Don't be too long. The dressmaker arrives within the hour."

"Dressmaker?" Why did she need a dressmaker?

"Did you bring a party gown? I forgot to tell you you'd need one."

"No. Why do I need a fancy dress?"

"A few dozen of my associates and their wives are joining us for supper tomorrow evening. I'd like to introduce you. There will also be an afternoon tea and other various events that require more formal attire than I believe you are accustomed to."

"You're having a dinner party here?" Paisley glanced around the suite. Though the rooms were large, they wouldn't seat half his guests by any means.

"No. At the castle."

"What castle?"

"Castle Rannoch, our family seat in Perth and Kinross."

"You live in a castle?" This was getting more and more bizarre. Next thing she knew, her father would be telling her his house was haunted.

Paisley set down her camera again.

"Aye, but I own three other estates as well," her father added in an almost apologetic tone.

She stared at him while her mind attempted to absorb the information. How many more surprises did he have up his sleeve?

"My wife uses this particular dress shop when she can't get to Paris." Her father checked his watch. "Her team arrives at half past."

"If a dressmaker is coming, I'll be quick."

Spurred to action, Paisley returned to her room for her tripod. Her heart gave a pang when her eyes landed on both cases standing side by side at the foot of her bed. She ran her fingers over the top of her battered luggage. Did her father plan to replace everything she owned with something shiny and new?

Chapter 9

A SHINY TRAY OF PIPING-HOT food was laid out on the coffee table beside a refolded newspaper when Paisley returned from her photoshoot. Her father must have read the paper while she was outside.

"I don't know your preferences, so I ordered a wee bit of everything," her father said.

"It smells delicious." Paisley helped herself to a poached egg and a slice of ham. Bypassing the gray glob of porridge, she poured herself a glass of juice. Curious about differences in American and Scottish journalism, she scanned the newspaper headlines:

Scottish wild cats found dead near Balmoral. Suspicious toxins at play.

Tourism down twenty-one percent in the last twelvemonth.

Body of lead investigator on WFB probe found floating in Loch Morar.

She cut a slice of ham, popped it into her mouth, and opened the newsprint to page two and read, *Sir Edmund Dalrymple, late of Mallaig, was found floating in Loch Morar in the wee hours by local fishermen. Sir Edmund was lead prosecutor in the investigation of World Finance Bank—WFB. Numerous allegations against said bank about skimmed funds have been placed on hold, pending further investigation into Sir Edmund's death.*

Her father appeared a bit shaken.

"Is something wrong?" Paisley asked between bites of her egg.

He indicated the newspaper she had just browsed. "Shortly before I picked you up, I had a bit of a dustup with a banker at WFB. One of my business accounts was affected."

"I'm so sorry. This is probably a bad time for me to visit."

"Nonsense. I've waited half my life to spend time with my daughter. Luckily, only one of my business accounts was drained."

Paisley swallowed as guilt assailed her. Her father had just forked out a huge amount on that trunk. "Maybe we should return my trunk."

Her father's brows wrinkled. "Whatever for?"

"So we don't waste your money."

Her father threw his head back and laughed. "You're a treasure, Paisley. I assure you that I am financially solvent. The bank is under investigation, and those of us whose accounts were emptied will, in time, likely receive a generous compensation."

He sobered and indicated the newspaper she had just browsed. "My main worry just now is for the lead investigator's family. Sir Edmund and I were acquainted."

"I'm so sorry." She had no idea what else to say in the face of her father's double tragedy.

A knock sounded on the door.

Her father checked his watch. "Right on time, I see." He went to answer.

Paisley folded the paper and rose to her feet. A plump woman with impossibly long eyelashes entered, followed by her attendants wheeling racks of clothing.

The chrome racks not only carried an assortment of formal gowns but also a plethora of jeans, blouses, tea dresses, outerwear, and tweeds.

Goodness. Paisley's eyes widened. She had to try on all that?

"Deb Ferguson, this is my daughter, Lady Margaret," Kinross said.

Evidently, when you had a title, it didn't matter what you were really called.

"Hi." Paisley nodded to the newcomers.

"Did my wife email you the list of necessities Lady Margaret will need during her stay?" Kinross asked.

"She did, Your Grace." Deb motioned for her assistants to place the racks along one wall.

"Good. Good." Kinross nodded to the room at large. "I've a conference call that should take the better part of two hours. Hopefully, we will conclude our business simultaneously." He entered his bedroom and closed the door behind himself.

"Well now." Deb circled Paisley like a prize fighter sizing up an opponent. "Kinross didn't mention that you were so petite. Let me get your measurements so we can find your size."

"I really don't think all this is necessary." Paisley motioned to the multiple racks of clothing.

"Nonsense. When Kinross asks, it's always necessary."

Paisley wandered to the closest rack and checked the tag on a Dolce and Gabbana black-and-white dress. Her eyes bulged at the price. She could purchase a season's worth of name brands at her favorite secondhand shop for that.

Deb's long lashes swept down, but Paisley caught the amused twinkle in her eye.

"Stop your worries. Kinross is as rich as Midas."

"I don't want him to waste that much on me."

"He's not one to squander his gold."

Paisley stiffened, unhappy to hear her father spoken of in such an offhand manner.

"Don't mind me. I'm far too outspoken. It's one of the reasons Kinross calls on me from time to time. That wife of his only wants Paris designers or something smart from London. Unfortunately, haute couture isn't warm enough for the Highlands, so I fill in the duchess's wardrobe gaps." While Deb talked, her fingers had run a measuring tape all over Paisley's body.

"Hmmm," Deb said when she finished. "I have a few items I'll send Mary back to the shop for. There are several lovely evening gowns in small sizes that might do nicely."

"Mary," Deb called over her shoulder.

"Yes, ma'am." Mary, a boney woman dressed in black spandex, came up alongside her.

"Take the van and bring back that shipment of size fours. We'll have to nip them in a wee bit, but a size two might be too small."

"A size four is too big. I wear a two," Paisley said.

"Trust me, lass. Sizing runs differently here. A two in the States is a four in the UK," Deb informed her.

"I'll be back in a few minutes." Mary let herself out of the suite.

"Why don't you try on some casual attire while we wait." Deb pounced on the rack closest to her.

A little self-consciously, Paisley removed her jeans and sweater. As an only child, she had never undressed, except for gym class, in front of others. She soon realized that this dressmaker viewed her body much like a doctor would a patient. It was an object to be clothed properly. Letting go of her inhibitions, Paisley gave herself up to the joy of trying on clothes she had only dreamed about.

Deb glanced at Paisley's bare feet. "I don't know what Kinross expects me to do about that. My stock doesn't run that small."

"I might have something in my room," Paisley offered.

Tired of short-people jokes all through school, shopping for heels had become a regular pastime. She had a large collection.

"Let's see what you have."

Paisley led Deb into her bedroom and removed three pairs of heels for her inspection. Whenever she had a spare bit of cash, she haunted the seventy-five percent off rack at top-end stores. Due to her small shoe size, she often found great bargains.

"You've some verra nice brands. Several of these will work." Deb nodded her approval.

"I'm back," Mary called from the outer room, making a loud noise as she dragged something across the floor.

Paisley left her shoes on the bed and followed Deb into the sitting room. Cocktail dresses, formal wear, and tea-length gowns crowded Mary's rolling rack.

Deb muttered under her breath while she pawed through the collection and removed several dresses that were as close to runway as Paisley had seen.

While Deb hunted down formal attire, Mary piled up tweeds, sweaters—which she insisted were jumpers—jackets, and an entire collection of riding apparel.

"Riding clothes?" Why would she need riding clothes? Paisley had only ridden horseback twice.

"You can't be a Douglas without joining the horsey set. Your father has one of the finest racing stables in Scotland. Haven't you heard of the Perth and Kinross Stables?" Mary set another "jumper" on top of the growing pile of casual wear.

"No." Paisley shook her head.

"One of your father's stallions took the silver cup last year at Royal Ascot. The duke put him out to stud this year and is making a small fortune off the fees. With your stature, you could pass for one of his jockeys, just like your wee granny did once upon a time."

A dull pang echoed through Paisley's heart and saddened her that she had never known her grandmother.

"Let's give these gowns a go, shall we?" Deb draped the formal wear over a chair.

A floaty dress in buttery yellow caught Paisley's eye. That cut might look nice on her. Deb slid the sumptuous fabric over her head and did up the buttons.

"Ah. No, definitely not," Paisley said after getting a good look at herself in the mirror. The dress was almost obscene. The plunging neckline exposed way too much of her assets, and a hidden slit almost reached her hip.

"I'd like something a little more modest," Paisley said as diplomatically as she could.

"The dress is fabulous." Deb busied herself around Paisley, tucking and straightening as she went.

"I'm not comfortable in it." Even though Paisley had the figure to pull it off, she had no desire to flaunt her wares.

"Lass, this gown was made for you." Mary seconded the shop owner's opinion.

"Let's try something else," Paisley insisted and tugged at the buttons.

"All right." Deb's voice was tight with disapproval.

She held up a red-colored gown with shimmery satin panels. The fabric was a little slinky, but the bodice was discreet enough. Paisley slipped into the dress and adjusted the capped sleeves just below the shoulder. The high waist hugged the bottom of her breasts but not indecently so. Though not formfitting, the fabric showed off Paisley's figure without making her cringe.

The room went dead quiet. Neither Deb nor Mary moved as they waited for Paisley's verdict.

"I like it." Paisley smoothed her hands over the satin material and smiled.

Deb helped her out of the dress. "You know, I don't agree with you on the yellow formal, but this dress . . ." Deb paused, obviously searching for the right words. "This dress was made for a duke's daughter."

***

During the three-and-a-half-hour drive to Castle Rannoch, Paisley's father peppered her with questions that were followed by long silences where he crossed and uncrossed his arms. Though Paisley answered him readily enough, something about his guarded, brown eyes kept her from asking him questions of her own.

The pastoral farmland surrounding Perth and Kinross gave way to dense forests and steep hillsides, which invaded both sides of the highway. The farther north they drove, the more rugged and less populated the landscape became. Soon her fingers itched to capture the view with her lens.

They crossed the river Garry, and Kinross rallied. "If the mist weren't coming down the glen just now, I'd have Hamish stop at the Queen's View so you could enjoy the vista, but I'd like you to see Castle Rannoch before the fog swallows it up."

"I'm sure there will be other opportunities." Paisley had a hard time absorbing the idea that her father was a duke and lived in a castle. To her, the entire scenario sounded like an alternate universe.

They drove past several lochs and played peekaboo with the river Tummel as the road weaved through the national forest and skirted through Kinloch Rannoch's quaint thoroughfare. Some miles past the village, Hamish stopped in front of a pair of wrought-iron gates with a large central crest emblazoned in gold and topped with acanthus leaves and spiked arrows. The electronic gates swung inward between the two stone pillars, and the SUV passed the empty gatekeeper's cottage.

"We only man the gatehouse for events," Kinross said when he caught Paisley eyeing the structure.

A sign for Perth and Kinross Racing Stables pointed toward a lane branching off the main drive. The stables must be one of her father's numerous businesses.

Hamish stepped on the accelerator, and the SUV shot down the lane. Paisley leaned forward, her eyes straining for the first glimpse of her father's home. The drive wound through woodland and rumbled over several flat stone bridges before the trees petered out.

Paisley caught her breath. "Ohhh."

On the rocky headland above a wind-whipped loch stood a medieval castle whose crenelated towers lent her imagination wings. Nearby oaks and rhododendrons danced wildly in the stiff breeze, almost as wildly as her beating heart. Opaque mist on the surrounding crags inched its way down the hillside, enveloping all in its path.

The car climbed the wide-sweeping drive and came to a halt in front of the castle's massive front door. Formal gardens of deciduous trees and shrubbery, interspersed with flower beds bare of blooms, were intersected by gravel walks, ending abruptly at the base of a forested hillside. The untamed beauty rippled through her senses and called to her soul more effectively than any siren's song. This was home.

A dignified man in his late fifties dressed in a kilt came down the steps as Hamish let her out of the SUV.

"Thank you, Hamish."

"My pleasure, Lady Margaret." Hamish went to the back of the vehicle and removed their luggage. "Henderson, I'll be taking these inside. Where should I leave them?"

"Set them in the hall. I'll have them delivered to Lady Margaret's rooms," Henderson said.

During their brief exchange, Paisley stood on the graveled drive, fighting to keep her hair from blowing into her face. She stared up at the battlements with her heart beating inside her throat. The sheer size of the castle made her feel small and insignificant.

"Paisley, this is my butler." Kinross motioned to the man called Henderson.

She quit her gawking and turned to the man beside her father.

"Henderson, my daughter, the Lady Margaret."

Henderson bowed neatly. "Welcome to Castle Rannoch, my lady. Won't you come inside?" He turned toward the door.

"Henderson keeps us sorted and running efficiently," Kinross said and accompanied his butler up the stone steps to the porch. "Where is the duchess?"

"Her Grace was unavoidably detained and sends her regrets that she was unavailable to greet Lady Margaret upon her arrival," Henderson said quietly.

Paisley caught the look that passed between her father and his butler. Evidently, her arrival at Castle Rannoch was not a highly anticipated event by her father's duchess, Munira.

Kinross turned back, waiting for her to climb the steps. When she reached him, his expression softened.

"Welcome home, Paisley."

Chapter 10

Paisley reverently fingered the bodice of her new gown before she went downstairs to meet her father's guests. The polished stranger in the mirror bore no resemblance to the fresh-faced, ponytail-loving woman who greeted her reflection each morning.

With naturally long, dark eyelashes, Paisley had never needed mascara and doubted she could replicate the look without putting out an eye. The results did give her an extra boost of confidence to meet her father's business associates, and that, she assured herself, was important.

"The duke will be well pleased." Her dresser moved back a step to appraise Paisley's appearance.

"Aye, that he will, Lady Margaret," the makeup artist agreed as she packed away the last of her cosmetics.

Why did Kinross's staff insist on addressing her by her title after she had asked them to call her Paisley? Did it have something to do with Kinross's elevated position?

"Thank you both so much. I've never looked so nice," Paisley told both women as they checked her one last time, then let themselves out of the ornate bedroom suite her father had assigned her.

To acquire a more sophisticated appearance, Munira's personal dresser and makeup artist had slathered her in creams, tweezed her thick brows, applied cosmetics, and piled her heavy tresses into an elaborate updo with enough bobby pins to set off a metal detector.

The ormolu clock on the mantle chimed the quarter hour. Since it was too early to go down to dinner, Paisley slipped on her heels and paced the gold-and-cream suite. The handcrafted bed was covered in pale silk and scatter cushions. Heavy brocade draperies surrounded the bed. Paisley paused at the window and drew back the curtains. A wall of shifting gray mist met her eyes. She sighed and dropped the fabric back into place.

With more than twenty minutes before she was due downstairs, Paisley determined to investigate the collection of antiquities lining the ground floor's main hall. She reached for the brass door handle, but subdued voices outside her room held her in place. Hesitant to interrupt a private conversation, Paisley opened her door a crack to see if they had moved off.

No such luck. A whispered argument appeared in progress between an elegant, middle-aged woman in a long cream gown and a younger man in a charcoal suit and blood-red cufflinks. Their backs were partially turned, and she could only see them in profile. Paisley didn't want to eavesdrop, but if she closed her door, the couple would realize she had overheard at least some portion of their disagreement.

"What you are doing is foolish," the woman hissed.

"Foolish? Me? I didn't marry a man I didn't love just to leave Uzkahzikstan."

"You'll not speak to me in such a way. At least Kinross is not the terrorist your father was. If you keep spending at this exorbitant rate, Kinross will cut you off. Where would you be without his support?"

"Threats, Mother?"

"If you like."

"Do your worst." The man peeled her fingers from his sleeve and left her to make her own way down to supper.

Paisley eased back from the door. That woman was her father's wife?

After that scene and the duchess's refusal to meet Paisley upon her arrival, tonight's gathering with its familial undercurrents sounded like a laugh a minute.

Paisley peeked through the opening to make sure the woman had gone. The corridor was empty. She slipped into the hall and eased her door shut. Turning in the opposite direction, she started down the wide hall. She recognized Cézanne's *Curtain, Jug, and Fruit* on the wall and stopped to admire the composition. Either that painting was an excellent replica, or it was the real deal. She leaned closer to get a better look at the signature. It appeared authentic. But what did she know?

A glance down the castle corridor with its ceiling fresco and gilded woodwork hinted toward the latter. When she had flown to Scotland, Paisley had worried about acclimating to the difference in culture, accent, wrong-side-of-the-road driving, and strange bathroom facilities. What she hadn't counted on was her father's wealth and title.

Kinross inhabited a world far removed from what she was accustomed to. How on earth was she going to adapt to this lavish lifestyle when half the time she couldn't remember that she and Lady Margaret were one and the same?

***

Paisley was lost. Strike that. Lady Margaret was lost. Referring to her titled self was enough to give Paisley an identity crisis and make her late for supper.

Her father had told her to meet him on the grand staircase landing. She had taken the staircase outside her suite only to realize it was one of four major stairways used by the family. A maid had found her wandering about and had taken pity on her. She escorted Paisley to the grand staircase, a fifteen-foot-wide affair with a landing larger than her bedroom in Virginia.

Sure enough, Kinross stood waiting alongside the stunning female of Persian descent Paisley had noticed earlier outside her bedroom suite. Paisley's mouth went dry.

"You look beautiful, my dear." Kinross addressed her with obvious pride. "Paisley, I'd like you to meet my wife, Munira, Duchess of Perth and Kinross."

"How do you do?" Paisley gave Munira her best smile. "I don't know the proper protocol. Do I curtsy or shake your hand?"

Munira held out an elegantly manicured hand. Though she greeted Paisley politely, Paisley's sixth sense prickled with unease. This woman did not approve of her. In fact, Paisley would venture that Munira strongly resented her presence in the castle.

Not one to give up easily, Paisley redoubled her efforts. "Thank you for sending your staff to help me dress."

"You are most welcome," Munira responded, her voice low and musical.

Paisley hadn't forgotten the woman's earlier upset outside her door or that her son had accused this woman of marrying Kinross for purposes other than love. Perhaps that was the way of the aristocracy. Since she didn't know Kinross or Munira, she was determined to remain objective.

She pushed a bobby pin into a more comfortable position, and in doing so, her eyes landed on the life-size oils hanging above the stairwell landing. One was of . . . *her*?

The shade of her prom dress had been altered to white, but she would recognize that gown anywhere. The artist had added a jeweled brooch and tartan sash to the ensemble. Paisley's brows squished together, and she turned toward her father for an explanation.

"All in good time, Paisley. Doubtless you will have many more questions in the days ahead. Right now, we have guests to greet. In the United Kingdom, we adhere to the order of precedence for royalty, position, and title. When supper is announced, you will follow Munira and me into the dining hall. The same applies to seating arrangements."

"Do I curtsy to anyone?"

Kinross shook his head. "No. Just nod graciously and say, 'How do you do?'"

"I can handle that." She flashed him a bright smile that belied the butterflies fluttering inside her belly.

"Kinross, it's time." Munira placed her hand on her husband's arm.

"Yes, my dear," Kinross responded, and the two of them descended the stairs to greet their guests.

Just as her father and his duchess turned down the hall, Paisley heard him say, "For once, Munira, can you rouse yourself beyond your own self-interest?"

If Munira's behavior was a precursor for the evening, Paisley seriously considered going back to her room. She hovered on the landing as a rare case of stage fright overwhelmed her. The murmur of voices reached her from the reception hall. A male laugh. A few titters. The wait staff her father had hired came and went past the bottom of the stairs to refill their hors d'oeuvres trays and aperitifs for Kinross's guests.

Lifting her long skirts with one hand so as not to catch her heel in her gown, she gripped the handrail and started down the last flight of steps. A man in evening attire crossed the hall below her and stopped at the newel post.

The fabric slipped from her fingers. "James? What are you doing here?"

It was James all right. Paisley would know him anywhere. Dressed to the nines in evening attire, his handsome face gawked up at her as though someone had impaled him with one of the ancient claymores hanging in the receiving hall.

After a couple blinks, the corner of his mouth lifted in a lopsided grin, and his eyes swept over her, taking in her gown and person. He propped his forearm on the newel post and emitted a low whistle.

"For a minute there, I wasn't sure it was you." He sounded breathless, as though he had jogged up a flight of stairs.

A frisson of energy zipped through her, puzzling in its intensity. James had never cast an admiring glance in her direction before. The situation was so foreign that she had no idea what to make of it.

"What's all that gunk on your eyelids?"

"It's called eyeshadow," she said dryly.

"To answer your question, Kinross is Dad's business partner on the resort build."

"No way. How do they know each other?" Paisley fought to keep her mouth from falling open.

"They met at some black-tie event in New York a million years ago."

Hurt washed over her, and she paced away, her fingernails digging into the palms of her hands. "Why didn't Richard say something to me? He knows I've wanted to find my father ever since I was a little girl."

"I know, Paise. Try to keep an open mind."

"An open mind? Richard could have told me who and where my father was and didn't. How am I supposed to take that?" Richard's betrayal stung a hundred times more than her father's. Kinross was still a stranger. Richard, well . . . *He* was family.

"There's probably a good reason for it. You know Dad loves you."

Paisley nodded. That was a given; Richard Pressley-Coombes had stood in for her father at every event that mattered. That's what made this scenario so painful.

"All I ask is that before you say something, give Kinross a chance to explain himself."

The hurt of being duped battled inside with a sense of fair play. Her anger and pain slowly ebbed and finally dissipated. James was right. These men loved her. She needed to hear both sides of the story before she made a judgment call. There must be a rational explanation for what they had done. At least she hoped so. She really, really hoped so.

"All right, I will." Paisley descended the last few steps.

Careful of her hair, James pulled her into a hug—not the shoulder-pat hugs from their growing up years, but an all-embracing one. She soaked up the solidness of his presence and the comfort he so generously offered.

Part of her mind refused to let go of what their fathers had done; both men had known about the connection for years. What could her father possibly say to justify his absence from her life?

She cast another glance at the oil, for the first time noticing the second picture hanging beside hers. Who was the boy? Why had he been given a prominent place beside her painting?

"Shall we?" James stepped back and held out his arm.

She placed her hand in the crook of his elbow and let him lead her to the reception hall. Inside her, unanswered questions still hummed and increased in volume like a hive of threatened bees.

Chapter 11

FORTY GUESTS CIRCLED EACH OTHER, their voices softly humming. Women in colorful gowns and conservative jewelry, along with their male counterparts, turned in Paisley's direction when she and James entered the reception hall and stopped beneath an impressive display of ancient weaponry. The coal fire in the massive grate did little to take off the evening chill.

Conversations petered out, and every eye fastened on her. Paisley swallowed. She was even more grateful for the new gown and makeover under such blatant curiosity.

"Smile for the nosy people," James whispered into her ear, a lopsided grin lifting one side of his mouth.

A small snort of laughter escaped her. "Stop it," Paisley hissed under her breath.

Kinross excused himself from a group of gentlemen and came to her side. "Paisley, there are some people I'd like you to meet. You too, James. Doubtless you will run across my associates on more than one occasion during your stay." Her father led them to a conservatively dressed couple somewhere in their late forties.

"Lady Margaret, may I introduce you to Lord and Lady Chatto?"

Paisley inclined her head and murmured all that was polite. Kinross moved on, working his way around the hall, introducing her to Sir This and Lady That until her mind was a muddle of names and disembodied faces. She'd never remember them all.

Finally, Kinross strode up to Munira and the man Paisley recognized from the corridor outside her rooms.

"Lady Margaret, this is Rahim Zamar, Munira's son." Kinross gestured toward the younger man.

"How do you do?"

"Welcome to Scotland." Rahim took her hand. As his eyes swooped over her body, his expression filled with blatant admiration. "Kinross, that oil painting of your daughter doesn't do her justice."

Rahim's white teeth flashed through his neatly trimmed beard, and his swarthy coloring emphasized his good looks. He leaned toward Paisley. "To say your father is delighted with your visit is an understatement. And I, for one, can only echo his joy at your recent arrival."

Paisley flushed at the blatant compliment and open admiration in Rahim's eyes.

James cleared his throat and took a step closer to Paisley's side, crowding Rahim and forcing him to drop her hand.

"This is James Pressley-Coombes," Kinross said. "He's over our marketing campaign for the resort build."

The two men shook hands. Paisley was surprised to find Rahim was several inches shorter than James. His personality had projected a much larger image.

James's greeting was abrupt and unlike his usual easygoing self.

"A word of warning." Rahim leaned forward and lowered his voice for their ears only. "Kinross's business parties are dreadfully dull. It's a pleasure to have intriguing new guests to converse with about things other than whiskey production, the price of beef, and tartan."

"The conversation can't be all that bad," James countered, eyeing the company at large.

"Close enough." Rahim snagged a tart off a passing waiter's tray.

The butler approached. "Dinner, Your Grace."

"Very good." Kinross turned to Munira, who had remained silent during the entire interchange. He held out his arm and led her inside the vast dining hall.

James smiled at Paisley, his intent to escort her to supper obvious, but Lord Chatto beat him to it. Rather than make an awkward scene, Paisley shrugged her shoulders at James and let his lordship lead her to her seat. Evidently, Lord Chatto outranked a mere mister, despite the fact that James's father was an American tycoon.

A collection of mounted hinds stared sightlessly at her from the walls when Paisley entered the vast dining room. The enormous table could easily seat fifty and was covered with so much silver that she was amazed it could bear the weight. Toward the tail end of the guests, James took a seat at the base of the table, but Rahim sat further still. No special concessions were made for Munira's untitled son.

Lady Chatto was aptly named, Paisley decided. Seated to Paisley's right, the woman chattered all through dinner, scarcely stopping to take a breath. Her good husband, a silent man, was seated directly across from her. With her ladyship monopolizing the conversation at their end of the table, Paisley had nothing to do but notice James in animated discussion with the attractive wife of the tartan manufacturer.

At one point during dinner, James glanced up and caught her look. Instead of smiling, he stared at her, his dark eyes intent. The same frisson of electricity she had experienced with him on the stairs zipped up her spine and out her extremities. She glanced away in confusion.

She had never considered James to be a stand-in brother, nor had she entertained romantic daydreams about him or Ben like all her friends—this probably had something to do with their incessant teasing. So why this tingle of attraction now? She shook her head, mentally denying her body's response. James was a familiar face in a strange setting; that's all it was.

She had tuned out Lady Chatto and all the rest of the room during her short internal deliberation. When her father rose from his chair, she glanced up at him in surprise.

"I'd like to propose a toast. To my lovely daughter, Lady Margaret." Kinross held his wine glass aloft and smiled down at her.

Everyone raised their wine glasses and looked at Paisley expectantly. While she had been woolgathering, one of the footmen had filled her empty glass with a burgundy liquid. Heat suffused her body, scorching her neck and face.

How could she extricate herself from this ticklish situation without offending her father? Paisley didn't want to damage their tenuous relationship, not after she had just met him, but her governing values demanded she remain true to herself. She didn't drink. Never had.

Her eyes darted down the table to James, pleading with him for help, even though the situation was hers to solve. He tapped his water goblet and gave her an intent stare. Relief poured through her at his "suggestion."

Smiling brightly at the company, she stood, taking note that Munira's goblet was the last glass to rise for the toast. "Thank you, Father. I'm glad to be here." She grabbed her water goblet and hurriedly pressed the glass to her lips.

A quick furrow came and went between Kinross's brows. Rather than make a scene, he sipped from his glass, the guests following his lead. Conversations resumed around the table, and other than catching a few raised brows, Paisley congratulated herself on evading a difficult situation.

She peeked at her father and noted the tightness around his eyes. Her heart sank. It was obvious he was not pleased with her. She had assumed because he and Richard were business associates her father was aware of her standards. Evidently, she had supposed too much.

While Paisley picked at her supper, she pretended a polite interest in Lady Chatto's discourse on the exquisite facial mask markings of her Himalayan Persian cats. Thankfully, the dinner party broke up not long after. Snow was on the way, and all wanted to reach their destinations before it stuck to the road.

James came alongside her and lowered his voice. "Sorry your dad put you on the spot like that. I think you handled the situation as well as possible."

"Thanks for that hint. My mind completely froze." She lowered her voice. "I think my father's still irritated."

"It will blow over." James stifled a yawn. "I'm going to call it a night. See you tomorrow." He gave her a hug, then thanked Kinross and Munira for a delightful evening and headed upstairs.

Henderson stood by the door, handing out coats and hats while Kinross and Munira wished the last of their guests good night and safe travels. Henderson bolted the locks.

Rahim loosened his tie after the door closed and approached Paisley. "If the weather clears tomorrow, might I interest you in a tour of the estate?"

Paisley opened her mouth to reply, but Kinross's hand descended on her shoulder. "Actually, I have plans to show her about the estate after breakfast. If I recall correctly, you have some deadlines to meet at the office."

Rahim's smile never left his face, but his eyes flickered. "Of course, how could I have forgotten? Perhaps a late lunch?"

"I would enjoy that. Thank you," Paisley agreed with a spurt of real pleasure.

Rahim bowed slightly in Kinross's general direction and wished his mother good night with considerable politeness. Evidently, their argument had blown over.

"Time for bed. Good night, Lady Margaret, Kinross." Munira nodded in that graceful manner Paisley could never hope to duplicate and glided toward the stairs.

"Paisley, might I have a word?" Kinross asked.

By the stiff set to her father's shoulders, Paisley had a sneaking suspicion that she was in for a lecture about her choice of toasting liquid. She followed him down a long corridor of paneled walls and dark oil paintings. How could she explain to a man who drank socially that she did not, nor ever would, partake of alcoholic beverages?

All her life, she had dreamed of connecting with her father. The reality of his stiff disapproval tore at her heart. More than anything, she wished to please him, but not if it came at the price of bending her own values. Perhaps if she could explain, maybe he would understand even though it was apparent he was used to having his own way. A Scottish duke related to the crown was high up the pecking order in the United Kingdom.

Kinross stopped at a door and punched in a code. When he ushered her inside, Paisley momentarily forgot her worries. She blinked, her eyes widening at the sight of her father's inner sanctum. The bright, modern room was stocked with the latest high-tech equipment.

Her father didn't wait before he addressed the reason for their private conversation. "I should like to know why you did not toast me appropriately in front of my guests? Your behavior embarrassed me. For years I have spoken to this group of your accomplishments. They were intrigued to meet you after all this time, and you went and made a fool of me."

"I honestly didn't mean to embarrass you, but I don't drink alcohol. I thought you knew that after being acquainted with Richard."

"I'd forgotten. In the future, I expect you to make an exception." He gave her a stern look, reminding her that he was a man of substance with hundreds of employees under his care. He treated her as though she was still a child and not a twenty-six-year-old woman.

She bit her lip and offered a silent prayer to give her the words to diffuse the situation without offending the man she yearned to know.

"I'm afraid that's not something I will make an exception about." Her heart thudded against her ribs as she drew her line in the sand.

"You won't enjoy a nightcap with me from our own family distilleries?"

"I'm afraid not." This was not an area she would acquiesce, but perhaps she could throw him an olive branch to soften the blow. "But if you stock up on diet soda and herbal tea, I'll be happy to join you."

Kinross tapped his bottom lip and eyed her. Paisley had no idea what he was thinking.

He let out a long sigh. "Munira doesn't drink either. Such a shame to be the only person in the house to enjoy the whiskey from our family distilleries. I'll speak to the housekeeper and have her stock up on herbal teas and such. You may be sure I'll be holding you to those nightcaps."

Paisley beamed at him, then offered up a silent, heartfelt thank you for her prayer's swift answer. Her eyes landed on the framed photos on the table beside her. She took a step closer. Was that a picture of her? She looked around the room, taking in the small, framed photos scattered everywhere. Pictures of her riding her bicycle, at the county fair, playing in the sprinklers on the lawn. Beside her photos were pictures of the boy whose portrait hung on the stairs.

"Are you paying attention, lass?" her father asked.

Paisley turned back. "I'm sorry. I was . . . How did you get these pictures of me?" She indicated the room at large. "Did Mom send them to you?"

"I hired a private investigator to take pictures of you every few months."

"What?" She looked around the room in confusion. Why would he hire someone to photograph her multiple times a year? She shifted uncomfortably, a little creeped out that someone had followed her all that time.

Unable to hide the unsettled emotions that information brought, Kinross took her arm and led her to one of the sofas.

"Richard said your mother had raised you with the impression that I had abandoned the two of you."

She nodded.

"When your mother and I married, we agreed that she would practice law for a decade before we moved to Scotland. My father's stroke forced me to return to Scotland much sooner than expected to run the family businesses. If I didn't, we would have lost our estates. Death taxes take a toll on properties this size, and we couldn't afford to hire someone to handle them for the next twelve years.

"I mistakenly believed your mother would understand the brevity of my father's situation and return with me. But that proved impossible, so I left, assuming I could break away to visit periodically until my father recovered. Instead of recovering, my father died. And I was inundated with the family businesses and the running of our estates.

"Your mother filed for divorce, stating abandonment. Because I was out of the country and unaware of her filings, I lost all rights to you. Immediately after the divorce, your mother changed your surnames and moved out of state."

The truth of his words sank in. Her mother had told her they were abandoned. She had changed their name and moved away, choosing the law over her marriage.

"Mom didn't know about your title or the estates?" Paisley asked, needing clarity.

"No. I'd been pursued since my late teens for both. It was one of the reasons I went to America for graduate studies. In the States, I dropped my title and was known as Cameron Douglas. Making friends on my own terms without all that was an exhilarating experience."

"Why didn't you tell Mom after you got serious?"

"Your mother and I met and married within a month. There wasn't time, and I'll admit, I was afraid she wouldn't accept me if she knew."

"Why?"

"From the beginning, your mother was set on practicing the law. *And* she was a stickler for the truth. She was introduced to me as Cameron Douglas, not Viscount Crieffmore as I was called in those days. I doubt your mother would ever have accepted a date if she had known. And I wanted to date her very much.

"You know the rest. It took time for my private investigator to locate the pair of you. The divorce decree kept me from making contact, but I've kept an eye on you over the years."

An understatement to be sure. Paisley's eyes strayed once more to the room filled with photos.

"When I met Richard at a fundraiser in New York and realized the connection, you cannae imagine my joy."

"Did you manipulate that meeting?" Paisley had to know if Richard had been involved in Kinross's "plot."

"No. It was purely chance that brought us together. Per divorce decree, I could not make contact, but I was not an absentee father, Paisley. Thanks to Richard and Dana, I was informed about your milestone celebrations and attended as many as I could." Kinross gave little away, but his tightened jaw betrayed strong emotion.

"Losing you hurt me in the worst possible way, and your mother knew it. I was the one who rocked you every night. I even made up songs for you. You loved my songs."

He hummed a few bars of a tune, and Paisley was suddenly transported back to a childhood where steady arms had encircled her with love and kindness. Her father's arms.

"Da." The word burst from her as tears blurred her vision and clogged her throat.

"You called me that long ago. Your mother tried to enforce the American *Daddy*, but you were too little and couldn't manage it."

A tear slipped down Paisley's cheek, and she sniffed, embarrassed at her show of sentiment.

Kinross handed her his monogrammed handkerchief and enfolded her in his arms. "Doubtless we'll muddle through this together." He patted her shoulder awkwardly and let go of her, his ears bright red.

She blew her nose on the pristine white fabric. It was soft and somehow comforting, smelling of his musky aftershave.

"Best be off to bed. It's late."

Rising to her feet, she started toward the door, but a picture of the little boy on the occasional table reminded her to ask.

"Who is that little boy?" Paisley pointed to the picture.

"That's your brother, Torquil, the Marquess of Crieffmore."

"I have a brother?" Paisley swayed and grabbed the edge of his desk for balance.

"A half brother to be precise. He's eleven."

"A brother," Paisley whispered to herself, her heart lifting. She had a brother.

"Aye, and you've a wee granny too. She has been ailing of late and keeps to her bed. She'd like to meet you after you've settled in."

Chapter 12

THE BED CURTAINS SURROUNDING JAMES's four-poster stirred from the breeze created by the partially open window. The storm, which had sent Kinross's guests home in a mad scramble, hurtled its gale-force winds against the castle, rattling windows, scattering snow, and snapping limbs from trees and flinging them against the castle walls.

For James, no matter what season, the walls shrank and boxed him in. He couldn't sleep without fresh air, even on a raw, blustery night like this.

He burrowed deep under the blankets, and a cocoon of warmth soon enveloped his body. The rhythmic rise and fall of his lungs lulled him into the pre-nirvana of sleep. A faint noise outside penetrated James's lethargy. He rolled over and tucked the duvet up around his ears.

There it was again—a slight whine between gusts. His eyes popped wide in the darkened room. If he wasn't mistaken, it sounded like a dog. A young one. What would one of Kinross's prized canines be doing out on a night like this? The castle kennels were over by the racing stables.

A weak howl rent the night.

James wanted nothing more than to snuggle back under the covers, but he'd never sleep with a helpless animal stuck out there.

"Stupid dog," he grumbled, then swung his legs over the side of the bed and fumbled for the light. His call to Ben after Kinross's dinner party had lasted long into the evening. Ben had sounded chipper on the phone, enthusing about his taking up climbing with Dad. The entire interchange had left James feeling more like an exile than ever.

Zipping up his fleece, he grabbed his waterproof jacket and tiptoed down the corridor to the stairs, ramming his toe into the newel post. He let out a grunt.

Reaching the entrance hall without further incident, he examined the plethora of rubber boots in the adjoining vestibule. After a few false tries, he found a pair that fit, then helped himself to a flashlight and went out to find that poor dog before it was injured by flying debris.

***

Paisley had long since given up all hope of sleep. Her father's revelations after supper, along with that weird zing of attraction between herself and James, had her as wired as if she had eaten half a dozen chocolate chip cookies.

She had a brother. And a grandmother.

All her life, she had observed her friends' families and had longed for one of her own. Those families cared about each other, fought with each other, and made up with each other. Would her father's people willingly accept her in their lives?

Dressed in a thick red robe and matching slippers, Paisley tiptoed downstairs and paused on the landing. She had only previously given her brother's painting a furtive glance. Now, she stepped close to study his likeness.

"Torquil," she murmured, tripping over the odd-sounding construction of letters. Other than the same dark, long-lashed eyes and silky brown hair that had a tendency to curl, she could see little resemblance between them. What kind of person was he?

More pictures were in her father's office. Curious, she grasped the rail and hurried down the last flight of stairs, her slippers making little sound on the polished wood floor and Turkish runners. Reaching her father's office, she found the door slightly ajar and pushed it open as the silver filigreed clock chimed three.

Every light in the room was on. Paisley recognized her father's tie and suit coat draped over the back of his desk chair. Of Kinross, there was no sign. He must have worked late into the night and forgotten to turn out the lights and lock the door when he went to bed.

She circled the room, examining the pictures. A half-formed thought took hold of her, and she carefully picked up every picture of her brother within easy reach. Gently, she placed the framed pictures on the surface of her father's desk and prized off their backs, then organized the photos into chronological order.

Her breath suspended at the sight of Torquil in a long, white christening gown. The lace appeared handmade and fragile, like it was a well-preserved family heirloom. Kinross, looking proud, held him in his arms while Munira, elegant in pale yellow, glowed about the eyes as though she, too, rejoiced in the occasion. A tiny woman with gray hair and a cane, whose dark eyes were as vibrant as Paisley's own, stood on Kinross's other side.

With an odd little catch in her throat, Paisley touched the aging face in the picture. That must be her grandmother. Paisley laid the professional photo on top of the desk and took a picture with her cell phone. Then she flipped it over and read, "Torquil's christening."

The next snapshot showed her brother in shorts, long socks, and a thick wool sweater. He ran across the lawn with a puppy nipping at his heels. Paisley smiled at the scene. Torquil appeared to be a happy, well-adjusted child.

She snapped another picture with her phone and moved on to the next photo and the next one after that—first a toddler in short pants, then Torquil progressed to long ones, his cherubic cheeks thinning in each successive picture.

The last image in the pile had Torquil in a school uniform with a full-grown English foxhound by his side—the only shot of him without a smile. A pang knelled inside Paisley's chest at the boy's obvious unhappiness. Eleven was much too young to leave home for boarding school. Yet ready or not, he had been shipped off to endure a regimented life far from home.

Paisley put the pictures back inside their frames, mindful to return them to their rightful places. Of her own photos, she did not look; she needed no reminders of her early life.

An all-too-familiar headache started behind one eye as anger stirred inside her breast. She squelched it. Nothing she did could erase her past. It was over and done with. All she had was the future—a future that included a father, stepmother, half brother, and grandmother.

But anger and jealousy pummeled her heart, stealing her breath and pushing her to the edge of her limits. She rushed out of the room as though the devil himself was at her heels, her focus on the one thing that had given her comfort over the years.

Up the stairs she fled, her panic a blind thing clawing inside her breast. She raced down the corridor and entered her room, closing the door with a loud thud. She grasped the wardrobe handles and flung them wide. Kneeling on the floor, she thrust her fingers into the dark compartment behind her shoes until her hand closed over the camera bag.

Her heart stammered as she unzipped the fastening and reached inside. Passing over her full-frame professional camera and lenses, her hands searched for the familiar shape of her first camera. She seized the small plastic housing, drew it out, and pressed it against her chest, her fingers running over the etched words.

Closing her eyes, she started to rock, humming the half-forgotten song her father used to sing to her—the one he had taught her before he left.

Chapter 13

IT WAS BLACK AS PITCH and colder than a polar bear's toenails. The wintry mix flayed James's exposed skin, and he tugged up his hoodie and tightened the fasteners under his chin. Bending into the gale, he battled his way around the side of the castle where the stone walls provided more protection. Two lights burned on the second floor. One he recognized as his own, and the other, he assumed, was Paisley's. The five-hour time change had probably wacked out both of their sleep schedules.

Clicking on his flashlight, he started his search along the castle perimeter, sweeping the beam over the ornamental plantings. The dog had probably hunkered down near the castle's foundation, or he never would have heard it over the storm. A downed limb from a nearby birch reminded James it wasn't entirely safe for him to be outside either.

His beam encountered, then bypassed, an oversized rhododendron. He whistled for the dog, but the wind carried the sound away the second it left his mouth. He called again and heard an answering yip. Pivoting, he retraced his steps, protecting his face from flying snow and debris.

He whistled again.

A whine came from inside the rhododendron. James pushed aside one of the branches and combed his light over the undergrowth. Ghoulish green eyes glowed back at him from the inky darkness, his flashlight singling out a very young puppy. By the size of him, the animal couldn't have been more than a couple months old. The pup lifted its head when the beam took him full in the face, then lowered it back onto his paws.

"Here, boy."

The dog whined but refused to leave the center of the bush.

Using one arm to hold the light, James crawled into the rhododendron. Dead branches scratched his face and hands as he forced his way through the thick undergrowth.

"Here we go, little fella," James crooned to the dog. "You are a fella, aren't you? I'd hate to injure your dignity by calling you a boy when you might be a lady. Girls don't take kindly to that, but then, little girls aren't as dumb as little boys about going on adventures in the middle of a storm."

The puppy whined.

By now, James had reached the pup, whose fur was so heavily caked with mud he couldn't determine its breed. The little scamp had probably burrowed out of the kennels.

He propped the flashlight against a primary branch to keep the beam steady, then scooped the puppy into his arms. The muddy fur was frozen in hard tufts that stuck out every which way. The puppy shook so violently James worried it would die of exposure before he reached the castle. Unzipping his hoodie and fleece liner, he shoved the pup under his T-shirt and zipped him in against his body.

Clasping his flashlight, James backed out of the foliage and started along the side of the castle for the great door. The puppy whined, and James stopped to check on him. Some of the frozen mud had globed onto James's skin, but a little dirt had never bothered him. He had spent half his childhood covered in it.

The puppy looked at him with big, sad eyes, and James's heart melted. "You're kinda cute. You know that?"

"Woof." Out came the tongue.

"No slobber. It isn't polite." He made a face and glanced at the castle. "We're all about fancy manners here." With that stern rejoinder, he hustled up the castle steps, his head and shoulders hunched against the storm.

James grabbed the iron handle and tugged. The door didn't budge.

Dagnabbit.

He'd forgotten to unlock it when he had gone out.

The main entrance was a good way from the family suites, and James doubted anyone would hear him if he banged. He patted his pockets for his cell phone, but he had dressed in a hurry and had left it in his room.

Paisley might still be awake.

With his eyes slit and tearing from the wind, he jogged back the way he'd come. The swoop and fall of his flashlight picked out shadowy vegetation and formal beds while he cradled the shivering pup with his opposite arm.

When he arrived beneath Paisley's window, her light was out. Now what? She couldn't be asleep. Not that fast. He squatted, careful of the puppy, and scrounged for pebbles.

Feeling like a stalker, he drew back his arm and tossed a few rocks at her window.

"Come on, Paisley," he muttered even as the image of her at dinner bloomed in his mind.

She had looked amazing tonight, and he couldn't take his eyes off her when she had descended that last flight of steps. Why had he never noticed her as a woman before?

He recalled his brother's and sister's words about the incredible zing of attraction they had each experienced when they met their significant others. James had scoffed. He had dated ten times the number of women as Jack and had never experienced it once.

Until tonight. When his eyes had connected with Paisley's, he could have sworn someone had shoved his finger inside a 220V plug. Later at the table, a similar current had hummed between them. For such a little thing, she sure packed a big wallop.

Why did that sizzley thing have to wake up inside him now? And why, of all women, did it stir for Paisley Clark? She was a freaking duke's daughter, for crying out loud—definitely off limits. He should run the opposite direction.

James stomped his feet to revive their circulation. Right now, they would pass for blocks of ice. He would freeze if he didn't get inside soon.

He clenched the pebbles inside his hand and looked up at Paisley's darkened window. A full minute had passed since he had tossed those rocks. Using a little more force, he chucked a few more stones and tried to will Paisley's mental image away.

It didn't work.

Nope. Nope. Definitely not.

Her father was related to the royal family and was his dad's business partner to boot, a double whammy as far as he was concerned. Besides, he had no intention of spending the rest of his life in this miserable climate. If he had read Kinross correctly tonight, that was exactly what Kinross intended for Paisley.

With his decision made, James peppered her window with the last of his rocks. He heard them strike over the noise of the storm. No way Paisley could sleep through that racket.

He bounced the pup to make sure the critter was alive and stomped his feet a few more times. Paisley had better not get the wrong idea about this. They were friends. Nothing more. He was *not* going to pursue her.

Golden light illuminated Paisley's room, and she came to the window, her head and shoulders peeping above the sill. He waved his flashlight to catch her attention, then lit up his face.

Drawing a blanket around her, she opened the window and leaned out. "James, what are you doing out there?" she called.

"I'm locked out. Let me in before I freeze to death," he yelled up to her, switching from one foot to the other.

"Which door?" she hollered over the wind.

"Main entrance. It's closer."

The wind whipped at her hair as she closed her window.

He juggled the pup's weight under his hoodie and blew on his hands, first one and then the other. One nice thing about Paisley was she didn't waste time arguing about stupid stuff. He went back the way he had come, dodging an obstacle course of shrubbery and formal plantings before he rounded the castle and trotted up the front steps.

On the porch, he paced in an attempt to keep his blood pumping. By the time Paisley opened the main castle door, he was positive he'd die of hypothermia. He slipped inside the vestibule while she banged the great door shut, then looked up at him expectantly.

Their eyes connected, and a buzzing started inside him. He had forgotten how tiny she was without those crazy big heels. He opened his mouth to speak, but her long hair distracted him. It cascaded down her back in dark shimmery waves against the deep red of her robe. His fingers itched to touch the glossy tendrils to see if the strands were as soft as they looked.

"What were you doing out in the storm?" she asked.

"Rescuing this." He unzipped his hoodie and fleece with stiff fingers.

The puppy had been silent for the last few minutes, and James was afraid he had been exposed too long to the elements. He shouldn't have worried; the puppy had fallen asleep nestled against his chest.

"Where did you find him?" Paisley reached out and petted the puppy's muddy head.

"I heard him yipping from my room." James's face was so stiff he was sure it was going to crack.

"Lucky little guy." Cooing, Paisley plucked him from James's arms and snuggled the sleepy pup against her robe, her expression tender.

Lucky dog. The words slid through his mind before he could squelch them.

"He needs a bath. The mud's frozen to his fur."

"I'll put him in my shower," James said.

"He'll howl and wake up the castle. I'm sure there's a sink in the kitchen scullery we can use." She started toward the corridor but turned back and said, "You'd better take off those rubber boots or you're going to leave a trail."

Too cold to care, he stared at her stupidly and saw her take in his situation. Placing the puppy on the floor, she helped tug off his boots and restacked them on the wooden poles inside the vestibule to dry. By now, the puppy was showing a little too much interest in one of the table legs. She scooped him up.

"Why didn't you wear socks?" Paisley nodded toward his bare feet.

"I didn't think I'd be outside that long."

"Come on, Superman. If you stand there much longer, you're going to turn into an ice sculpture. Why don't you go upstairs and shower while I clean this little guy up."

"I'm good. I just need to move is all."

They made their way through the entrance hall to the green baize door he'd seen the waiters use last night when they had gone to refill their trays. He held it open for Paisley.

"Thank you. I'm sure the scullery is down here somewhere."

At the bottom of the stairs, a wide hall ran the length of the castle. A row of bells covered a section of the wall, each labeled by room.

The castle was considerably less ornate behind the green baize door with exposed plumbing running along the ceiling and walls. The gleaming hardwood floors above stairs gave way to serviceable tile. And the gilded fixtures had been replaced with utilitarian fluorescents.

"So, this is how the other half lives," James said, looking around.

"I wouldn't know. I've never been down here." Paisley blushed, the added color highlighting her delicate features.

His gaze turned into an outright stare, and he couldn't believe he had never noticed how lovely she was. Paisley refused to meet his eyes, but her cheeks deepened from pink to rose. Interesting. Maybe she was experiencing that peculiar sensation between them too.

A light shone under the door on the opposite side of the wide corridor. Paisley pushed it open and peered inside. "I found the kitchen. Here, take him while I go fill the basin." Paisley pressed the puppy into his hands.

"Why don't you just put him down?"

"Because he'll chew on something or piddle on the floor." Paisley took two steps inside the kitchen and stopped dead.

"Oomph." James ran into her, and the puppy let out a whine.

"What are you doing up so late?" Paisley asked, her voice a little breathless.

Kinross stood at the kitchen worktop, a bottle of whiskey in one hand and two shot glasses stacked one inside the other. He raised a brow at Paisley's robe and James's bare feet and disheveled appearance. "I might ask the same about the pair of you."

Chapter 14

James didn't care for the look in Kinross's eyes. If ever an overprotective papa stared him down, it was Paisley's dad.

Kinross set the whiskey bottle on the worktop with more force than necessary. Ward MacKenzie, a dark-haired Scot who had grown up in the glen, cleared his throat from his seat at the kitchen table.

"This isn't what it appears." James wasn't about to let Kinross or MacKenzie jump to the wrong conclusions.

"And what might that be?" A slight edge laced Kinross's words.

Before James could answer, Paisley snatched the puppy from his hands and held him up for her father to see.

The pup wriggled and began to slip. James retrieved him before Paisley dropped the puppy on the flagstone floor.

"He was out in the storm. We came down here to give him a bath so we wouldn't wake anyone up if he howled."

"Is that one of Thistle's litter? How the devil did he get out?" Kinross squinted at the dog.

"Dug, by the look of it," Ward MacKenzie said.

James whipped his head in MacKenzie's direction. Kinross and his CEO were obviously holding a late-night confab if the partially empty whiskey bottle and half-eaten plate of hors d'oeuvres from last evening's festivities were anything to go by.

"A shame. We can't have a digger. He'll teach the others, and we'll never keep them penned." Kinross crossed to the table and plunked the bottle of whiskey onto its surface.

"Could I keep him?" Paisley spoke up, her voice small, as though she expected a refusal.

"You want a puppy?" Kinross asked.

"Please don't put him down. He's just a baby." Paisley's eyes were bright and pleading.

"Do you know how to take care of a dog?" Kinross challenged, his brows rising.

"James can give me pointers. He grew up with a houseful of pets."

James cleared his throat to protest, but Paisley stomped on his bare foot with her slipper to shush him.

"Och, lassie. I don't think it wise," Kinross objected.

James couldn't have withstood Paisley's pleading expression, and neither could her father. His stern expression melted like butter near a hot stove in something like two seconds flat.

Kinross glanced at MacKenzie, whose eyes glinted with amusement over the rim of his whiskey glass.

"All right, lass. You can have him."

"Thank you." Paisley beamed her delight and ran across the room to Kinross's side. Rising on her toes, she kissed his cheek.

For two beats, Kinross stood utterly still, his eyes on his wedding band. "I had no idea muddy pups could have such an effect. The duchess didn't show that much enthusiasm last Boxing Day when I gave her a diamond choker." Kinross made a fuss of recapping the whiskey bottle. "Be off with you then, lass, and clean that wretched animal."

Paisley fairly danced across the room and took the puppy from James. She left the kitchen without another word. A few seconds later, water started in the scullery sink.

James wasn't fooled. Paisley's behavior had touched a deep chord inside her father. And by the look of it, Kinross was ill-equipped to deal with the emotions she had aroused. If it hadn't been completely ridiculous, James would almost think the man was starved for love.

Kinross took a bite of salmon pâté, chewed, and swallowed. "James, I need to meet with you first thing tomorrow morning at the office complex." He appeared in control of himself once more.

"Of course." James darted a look between Kinross and MacKenzie, and his senses went on red alert. Whatever had brought the two men to the kitchen tonight couldn't be pleasant, not if their sober expressions were anything to judge by.

"James," Paisley called from the scullery. "I need your help. He won't sit still."

James nodded to both men and started for the scullery. Before he slipped through the door, MacKenzie said, "Sharp lad, that. He knows something's afoot."

***

James traversed the half mile between the castle and Kinross's headquarters, his feet crunching on the thin dusting of snow. Clouds of condensation burst from his mouth in the sharp, frigid air. He suspected this meeting had something to do with the three a.m. powwow he and Paisley had interrupted in the castle kitchen.

He stomped his feet and let himself inside the former stable block. Kinross's personal secretary, a plump woman in her forties, took his coat and scarf and hung them on the hall tree.

"Are you enjoying your stay in Scotland, Mr. Pressley-Coombes?"

"I am." James took in the wedding ring on her hand, and his eyes dropped to the nameplate on her desk. "It's a beautiful country, Mrs. Campbell."

"That was quite the party up at the castle last night. I've heard the duke's daughter is a bonnie wee thing, like her granny before her."

"You knew Paisley's grandmother?" James leaned against Mrs. Campbell's desk.

"Aye, I'm acquainted with the dowager duchess, Lady Margaret's wee granny," Mrs. Campbell corrected. "The dowager duchess is still with us, though no one sees her these days. She's crippled with arthritis and does poorly."

Gently put in his place for not referring to Paisley and her grandmother properly, James vowed to do better. This wasn't the US with its casual attitudes. People still dressed for dinner and bowed to their betters. At least they did in Kinross's circles. The sooner he remembered that, the better off he'd be.

Mrs. Campbell excused herself and rapped on Kinross's door. No buzzing of phones for her.

"Come." Kinross's voice was muffled by the door.

Mrs. Campbell poked her head inside. "Mr. Pressley-Coombes is here, Your Grace."

"Send him in, Elspeth."

"He'll see you now, Mr. Pressley-Coombes." Mrs. Campbell nodded to James.

James was taken aback when he entered Kinross's domain. In no way did the space resemble the duke's state-of-the-art office at the castle. The smallish room's single window overlooked the forested hillside. Several computer screens stood side by side on top of a square walnut desk, and two leather chairs sat against the near wall for visitors.

James shook hands with the duke and took the nearest chair, noting the dark circles under Kinross's eyes. After only two hours of sleep, James sympathized with the man. Kinross remained standing.

"We've a bit of a conundrum on our hands. My startup fund for the resort build has gone missing." Kinross paced the small space, his hands clasped behind his back.

James's lungs deflated as Kinross's words sank in. He inhaled sharply. "What happened?"

"My business account was emptied just before I collected Paisley at the airport. I've gone over the events leading up to my appointment at least a thousand times. As far as I can detect, only a bank employee or one of my own could have done it. A stranger could not replicate the sound bites required to authorize the transfer or access my security codes."

James looked down at his lap. This theft spelled disaster for their project.

"I should tell you," Kinross continued, "the theft was done through an intra-bank transfer, which sustained no holds, then splintered to thirty separate accounts in the Middle East."

James jerked his head up. "You're saying someone laundered your seed money to a terrorist organization?"

Kinross stopped pacing and nodded. "It appears so, and I'm not the only one who has lost funds at WFB. Other aristocrats and financiers have been targeted over the last few months."

"What does WFB stand for?"

"World Financial Bank. They are the premier institution for those who procure business transactions across the globe."

"Have the authorities—?"

"I assure you I have filed a complaint. My grievances have been added to an ongoing investigation against WFB." Kinross sat in his chair and steepled his fingers. "After I took time to think, I've realized the theft must have been a combined effort between someone on the estate and the bank."

"What makes you think that?"

"I was delayed from my appointment by three seemingly innocuous events. Those holdups granted the thief extra time to complete the transaction."

Simple and diabolically clever. James curled and uncurled his toes inside his dress shoes. Without Kinross's million, the resort build would be placed on hold or cancelled altogether.

His mind sped over the ramifications facing them: heavy fines, contractor fallout, artisan cancellations, disruption of supply deliveries, new permits for construction, food and alcohol reorders, delayed shipments . . . the cancellations and reorders to jumpstart the production schedule after such massive changes would set them back months. In an area so sparsely populated, they would be hard-pressed to re-earn local trust to pick up other bids.

And that was just the tip of the iceberg.

What would become of his father's and Kinross's partnership? Dad didn't mess with financials. Not ever. Undoubtedly, their partnership would dissolve, and James would return home without achieving what he had set out to accomplish: proving to his father that he was as valuable to Coombes Enterprises as his twin.

And what of Paisley? His mouth thinned, and his stomach knotted. This would affect her harder than anyone. With both father figures at odds with one another, the situation would wreak havoc on her sensitive soul.

"Is it possible to raise the necessary cash before the start date?" James asked.

"Ward and I were crunching numbers last night when you and Paisley showed up. We might have a solution of sorts. It requires a few concessions by our general contractor. I'm short $300K. If necessary, I can liquidate a personal asset to make up the difference, but it will take time—time we don't have. If Coombes Enterprises would consider advancing $300K, I will repay the corporation and cover extra expenses accrued during the build."

James barely kept his mouth from falling open. Kinross wanted them to cover the extra expense? He doubted Richard would go for that.

"Without raising a fuss, I would like to quietly investigate employees on the estate. I understand you have computer skills. If you would like to poke around my corporate database, be my guest. Fresh eyes are most welcome."

"I'd be happy to take a look." James shifted his feet. "Is my father aware of the theft?"

"I plan to call him this afternoon." Kinross's jaw tightened, but his face remained poker smooth, giving away little. "Doubtless you will be hearing from Richard with your own instructions on behalf of Coombes Enterprises."

"Yes, Your Grace." James pushed out of his chair and prepared to leave.

"Before you go, there is a small matter I would like to discuss." Kinross rose to his feet, his fingers idly touching the mouse on top of his desk.

"What is it?"

"I am aware of your reputation with the ladies. I'll not have you toying with my daughter's affections."

Kinross's words, though unexpected, did not anger James. In fact, he found himself in perfect harmony with the man. Kinross obviously loved his daughter and wanted to keep her safe from unnecessary pain.

"Your Grace, I would never hurt Paisley in any way."

Chapter 15

Paisley followed Rahim into McKay's, a lovely restaurant with double bay windows in the Victorian village of Pitlochry. It was thoughtful of Rahim to have invited her. At least *he* hadn't forgotten their date.

After breakfast, Kinross had left for his office without mentioning their planned tour of the estate. Due to his pressing business, their outing had apparently slipped his mind. Paisley made the typical excuses, as she had so often done for her mother: he was busy, they'd had a late night, issues with the bank, etc. But the pain lingered.

She'd been quiet all the way to the restaurant, trying to force the hurt away and focus on her companion.

"Table for two by one of the windows," Rahim told the hostess, a middle-aged woman with a gap between her front teeth.

The hostess led them to a table in one of the bays and passed them their menus. "May I interest either of you in a dram of our own whiskey from the Blair Athol Distillery?"

"Water for me, please." Paisley eyed her menu.

"Make that two waters," Rahim added. "And a side order of haggis for us to share."

"Haggis?" Paisley had heard rumors about the infamous seasoned oats and organs cooked in a sheep's bladder.

Rahim gave her a direct stare. "No self-respecting Scot or half-Scot visiting the Highlands would leave without giving it a try. Isn't that right, ma'am?" he asked the waitress.

"I'm staying out of this," the waitress said.

"Is it a rite of passage or something?" Paisley asked.

"Not exactly, but where else will you find it? In my opinion, foreigners are too tentative about giving it a go."

"So, this is a dare?"

"Perhaps." Rahim glanced briefly at the menu. "I'll have the Scottish salmon in honey glaze." He gave his menu to the waitress with a flourish.

"I'll have the sea trout." Paisley handed over her menu as well.

"So." Rahim grinned at her, his white teeth flashing against the close-cropped beard. "Tell me about yourself, Lady Margaret."

"There's not much to say. I grew up an only child of a single mother."

"I heard she's a barrister."

"Something like that." Paisley didn't want to get into legal comparisons over lunch.

Rahim cocked his head to the side. "What do you do for a living?"

"I'm a photographer."

His eyebrows shot up to his hairline.

"Is that a bad thing?" She crossed her ankles to a more comfortable position.

"Not at all, just surprising. I would have taken you for a principal dancer in a ballet company, a news anchor, or," he wiggled his brows, "a personal assistant."

Paisley laughed outright. "That covers a broad spectrum of professions."

He shrugged. "I have a big imagination. Do you have a specialty?"

"Family portraits and weddings are my bread and butter, but I'd like to branch into landscapes while I'm here. Scotland is stunning."

"I agree. This country is much more beautiful than where I'm from."

"Where is that?"

"Uzkahsikstan."

"I thought you were British?"

"I am. I grew up here. My mother and I met Kinross in a refugee camp when I was six."

"You were so young. Do you remember much?" Paisley toyed with her napkin.

"Not really. Just the fear and sound of gunfire."

"How horrible."

"When I came of age, I became a British citizen."

"Did you convert to Christianity as well?" Paisley regretted her words immediately. Rahim was so easygoing that she hadn't considered how personal her question was until it sprang from her lips.

"Mother did. I, however, am Muslim."

That explained why he didn't drink.

The waitress approached, carrying their meals on a large serving tray. Paisley's stomach growled at the mouthwatering aromas. The trout looked delicious; she couldn't wait to dig in. When the waitress set the haggis beside her plate, Paisley eyed the grayish-brown lump with suspicion.

"I saw that look." Rahim picked up her fork and scooped a small piece on the end of her utensil. "Try it. Just one wee bite."

Instead of handing her back her fork, Rahim fed her, his dark eyes unfathomable. She squirmed in her seat but, in the end, opened her mouth obediently.

"Not too bad?"

She chewed the salty lump of oats and swallowed. "It's much better than I thought it would be." She took her fork back from Rahim, careful not to touch his fingers, and scooped up another bite.

Paisley studied Rahim under her lashes. He was a handsome man, every bit as good-looking as James, with an attractive vitality she hadn't encountered in anyone else. His natural charm drew her like a moth to a flame. When she spoke, he listened intently—a novel and highly flattering experience.

Retaining her fork, she picked up her knife and cut into her trout.

"Try not to be too upset with Kinross."

Her eyes flashed up from her plate. How had he read her so easily? She had done her best to hide the emotions her father's forgetfulness had caused.

"Your father's rather preoccupied at the moment. The seed money he set aside for the resort build was drained from his business account."

"Was it a lot of money?" Her father had never mentioned the amount but had focused more on the death of his friend.

"A million pounds or so."

Paisley's stomach dropped, and she set down her utensils. *A million pounds?* "How do you know this?"

"Mother told me about the issue this morning."

What would the loss do to the resort and Kinross's partnership with James's family?

Over lunch, Rahim tried to jolly her out of her worries. He shared a story about his first fishing expedition at which he had slipped on a rock and was swept downstream. Partway through the tale, the wail of a bagpipe filtered through the closed window.

Paisley glanced across the narrow street to where a piper, in full kilt, stood playing in front of the bank. A tourist dropped coins into the open case at the piper's feet. The piper's dog lay on the ground beside him, his tail thumping when the tourist spoke to him.

Few would brave the elements with a storm threatening. The bagpiper must need the cash badly to play on such a cold day.

The tourist moved off, and the piper switched to a new tune, one Paisley recognized. She set down her silverware to watch. The wind tossed his colorful kilt, flapping the tartan about his knees. Leaves whirled around the corner amidst a cloud of white dirt and enveloped the man and his dog before it dispersed.

"Do you like bagpipes?" Rahim asked.

"Very much so."

"Tourists either love them or hate them. It's the national dress I take issue with."

"Why?"

"The weather here is too wet and cold for a skirt." Rahim's white teeth flashed, and he gave her a self-deprecating smile.

The wind picked up, and rain spattered against the bay window, emphasizing his words. A few seconds later, the pipes fell silent. Paisley glanced across the narrow street. The piper was sitting on the ground, his instrument beside him.

"He looks ill," Paisley said.

As if on cue, the piper leaned forward and retched in the gutter.

"He probably had too much whiskey," Rahim said without concern and took a sip from his glass.

Astonishment rounded her eyes.

"People drink heavily in the UK, especially Scots. You've seen the distilleries."

Rahim was probably right. Almost every town of any size had a distillery.

The piper heaved again and collapsed on the pavement. Paisley rose from her chair.

"Where are you going?" Rahim's brows snapped together.

"To see if that bagpiper is all right. It's raining outside. Whether he's drunk or not, I can't just leave him there." She hurried to the exit and spoke to the waitress on her way out the door. "I'll be right back. The man across the street needs help."

Freezing-cold rain soaked through Paisley's clothes as she waited, bareheaded, to cross the street. A man exited the bank, took one look at the piper, and knelt beside him.

"Ian, can you hear me?"

Paisley ran across the road and reached the downed piper, but she wasn't sure what to do. A short, redheaded woman burst out of the shop next to the bank. She knelt on the pavement beside the bank customer and helped roll the piper onto his back, then checked his pulse.

"Someone call an ambulance," the woman cried.

Thoroughly soaked and unable to help, Paisley stepped out of the way. At her feet lay the terrier. The dog's eyes were open and stared glassily at the sky while rain pelted his fur.

Paisley squatted beside him and waved her hand in front of the animal's face. No response. Tentatively, she touched the terrier. He was warm, and his coat felt a little gritty, as though he had rolled in dirt. But his chest didn't rise, and his heart didn't beat.

The dog was dead.

"Lady Margaret, come away from there." Rahim took her arm and pulled her to her feet. He must have followed her when she crossed the street.

She started to wipe her hands on her pants, but the grit was gone—dissolved like magic.

"The dog—he's dead." Paisley blinked the rain out of her eyes. "He was fine a few minutes ago."

The wail of a siren and flashing lights coming up the road diverted her attention.

"Let's get out of this rain. There's nothing we can do here."

***

There was nothing James could do. Kinross's confession about his financial issues had placed the entire resort build in a state of flux. James needed to punch something. For all he knew, he could be packing his bags in a few hours for the States.

After this morning's discussion with Kinross, he had returned to his suite at Castle Rannoch to prep slides for his upcoming marketing presentation in Amsterdam. Who was he fooling? The whole campaign was probably a waste of time.

He saved his work, turned off the computer, and rolled his chair away from the desk. Checking the time, he was unable to postpone the inevitable any longer. Dad needed to hear about the theft. James picked up his cell phone and dialed his father's private number.

"James," Richard answered, his pleasure pouring through the line.

"Hi, Dad. Got a minute?" James fidgeted with the computer cord, absently swinging it with his free hand.

"Absolutely. How are things in Scotland? How's Paisley?"

Though James's stomach roiled with his sour news, he was temporarily diverted by Richard's question. "About Paisley, Dad," he started. "You knew how much finding her father meant to her. Why didn't you tell her you not only knew where he was but that you had partnered with him?"

"Son, that wasn't my story to tell. When Cam and I discovered our connection, he asked if your mother and I would regularly send him pictures of Paisley. His request was so sincere that your mother didn't have the heart to turn him down. Cam worried about Paisley, but he didn't believe his home environment with his second wife would be an improvement for Paisley if he contested the court ruling. She was only four when he remarried. Now that she's an adult, he and Paisley have the opportunity to get to know each other and bond as father and daughter."

"All right. I'll drop it." James still had a beef with Kinross about it, but this morning, he had other things to address.

"Is that why you called?"

"No. I still disagree with how Kinross handled things with Paisley, but I called about something else. We've got a big problem on our hands. Kinross said he would get hold of you later today, but I wanted to reach you first so you aren't caught off guard." James updated Richard about Kinross's emptied resort account. "Kinross has scraped together $700K and is willing to pay all fines and added expenses if the contractors agree to move forward without delays. He's talking to the project manager as we speak."

"And if the contractor doesn't agree?" Richard asked.

"Kinross said he could liquidate a private asset, but it will delay our start date and accrue heavy fines. He's asking that Coombes Enterprises front him the missing $300K, and he will reimburse us later with interest."

Dead silence on the line.

"Dad, are you there?"

"I am." Richard cleared his throat. "I'm sorry to hear about the theft, but Kinross has placed us in a difficult position. This is not what was agreed upon."

"Do we have the extra $300K to front Kinross until he can liquidate those assets?" James tugged on his computer cord and accidently unplugged it from the wall.

"We do, but that's beside the point. Having never walked the resort site, I can't determine if the location is a competitive corporate draw like we hoped, or simply a nice place for families to vacation. I'm counting on you to determine what's best for the company. Perhaps you can market the corporate center with a few extra perks others don't offer."

James's pulse accelerated, unable to believe what he was hearing. Dad trusted him to make this decision? "If we pull out, our main contractor has every right to sue us for breach of contract. I guess what I need to know from you, Dad, is if Kinross is good for it if we front him the money? You're the one who has dealt with him in the past and know his track record."

"He always pays on time and has never given me a reason to doubt his integrity. Nothing like this has ever happened before. If Coombes Enterprises has to suck up that $300K, I need to know if that job site is worth it—that we can recoup the loss over time if Kinross doesn't come through. You are the only one from Coombes Enterprises with physical knowledge of that resort site. You also understand what a loss like this can do to our construction teams here in the States." Richard's voice was calm, but he had reminded James of how many families would go without work on both sides of the pond if this resort build failed.

James weighed the ramifications should the contractor refuse Kinross's offer, or the duke didn't repay Coombes Enterprises in comparison to the positive responses on the resort build's online marketing campaign.

In some ways, it would be best if they pulled out and swallowed their losses, but James hesitated to do so. Based on his initial projections, this resort had all the makings of a gold mine.

As he teetered on the razor's edge, Paisley came to mind. If Coombes Enterprises pulled out of the resort build, she would be forced to choose between her surrogate father and Kinross. He couldn't do that to her.

James raked his free hand through his hair. "Dad, I think we need to stay." At least for now, James would delay on the side of mercy and see what Kinross came up with. Later, if things didn't improve, he would remove Coombes Enterprises from imminent disaster.

Chapter 16

Some people would reassess owning a puppy after two accidents in one night. Not Paisley. Though she remained abysmally ignorant in the way of pets, she was trainable. For instance, when her Australian shepherd sniffed in a circle on her bedspread, that meant her black, gold, and white doggie needed an immediate transfer to newsprint.

Paisley woke late. Having showered the night before, she climbed out of bed, threw on some clothes, and tossed her hair into a ponytail. With her camera bag over one shoulder, she headed outside into the brisk day to give the pup some much-needed exercise.

Most of the snow from last evening's dusting had already melted. She followed the track through the conifer plantings to the loch, her eyes sweeping over the sea of tinted white pines creeping up the glen's forested slopes. When they reached the water, the puppy flopped onto the dock's rough wooden slats and promptly fell asleep.

Paisley removed her camera and adjusted the lens. White peaks surrounded the glen. On the valley floor, the oaks looked sadly tattered after last night's storm. Only the loch lay dreaming under a blue-and-white sky, indifferent to the sudden changes around her.

Overwhelmed by the sheer magnificence of the view, Paisley captured several shots of the loch while the sun played peekaboo behind fluffy white clouds. A soft breeze ruffled the water, shimmering its reflective surface like an impressionist painting.

Paisley changed out her lens for a few long-distance shots of the snowcapped peaks. Her focus, a derelict crofter's cottage on the slope just above the tree line, added depth and interest to the perspective. In the next three months, she planned to rebuild her portfolio, adjusting her photos to include dramatic landscapes and pursue her dream of holding an exhibition.

Adjusting her shutter, she took a series of photos at high speed until a reflection inside the woods ruined her shot. She lowered her camera and turned away to pack up her gear, but the beauty of the glen sang to her soul. Heedless of the cool temperature, she sat on the dock, placed the pup on her lap, and absently stroked his soft, multi-colored fur.

If the Aussie accompanied her on her daily excursions, she'd need to order a rucksack. He was too young to keep up. Her father wouldn't be happy if she left a whining puppy behind to disrupt the staff while she hiked the glen.

Paisley sighed. Her father still hadn't remembered his offer to show her the estate, and she'd been left again to her own devices. Good thing she was used to entertaining herself.

The sun climbed higher in the sky. She checked her watch and groaned, rising to her feet in one fluid motion. If she hadn't promised to meet her father, Munira, and James for brunch, she would have skipped eating altogether and gone upstairs to upload her pictures onto her computer.

"Time to go." Carrying the Aussie, she retraced her steps along the track that bordered the conifer plantings partway back to the castle. On the front porch, she scraped the mud from her boots and entered the vestibule to shed her outerwear. The puppy, revived from his snooze, gamboled about the small room with an occasional stop to nip her ankles.

Paisley reached down and rubbed his ear. The Aussie leaned into the caress and tumbled over, then sat up and shook himself. Paisley giggled, falling more in love with him by the minute.

Locating a bench, she removed her rubber boots and slipped into her heels. A row of wellies hung upside down on drying stands. She added hers to the mix while the puppy sniffed one of the wooden pegs and chewed on it with his sharp little teeth.

"Naughty boy." She picked him up before he could do further damage, crossed the entry hall, and gave him to one of the maids to put in his crate before she continued to the small family salon.

The small salon was half the size of her mother's townhouse. James hadn't arrived yet, but her father and Munira sat at the far end of the room beside a tea trolley loaded with sliced fruit and breakfast pastries.

"Paisley, just the person I wished to see." Kinross set his spoon beside his teacup and motioned for her to join them. "Our annual charity gala ball is next week. We must get a dress sorted for you."

Munira laughed, her voice reminding Paisley of a soft wind chime. "You men are so simpleminded. This is Scotland's premier ball. The best designers have been back-ordered for months."

"Let her borrow something of yours, then. You have a closet full of gowns," Kinross said dismissively.

"I'm several dress sizes larger than she is," Munira said.

Kinross looked nonplussed. "Can we send to London for something?"

"No time for fittings." Munira's perfectly formed lips lifted smugly.

Paisley's heart sank. The closest thing to a ball she had attended was her high school prom. Even she knew how long it took to find the right gown. With her small size, it would be downright impossible to purchase and fit a dress in that amount of time.

"It's all right," Paisley interjected. "I don't need to go."

Munira's eyes gleamed with triumph when she turned in Paisley's direction. Paisley stiffened as though she had been slapped. She'd bet her brunch her father's wife had realized Paisley's need for a ballgown and had done nothing to prevent it.

"Nonsense. Both my children will attend," Kinross said.

"Torquil's coming?" Munira's brows rose.

Apparently, Kinross had not filled her in. Somehow it eased the hard, little knot inside Paisley's chest.

"Of course. I arranged it with the headmaster."

"He'll get behind in his studies. You know how he struggles." Munira stirred her tea, a frown marring her perfect complexion.

James entered the room and came up beside Paisley. She gave him a brief smile in greeting. He looped his arm around her shoulders and gave her a side hug, his touch a comfort after Munira's betrayal. The scent of his woodsy aftershave teased her senses.

"If Torquil brings his schoolwork home, I'd be glad to help him out," Paisley said, offering Munira an olive branch instead of reciprocating hostilities.

Munira eyed her for the first time without cold haughtiness etched across her features. Paisley could now see why her father had fallen for her.

"That's kind of you, lass, but British schools aren't like American ones," Kinross said dismissively.

"Paisley could figure it out," James informed the room at large. "She's an exceptional student."

A glimmer of pleasure rippled through Paisley at James's defense of her abilities. Her eyes locked with his, and the air fairly sparked between them.

Kinross pressed his mouth into a firm line and looked away.

James lowered his head and whispered, "Have you decided what you are going to call our baby?"

"*Our* baby?" His words effectively doused the currents circling Paisley's system. She wasn't sharing her dog with anyone.

"I saved him." James all but beat on his chest. "You're taking care of him. That makes him *our* baby."

She ignored his claim to *her* dog. "I haven't decided on a name yet."

"Baby has a nice ring." One side of James's mouth quirked up into a lopsided grin.

Paisley frowned. How could James behave like nothing was shimmering between them? Didn't he feel the current of attraction? One minute she thought he did, but in the blink of an eye, the valve turned off, and James was his normal teasing self again.

"Baby is too girly for a male dog." She lifted her chin.

"How about Digger?" James wiggled his brows.

Paisley fought the urge to roll her eyes.

"C'mon, Paise. Digger's a great name for that dog."

"Okay. Just give me a minute." She screwed up her face in concentration. "How about Scot or Burns?"

"That's lame."

"Stormy?"

He gave her a dark stare. "What's wrong with Digger?"

She had to admit that Digger definitely suited the little rebel, and James, with his marketing skills, knew it. "All right. Digger it is."

James smiled as though he had conquered the world, even though all he had done was name a dog. Men and their silly egos. Paisley turned away. At least that had solved one problem. Unfortunately, she had no idea what to do about a dress.

***

Shortly after lunch, Henderson escorted Paisley to an area of the castle she had never entered. Views through the tall casement windows framed the loch and Schiehallion, a conically shaped Munro known as the Fairy Hill.

"Why are my grandmother's rooms so far from the rest of the family's?" Paisley inquired as Henderson stopped in front of a large door in the middle of the second-floor gallery.

"Her Grace, the dowager duchess, suffers from rheumatoid arthritis and other ills. It is easier to heat this area to her doctor's specifications and use the lift to transport her to appointments."

Henderson opened the thick wooden door that led down a long corridor. Warm air rushed out like a blast from the tropics.

"Does my grandmother ever go downstairs?" Paisley peeled off the wool sweater that covered her blouse.

"Not in the last few months." Henderson marched down the hall and rapped on a door.

While they waited for a response, Paisley noticed the elevator opposite her grandmother's suite. The wall surfaces surrounding the lift appeared new and not in keeping with the roughly plastered walls of the rest of the corridor.

"Come," a strong voice called on the other side of the double doors.

"The dowager duchess tires easily. I will return to collect you in thirty minutes," Henderson informed her before he let Paisley enter.

Despite the lofty ceilings and tall leaded windows, the suite was stifling. A tiny woman with grayish-brown hair sat in an enormous bed draped with embroidered velvet curtains.

A flat-screen television emitted a series of dings, and a gameshow contestant jumped up and squealed.

"Your Grace, the Lady Margaret." Henderson bowed, then closed the door.

"Come here, lass, and let me get a look at you." Large dark eyes in a wizened face pinned hers.

Paisley negotiated her way around the great bed to the side closest to her grandmother.

"Ah." Her grandmother's eyes gleamed with unholy delight. "Would you be so good as to turn that noisy thing off and fetch me the photo on the dresser?"

After turning off the television, Paisley went to the dresser. Two framed photos stood side by side. Not knowing which one her grandmother referred to, Paisley took the one closest to her.

"Not that one—the other." Her grandmother made an impatient gesture toward the second photograph.

Paisley brought the framed picture to her grandmother.

"They tell me you are called Paisley."

"Yes, Your Grace."

"That's rather a strange name for a female."

Paisley ducked her head, her lips twitching.

"You think that's funny?"

"I do," Paisley answered. "And what am I to call you?"

"Grandmother or Granny. That is who I am."

"Granny," Paisley said, deciding.

She studied the photograph in her hand of a small dark-haired woman with luminous eyes and pale skin. The nose and mouth were different, but the eyes, facial structure, and coloring definitely bore a strong resemblance to her own.

"I was about your age then."

"Now I know where I get my height and coloring from," Paisley said. Her mother was five inches taller than her own diminutive size and was a redhead to boot.

"Our height has been tampered with by fairies. There's a story that the fairies kiss the female bairns in our family to steal them from their parents. But our human blood holds true, and we remain in the land of mortals until they return to take us home to the Fairy Hill."

With superstition rampant in the Highlands, Paisley was not entirely sure if Granny was serious or not, so she refrained from commenting.

"You're a bonnie lass. Much bonnier than I ever was—definitely an improvement on the old stock."

"Thank you. You can blame that on good genes." Paisley wandered to a glass-fronted cabinet. Inside appeared to be collections of photographs and several small baskets of polished stones.

"Are these your treasures, Granny?" Paisley pointed to the shelves.

"Aye."

"Do you mind if I look at them?"

"Be my guest. Only you and Torquil have ever asked to see them."

Paisley opened the cabinet. "What is this?" She touched a polished violet rock.

"You've heard our Scottish expression of Munro bagging, haven't you?"

"That's when a person climbs to the top of a mountain, isn't it?"

"Aye. Your grandfather and I were avid hillwalkers. Whenever we reached a summit, we brought back a souvenir. The stones inside that cabinet represent every Munro we bagged over the course of our marriage."

Deeply touched by her grandmother's sentimentality, Paisley fingered the smooth rock. When she set it down, her eyes landed on a snapshot of her eight-year-old self sitting on her mother's small patch of lawn holding her first camera. Paisley's breath hitched, and a huge lump formed inside her throat. She blinked rapidly against the sudden sting of tears.

"You have a picture of me in here," Paisley said when she had sufficiently recovered.

"Och, lass. Of course I do. You're my only granddaughter. I stole it from your father's collection. It fair broke his heart to leave you behind when he returned home." Granny's gruff tone softened. "Come sit with me."

Her words were more of a command, but Paisley was starting to understand her grandmother a little. That brusque manner of hers covered a sentimental heart. Paisley closed the cabinet and climbed onto the bed.

"Are you going to attend the charity gala ball next week?"

"Will you be there?" Too late, Paisley remembered her grandmother stayed in her rooms.

"My dancing days are long over, and I no longer abide insipid conversation. I'm sure Kinross plans to present you to the who's who of Scottish society."

"Fancy dances aren't really my thing." Paisley recalled her prom date with Jack. He and his friends had talked cars all evening while she watched her friends dance. A root canal would have been more entertaining.

"What's not to like about dancing with handsome young men? You must make the most of your youth, lass. It fades soon enough."

Paisley made a face. "I don't know the dances."

"Would you go if you did?"

"There isn't time to shop for a dress." Paisley worried at a snagged fingernail and avoided Granny's eyes.

"Nonsense. I have trunks full of ball gowns. One of them is bound to fit you."

A spurt of hope infiltrated Paisley's heart, and she lifted her head. "Won't they be a little outdated?"

"Have you no imagination, lass? There's a seamstress in Perth I've used for years. If I ring her, she would be happy to freshen one of them into the latest style."

"But what if—?"

"No more of that. Do you or don't you wish to go?"

"I do want to go."

"Then let me play fairy *grandmother*." Granny rubbed her hands together.

Until that moment, Granny had kept them carefully hidden under the covers. Her fingers were gnarled, twisted things that could not function normally.

Paisley lowered her lashes. Were Granny's legs in the same condition? Was that why she kept to her bed?

"Ring that bell, would you please? I'll have my assistant bring my trunks down from the attics. You will attend the charity gala ball in the height of style. Munira's nose will most definitely be put out of joint," Granny cackled.

Granny, it seemed, had no liking for her daughter-in-law. When Paisley had arrived at Castle Rannoch, she had held high hopes that she and her father's duchess would hit it off. After brunch this morning, it was a foregone conclusion that Paisley's attendance at the ball would only deepen Munira's animosity.

"Munira lords it over the women as being the best-dressed female at every function. It will be a braw day indeed when she topples off that dais," Granny said with a wink.

Evidently, Munira had not only alienated herself from Granny but others too.

Henderson returned with a maid. "Lady Margaret, your time is up."

"Did my son send you to play watchdog, Henderson?" Granny asked.

"You know how visitors tire you, Your Grace." Henderson neither denied her claim nor agreed.

"This is a good kind of tired. It's not every day one meets their granddaughter. Come here, Paisley, and give me a kiss."

Paisley obediently kissed her withered cheek.

"Return tomorrow at ten; I'll be waiting for you," Granny whispered.

"I will."

The dignified Henderson led Paisley from the room. Just before he closed the door, she peeked over his shoulder to wave, but Granny had already closed her eyes.

Chapter 17

ACHMED WAS A CREATURE OF habit. He arrived at Kinross's offices often before Gerry, the night watchman, completed his rounds. Achmed rapped on the outer glass door and waited to be let inside the stable block.

The minutes lengthened. He cupped his hands on either side of his face and peered inside, his breath fogging the glass. He tapped the surface with his keys to catch the guard's attention.

A second later, Gerry appeared.

"You weren't out here long, were you, Mr. Razool?" The Irishman's blue eyes held a pucker of worry.

Achmed hung up his coat and forced a polite answer. "Nothing to worry about."

Gerry was doing his level best on that new prosthetic leg. The man was not to blame for Achmed's inability to sleep. He took full responsibility for the wrong choices that had placed Padma in the hospital and kept him up at night.

Once Achmed arrived at his workstation, he booted up his computer and was soon absorbed with projections and developmental charts. He scarcely noticed when his coworkers arrived.

"Good morning." Rahim knocked on the side of Achmed's cubicle, a friendly smile on his face. "Did you arrive at the crack of dawn per usual?"

Rahim raised the office morale wherever he went. If Achmed had a friend at headquarters, it was Rahim. The two Persian men had both emigrated to the UK as children from war-torn nations and considered themselves British, both having become citizens once they reached adulthood.

"How's your sister?" Rahim asked.

"She's holding her own, thank Allah. In time, she should recover."

"That's fantastic news." Rahim's white teeth flashed.

"How's that racehorse of yours? Are you going to enter him at Ascot next year?"

Rahim owned several racehorses and boarded them at Kinross's racing stables on the far side of the estate. He took long lunches to oversee their daily exercise.

"I'm considering it." Rahim's mobile alarm went off. "Duty calls."

Rahim headed off to attend one of his myriad meetings. As Kinross's stepson, he had been groomed to take his place in the company. Though Rahim was talented—brilliant even—Achmed had to admit his friend was sporadic on the job, preferring to be out with his horses.

Achmed returned to his charts and was totally submerged in another graph when his mobile pinged. He glanced at the screen lying on the desk beside him.

Destroy Lady Margaret's camera.

Achmed tensed. The blackmailer had breached his electronics—not just his work computer, but his mobile as well. How else had the person known about his scheduled birthday appointment with Padma the day of her accident? Achmed had ensured that his calendar app on his phone did not transfer to his computer.

He lived alone and rarely socialized, which meant the blackmailer must be a coworker. Achmed glanced around the office, his eyes darting from one employee to the next. How had one of them found out he had skimmed Kinross's funds?

His one moment of weakness had turned him into a puppet for an evil he abhorred. Most mornings he could scarcely look at himself in the mirror. To save his sister, he would do their bidding and jerk to the twitch of their strings, but his self-loathing increased each time he did.

He pocketed the mobile. How was he to steal Lady Margaret's camera? He had never so much as spoken to her, nor did he have access to the castle where she lived.

Unable to focus on the graph, Achmed went to the employee lounge to clear his head. Removing a glass from the cupboard, he turned on the tap, and stared out the window.

And there she was, not even one hundred yards away. Lady Margaret headed down the track in the direction of the loch with one of the duke's purebred pups at her heels. She bent to pet the dog, and her camera bag swung forward.

He stiffened like a pointer. Allah be praised. Without conscious thought, he grabbed his coat and slipped out the side door. Following Lady Margaret at a discreet distance, he kept to the sodden grass to ensure no sound alerted her to his presence. Another fifty yards and he reached the conifer plantings on the south side of the track. He entered the thicket and used the evergreens to shield him from detection.

The puppy's gambol flagged to a walk. By the time Lady Margaret obtained the dock, the dog gave out altogether and sprawled on the wooden slats, his tongue lolling.

Lady Margaret knelt and ruffled the dog's fur. "Poor little Digger." Her voice traveled in the clear morning air.

Achmed pushed aside a branch to get a better view of the dock.

Lady Margaret placed her bag on the wooden planks and retrieved her camera. Making several adjustments, she set off along the shoreline, stopping every once in a while to take a shot. The whir and click of her camera carried in the silence.

A gull cried as it flew low over the water.

When Achmed had first arrived in Scotland as a refugee, he had disliked the damp and blustery climate. Over time, he had grown to appreciate, then embrace, Scotland's moody skies, abundant lochs, and snowcapped Munros.

Now, this was home, and the war-torn, sunbaked deserts of Syria were but a memory. He had adapted, even enjoyed his new country until the first message had arrived on his computer.

Woof. The dog sniffed the air, then clambered to his feet. *Woof.*

Achmed dropped the branch and prayed the dog would not come this way.

Lady Margaret glanced over her shoulder from where she knelt. "Come here, Digger." She patted her leg.

The dog barked again and stared at the pines where Achmed had secreted himself.

"Digger, come," Lady Margaret commanded.

The dog gave another half-hearted bark and trotted obediently to her side.

Achmed expelled a pent-up breath. That was close.

The dog followed Lady Margaret's general progress along the edge of the loch, sniffing at reeds and barking at the occasional bird. Leaving the shoreline, Lady Margaret hopped from rock to rock until she reached a large boulder and knelt to fiddle with her camera.

Achmed's eyes rested on her small, dainty form, and a twinge of guilt pressed upon him. At least today's demand would have little impact on her. A camera was easily replaced. Achmed had no idea why he needed to destroy it, only that he must. Perhaps Lady Margaret had inadvertently taken a picture of something she shouldn't have.

A splash took him completely off guard, and his eyes snapped to the loch just as Lady Margaret cried out.

In an attempt to reach his mistress, the dog had fallen in and now paddled about in the frigid water. Instead of swimming to shore, the puppy headed in the wrong direction.

"Digger, here boy," Lady Margaret called. If she couldn't get her dog out of the water, he would succumb to hypothermia.

Lady Margaret worked her way back to shore, then ran for the dock where a weathered rowboat was lashed to a piling, slipping in her haste. Placing her camera inside her bag, she left it on the dock. She obtained the boat just as the puppy began to flounder.

Her fingers made quick work on the ropes. She jumped into the rowboat and pushed off, her oars slapping the water in quick succession.

Achmed darted from the evergreens and reached the dock before Lady Margaret pulled the animal from the water. His hand plunged inside her bag and closed over a strap. In the process of yanking it free, the bag tipped on its side.

He hesitated whether to toss the camera into the loch or flee. Taking no chances that the camera might float and Lady Margaret would see it, he darted, quick as a hare, for the trees, the camera firmly clasped in his hands.

He arrived at the conifers just as Lady Margaret turned the boat toward the dock. The scent of pine engulfed him, and the needles under his feet muffled all sound as he took the shortcut through the trees back to the offices. He glanced at the small camera in his hands and wondered yet again why he had to destroy it.

When Achmed arrived at the corporate car park, he placed the camera on the gravel, directly behind his back tire and wedged it in place. Climbing inside his battered Vauxhall, he fired up the engine. Placing the stick shift in reverse, he backed up.

Pop.

Achmed rocked the wheels back and forth a few more times, just to make sure the camera was unrecognizable. Satisfied that he had pulverized the device beyond recognition, he moved his car to another spot and parked.

Pocketing his key fob, he started toward the office. Though he wasn't exactly proud of himself, he could live with this morning's work. After all, what other option did he have?

Chapter 18

JAMES HAD ALWAYS SUSPECTED GOD had a sense of humor. Now he was sure of it.

He leaned back in his chair and stared out the office window. Of all the women on the planet, why did he have to fall for the one female who had watched him flirt with most of her friends?

Paisley even knew his dating routine. Flowers. Dinner. Movie. Bored. Actually, bored usually arrived somewhere between hors d'oeuvres and the main course.

The last few nights, he had lain in bed listening to the clock chime the quarter hour, waiting for the sun to rise so he could sweat off his frustration in the castle gym. James had no idea how to pursue Paisley.

And it was killing him.

To top it all off, Richard had left the decision in James's court on whether to withdraw Coombes Enterprises from the resort build if Kinross couldn't cough up the $300K. As he had teetered on the precipice of which way to lean, James had driven up to the building site for inspiration.

Situated off the B846 near the village of Kinloch Rannoch, the spectacular views of Schiehallion and Loch Rannoch had fired his imagination. The place was every bit the gold mine he had imagined.

In this flagging economy, his decision would place hundreds without work if he cancelled the contract. He would also force Paisley to choose between the father she had longed to know and the surrogate one who had attended her every milestone.

The choice left him seesawing multiple times each day. He tapped his pen on the edge of the desk as he contemplated the stats on his monitor. The numbers were close but still favored disbandment unless Kinross could procure the missing $300K of the original agreement.

Kinross hadn't said specifically where he would obtain the extra $300K, but James had a sneaking suspicion from the duke's reluctance that Paisley was about to lose a substantial portion of her inheritance.

After a conversation with Nick, James understood the winds of British primogeniture law was shifting, but as of now, the legislature held fast. The firstborn legitimate son of an aristocrat inherited his parents' entailed estates. In Scotland, forced heirship laws required that a portion of the finances outside the entail be divided among the deceased's children, therefore keeping the property intact for future generations.

Paisley's inheritance wouldn't be tied to Kinross's estates like Torquil's and, therefore, was accessible for liquidation. If Kinross pilfered her funds, law required he repay them, to some degree, before his death.

James stared at the monitor and tapped the metal cap of his pen against the edge of his desk. He didn't like this situation one bit. If Kinross couldn't guarantee Coombes Enterprises a reimbursement for fronting the duke's missing funds—with interest—James was honor-bound to remove their corporation from the resort build.

Great choice.

He went over the graphs one last time and compared them to his findings at the resort site. As he stared at the charts, a corporate marketing idea came to him with blinding clarity. He could make this work. All he needed was Kinross's guarantee of reimbursement, and James would bet his own shares in Coombes Enterprises that Kinross would come through.

He tapped his pen cap on the edge of the desk. The thing that worried him was Kinross's suspicions that an employee on the estate had taken part in the theft.

James believed him. The timing was too coincidental.

While authorities scoured WFB records and wire transfers, Kinross had given James passcodes for the estate mainframe, which encompassed emails, financials, and Kinross's electronic calendar.

James had located a few interesting patterns, but he wasn't proficient enough in code to back up his theory. What he needed was a computer geek he could trust to explore employee algorithms the day of the theft.

He tapped his pen again. A few months back, Jack had let something slip about Davis Racing's server being hacked. When James had questioned him about it, Jack played it down, but James had known he was evading the truth.

Leaning back in his chair, a smile lifted one corner of his lips. If hacking had occurred at Davis Racing, Jack must know someone with legit computer skills.

When break time rolled around, James went outside and called his brother. The call went straight to voice mail.

"Jack, give me a buzz when you get a minute," James said and hung up.

Wind ruffled his hair and sliced through his wool coat as he strode the perimeter of the parking lot. He stopped, his eyes sweeping the hillside and taking in the folly, a small, single-turreted affair partway up the Munro.

Something sharp poked the bottom of his shoe. He lifted his foot and found a piece of thick black plastic stuck into the sole. He removed it and tossed it to the ground, careful to step away from other bits of broken glass and black plastic shards. A grimy strap, almost obliterated of color by last night's rain, lay alongside the pile of plastic and glass. He nudged the strap with the toe of his shoe, exposing orange neon striping on the underside.

Goosebumps broke out and slithered across his skin while his heart clanged inside his chest like the knell of a graveside service. He had seen that strap in Paisley's hand hundreds of times. Reaching down, he picked it up. A shard of black plastic was still attached to its clip. Even though the camera was outdated and she had replaced it with a fancier model, Paisley carried that camera with her wherever she went. He raked a hand through his hair and exhaled sharply. How had Paisley lost it?

Puzzled and not ready to return to work, he started up the track toward the promontory where the folly topped a knoll with views of the loch. He kept to the middle of the dirt lane to avoid the worst of the mud.

When he reached the folly, he clattered up the steps with the camera strap still in his hand. He tugged open the door just as his phone buzzed.

"How are things in the far north?" Jack's voice asked through the line.

"Blustery and damp," James said absently, his mind still on the camera.

"Wish you were back in Virginia?"

James took in the view of the loch, surrounding hillsides, and the scudding clouds. "I thought I would, but I can't get enough of the scenery."

"How's Paisley?"

James fingered the muddy strap. "You mean Lady Margaret?"

"Crud. I forgot Paisley went aristocrat on us. What did she have to say when she found out her dad was a duke?"

"I'm not sure she's absorbed it yet." James compartmentalized his discovery and switched to the subject for his call. "I need you to keep something on the lowdown."

"And that would be?" Jack sounded suspicious.

"Did Dad tell you that Kinross's funds for the resort build were funneled from his bank account to the Middle East?"

A quick intake of breath. "No, he didn't."

"There's a chance one or more of Kinross's employees might be involved," James said. "I've been checking electronic appointments, corporate emails, and Kinross's financials. I think I found a discrepancy, but I need a computer expert to verify."

"Did you call the police?"

"There's an investigation going on at the bank level, but Kinross doesn't want publicity here in the glen. If word gets out that police are nosing around and asking questions, the construction workers Kinross hired for the resort build will catch wind of it and seek employment elsewhere—if they can. Positions don't backfill easily here; there isn't enough of a population base."

"Why are you asking me for help?" Jack's slow drawl reached out through the line.

"Your company had a computer breach. With designs worth millions, you must have used a computer geek to find it. I need a trustworthy, out-of-area individual to check Kinross's mainframe and see if someone hacked into his server before the theft."

"I do know someone, but I'm not sure if she's available. I'll give her a call and find out if she has some spare time. If she does, I'll have her contact you."

"Deal. Does this person have a name?"

Jack laughed. "Yeah, several of them."

"Are we talking plural aliases?"

"Don't ask any more questions or I'll have to lie."

What exactly has Jack been involved in?

"Trust me, someone will be in contact. Words like *Middle East* and *money funneling* are an open sesame to this bunch," Jack said.

"Thanks, man. I look forward to hearing from her." James took a seat on a dusty lawn chair and gazed out the window at the loch. "So how are things?"

"Busy. I had no idea department managers attended so many meetings. Gillian says it's good for me."

"How come?"

"It forces me to communicate. Gillian said it's rubbed off at home, and she doesn't have to guess what's going on inside my head."

James bit back a laugh. His taciturn brother was notorious for long silences. "How's Thierry handling school this term?" Thierry, Jack's adopted daughter, had suffered some trauma a few months back.

"She has a rough day every once in a while, but the primary school is working with her."

"And Gillian?"

"The doctor says she's through the worst of her morning sickness."

"Morning sickness?" James straightened. "You're going to be a dad?"

"I'm already a dad," Jack reminded him with a growl.

"You're right, sorry." *Holy moly.* Jack sure got prickly when it came to his family.

"It's okay. I think Thierry's more excited about this baby than Gillian and me."

James could hear the exuberance lapping through his brother's words. Truth be told, it made him a little jealous, like he was stuck outside a sporting goods window looking at baseball equipment he couldn't afford.

Abruptly, he changed the subject. "I'm thinking about taking up climbing. Did you know that Dad and Ben go every Saturday?"

"I heard. Are we going to let them show us up?"

"Are you interested?"

"Heck yeah. I've wanted to climb for a while, but I didn't have a partner. Gillian's idea of exercise is a three-mile loop around the lake—at a fast walk. When she's really serious, she takes the switchbacks, but they make her grumpy."

"Gillian, grumpy?"

"Dude, pregnant women are crazy weird. One minute Gillian's giggling, the next she's bawling."

"You're not making the future sound all that appealing."

Jack laughed. "So how do you like dating Scottish women?"

"I wouldn't know. I've been busy."

"Too busy to date? What's the matter, are the Scottish lassies smarter than Southern belles?"

"I've never asked one out." James tugged at his shirt collar.

"Come again? I think there's something wrong with this connection."

"You heard me."

"Are you sick or something?"

Something was definitely the operative word for it. The last few days, James hadn't been able to sleep or focus. All he could think about was a pair of dark eyes.

James cleared his throat. "When did you know Gillian was the one?"

A slight pause.

"Like that, is it?" Jack finally asked.

"I'm a walking zombie and can't focus on work. How do I get her to consider me romantically when I've dated all her friends?"

"You fell for Paisley?" Jack's laugh almost blasted out his eardrum.

"What's wrong with Paisley?" James asked, hackles rising in her defense.

"Nothing's wrong with Paisley except she's seen you flirt since you hit puberty." Jack chuckled again, clearly enjoying himself. "You making any headway?"

"Are you kidding?" James raked a hand through his hair.

"That would be a no. Why are you asking me anyway?"

"I need advice. You're my only married brother."

"I'm not the best person to ask about this. For the record, I blew it twice."

"It was a miracle you and Gillian ever got together." James shook his head.

"Pretty much," Jack drawled, elongating his vowels. "Paisley won't make it easy for you. You know that, don't you?"

"Believe it or not, I did manage to figure that out for myself."

"How are you going to convince her you're serious?"

Good question. James had absolutely no idea. "Her dad's already warned me off."

Jack roared with laughter, and James had to hold the phone away from his ear. His brother was enjoying his downfall way too much.

"Get her some flowers. Gillian always goes . . . never mind. She likes them a lot."

"Kinross grows his own. They wouldn't be special." James ran his finger along the windowsill.

"Yeah, but they would be from you."

"Kinross is distantly related to the royal family."

"So what," Jack said.

"In the States, that's no big deal, but over here, it matters."

"We're related to the Earl of Rivendon. That has to count for something. And our family isn't exactly living paycheck to paycheck."

"Kinross's property puts Ashford Priory to shame."

"They're still people, James. They put their pants on the same way as you and me—oh wait. Maybe not. They wear skirts up there, don't they?" More laughter blasted through the line.

James shook his head. He should have expected this reaction from Jack.

"So Paisley lives in a fancy house, and her daddy has money. Big deal." Silence for a heartbeat, then Jack inquired softly, "Do you love her?"

"If staying up most every night and not being able to down a good steak when it's cooked to perfection and losing my train of thought is love . . . then, yeah."

"That's a start in the right direction."

"You mean it gets worse?" A shudder rippled down James's spine. He couldn't take much more of this. Falling in love had destroyed his peaceful existence.

"Dude, you've got a good dose of infatuation. When it gets to the point where you want Paisley's happiness before your own and would do anything to make her smile and want to spend every minute with her until you're old—then you're in trouble."

James sat. The idea of Paisley hunched with age and covered with wrinkles sounded kind of cute. James's mouth curved, then slowly straightened. If he ended the contract, who would watch over her when he went back to the States? Kinross was too busy, and from what he'd observed, his duchess wouldn't lift a finger to assist her.

His head itched. James held his cell between his neck and shoulder and ran both hands through his hair. If he kept this up, he'd be bald.

When he had left Paisley behind in Virginia, he had worried about her. He always worried about her. James looked at the soiled camera strap in his hand, then shoved himself out of the chair and stared out the window at the wind-whipped loch.

Jack's voice faded into the distance.

He had worried about Paisley since the second grade. The only time he had laid violent hands on Ben was when his twin had teased her too much. No one ever came between him and Ben—no one except Paisley.

She was the only person who . . .

Sheesh.

James hit his forehead with the palm of his free hand. "I gotta go." He disconnected without waiting for Jack to say goodbye.

Chapter 19

An act of Parliament might have been easier for James to arrange than getting Henderson to lead him to Paisley's grandmother's rooms. Usually, he had a way with people, but James had almost resorted to bribery before Kinross's butler had acquiesced. James took in the rigid set of Henderson's shoulders as he followed the man through the upstairs gallery. He had no idea what he had done to set the butler against him.

James passed the Douglas family portraits of stern-faced individuals in funny wigs to a connecting door. Entering yet another corridor, Henderson stopped at a double set of doors across from an elevator. A laugh rang from within. James recognized it as Paisley's.

"The dowager duchess is verra busy," Henderson informed James as he rapped on a wooden panel.

James rocked back on his heels and held back a sarcastic remark.

A young, redhaired woman dressed in a navy pantsuit with the duke's coat of arms emblazoned on her jacket breast answered. A blast of hot air from the open door rushed out.

"Mr. James Pressley-Coombes wishes an audience with Lady Margaret," Henderson said stiffly.

The redhead eyed James with open curiosity. "I'll see if Lady Margaret is available."

James ran his fingers over the camera strap inside his pocket. He didn't want to be the harbinger of bad news, but Paisley's camera was important to her. Perhaps he could take her to lunch before he filled her in. He brightened perceptibly. Anything to postpone the inevitable sounded like a good plan.

"Is this really a dress?" Paisley giggled from somewhere inside the cavernous suite.

"That design was all the rage once," an older voice responded.

"Your Grace, Mr. James Pressley-Coombes is here to see Lady Margaret." The maid's words carried to the doorway where James waited beside the frowning Henderson.

"This isn't a good time," the older woman answered.

The maid soon returned to the door. "I'm sorry, Henderson. Her Grace isn't receiving."

"Verra good." Henderson moved to close the door.

"Wait," Paisley called. Her voice was followed by quick footsteps.

Henderson pushed the doors wide, nodded briefly to James, and started for the stairs, disapproval etched on every feature.

Paisley appeared in the doorway dressed in a fluffy netted gown that resembled a turquoise Brillo pad. James's eyes bulged.

"Come in."

James followed her, stopping just inside the doorway. "It's a little early for Halloween, isn't it?" he asked, his eyes still on her netted gown.

"I don't have a dress for the ball, so Granny's letting me try on her dresses."

"And that's your choice?"

Paisley snorted. "Hardly." She glanced over her shoulder, then turned back and lowered her voice. "Sorry, you'll need to be quick. Granny tires easily."

"Who is this young man?" Granny called.

"It's my friend James."

"Where are your manners, Paisley? Bring him over here and introduce us."

Paisley grabbed his arm and brought him to the bed, where a small woman with Paisley's dark eyes looked him over.

"Granny, this is James. We grew up together."

"You must be the American Cam has told me about. Welcome to Castle Rannoch."

"Thank you." James gave her his best smile. "Sorry I've interrupted your fun. I'll come back when Paisley's finished. It was a pleasure to meet you, Your Grace."

"And you as well, young man." Paisley's grandmother nodded.

Paisley followed him back to the door. At the door he turned, taking in her shining eyes and the long, dark hair that had a tendency to curl. His heart gave a huge thump. No wonder no other female had ever held his attention. He had unknowingly attached himself to Paisley when he was knee-high to a grasshopper and too young to recognize his emotions. How could he have gone so long without recognizing his feelings for her?

"I need to talk to you when you finish."

No way would he deliver bad news with witnesses around. Paisley had always valued her privacy, and this, he sensed, would not go well. He had just the place to tell her without anyone the wiser.

"I'll text you when I'm done."

"Sounds good." James squeezed her arm and pulled the door shut between them.

***

After much deliberation, Paisley settled on a pale gold, A-line Dior ballgown. The sweeping train and off-shoulder bodice covered in handmade lace and crystals offset the full organza skirt with crystal appliques. The color brought out the natural highlights in her hair and made her skin glow.

"That was always one of my favorites," Granny said approvingly. "The full skirt is perfect for dancing reels."

Standing in front of the long, three-way mirror, Paisley touched her exposed collarbone. "Do you think there's enough material in the train to make sleeves or a jacket?"

Esme McMurdie, Granny's dressmaker, circled Paisley with a considering expression.

"I think so. I could finish the sleeves with crystal beading from the train. What type of jacket do you have in mind, lass?"

"She doesn't need a jacket. There's a matching cape in those trunks you can use," Granny said, her voice a little frayed around the edges.

Paisley exchanged a smile with Esme.

"That will save us some time," Esme said.

Paisley turned this way and that in the three-way mirror, admiring the gown's sparkle under the lights. "I love it." Nothing had suited her small frame more.

She texted James, then slipped out of the gown and changed back into her skirt and blouse.

"What do you have in the way of shoes?" Granny's voice sounded weaker.

A furrow etched Paisley's brow. "I think we can discuss shoes another time."

"Nonsense," Granny said. "Shoes are important."

"Well," Paisley said, her mind running over the collection of heels she had brought with her to Scotland. "I have a gold pair of peep toes with ankle straps."

"Sounds lovely." Granny closed her eyes for a moment before she opened them again, and a spark of curiosity swirled in their depths. "Where did you meet your young man?"

Paisley's heart skipped a beat, and she blushed. "James isn't my young man. We grew up together. We're friends."

"That isn't what I saw," Granny said softly, a wicked gleam in her eyes.

Since the night of the supper, James had behaved differently, his eyes following her whenever she entered a room. At first she thought she had imagined it, but evidently, Granny had noticed too.

On impulse, Paisley went to the bed and kissed her grandmother's cheek. "Thank you for the dress, Granny. I've never had anything so beautiful."

Granny fidgeted with the duvet that covered her legs. "There, there. It's just an old dress."

Despite Granny's weak protest, Paisley had a feeling her grandmother was secretly pleased.

A smart rap sounded on the door.

Granny's eyes brightened, and a little smirk played about her mouth. "Americans are such an impatient breed."

***

"Aren't we taking Digger?" Paisley asked as she accompanied James past the castle's treasure trove of art lining the main corridor, ranging from ancient Egyptian sarcophagi to oils by Georgia O'Keeffe.

"Hamish put a crate and dog supplies in the scullery this morning while you were sleeping. Mrs. Grant has already moved Digger's crate into the kitchen and has been sneaking him table scraps."

"What were you doing in the kitchen?"

"I heard a rumor that Mrs. Grant hands out scraps to all the strays, human or canine." James gave her a lopsided grin. "I had to check it out."

Paisley shook her head. *Unbelievable.* James had been here no time at all and already had the cook wrapped around his little finger. When Paisley had arrived at the castle, Munira had informed her that snacking was heavily discouraged as Mrs. Grant and her staff were paid to produce meals, and the family was expected to eat them.

Paisley glanced at James out of the corner of her eye. He had fallen silent during her musings. His expression was more serious than she had ever seen him wear. Had he received bad news from home?

The muted golds, blues, and greens of the Turkish carpet muffled their steps as they entered the entrance hall and crossed to the coatroom annex. The vast array of ancient weaponry in starburst patterns on the walls made her shudder.

She had reason to know that those battle axes and broadswords had seen heavy action.

"I thought we could hike up to the folly." James helped her with her coat when they reached the vestibule. "We can have privacy there."

Privacy? Her heart squeezed painfully. Had he pulled Coombes Enterprises out of the resort build? She couldn't bear the thought of him not being here at the castle. As much as she loved her father, he hadn't been available. It was James who had carved time for her from his busy schedule during the bewildering transition from American pauper to Scottish aristocrat.

He refused to take her new lifestyle too seriously. A castle, mansion, or cottage to James was simply a place to live, and an aristocratic title was just another name. His sense of normalcy in this maelstrom of preferential treatment had helped her maintain her sense of self.

As to the other emotions that had recently surfaced for him, she refused to dwell.

They left the castle and clattered down the porch steps to the drive, James slowing his stride to accommodate her shorter one. In silence, they cut through the formal gardens whose deciduous shrubs and perennial beds were bereft of leaves.

Veering off the main drive, they merged onto a steep track that wound its way up through the forested hillside filled with the pungent scents of moss and pine. The toe of her boot dislodged a loose pebble and sent it bouncing down the slope behind her.

The snow had melted, and the hillsides were ablaze with autumn's last hurrah. Her fingers itched for the camera she had left in her room. A steady stream of condensation puffed in front of her lips as she hiked up the track. The wind had not warmed since Digger's mishap that morning.

A crossbill startled from a nearby pine and shot into the air, its cry similar to that of a sparrow's. They came out above the tree line and continued along the ridge toward the folly, a minuscule castle with a lone turret.

James went up the stone steps and opened the door to the one-roomed structure. Paisley blinked in surprise. She had half expected the faux ruin to be open to the elements, but Castle Rannoch's folly was more in the line of a studio apartment.

Cautiously, she entered the vaulted space, her boots echoing on the chilly stone floor. Cushioned rattan sofas and chairs were arranged to take in the view of water and hills. A rustic farm table stood on the far side of the room, adjoining a small galley kitchen. Paisley turned slowly. The folly was cold and in need of a good dusting.

One glance at James's serious expression told her she was on the precipice of something unpleasant. She had learned over the years that delay tactics didn't work on him. James, though kind, was as stubborn as an old hickory stump. Once his mind was made up, there was no budging him.

She squared her shoulders and bit the inside of her lip. He took her hand, his eyes suddenly full of tenderness. Despite the worry swirling inside, Paisley's pulse quickened at his touch.

He led her to the sofa and pulled her down beside him, the view from the windows facing the Fairy Hill on the far end of the loch. He ran a hand over his jaw and met her eyes.

"I found something today."

He removed a soiled lanyard from his jacket with a small piece of jagged plastic attached to the end and placed it gingerly in her lap.

"What's this?" Paisley nudged it with her finger.

The material rolled on its side and exposed a bright neon-orange interior. She swallowed. *No.* It couldn't be. She looked away, refusing to accept the evidence before her.

That filthy thing couldn't be her camera lanyard. It couldn't. She kept it with her always. She had all but slept with her father's gift since childhood. The camera had been her talisman throughout the years of her mother's neglect, the only proof of her father's love. Now it was gone?

Paisley lifted the lanyard as though it would bite her and examined the jagged piece of camera housing attached to the clip. She shook her head violently and tossed the lanyard onto the cushion beside her.

"No. That's not mine. You're wrong." The words spilled out, broken and sharp as the jagged piece of plastic.

"Paise, I found it crushed to bits in Kinross's car park." James put his arm around her and squeezed her shoulders, his eyes filled with compassion.

"You're wrong," Paisley whispered. "It's in my room."

She jerked free and ran to the window, tears splashing onto her cheeks. She heard the sofa scoot on the stone floor as James rose to his feet. Without a word, he came up behind her, turned her around, and pulled her into his arms.

"Go away." Her hands clenched into fists.

"No. I won't leave you like this."

Unable to keep the pain at bay, she buried her face in his jacket and sobbed quietly. He rubbed her back and let her cry out her grief. Briefly, she felt the pressure of lips against her temple and wondered if he had kissed her.

When she finished, he settled her back on the sofa and hurriedly retrieved several napkins from the kitchen, pressing them into her hand. She used them to blow her nose.

Paisley couldn't figure out how her camera had ended up in the car park. Unless she left it inside her room, she never let the bag out of her sight. She remembered touching the camera briefly before she and Digger had set out for their walk. Digger had fallen in the lake and . . .

She lifted both hands to her cheeks. "I left my camera bag on the dock this morning when Digger fell in the loch. I used the boat to get him. The bag was tipped on its side when I returned. I didn't think anything of it at the time, but someone must have removed it when I was in the boat during those few minutes."

"Could you have dropped it on the way to the loch?"

She shook her head vehemently. "You've seen my bag—the opening is narrow and curves at both ends. Even when it's unzipped, it's impossible for the camera to fall out unless I purposely dump my bag upside down and shake it. Whoever took it must have been nearby—watching." Chills rippled up her arms.

"Are you sure?" James's eyes pierced hers.

"I'm positive. That was the only time I didn't have the camera bag in plain sight." She tucked a dark strand of hair behind her ear. "How did you know it was mine?"

"I recognized the strap."

Her body shook, and she clenched her teeth to keep them from chattering. James pulled her back into his arms. But even with his additional body heat, she couldn't get warm. Whoever had done this had followed her, watched her, then had deliberately stolen and destroyed her personal property.

Resentment warred with grief. Anger won. And fury like she had never experienced before rose up and choked her. She recognized it for what it was, the reaction of being victimized as the target of an intentional act.

Paisley lifted her chin and met James's eyes. "I want to find out who did this."

Chapter 20

LAMPLIGHT REFLECTED OFF THE EMPTY superglue tubes at the bottom of James's bedroom wastebasket. He dipped his fingers in a bowl of acetone and stared at the black plastic fragments on top of his desk. He had always enjoyed a good puzzle, but putting Paisley's camera housing back together just about had him stumped.

He had walked Paisley back to the castle just before supper. After escorting her to her room, he had borrowed a flashlight (Kinross insisted the thing was called a torch) from the coatroom and returned to the car park to gather up the remains of her camera.

He had known how attached Paisley was to her father's gift, but it wasn't until he glued part of the back casing together that he found the etching "Love, Dad."

James exhaled sharply, grateful he had gone with his gut and had retrieved the remains. Now, more than ever, he was committed to this project. Lifting his fingers from the acetone, he scrubbed the adhesive from his skin.

If he lived to be ninety, he would never forget Paisley's anguished expression when she realized what had happened to her cherished camera. It would haunt him forever. While nothing could replace her loss, perhaps he could soften the blow by piecing together the outside housing.

Someone had wounded her deeply by destroying that camera. Had malicious intent been their aim, or had they simply wanted to get rid of whatever was on her SIM card?

Except for Munira, he couldn't think of anyone in the castle who didn't like Paisley. The Duchess's cold behavior had been noticeable from the start. Was she the responsible party? Somehow, he couldn't see the elegant Munira skulking behind pines, lying in wait. But the fact remained that she was one of the few who knew Kinross had gifted the camera to his daughter.

James worked at another blob of glue on his finger. He'd hate to be Kinross right now. The destruction of his daughter's old camera was small potatoes in comparison to his financial loss. Since the bank theft, Kinross was positive someone on the estate had delayed his departure on the day of the transfer. James wouldn't want to be in their shoes when Kinross figured it out.

Dipping his hand back inside the bowl of acetone, he stared unseeing at the black plastic casing. No one entered the duke's estate without a code, which meant if Kinross's assumptions were correct, whoever had stolen the resort money had an accomplice, and it had to be either an employee or a member of the family. If that was the case, Kinross's troubles had only just begun.

***

After an impromptu marketing meeting following supper, James left Kinross's office in search of Paisley. He found her outside the dowager duchess's suite. Paisley's eyes were still bloodshot from the afternoon's crying jag. She looked exhausted.

"Are you doing okay?" James clasped Paisley's upper arm when she passed him in the hall.

She hesitated, then said in a rush, "I'm fine. Thank you for being so kind about my camera today." Her hand made a restless motion.

"Where are you off to?"

"To see if Munira needs help with the RSVP list for the ball."

"Have you toured the estate with your father yet?" he asked, knowing Kinross had been swamped liquidating assets since the loss of the resort funds.

"He's been a little busy." Paisley wouldn't meet his eyes.

"He has," James agreed, but he was disappointed in Kinross all the same. Despite his issues, certainly the man could carve out some time for his daughter after bringing her here instead of letting her wander the castle by herself.

James took in Paisley's downcast features. Granted, he didn't know the estate like her father or Rahim, but James had a stack of travel brochures inside his desk drawer. One of them offered an air and sea trip to the Western Isles, complete with picnic lunch and supper at a luxury restaurant. He had tentatively booked the excursion in the hope of taking her. After her rotten day, she needed a complete change in scenery.

"I'm touring the Western Isles tomorrow—weather permitting. Why don't you come with me? I hear the scenery is spectacular."

"I'd like to, but Dad's ball is in three days. Munira might need my help."

"So, you're going to let me spend an entire day wandering around the back of beyond by myself?"

She shrugged, but at least a little something flickered in her eyes before she glanced away.

Stubborn woman.

"Let me ask you this—when do you think your dad is going to give you a tour of the area?" James hated to grind her nose in it, but he doubted Paisley would go out with him unless he pushed. "Come with me. It'll be fun. You know it will. And when we return, you can tell your dad about our day trip. Maybe it'll jog his memory, and he'll give you that promised tour. If it doesn't, I'll take you around the estate myself."

"You're almost as unfamiliar with it as I am."

"Wrong. I've been all over this property. While I'm not versed in clan history, I have a general idea where most things are located."

"Hmmm."

"C'mon, Paise. I wiped snot off your face. The least you can do—"

"You did not." Paisley huffed indignantly.

"I got you napkins for your runny nose. That's almost the same thing."

"Would you have wiped my face if I had let you?"

He squirmed. The bad part of trying to date someone you had known since your single digits was that they knew your history. He couldn't stand goop—not on his hands or anywhere on his person.

"Will you come with me tomorrow or not?" he asked, refusing to answer her question.

She blinked those large brown eyes of hers several times and sucked in her mouth, hollowing her cheeks. He would have laughed if her answer hadn't been so important.

"Well?" He raised his brows and waited.

"I'll go. When are we leaving?"

"Around first light." Satisfaction hummed through his body. "I'll meet you on the landing."

***

Paisley stood on the end of her father's dock in the chill, gray dawn and eyed the bobbing gold Cessna floatplane. Her lips quivered at the corners when she caught sight of the words *Nessie Fodder* painted jauntily on the fuselage. The pilot must be a real character.

Wind gusted across the water's surface and unleashed its icy talons. She shivered and huddled deeper into her waterproof coat. Even the thermos of hot chocolate James had provided did little to warm her.

"Are you excited?" James asked before he finished his hot chocolate in one long swig.

"I am. But how do we get inside that thing?" Paisley didn't see any stairs.

The pilot, a thin man in his thirties with a full, untrimmed beard, jogged down the dock. "Well now," he said when he reached them and checked his clipboard. "You must be Lady Margaret and James Pressley-Coombes?"

"That's us," James said.

The pilot stepped off the dock onto the nearside pontoon skid, the flotation device which allowed the plane to take off and land on water, then he reached for her hand.

Paisley clutched her camera bag to her chest and stepped onto the skid beside the pilot. The plane rocked subtly under her weight. "That's a bit of a wobble," she laughed.

"Up you go. Mind your step," the pilot said, indicating the Cessna's four-foot-wide built-in ladders—two per side—connecting the fuselage to the pontoons.

Paisley scampered up the nearside ladder and took her seat kitty-corner to the pilot and buckled up. James took the spot beside her. The pilot climbed aboard, put on his headset, and punched a series of buttons. Seconds later, the engine sputtered to life, and the plane began to taxi.

The skids bounced across Loch Rannoch's surface before the pilot turned a few knobs on the instrument panel, and the engine dropped several decibels, then picked up speed, flinging white spray in their wake. A spurt of adrenaline coursed through her, and she couldn't hold back the grin.

The Cessna lifted off into the headwind, circled, gained altitude, and turned toward the Hebrides, a series of islands off Scotland's west coast.

Flying across the Atlantic in a 747 was smooth compared to buzzing about the Western Isles in nothing sturdier than a tin can with wings. The plane made so much noise, the aircraft sounded like it was going to fall apart.

James's eyes were hidden behind dark shades, but an answering grin tipped up one side of his mouth as the plane bucked about and items rattled in the locker behind her seat.

Soon they would be swallowed in mist if that bank of gray clouds was anything to judge by. Why had she let James talk her into coming? She glanced at him briefly. His head was turned to the window, his eyes on the view below.

Of the three Pressley-Coombes brothers, she had always considered James the handsomest—though why she did often puzzled her. He and Ben were identical, and Jack, though younger and a few inches taller, was so similar in looks that people often mistook him for one of the twins. It must have something to do with James's personality. Though perplexed why he had insisted she accompany him on this sightseeing trip so close to her father's ball, she had agreed due largely to the fact that she had cried all over him yesterday.

"It's a bonnie day for a flight," the pilot yelled back to them, his voice barely discernible over the noise inside the aircraft.

Paisley didn't roll her eyes—not exactly. But it was close. She hadn't been in Scotland long before she realized its weather was ambivalent at best. Just this morning, the temperature on Mull had registered three degrees Celsius with winds at eighteen knots. Rain was a given, especially in the Highlands, and she had dressed accordingly: wool thermals, waterproof gloves, hat, coat, pants, and boots.

James had secured reservations for an early dinner at a luxury hotel and restaurant on Loch Awe, whose jetty accommodated floatplane aircraft. Since James was not given to large expenditures, Paisley had been nonplussed after she had mentally tallied the cost of this excursion. Why had he blown $3K for a bouncy ride in the rain?

This went against the principles and hard work ethics Richard had instilled in his children. Richard did not coddle his offspring like those of his privileged associates, the majority of whom had lost their financial standing in one generation due to parental handouts. Though the Pressley-Coombes family was about as down-to-earth as any regular Joe, they were loaded.

Growing up alongside them, Paisley had been self-conscious that the Pressley-Coombes family and hers lived under two different tax brackets, but mostly, her issues had stemmed from her abysmal attempt at a startup business. Her efforts had proven how inept she was in comparison to their superior skill sets.

Paisley looked out the window. Her visit to Scotland had come at an opportune moment, for which she was most grateful, but she couldn't continue to live off her father's charity. She had a business to rebuild. The recent shots she had taken of the Scottish countryside might sell for enough online to provide collateral for that venture.

The plane jostled. She glanced at James again as questions circled inside as to why he had forked out so much money for this day trip. This wasn't a date—she had witnessed firsthand his smitten behavior before he asked women out. His conduct toward her hadn't come anywhere close. Today must be his way of taking her mind off her broken camera.

He turned his head toward her and gave her that endearing lopsided grin.

"If this is what you do for friends, I can't imagine how much you spend on your dates." The words burst from Paisley before she thought them through. Her cheeks flamed, and she could have swallowed her tongue.

He removed his sunglasses and gave a self-deprecating laugh. "I take my dates to dinner, but I'm usually bored before the main course is served."

His eyes had darkened, reminiscent of the night of her father's business supper. A tug of attraction shot through her belly and knotted her tongue. She couldn't speak if she tried.

"If you think today is some kind of pity outing, think again," James continued, accurately reading part of her tangled thoughts.

The old Paisley would have demanded to know what today's outing was all about, but an unaccustomed shyness gripped her. Things had shifted between them, and it had left her with the sensation of walking on quicksand, fearful and unsure of the terrain.

The plane banked sharply, but she hardly noticed.

"Don't you want to know why?" James cocked a brow, then wiggled it at her.

She nodded, still riding that wave of nervousness.

"I wanted to spend the day with you."

Her heart gave a jolt. Today really wasn't a kindness then, but something else altogether? She glanced away, her mind whirling. Perhaps that little zing arcing between them hadn't been as one-sided as she had imagined.

Paisley was unbelievably tempted to give her crazy response to James a try. But deep down, she didn't trust his lack of staying power. One at a time, all her friends had fallen for James. She had witnessed their euphoric responses when he asked them out and the tears afterward when he didn't call. Some of them had dubbed him a player, but Paisley knew otherwise. James was in earnest every single time with each of them—for all of two minutes.

In the end, he would jettison her like all the rest, and the fallout for her would be ten times worse. She had no intention of having her heart dashed to pieces. No matter how attracted she was to James, Paisley couldn't jeopardize her relationship with his family for one of his two-hour attractions.

The plane shuddered, then side-crabbed as she watched James's reflection in her window. A furrow marred the skin between his brows, and the teasing light had gone from his eyes. He looked serious and uncertain—not a common state for the confident and easygoing James.

Paisley's breath hitched, and her heart swelled. Was James zeroing in on her?

The pilot yelled from the cockpit. "Below us is the island of Mull. You can see Duart Castle on that promontory above the sound. In the distance are Coll and Tiree."

Paisley peered through the window. James unbuckled his seatbelt and crowded beside her. The plane tilted from the weight shift, and James's woodsy aftershave enveloped her.

"Return to your seat, sir," the pilot said sharply.

"Sorry." James reclaimed his seat, his eyes twinkling, not the least bit repentant.

She shook her head and fought back a giggle.

Under James's playful exterior lurked the heart of a caring man. The woman who snared him would need to challenge, intrigue, and shake that keen intellect of his to keep him on his toes—a tall order when he had the attention span of a gnat.

She lowered her head, her hands hanging limply at her sides. For her, the risk of failure was simply too great.

Chapter 21

THE FLOATPLANE TOUCHED DOWN ON the far side of Mull with all the subtlety of a rockslide. Paisley grinned as the Cessna bounced from one swell to the next before it slowed to a more sedate pace. This was better than any ride at Kings Dominion, the amusement park closest to her home in Virginia.

Dark polygonal pillars of basalt jutted straight from the sea, forming an eighty-foot-high cliff capped by mushroom-shaped rock topped by a greensward of peat. Paisley caught her breath and stared at the Norse-named Staffa while the plane taxied slowly through the swells and troughs, dipping and bobbing like a gull on the sea.

The large opening of Fingal's Cave at the southern tip of the island, whose natural cathedral and melodious cavern had inspired the first few bars of Felix Mendelssohn's overture, yawned wide.

Tingling with excitement, Paisley grabbed her camera, swung the strap around her neck, and unlatched the door beside her. Unmindful of the dip and roll of the sea, she climbed partway down the four-foot-wide ladder, wrapped her legs through the bars, hooked her ankles, and hung outward, straining for the right position.

"Are you crazy?" James shouted to her over the noise of the engine.

She blinked up at him, then realized her position. Her heart gave a lurch but righted almost immediately when she turned back to the incredible view. Without a glimmer of worry, she zoomed her lens on the multi-toned water at the cave entrance and turned off her flash for greater depth of field. Waiting between swells, she clicked the shutter in rapid succession.

The metal rungs of the ladder vibrated as James climbed partway down and grabbed the back of her belt, apparently ready to hoist her inside the cabin.

"I need another shot," Paisley yelled and leaned further out to capture the wave as it crested, then crashed on the rocks at the cave's mouth.

"Your little stunt almost gave the pilot a heart attack," James bellowed with narrowed eyes, and his hand on the back of her belt shook.

"I'm totally fine," she yelled as water sloshed over the pontoon skid beneath her.

Her comment had no visual effect on him. She hadn't meant to upset James, or the pilot for that matter. She had simply seen a spectacular shot and had taken it before the light changed. It was always the same; nothing existed but the view through her lens. If one of those shots paid off, it could reboot her career.

Paisley's eyes swept over her awkward position. Below her, the ocean rose and fell, frothing at the base of the pontoon skids. Both of her legs were woven through the rungs. She was in no danger, especially now that she had James's added support, but the firm expression on his face had her untangling her legs and straightening on the ladder.

"The pilot needs to taxi, but he's afraid he'll dump you in the sea."

Careful not to let her camera hit the side of the plane, she started up the ladder, still high on that incredible euphoria that had whisked her out of the cabin for those shots.

When they retook their seats, James addressed the pilot. "When she has a camera in her hands, she has no concept of what's around her."

A flush covered Paisley's body as she buckled up. "Sorry," she mumbled.

"If you are quite ready, we will proceed, Lady Margaret." The pilot spoke in a deadpan manner, but his eyes glittered with suppressed emotion. He turned back to his controls and spoke into his headset. "Had a slight hiccup. Passengers will be at the jetty in five."

"You could have fallen in and died of hypothermia before we fished you out." James grabbed the camera from her hands and put it away—setting the bag on the far side of his seat.

"I was completely safe," she said, oddly touched by his concern.

The pilot looked as though he had more to say but refrained as they neared the drop off, a large cement platform with moorings for boats and floatplanes. A small wooden boat lay anchored two hundred yards away.

"Your ride is here." The pilot climbed out and secured the plane to the moorings.

"Aren't we going to explore the island first?" Paisley asked.

"There isn't time, not if you want to see the seals." James checked his watch. "The best views of Staffa are from the sea, according to the pamphlet."

"Oh. Then I'm glad I took those shots," she said.

That comment earned her another furrow between James's brows.

"I'll go first. That way, if there's a problem, I can catch you." James lifted the backpack with their picnic lunch and slipped it over his shoulders.

"Okay." Paisley chose not to mention the fact that of the two of them, she was the more sure-footed. Instead, she picked up the camera bag that James had left on the far side of his seat, draped it crosswise over her body and clattered down after him.

***

James grasped the support pole behind the captain's chair and stared out the salt-stained windows of the blue tourist boat as it plowed through the murky Atlantic. Despite the cold weather, the captain kept both doors open to dispel the heavy fuel fumes.

James's nostrils flared, and he jerked the zipper on his three-in-one jacket repeatedly. How could Paisley not be aware of the danger when she had climbed out of the plane?

When he and Paisley had boarded the boat on Staffa, James had opted to stay in the cockpit with the captain, Jock Robertson, and his eighteen-year-old son, Rod—a thin youth with brilliant blue eyes and the soft voice of the islanders. Paisley had gone below into the observation lounge, a fancy name for several rows of wooden benches with windows just above sea level in the freeboard sector.

An outcropping of rock rose from the seabed on the starboard side, the first sign that they had entered the Treshnish Isles, an archipelago of small islands and skerries within the Inner Hebrides. Lunga, their destination, the largest in the chain, provided a breeding habitat for seabirds and marine mammals.

He had booked the trip to take Paisley's mind off the loss of her camera plus remove her from Rahim's orbit. Munira's son had shown a keen interest in Paisley of late, and James didn't like it one bit.

"You'd better keep an eye on that one." James nodded down the short flight of steps into the lounge where Paisley sat. "If she sees anything of interest, she'll be out on the bow before you can stop her."

"That wee lass?" The captain's tone scoffed. "It's misting out. She'd slip on the deck and fall into the sea."

"You've been warned," James said darkly and returned his gaze to the rise and fall of the swells.

The captain and his son exchanged a look, but neither of them said another word. James knew he'd spoken out of turn, but his temper—once fired—took a while to cool.

Movement on one of the low-lying rocks caught James's attention. He edged closer to the window and braced his legs for balance. Divers? At this time of year? Their wetsuits would have to be at least seven millimeters thick to handle the temps.

A head broke through the surface and bobbed above the waves. Was he seeing things? James rubbed the glass for a better view, but the head disappeared beneath the waves. He kept his eyes on the area where he had last seen movement. Within seconds, two sleekly shaped heads emerged from the swells.

"Seals?" James asked.

"Aye. We're getting close to Lunga."

"Autumn's the best time for Atlantic Greys. The colony's gone to shore to breed." Rod jerked his chin toward the island.

"A seal!" Paisley squealed from the observation lounge.

"Watch your exits." James met Rod's eye.

A second later, Paisley clattered up the stairs and darted for the closest doorway, her camera swinging from its strap around her neck.

Rod stepped in front of her. "Och, lassie. Cool yer jets. Ye'll not be going out on deck in this mist. Ye'll fall in for sure."

She made to move around him.

"You'll have plenty of photo ops once you reach shore." The captain slowed the engine.

The fervid light in Paisley's eyes leached out. "I did it again, didn't I?" She looked at James for confirmation.

"Yeah."

Paisley looked so woebegone that the anger inside James fizzled and died.

She exhaled loudly. "Sorry."

James wrapped an arm around her shoulders and squeezed it. "I'm beginning to think I need to carry the camera. That way, I'll be warned before you do something crazy."

Rod's mouth twitched as he went out onto the bow.

The captain steered the vessel to a floating platform anchored a good distance from the rocky shoreline. Rod jumped from the bow onto the platform, secured it vertically to the front of the boat, and pulled anchor. The result somewhat resembled a narwhal and its tusk in appearance.

Pressing a few levers, the captain veered the watercraft toward the boulder-strewn beach and wedged the platform onto the rocks.

"That's quite an engineering feat." James was duly impressed.

"There aren't any good landing places in the Treshnish chain. We've built several docks over the years, but winter storms wash them away. So, I came up with this idea and charge competitors a fee for its use." The captain tapped his temple and winked. "Canny, aye?"

"Definitely," James agreed.

Rod returned to the cabin. "Ready? We'll return in an hour and a half to collect the pair of you." He glanced at the glowering sky. "The weather should hold until then."

"Are there any special sights not mentioned in the brochure?" Paisley asked as she swung her photography bag over her shoulder.

The captain swiveled his chair in her direction. "There are a few unmarked caves on this side of the island."

"They're more like cubby holes," Rod said to no one in particular, his voice dry. "Not like what you've seen on Staffa."

"Paisley's more interested in photographing wildlife," James said hastily. No way was he going to enter a small, enclosed space.

"You'll likely spot the seal colony from up on the cliffs." The captain flipped open his logbook and made a notation. "But you might want to keep an eye on the sea. Every once in a while, we spot an orca."

James tightened the strap on his backpack, anxious to be on his way. He started down the companionway a few steps ahead of Paisley and hopped off the end onto a large black boulder. She jumped down beside him, her hair flying out in all directions in the stiff breeze.

He scanned the cliffs, searching for the small caves the captain had mentioned. If there were any, they were well hidden. Good. He didn't want Paisley getting any ideas.

Charcoal-gray boulders covered every conceivable inch of the "beach," which gave way to green turf before the terrain rose steeply, culminating in rocky cliffs. He reached out and took Paisley by the hand, their touch shooting tingles up his arm. He opened his mouth to tell her how he felt but held back, waiting for the perfect location before he laid his soul bare.

Together they made their way across the rocks. By the time they reached the turf, the wind had numbed his face. He retrieved his fleece-lined beanie from his pack and shoved it down over his ears.

He glanced at Paisley and caught his breath, his heart thundering painfully. The breeze had whipped color into her cheeks and tossed her long, dark hair about her face. Words eluded him, and he stood transfixed by the foreign emotion, unable to take his eyes off her. If someone had asked his name just then, he would have struggled to answer. He couldn't think of anything but Paisley; she consumed his every thought.

Why hadn't Jack warned him that falling in love messed with your brain? He couldn't focus on his upcoming marketing presentation or work the simplest Sudoku if he tried.

"Earth to James. Are you ready?" Paisley asked. Her voice sounded concerned.

"Yeah, sorry I spaced out on you. I've got a few things on my mind."

"I can imagine. Are you worrying about that upcoming presentation of yours?"

"Something like that."

She cocked an eyebrow, but he refused to elaborate. How could he when she was the root of his inability to focus?

Behind them, the boat started up, then slowly headed to open water, towing the platform with it. Geese flew in V formation above the speckled cliffs, their honks muffled by wind and sea. Dark clouds scudded on the horizon, and he hoped the rain Rod predicted held off until they were through exploring.

"What do you want to do first?" he asked.

"I'd love to get some shots of the seals, then maybe picnic up on the cliffs?"

"Sounds good to me." He took her by the hand and started across the turf toward a narrow trail.

The wind shifted, and the smell of guano hit him like a brick wall. James held his breath and tried not to breathe.

Paisley crinkled her nose. "What is that awful smell?"

"At a guess, I'd call that *Ode d'Birdie* or *Sea Spray Guano*. Do you have a preference?"

"I think I'll pass." Her eyes swept the coast. "I don't see the colony."

"Let's climb to the top and have a look around." He jerked his chin toward the cliffs. "If the seals have moved to one of the closer skerries, we should be able to spot them through one of your lenses."

Single file, they hiked up the ravine trail—a narrow, one-person path that wound through massive boulders, the turf and rocky soil slippery from the mist. At times, the angles were so steep it required both hands to keep from tumbling. When James reached the top, he placed his hands on his hips to catch his breath. The breeze, though cold, was exhilarating.

He rotated in a slow half-circle, taking in the green meadows and rocky crags. To the north, the islands of Rum and Eigg were nothing more than gray silhouettes rising from the Atlantic. On a clear day, he couldn't imagine anything more beautiful, but just now, the monochromatic palette did little to inspire a declaration of love.

Chapter 22

THEY HAD LUNGA ALL TO themselves. James hiked up to the next meadow and headed for Harp's Rock, making sure to stay back from the myriad burrows lacing the cliffs. The rock faces were stained white in the steep gorge. The place had to be crawling with birds each spring and summer. Right now, only the lonely calls of gulls and geese made themselves heard.

Paisley joined him and set up her camera to take a few random shots to check her lighting. He wandered off a dozen yards, his eyes on the small skerry between Lunga and the next isle to the north.

Bending over a clump of sea pinks, Paisley adjusted her lens, absorbed in the task.

Was that a helicopter? What would tourists be doing there? The small spit of land had nothing to recommend it unless the seal colony had moved locations.

"Hey, Paise?"

"Yes?"

"Did you bring your telephoto lens with you?" That got her attention.

She lifted her head. "I did."

"I think the seal colony is on that little skerry just north of us. Care to check it out?"

She nodded and changed out her lens.

"I can't tell from this distance, but a helicopter's over there. I assume they are taking photos." The chill wind swept over the cliff face, and James shoved his hands inside his jacket pockets.

"It's probably a filming crew." Careful to stay back from the puffin burrows, Paisley zoomed her lens to where he pointed. "I see seals!" she squealed.

He laughed aloud at her obvious delight, grateful he had insisted on bringing her.

"Oh my gosh." Her forehead wrinkled. She grabbed his arm and pulled him down to the sward beside her.

"What?"

Instead of answering, she handed him the camera and pointed to where she wanted him to look.

He held the viewfinder to his eye. The helicopter was unmarked. *Odd.* A discordant note of uneasiness shot through him. Using the lens, he followed the shoreline until he found the seals, lying still among the rocks. He zoomed in further, focusing first on one bull, then another. Not one of them moved—not one tiny twitch.

Amongst the seals, three figures in white jumpsuits with their faces covered in gas masks sprayed a white substance into the air. A fourth man, dressed in similar attire, stood on a promontory with a pair of binoculars pressed to his gas mask, moving slowly in his and Paisley's direction.

"Get down." He pushed Paisley's face into the damp turf and joined her. Whatever those men were up to, he strongly doubted it was government sanctioned. "We've got to get back to the boat before we're seen."

"I need to document this first." Paisley reached for her camera.

She was right—they needed proof before they reported this to the authorities. With nothing but turf for cover, he and Paisley would be easily spotted if the helicopter took off. And if the wind shifted, they were in genuine danger of suffering the same fate as the sea mammals.

James raked his eyes over the terrain for another way off the cliffs while Paisley snapped a few photos on high shutter speed. She checked her images quickly, then packed away her camera.

"Ready?" James asked.

"Yes."

Crouching low, they moved back from the cliff face and hunted for another way to the shore out of sight of the helicopter crew.

"No chance the government is culling part of the seal population?" she asked.

"Not a chance." James's voice was firm. "The UK has very stiff environmental protection laws. No doubt whatever they're spraying on those seals will harm us too. We've got to get off this island."

She checked her watch. "The boat doesn't return for another hour."

"We'll signal the captain from shore," James said, putting confidence in his words.

"The boat's a good way out. Do you think they'll see us?"

"No idea, but we've got to try. If not, we'll need to find cover."

"Give me your scarf." Paisley held out a hand for his dark wool scarf.

He half expected her to wave it in the air to flag the boat. Instead, she took the fabric and covered his nose and mouth and knotted it behind his head, then she did the same with hers.

"Precautionary tactics." Her eyes crinkled above the red tartan material.

"Good idea." James's scarf muffled his response. He jerked his head toward a steep crevice formed by erosion. "This ravine will place us on the shore."

Paisley's eyes narrowed, luminous and disbelieving.

"Do you have a better idea?" His words were terser than he had intended, and he hoped she didn't realize how worried he was.

"No."

He led the way down the steep incline, climbing and semi-sliding on his backside, dislodging stones as he went.

"How are you doing?" James turned back to check on her while his ears strained for the sound of a helicopter.

"Fine." She stopped to examine her hands, hesitated, looked up at him, then wiped them on her waterproof pants.

James eyed the distance between the boat and shore.

"Do you think those men will hear us if we yell?" Paisley asked.

"I doubt it, but I'm not willing to take a chance our voices will carry. Are you?" James removed his backpack, grasped both straps firmly in front of him, and hoisted it high above his head.

"What are you doing?"

"Trying to attract the captain's or Rod's attention."

"Good idea." She followed suit, taking off her jacket and waving it over her head.

No movement on the deck. The men were probably in the observation lounge. James lowered his backpack and took out his cell phone to check reception. No bars. The inhabited isles were simply too far away for any type of connectivity.

He rolled his shoulders, and the beginnings of a tick started beside his left eye. "We'll need to find cover in case that helicopter does a flyover." James didn't add that if those men were running an illegal experiment, nothing stopped them from dropping their magic powder on him and Paisley to remove all witnesses.

"If they do a flyby, won't they see the boat and know someone's on Lunga?"

"They might think the boat just arrived, especially if they don't see anyone on shore."

"Where do you suggest we hide?" Paisley turned toward the cliffs they had just descended. "There's not a tree or bush on this entire island."

James's mouth went dry, and he cleared his throat before he could speak. "In one of the caves."

They started down the shoreline, climbing over boulders, their eyes trained on the cliffs.

"That looks like a cave." Paisley pointed to a slightly darkened hole about eight feet above their heads. The opening was nearly obscured by clumps of sea pinks.

He swallowed. That couldn't be the captain's idea of a cave, could it?

"I'm going to check it out." She placed her photography bag at his feet and started up the cliff face, her hands reaching for holds in the rock. A few loose pebbles tumbled.

"Careful, Paise," James called softly.

The climb wasn't bad, and she made it look easy. When Paisley reached the hole and disappeared from view, his chest squeezed and limited his air intake—a precursor of things to come.

Almost immediately Paisley reappeared, her head poking out above the clumps of thrift. Her scarf had slipped, and he could see her smile. "Come on up; there's enough room for both of us."

The shore looked mighty appealing all of a sudden.

The whir of blades and throb of a powerful engine changed his mind. James picked up Paisley's camera bag, slung the strap over his neck, and reached for the first rock. The helicopter entered his peripheral vision, pointed northwest as though making for the mainland. James clung to the side of the cliff, unsure what to do. If he moved, would they see him?

"Hurry. They're turning." Paisley's eyes were on the chopper.

He glanced over his shoulder. Sure enough, the helicopter had started to swing about.

"Get inside," he hollered.

James scampered up the face of the cliff like a chamois, his hands finding the holds to pull himself up the wall.

"It's a lot bigger in here than it looks from the entrance." Paisley's voice echoed oddly from inside the cavern.

The inky-black hole was no more than two feet by three. Bands of steel pressed against his ribs, making it impossible to fill his lungs with air. Dark spots danced before his eyes. He couldn't have a full-blown attack in front of Paisley. She'd think he was a wuss.

"Hurry." Her small hand appeared from the dark depths of the cave and tugged on his arm.

He'd rather take his chances with a copperhead than climb inside that dark hole. Unfortunately, if these men were hostile, his location would give Paisley's away. So, he scooted inside, feet first, facing the ocean, and prayed that would stem off the feeling of entombment.

"You're claustrophobic, aren't you?" Paisley asked quietly when his head and shoulders were finally inside.

"Yeah," he rasped out on a half-choked swallow of air and kept his eyes on the cave entrance, willing himself not to fall apart. The panic attack wasn't near as bad as others. If he kept his eyes on the sea, he could work through it. Sucking in a deep breath, he expelled it slowly and took another.

Paisley didn't say anything, but her hand settled on his upper back and began to rub in circles, small at first, then widening out and kneading into the muscle.

After a full minute of focused breathing, his attention shifted to the pleasant sensation of her touch.

"Ben locked me in a trunk when I was four," he wheezed.

Just then, the helicopter buzzed the cliff face, flying low, its blades a blur as it headed toward the boat. Rod came out on deck, his face turned skyward. James could tell it was Rod by the yellow sweater he wore.

While the helicopter circled the watercraft, its side door opened, and a man leaned forward, his thigh and upper torso visible. The chopper did another slow loop, its propellers whipping the water around the boat.

Rod waved his arms above his head in an obvious signal for the helicopter to move away. Either the chopper pilot did not see Rod or chose to ignore him because it continued to circle. James had a clear view of the man seated inside the open door behind the pilot—so did Rod. He hastily skidded across the deck, darted inside the cabin, and slammed the door behind him.

The man seated behind the pilot was harnessed, undoubtedly to his seat. He leaned out while the chopper hovered—less than a hundred feet above the waves—an automatic weapon in his hands. A *rat-tat-tat* carried across the water. Holes peppered the bow of the watercraft and shattered glass.

James stared—unable to blink, his panic attack in full arrest as his mind scrambled to accept what was happening.

Paisley's hand stilled on his back. "What's going on?"

The helicopter swung about and faced the stern, its windshield pointed toward the cliffs. James flattened himself amongst the thrift, the pink blooms tickling his nostrils.

The shooter let loose a second round. *Rat-tat-tat.* The noise ricocheted off the cliff face as a rain of bullets splintered the boat's thin wood. Helpless fury bubbled inside James as he watched the deliberate attack on two innocent men.

The boat engine was located directly below the stern. Marine fuel, a highly unstable mixture, only needed one spark to ignite. That was obviously what the chopper was counting on.

"That sounds like gunfire," Paisley said, trying to squeeze up beside him in the tight space.

"Stay put." James placed the palm of his hand directly on top of her head and pushed her back none too gently. No one should witness this horror, especially not a sensitive person like Paisley.

"Let me see." She swatted ineffectually at his hand.

"No."

The helicopter gained altitude, and James breathed a little easier. Perhaps the chopper only meant to disable the watercraft. Before James had time to appreciate that concept, another stream of bullets sprayed the stern.

One second the boat was there—then *boom.*

Wood and decking shot in the air, blown to bits like a bomb. Yellow and red flames engulfed what was left of the hull.

In his horror, James had scooted out of the opening, his eyes on the waves, searching for survivors. Neither Rod nor the captain surfaced. Paisley lay in the cave entrance, her eyes filled with sorrow.

The helicopter backed off—the whir and throb of its powerful engine magnified by water and cliff. It hovered while the boat burned. Were they waiting to see if there were survivors?

Evidently satisfied, the chopper lifted, making an arc in their direction.

"Get back inside." Paisley had the presence of mind to tug him backward into the cave before they were seen.

A hum and pulse of a powerful engine. The helicopter buzzed the shoreline, flying low, obviously looking for tourists. James lost sight of it as the chopper lifted above the cliffs. From time to time, they heard the whir of blades as it covered Lunga's terrain.

"What if they land?" Paisley's voice trembled.

"I doubt they'd find us." Worry for her safety kept his thoughts off the tight, dark space.

"Are Rod and the captain dead?" Paisley's voice shook.

"Yes."

From what he could tell, once he got past the narrow opening, the cavern was about fifteen feet deep and half again as wide. He couldn't fully stand, but the cavity wasn't nearly as bad as he had initially believed. He reached out and found Paisley trembling, her arms wrapped about her knees. He pulled her up beside him, then slipped his arm around her and drew her close. She came unresisting.

"I'm sorry, Paisley." He touched her face and found it wet. His heart constricted.

"It's not your fault. No one could have anticipated . . ."

His arms tightened in an attempt to comfort. She snuggled closer, her own arms cinching around his waist. The heady scent of coconut, lime, and verbena filled his senses. Aching with the need to kiss her, he nuzzled her neck, then drew back with an internal groan.

When he kissed Paisley—and he would, of that he was certain—he wanted no other contributing factors involved. If she kissed him now, he would always wonder if she had responded from the horror of their situation or from the euphoria of survival.

Cocooned as they were from sight, the severity of their situation began to sink in. Overnight temperatures hovered around freezing, but he and Paisley might be all right inside the cave, especially if they covered the entrance. Could he handle a blocked exit? He didn't know. His hand brushed against the noisy Gore-Tex of her waterproof jacket while his thoughts raced. He let go of her to peer outside.

The helicopter passed overhead, this time moving toward Fladda, the next island north in the Treshnish chain and continued northeast toward the mainland. He watched it go and speculated where it would land. The Highlands were a vast territory without many inhabitants, a perfect place for a militant group or terrorist cell to go undetected.

Maybe he had read too many thrillers, but this entire scenario had big-time taboo written all over it. Local cops were not equipped to handle this situation. They would pass it to someone higher up the UK security chain.

His gaze raked the ocean where the boat had anchored. Little was left of its blue-painted hull. Nor was there movement in the water, but he had to be sure. "Hand me your camera."

The rustle and zipper of her bag filled the small cavern. She thrust the camera into his hands. Though he didn't have her professional skills, he knew his way around the apparatus well enough. Wrapping his scarf tighter, he checked Paisley to make sure she wore hers. He scooted onto the ledge, adjusted the lens, and zoomed in on the wreckage.

Bits of flotsam and jetsam bobbed on the sea. There was no other sign of life. Not even a stray seal in the waves.

If he and Paisley hadn't taken cover, they would be dead. By the grace of God, they had survived. But they weren't out of the danger. The wind might shift and those toxins could poison them before help arrived.

Few visited the islands late in the season. In two days, ferry service would slow to a crawl while the Western Isles hunkered down for the winter.

A cold droplet of water splashed on his nose. He looked up at the gray clouds just as they opened, releasing a deluge of rain. James scooted swiftly inside the cave, wiped the rain from his face, and did his best to dry the camera.

Paisley sat huddled near the back wall, shivering. She lifted her head and looked at him across the dimly lit space. Her face had blanched of color, her eyes dilated with shock. "Why would someone kill them?"

"I don't know." James hesitated, then said, "I believe the Robertsons were murdered to hide whatever those men were doing to the seals. We need to inform someone higher up than the local authorities with this information. Do you think your dad could pull a few strings?"

Paisley snorted. "He's distantly related to the crown. If needed, he could be patched through to Buckingham Palace."

Yet again, James had forgotten her status. To him, she was Paisley, the woman he loved and his longtime friend. Now, he admitted her being the daughter of a duke did have some perks.

"Any idea how we're going to get off this island?" she asked.

"When we don't show up on Staffa, the pilot will look for us." At least he hoped so.

"He will?"

"Of course he will."

When Kinross realized his daughter was missing, he would throw out all the stops. All James and Paisley had to do was survive the overnight temps and pray that whatever had killed those seals didn't blow in their direction.

Chapter 23

Paisley's night on Lunga was not romantic. Though grateful for the cave's shelter, the stones underneath her were cold and jagged. The rain poured for hours and let up just after dark.

James blocked the entrance with the outer shell of his 3-in-1 jacket to keep out the wind. But she could tell it was difficult for him to stay inside without a visible exit, even if it was only a mental one, so she had insisted he take it down.

James stirred restlessly beside her. "You awake, Paise?"

"Yes." It was black as an oil slick inside their hidey-hole. She hated to admit it, but she was scared. What if that powder didn't dissolve with the rain and blew inside the cave? Then what? She'd grown slightly nauseous just thinking about it. "James?"

"Yeah?"

"What if we get sick?"

"We're going to be fine." James's jacket rustled, and his arm slid around her. "Would you like me to say a prayer?" he asked.

"Yes."

His offer was like a lifeline. She'd been praying silently for the last few hours, but her fear had overcome her faith.

He took a second before he began.

"Dear Heavenly Father." James's deep voice filled the dark cavern as he approached Deity. "We come before you this night with troubled hearts, unsure of what lies ahead. Thank you for your protection this day and for providing us a place to hide and shelter from the elements. Will you please keep us safe till morning and alert those who can rescue us from this island?

"We pray for peace and ask that those who notify the Robertson family of their loss will be compassionate in their delivery. We ask that thy grace will encircle them in their time of grief. In the name of thy beloved Son, Jesus Christ, amen."

Paisley sighed, letting the calm assurance that God was aware of their needs envelope her. "Thank you, James. I feel so much better turning our situation over to Him."

"Good." James hugged her close. "Everything is going to be fine. You'll see."

The Lord might not always answer prayers the way she expected, but she was willing to trust in His greater understanding.

They sat for a time listening to the ocean crash on the rocks below.

After a while James broke the silence. "Did you know a perfect crime was committed the other night when thieves broke into Scotland Yard and stole all the toilets? Police say they have absolutely nothing to go on."

Paisley rolled her eyes. She'd forgotten about James's warped sense of humor and braced herself for another poke at life in the UK.

"What do you call a good-looking guy in Britain?" James asked.

"I don't know. What?"

"A tourist."

"Very funny." Her voice dripped with sarcasm. "Somehow I think Nick would take exception to that. Where did you come up with these? They're awful."

"You don't like my jokes? I'll have you know that once upon a time, I was going to do stand-up comedy."

"It's a good thing you didn't," she muttered under her breath.

"I'll pretend I didn't hear that. All my friends thought I was hilarious."

"How old were they, nine?" Her mouth curved in a smile.

"Eight. We were mature for our age."

"I don't remember much from back then. You were a lot older than I was. What else did you do besides tell rotten jokes?" She settled against his shoulder, happy to take her mind off their predicament.

"We pranked Catherine."

"You weren't very nice brothers."

"Yes, we were. Ben and I never let anyone else prank her . . . except maybe Jack when we were in a benevolent mood. But that little punk usually took Catherine's side."

"Catherine's almost four years younger than you and Ben."

"Three and a half, but who's counting? Besides, she always got the best of us."

"How?"

Catherine had been the epitome of graciousness whenever Paisley had visited the Pressley-Coombes home.

"She got us in ways we least expected."

"If you knew she'd get you back, why did you keep doing it? Didn't Einstein refer to that as a form of insanity?"

"Behind Catherine's ladylike demeanor lurks a calculating mind. The suspense was addictive."

"When did all this start?"

"I don't know. I think Ben and I were tenish."

"You deliberately tormented a six-year-old?" Her voice rose an octave.

"She was a nuisance—always following us around, heckling us to let her play ball. Mom felt sorry for Catherine and forced us to let her play. So, we got her back."

"What did you two crazies do?" Despite herself, Paisley was fascinated.

"One night after dinner, I slipped under Catherine's bed and waited for lights out. Ben went outside and borrowed Dad's ladder. When he scratched on her window, I shook her mattress and moaned."

"How horrible." Paisley would have died of fright if anyone had done that to her.

"I felt kind of bad when she cried, but then she ran for the phone and dialed 911 and told the dispatcher someone was trying to break into the house."

"Why didn't you stop her?"

"I thought it would be funny if Ben got arrested."

"Did he?" Paisley was suddenly grateful to have grown up an only child.

"No, but they caught him outside her window, and he had to explain what he was doing out there. Mom was so angry that she grounded us."

"Where was your dad?"

"Laughing. He backed Mom up though. Catherine can do no wrong in his eyes."

"Catherine didn't pull that prank; you two numbskulls did."

He poked her in the side. "Hey, whose side are you on, anyway?"

"Catherine's."

"Why?"

"She was six years old." Did Paisley really have to spell it out for him?

"Catherine has nerves of steel. You heard what she did to her kidnappers, didn't you?"

"I did." Paisley's teeth chattered.

"I rest my case."

They huddled together to keep warm, but the rocks were too sharp to find a comfortable position. Every time Paisley shut her eyes, the sound of the explosion and the sight of bits of flotsam and jetsam on the sea crowded her mind.

After a while, James nodded off, and sometime in the middle of the night, she passed out from sheer exhaustion. When she woke at first light, James was gone.

She knotted her scarf around her neck, pulled up her hood, and crept out onto the ledge to see where he had gone.

"Good morning," James said.

She craned her neck in the direction of his voice. He stood a good fifteen feet above her on the lip of the cliff. "I was wondering where you were."

"Cover your face."

"After last night's storm, those toxins are long gone. Besides, the wind is blowing in the opposite direction."

Dirt, rock, and thrift gave her the necessary handholds, and she easily made the ascent. When she neared the top, James reached down and hauled her up the rest of the way.

The panorama of green turf meadows, rain-washed sky, and dark-blue sea captured her attention, a salve to her distressed nerves. She refused to look where the boat had anchored the day before. Nor did she glance to the north where the seals lay unmoving on the low-lying rocks.

To the west, she made out the vague outlines of Coll and Tiree, the last bastions of land between her and the US. If the plane didn't come looking for them, she and James were truly stranded on this isolated patch of earth.

They had eaten their sandwiches the night before but had saved their oranges for breakfast. If it didn't rain, they only had half a bottle of water between them to get through the day. She wasn't too worried—yet.

The turf was slick underfoot as she made for a likely outcropping of rock to relieve herself. The only sounds to break the silence were the slap of the sea against the rocks below and the occasional cries of geese and gulls.

One of her favorite party games as a teenager had been the inevitable "If you were stranded on a desert island, who would you bring?"

Though Lunga wasn't anywhere close to the tropics, it would do in a pinch. And if one of her girlfriends were there to ask her now, the answer would unequivocally be James. Sometime in the hours before daybreak, it had come to her that the zing buzzing between them wasn't a weird streak of attraction due to homesickness but the real deal.

She loved him, truly loved him.

And she was fairly certain it was reciprocated, though she couldn't say why she was so sure. James hadn't flirted with her—not even overtly. He had stayed inside the cave with her when she knew everything inside him had urged him to leave. Two days ago, she had cried all over him with goop on her face. James did not do goop, not with that queasy stomach of his.

Granted, he had looked a little green when he had handed her napkins, but he hadn't complained. Then there was last night. Even though the attraction between them was strong, he hadn't once made her uncomfortable or taken advantage of their situation. He had a habit of sacrificing himself to smooth the bumps for others—often at his own expense.

Why hadn't she noticed that about him before? James was a true gentleman in every way that mattered; his mother would have been proud.

She wandered the cliffs toward an outcropping of rock and stopped to admire the seabirds as they swooped for breakfast amongst the waves. James came up beside her and slid an arm around her shoulders. She leaned into him, enjoying his nearness.

The lavender sky turned pink before the sun's golden globe bathed the world with its rays. For once, she didn't itch for her camera. For once, this was enough.

Never had she considered the kind of man who would capture her heart. All her life, she had focused on two things: trying to make her mom love her and setting up a lucrative photography business to support herself.

A family of her own, with a husband and children, had never once factored into the equation. Other than by observation, she didn't know how real families functioned. And James had family written all over him. Once he fell in love, he would be just like the rest of the Pressley-Coombes clan—*bam*, a mad dash to the altar.

Paisley took a deep breath and exhaled slowly. The idea of marriage made her want to run in the opposite direction. But even stranded on an uninhabited island in the middle of nowhere, without a rescue in sight, she was happy. Happy to be with him. Happy he hadn't gone on this excursion alone. And happy that even in their dire circumstances, she still experienced that persistent tingle of attraction.

Did love make an unfathomable future palatable? She had no experience to pull from except the typical high school crushes and short-term college romances.

Paisley glanced up and caught James's intent gaze. He looked like a gypsy with the lower half of his face dark with stubble. Her belly flipped, and a little zing of awareness shot through her. Was he going to kiss her? Right here? Right now? She looked a mess, and her breath was sour. And she—

"I love you, Paisley."

Her eyes searched his face, and his expression turned her insides to goo. James was in earnest. The words he had never uttered to any of her friends were hers, and hers alone. He loved her. Her heart soared, and the void she had lived with all her life suddenly filled. She was loved. Unable to hide what was in her heart, the yearning and the reluctant affection that persisted in blooming, despite her best efforts, she said, "I love you back."

His eyes darkened with purpose and stilled the very air between them. Slowly, he dipped his head and met her lips with the lightest of kisses, his cold nose bumping against hers.

She closed her eyes and absorbed the sensation of his warm lips against her own. He lifted his mouth the merest fraction, tilted his head further to the side, and kissed her again, this time with much more finesse.

She tingled right down to the tips of her toes.

A low hum interrupted her fractured thoughts. In unison, she and James turned toward the mainland. Flying low above the water, with the hills of Mull behind, gleamed the bright paint of the *Nessie Fodder*.

"Looks like we have company," Paisley said with a sinking sensation.

"Looks like." James kissed her briefly one last time and said, "That pilot has horrible timing."

Chapter 24

James's shoes squished as he crossed Kinross's plush office rug, his hand at the small of Paisley's back. They stopped in front of the duke's desk, but James's eyes slid to the crackling fire with longing.

"Where were you last night?" Kinross motioned toward Paisley's damp attire.

"Men with automatic weapons shot up our boat. We were stranded on Lunga until our pilot came looking for us this morning," James answered, determined to draw the duke's ire away from his daughter.

Kinross's jaw tightened. "Codswollop. Do you expect me to believe that twaddle? Every movement our family makes travels like lightning through the glen. When you didn't come home last night . . ." Kinross tugged at his collar. "With Mr. Pressley-Coombes's reputation, I naturally presumed . . ."

"You assumed the worst." Paisley lifted her chin.

"Paisley, I don't care if James is the son of an old friend. If that lad has touched you, I'll . . ." Kinross set his pen beside his papers.

Fury bubbled inside James. "Neither one of us is the kind to give way to that type of behavior. If you think for one minute that I would disrespect your daughter—" James bristled.

Paisley placed her hand on his arm and shook her head.

Kinross's eyes narrowed at Paisley's gesture, and he glared at James over the top of his glasses.

"Stop it, both of you," Paisley commanded, her eyes shooting sparks. "We really were stranded." Her voice hitched. "People died."

Kinross's eyes darted first to James, then back to Paisley, and the glitter inside those dark depths softened. "I'm verra sorry, lass. You cannae blame a father for worrying. What really happened?"

Paisley's face looked pinched, and she swayed on her feet. James led her to the fire before he answered.

"We visited the Treshnish Isles yesterday. When we went ashore, a chopper was on a small skerry just north of the island. It wasn't visible from where we landed." James shifted, twitching his shoulders to loosen the damp shirt from sticking to his body. "We noticed it when we hiked to the top of Lunga. Paisley took photos of men spraying a white substance on the beached seal colony, killing the mammals."

James widened his stance in front of the hearth and folded his arms across his chest. "If the wind had shifted, those toxins would likely have killed us. So, we slipped down to the shore to signal the boat." James continued the tale, filling in the rest of the details.

"Were you seen?" Kinross asked sharply.

"No, sir," James said, darting a look at Paisley.

"We sheltered all night in a cave. Early this morning, our chartered flight came in search of us."

"We owe your pilot a verra great debt of gratitude," Kinross said.

"I agree," James nodded.

"James has a theory why those men killed the seals and then destroyed any possible witnesses." Paisley glanced at James. "And I agree with him."

"Let's hear it."

"I'm not big on conspiracy theories, sir, but nothing else makes a whole lot of sense. What if those toxins were used by a terrorist cell? A trial run, per se. What happens if they plan to use them on a population base? Why else would they murder those people on that boat?"

"Those are a lot of what-ifs."

Color burned in James's face. The duke didn't appear to buy his theory.

"I assume your pilot contacted local authorities?"

"Yes, sir. Debris from the explosion will prove our story," James added, his tone crisp.

"I know what we've told you is hard to believe," Paisley jumped in and added, "but one of the men on that helicopter shot up the gas—petrol tank and blew up the boat while the captain and his son were on board."

"A terrible tragedy." Kinross rubbed his temples. "Paisley, you have dual citizenship, but the American consulate will need to be notified because James isn't a British citizen. I'd be happy to place some discreet calls."

"No offense, sir, but I can make the call after I change." Kinross might be Paisley's father, but James didn't need anyone to hold his hand.

"Hmmm." Kinross's mouth flattened. "It appears you've a capable champion in your young man, Paisley. I'm dreadfully sorry for my abrupt behavior, James. That was verra bad of me to attack you like that."

A log in the fireplace popped. James nodded, accepting the man's apology.

Paisley stared at her hands, an arrested expression on her face. She looked up. "I just remembered something. I might have seen another animal die in a similar way."

"When?" James and Kinross both asked at the same time.

"In Pitlochry, Rahim took me to lunch shortly after I arrived. A bagpiper was playing across the street from the restaurant. It was windy, and leaves and dirt swirled around the piper and his dog . . ." Paisley hesitated and tilted her head to the side. "I think white powder might have been involved then too. The piper collapsed, and they called an ambulance. When I knelt to check his dog, the dog was dead. The animal's fur was covered in a light-colored, fine grit. I thought it was dirt. The stuff was all over my hands, but the rain dissolved it. I'd forgotten that detail until just now." Paisley's eyes were huge and filled with self-recrimination.

James slid an arm around her and pulled her close. Thankfully, the heat of the fire had returned the natural color to her lips, but both of them were in dire need of dry clothing.

"Why don't the two of you go change before you get sick." Kinross picked up his landline. "I'll make some calls while you do. There are bound to be interviews."

James couldn't tell if the man believed them or not, but at least Kinross was no longer antagonistic. And despite James's desire to make his own phone calls, Kinross was not a man to step aside. As a guest in the duke's household, James had a certain obligation to acquiesce, at least on the surface.

Without further protest, James and Paisley started for the door. Paisley halted halfway across the room and asked, "If I give the police my SIM card, they won't take my camera as evidence, will they? James went to a lot of trouble to keep it dry when he swam out to the plane."

"I can't imagine the authorities will need anything other than the card." Kinross glared at the arm James had encircled around Paisley's waist.

It was obvious the man did not care for this new development. Not one "wee" bit. *Too bad.* Because James had every intention of becoming a permanent fixture in Paisley's life.

***

Paisley lifted her foot from the bathtub and pressed the tap lever to add an infusion of hot water. She leaned back drowsily and relived James's kiss. All his years of dating had certainly paid off. He was a yummy kisser. The man had obviously had a lot of practice.

She scowled, and the happy moment shattered. Just how many women had he kissed?

Paisley sat up in the tub, water pouring off her body. The abrupt movement dislodged the knot of hair on top of her head, and it tumbled down her back. While she scrambled to repin it, one of the upstairs maids knocked on her bathroom door.

"Lady Margaret, you're needed in the conservatory."

"Right now?"

"Aye. It's most urgent."

"All right. Thank you." Paisley pulled the plug, a rubber stopper with an attached metal chain, and reached for her towel.

Had her father already heard back from the authorities? She climbed from the tub, water trickling all over the tiles.

***

The sound of trickling water greeted Paisley when she pushed open the conservatory door and warm, humid air, not unlike the Virginia summers of her youth, made its presence felt. Through the jungle of greenery, subdued voices reached her.

She skirted a koi pond and brushed against the encroaching leaves of gunneras and cascading ferns. Palm trees soared toward the domed ceiling above her, and the fragrance of star jasmine perfumed the air.

On the far side of a bank of camellias, James conversed with an attractive couple. Kinross was nowhere in sight.

The woman was beautifully formed with a thick mane of red hair and pale-blue eyes. Her companion was half a head taller, well over six feet, with the erect posture that reminded Paisley of military parades.

The man's gray eyes swooped in Paisley's direction and pinned her like a deer in the headlights.

"There you are." James reached out a hand and drew Paisley forward. "Lady Margaret, I'd like to introduce you to Agents Taylor and Benson from Her Majesty's Secret Intelligence Service."

Paisley's eyes widened.

"Americans know us as MI6," Agent Benson said.

Paisley swallowed. "Nice to meet you." She glanced at James, her mind full of questions.

"Shall we take a seat?" James indicated a group of wrought-iron chairs.

Paisley whispered softly before she sat, "Why are they here? And why are we in the conservatory?"

"All in good time," James assured her.

"Your father, the Duke of Perth and Kinross, made a few well-placed telephone calls," Agent Benson informed her.

"We understand that you witnessed a double homicide and the decimation of a seal colony." Agent Taylor's eyes strayed to, then rested on James for a moment. Her accent was slight, but Paisley caught the Scottish lilt.

"Could I see your identification, please?" Paisley held out her hand.

Agent Taylor glanced at her companion before she pulled out an ID card from a generic HM service leather. Agent Benson followed suit.

Paisley inspected their cards and nodded. "Thank you."

Agent Taylor's eyes assessed Paisley while she returned the ID to her wallet.

"We need to ask you a few questions," Agent Benson said.

"Of course," Paisley said.

Agent Taylor turned on a handheld device and spoke into the mic, her speech well-modulated. "October 30th, four o'clock. Interview with Lady Margaret Douglas, Castle Rannoch, Perth and Kinross." Taylor turned to Paisley and asked, "Could you explain in your own words how the murders of Captain Jock Robertson and his son, Roderick Robertson, occurred?"

Paisley cleared her throat. "We climbed to the top of Lunga to locate the seal colony. I hoped to photograph them in the wild . . ." James took her hand and squeezed it as she proceeded to give her statement, even adding the part about her lunch date in Pitlochry.

After she finished, Agent Taylor turned off the recording device.

"May I ask a question?" Paisley had no idea if this was proper, but she had to know.

"You may, but you will understand if we cannot respond." Benson leaned back in his chair and folded his arms.

"Why is MI6 involved in this investigation instead of homicide detectives?" Paisley prayed James's suppositions were off the mark, but why else would MI6 be involved?

Agent Taylor crossed a booted leg. "Technically, the authorities in Argyll and Bute would handle the double homicide, but due to particular aspects of this incident, we would have taken over eventually. The duke's calls accelerated the process," Agent Taylor informed them.

"Which aspects?" Paisley asked.

"The unmarked helicopter did not appear in any known flight logs, nor did it land at any airfields. Automatic weapons were also involved. Those firearms are only purchased via the black market by militant groups or terrorist cells.

"For the last several months, Agent Benson and I have been in the Highlands monitoring radicals suspected in the Copenhagen Metro bombing. When the duke notified government officials this morning about automatic weapon activity and the decimation of a seal colony by a suspicious white powder, we came at once." Taylor tucked a strand of red hair behind her ear.

"We believe this tragedy is linked to other mammal deaths in the Cairngorms," Agent Benson said, tapping the armrest on his chair.

"And?" Paisley wanted the agents to verbalize what she and James suspected.

"This means, Lady Margaret," said Agent Benson, then glanced at his partner, who gave him a nod, "that we have an active terrorist cell operating in the Highlands. We believe they have set up a lab and are experimenting on mammals before targeting a significant population base.

"Whatever killed the reindeer and wildcats in the Cairngorms is highly toxic. As we speak, forensics is performing autopsies on several retracted seals to see if they died of similar causes. If so, you two are our only witnesses that a substance was used to destroy them," Benson said evenly, his eyes grave.

"The powder you observed appears to be water-soluble." Taylor's face remained impassive.

"And Scottish weather has erased all evidence." Paisley's head started to throb, and the trickle of water in the background did nothing to soothe it.

"If this substance is utilized on a large population base shortly before a storm, it will leave no trace. There would be no way to identify the properties in time to create an antidote," Benson stated, his eyes on the koi pond.

"That's diabolical," Paisley said.

"It is imperative neither of you share what you witnessed or that you were anywhere near that island. We've already spoken to the floatplane pilot and your father. They understand what is at stake." Agent Benson's gray eyes bored into hers.

"What about my other suspicions?" James spoke up for the first time in several minutes.

"That Kinross's financial thefts from WFB are somehow related?" Agent Taylor shrugged, a purely Gaelic movement. "That's sheer supposition."

"The money was funneled to the Middle East most likely by someone who works for Kinross. You mentioned that you were monitoring radicals suspected in the Copenhagen bombing living here in the Highlands. What if these incidents are connected?" James leaned forward in his seat, elbows on knees.

"That's highly unlikely. But hypothetically, if both issues are linked, we may be dealing with a new terrorist regime instead of a cell," Taylor said.

Chapter 25

"That woman stared at you," Paisley informed James as they stood on the front steps of the castle as the MI6 agents drove away.

"What can I say? I'm irresistible to women." James thrust out his chest and flexed his muscles.

Paisley hit him on the arm. "And your head is the size of a Goodyear Blimp. Your brothers are every bit as good-looking as you. In fact—" She gave him a saucy smile. "Jack has you and Ben beat; he has a dimple."

"A dimple? That girly dent in his face?" James sounded disgusted as he started along the path, pea gravel crunching under his loafers.

"Women love dimples."

"Huh." James was silent as they rounded the corner of the castle and started down the path of formal plantings.

"You really think that Jack is better looking than I am?" James sounded just the least bit insecure.

Her mouth twitched, and she shrugged.

"You're messing with me." James nudged her in the ribs.

"You needed to be taken down a notch. Admit it."

He slid an arm around her waist. "Probably. When it comes to you, I don't mind so much. You're good for me." He looked deep into her eyes, and she could see the olive-green flecks inside the brown of his irises. "I think we should always be honest with each other."

"I agree."

"And I think you should admit that I'm good for you too."

"You are? How's that?" She stopped on the path beside a giant rhododendron and looked up at him.

"You, my love." He placed the palm of his hand around the back of her neck and stroked it with his fingers before he dipped his head and kissed her, a feather-light meeting of lips. "You could use some spoiling and need to be told every day how special you are—how much you are loved."

The tenderness in his eyes almost undid her. James, for all his inexperience with girlfriends, knew her down to the base of her soul.

"I have everything I need."

"I'm not talking about tangible spoiling, Paise. It's love and affection—you haven't had enough of that in your life." He opened the wooden gate for her into the walled vegetable garden.

"Oh ho, so you think you're here to fix all that?" She tried to laugh it off while her nerves arced like an exposed wire. James saw too deep.

"I am." He wiggled his brows, his playfulness lightening the atmosphere.

They wandered along the exterior wall of the castle, and James opened the door that led straight into the kitchen.

She followed him inside and unzipped her jacket. Mrs. Grant, her father's cook, a rotund Scotswoman with a motherly heart, had just finished filling a platter of scones on the kitchen worktop.

"Help yourself," Mrs. Grant said, then turned back to the stovetop and stirred something inside a large stock pot.

James snagged a scone off the platter and took a healthy bite. The man could never resist home-baked goods.

Paisley went into the scullery, lifted Digger's lead from the shelf, and freed her puppy from his kennel. Digger jumped on her knee and whined, his tail and body wagging so hard he fell over. She picked him up and gave him a cuddle before she clipped on his leash.

When she returned to the kitchen, James had advanced to his second hot buttered scone and was teasing Mrs. Grant.

"The scones smell delicious, Mrs. Grant," Paisley said.

"You'd best try one before Jamie here eats them all." Mrs. Grant pushed the plate toward her.

"Jamie?" Paisley asked.

"Aye. It suits him."

Paisley supposed it was to be expected that James would be dubbed by Kinross's cook, a local woman who loved to feed anyone who ventured into her domain.

Leaning across the table, she helped herself, breaking open the heavy sweet bread. She bit into it and closed her eyes as she chewed. "Mmmm. This is delicious, Mrs. Grant."

"It's glad I am to hear it, Lady Margaret."

Paisley took in the empty kitchen, devoid of extra help. "I thought you'd have a full staff to help prepare for tomorrow's Charity Gala Ball?"

"The duchess uses a caterer from Edinburgh for these events. They bring their own equipment and set up a cooking station in the breakfast room." Mrs. Grant opened her mouth to say more, evidently thought better of it, and closed it again.

Paisley took another bite of scone, then headed for the door with Digger.

"Come along, Jamie lad," Paisley said and sauntered outside.

She hadn't gone ten feet when she heard the door slam behind her, and James's arms seized her around the waist and spun her around.

"Hey, where are you going? I want a kiss."

She purposely took another bite of scone and gave him a naughty smirk.

"Playful, eh?" James said. "You must be fully recovered after our overnight campout."

Paisley sobered immediately and swallowed. "No. That's not something either of us will ever forget. What do you make of our MI6 visitors?"

"You won't like it," James warned.

She tilted her head to the side. "You're stalling."

"Okay. Don't say I didn't warn you." The wind whipped James's short hair. "You heard me earlier. I really do think there's a terrorist cell in the Highlands and that your father's missing funds are somehow linked to it."

"Ugh." He was right, she didn't want to hear anymore.

"I told you you wouldn't like what I was thinking, but hear me out. We know your father's money went to the Middle East. The location alone leads me to believe it funded a terrorist organization."

"My father mentioned one of his business accounts had been drained, but he said in time he should get it all back."

"That's probably true, but those funds won't be reimbursed from the Middle East. The bank will cough up heavy fines if the patrons' case is proven."

"The agents' questions focused more on the explosion and seals."

"Paisley, they were hedging. Those spooks didn't seem the least bit surprised about those seals. Something else is going on. If an international bank branch located nearby is being drained of funds and the money is being wired to the Middle East, why would MI6 be poking their noses around the Highlands? They'd be overseas. It's a good bet that a terrorist cell is operating close by. Why else did SIS send MI6 instead of MI5? MI6 only deals with international threats."

"They said they were monitoring radicals in the area. Do you really think the two incidents are related?"

"I hope not." James leaned against a tree while his gaze wandered to the raised beds.

"Did you express your concerns during your interview?"

"I did."

"What did they say?"

"Just what you heard; they don't want us to let anyone know about the incident." James plucked a limp piece of oregano from the kitchen bed closest to him and crushed it in his hand, the savory scent filling the air around them. "Those agents have the best poker faces I've seen in years."

He crossed to where she stood. His fingers grazed her chin, then cupped her cheek, rubbing her skin with his thumb. Tingles erupted all over her body.

"Are you finished with that scone yet?" he asked, his eyes on her lips.

She glanced at him through her eyelashes. "Maybe."

"Good." He took her by the shoulders and leaned in, his mouth hovering over hers while their breaths intermingled for the space of a heartbeat before he lowered his mouth to hers. His lips teased hers with soft, swift kisses until she fairly begged for more. Fingers tangled in her hair, and his mouth settled on hers in a way that stole her breath and spun her senses. Both hands circled her throat, then skimmed her cheekbones and deepened the kiss.

Time suspended, and warmth infused her body, erupting flutters low in her belly. Nothing existed but his mouth on hers.

Digger jumped against her legs and snapped her back to reality. Paisley pushed against James's chest and stepped back.

"Whoa," she said when she could think straight.

James's eyes were almost black, and he looked as shell-shocked as she felt.

"Are you all right?" She ran a shaky hand through her hair.

He nodded.

"Then say something."

"I think we need a chaperone." James turned on his heel and started for the kitchen entrance.

"James!"

He stopped at the wooden door, his hand on the casing, and glanced at her over his shoulder. "I mean it, Paisley."

Chapter 26

Achmed lifted his sister's head from the hospital pillow and adjusted the straw in her drink to reach her mouth. She was more alert today. He had seen glimpses of her old self surfacing above the pain and medication.

"Do you want more?" he asked.

"No, thank you."

He set her drink on her tray table.

A nurse bustled inside Padma's room. "This came for you." He handed Achmed a sealed envelope.

Puzzled, Achmed opened it and read, *Remove Charity Gala Ball donations from Kinross's safe before the ball ends. Codes are listed for remote deposits.*

An account number at WFB was printed on the bottom of the page.

Achmed crumbled the letter and paced to the window overlooking the mechanical systems. This nightmare would never end. He was trapped.

"Is something wrong?" Padma moved restlessly, and her heart-rate monitor increased its beeping.

"Nothing is wrong. It's just something I have to do for work." He shoved the wadded-up note inside his pocket and returned to her bedside.

How could he do what they asked? Many times he had considered confessing to Kinross and taking his medicine. Prison would be a welcome reprieve after the mental anguish of the last few weeks, but he couldn't leave Padma unprotected if he turned himself in.

Since the first message had appeared on his monitor, Achmed had watched his coworkers to the point of obsession. No one appeared the smallest bit interested in him or his job.

But it must be one of them. How else had they gotten inside his computer? Someone had hacked into the mainframe and accessed Achmed's computer along with the database codes Kinross kept under secure wraps.

Achmed cycled through what little information he had on the blackmailer until he thought he'd go mad. Now they wanted him to siphon donations from the charity ball before the banks opened the following morning. Even with the codes, how could he break into Kinross's office unseen? The duke had hired extra security for the event.

"What is troubling you, Achmed? You aren't yourself," Padma asked, her voice filled with concern.

"Everything is brilliant." When she just stared at him, he added, "Truly, it's nothing to worry about—a storm in a teacup."

She closed her eyes, and presently, her breathing evened out. Achmed lowered his head into his hands as a wave of despair washed over him. He wasn't stupid. When he was no longer of use, the person behind his sister's accident would kill him and most likely her too.

An alarm went off outside his sister's room, and a voice over the PA system said, "Code blue—room 1271." Shoes slapped against the laminate floor as medical personnel rushed down the hall.

Achmed spared a thought for the unfortunate individual and their family before he returned to his troubles. His gambling had landed him and his sister in this mess, and it was up to him to get them out. He bent over Padma and kissed her forehead. She didn't stir.

Taking one last look at her, he went into the hall and pulled out his mobile. His actions had forfeited his right to a peaceful future, but he could protect his sister. Carefully, he scrolled through his contacts and pressed the number he had promised himself he would never call.

***

Achmed rubbed the edge of the battered table inside the local police station. A beetle, his only visitor, wandered the perimeter of the interrogation room and disappeared into a crack beneath the gray walls.

He'd been sitting for hours, refusing to tell the police anything until they proved his sister was safe. From what he had gathered, the police had passed his situation to Scotland Yard. So, where were those who would assist him? London? Is that what was taking so long?

Achmed unscrewed the water bottle the station had provided and chugged. Two dog-eared magazines sat at his elbow, untouched. He had no interest in what ribbon-cutting ceremony the British royal family had taken part in or how many squats a day he needed to do to keep in shape, not when Padma's life hung in the balance and his own choices had put her there.

A nondescript man in business attire entered, a file in one hand. Nothing about him stood out. He was average in every conceivable way: height, coloring, mannerisms. Despite his mediocre appearance, Achmed had the distinct impression the man missed little and carried great power.

Without thinking, Achmed rose from his chair.

The man placed the folder on the table and held out his hand. "Nigel Thatcher. MI6."

MI6? Achmed shook the proffered hand while his mind spun. Were they going to lock him up for treason?

"Please, have a seat, Mr. Razool. I understand we have much to discuss."

"Before we begin, I need confirmation that my sister is safe."

"Of course." Thatcher went to the door and held a short conversation with someone in the corridor before he returned to his seat. "Two of my agents will be with us momentarily."

A soft tattoo on the door.

"Come," Thatcher said.

A man and woman entered, both exceptionally tall. The woman, a stunning redhead with a pelting of pale freckles, was dressed in black leather and biker boots. Her companion, a man with short sandy hair and gray eyes, carried himself with military precision. He smiled at Achmed and exposed a crooked incisor.

For some unknown reason, Achmed liked him for that imperfect tooth and relaxed a tad as Thatcher made the introductions.

"Agents Taylor and Benson, Achmed Razool."

The newcomers nodded to Achmed politely.

"My agents have just returned from transporting your sister." Thatcher tapped the folder.

"Were you followed? Padma has been watched since this began," Achmed informed Taylor and Benson.

"Undoubtedly so," Thatcher agreed. "We switched your sister's gurney in the elevator with that of a decoy, and then whisked her up a janitor's elevator to her new room. She has been expunged from the system and readmitted under a numerical code. Miss Razool is in a private sector behind several locked and coded doors. No one can enter that floor. Access to the premises requires fingerprints, along with other forms of ID."

"You're saying she didn't leave the hospital?" Achmed asked, somewhat floored.

"No. Her lungs could collapse at any given moment."

"If you'd like, I have a video of the entire operation. Your sister was heavily sedated to ensure her comfort during transport to her new room." Agent Taylor stepped forward and pressed a video feed on her mobile.

Achmed watched the video as Padma was sedated. Agents Taylor and Benson, dressed in scrubs, wheeled her into a waiting elevator, where they exchanged Padma to guards dressed in scrubs who whisked her through the surgical wing and up a janitorial elevator to the secured floor with an armed guard. Meanwhile, according to the timestamp on Agent Taylor's mobile, she and Benson wheeled the fake Padma to a waiting ambulance.

Once they placed the imposter inside and closed the doors, the ambulance drove away. Agents Taylor and Benson returned to the hospital and rode the elevator up to an undisclosed floor.

When they exited the lift, the corridor was quieter and more secluded than Padma's original one. At a double door, two armed guards stood at attention. The video feed ended.

"When your sister is sufficiently recovered, she will be transported to a safe house in the Lake District." Nigel Thatcher folded both hands over the folder and bent his mild gaze on him. "Satisfied?"

"Yes," Achmed said.

Thatcher leaned forward. "Now, tell me what you know about this blackmailer."

***

A little after seven the next morning, before the sky turned pink, Paisley rapped on Munira's refugee charity office door inside Kinross's corporate complex.

"Come in," Munira's musical voice sounded from within.

Taking a deep breath, Paisley turned the knob and let herself in, her feet stepping onto a bright, hand-knotted Turkish rug. Munira sat at a small escritoire, entering a long list of handwritten notes onto her computer. She did not look up from her task.

The bright room was painted in soft umber, with a curtained window on the far wall draped with green fabric embroidered in gold, reminding her of a Turkish caftan. Colorful lamps with pointed tops and bottoms of heavy brass filigree dangled from the ceiling, and a hand-hammered mirror hung on the wall.

Paisley rocked back on her heels as the silence dragged on. Perhaps coming was a bad idea after all. Finally, Munira lifted her dark almond-shaped eyes and set her stack of papers aside. She neither greeted nor invited Paisley to sit on the only spare chair available.

Paisley broke the silence. “I came to offer my assistance with the ball.”

“Who told you that I need your assistance?” Munira raised her finely arched brows.

It was hard to believe such a musical voice could be so cold. Paisley shook her head, already regretting her overture at friendship.

“No one. But I have spare time on my hands—”

“So, you are bored and seek entertainment by offering your services?”

Heat suffused Paisley’s cheeks. It seemed the woman was deliberately misunderstanding her.

“I simply wanted you to know that I’m available to help if you need an extra pair of hands. That’s all.”

“How charitable of you.” Munira’s words were laced with acid.

“I’m sorry I bothered you.” Paisley wrapped the last vestiges of dignity around herself.

A woman entered dressed in a black abaya with a hijab over her head.

“Your Grace, the truck has—” The woman stopped speaking when she caught sight of Paisley.

“It’s all right, Alhava. Lady Margaret was just leaving.”

Paisley nodded as she passed the newcomer on the way out. She blinked rapidly, unsure whether to laugh at both women’s hostility or shake her head. Never had she been treated with such rudeness.

Not for the first time did she wonder why her father had married such a woman. In Virginia, Paisley had several Muslim friends; they were warm and engaging women. Munira and Alhava’s behavior was ill-mannered and rather suspicious. Why did Alhava stop speaking about a truck the second she realized Munira was not alone?

***

Morning sunlight filtered through the stained-glass windows as Paisley almost, but not quite, stomped up the castle’s main staircase. Munira had coolly rejected her offer to help with the Charity Gala Ball preparations—again.

Huffing with indignation, Paisley entered her bedroom suite and banged the door shut behind her. Her eyes swept over the lush fabrics and scatter cushions on the bed. She might be a duke’s daughter, but her father’s duchess had ensured Paisley would remain a visitor under his roof.

Kinross wanted her to extend her time at Castle Rannoch, but his wife most decidedly did not. Unless Munira’s opinion of her changed, Paisley’s visit would remain just that—a visit. Her presence must have threatened the duchess in some way, but Paisley refused to run tattling to Kinross and cause further trouble between him and his wife. Things were tense enough between them.

Paisley twirled a strand of hair. Perhaps the sooner she amassed her photography portfolio and returned to the States, the better. She strode to the adjoining study and booted up her computer.

Clicking the mouse, she opened her portfolio. The collection was large enough to accommodate a photography exhibition, a secret dream of hers, and allowed her to be selective. Right now, she'd peddle her pictures to anyone who showed interest. Two sales would fund her flight home and set her up in a studio apartment. She would not ask Kinross for help. She hadn't come to Scotland to cash in on his wealth and celebrity, but merely to meet him and build a relationship. So far, she wasn't any closer to the man than on the day of her arrival.

Her shots of Scotland's mercurial weather, shimmering lochs, rugged hillsides, and moody panoramas stunned the senses. And her ad-lib photos were whimsical and endearing, featuring Highland cows, Digger, red deer, and other Scottish wildlife. With a few enhancements on some of these, she could create an online gallery for purchase. Perhaps James would give her a few marketing pointers.

She clicked on a picture of Loch Rannoch and Schiehallion, the conical Fairy Hill beyond. It was a lovely shot, with the shimmer of water and vibrant fall colors found in Perthshire's Big Tree Country. She doubted it would bring in a great deal on its own, but if she did an entire series of the glen all the way from the Queen's View on Loch Tummel to the Falls of Bruar, she might attract the attention of the Scottish National Gallery.

The next shot was taken from the dock and accentuated the pebbled shore and snow-topped Munros above the castle. Sugarcoated in white, the hillsides and semi-ruined cottage drew the eye. The photo showed real promise. She tilted her head and considered how best to enhance the lighting. Perhaps a black-and-white would do it justice.

Her cell phone alarm rang to remind her to take Digger for a walk. She pushed back from the desk while her eyes remained on the screen. Was that smoke rising from the derelict cottage's chimney? How odd.

If only she had more time for her art, but if she didn't take Digger now, he would set up a ruckus in Mrs. Grant's kitchen. All she needed was a whining, barking puppy to add to her demerits with Munira.

She shut down the computer and promised herself she would finish the batch when she returned.

Chapter 27

PAISLEY TRUDGED DOWN THE LANE with a rucksack strapped to her back. Digger ran ahead, straining against the lead, his tail wagging like a metronome. Still embarrassed about James's comment outside the kitchen last night, she headed toward the castle's main gates, as far from the corporate office complex as possible. *Chaperone indeed.*

A few hundred yards before she reached the gatehouse, a sign said, *Perth and Kinross Racing Stables*. Curious, she followed the lane when it branched off the main drive.

The crisp air made her glad she had her coat. Birds warbled high in the Caledonian pines where the sun's first rays lit their tops. A stream babbled beside the tarmac, pouring over stones on its way to the loch.

She filled her lungs with the sweet scent of fir. Sometime today, amidst the last-minute bustle of charity ball preparations, her brother, Torquil, would arrive. She didn't resent Torquil, his title, nor their father's entailed estates. British primogeniture laws had been in effect for centuries and had nothing to do with him.

Torquil belonged here; this was his home. Paisley had no beef with that. But when she had seen her brother's photos scattered about Kinross's office, jealousy's green-eyed monster had pounced out of nowhere and had taken her hostage.

Despite her birthright, she was an outsider, barely tolerated by her father's wife. Paisley halted on the drive as her eyes swooped over the gnarly old trees growing next to their sapling descendants.

Since Paisley's arrival, her father's financial loss had him scrambling to meet his obligations. She had seen very little of him. But surely he could squeeze in a little time for her, couldn't he?

Both of her parents, in their own way, were as un-get-at-able as the other: her mother with her myopic passion for the law and her father with his constant corporate demands. Though she had moved to a foreign country, nothing had changed in her familial ties. She was still alone.

James had told her he loved her, then tossed her aside after that kiss.

A tear coursed down her cheek. She switched Digger's lead to the opposite hand and dashed the moisture away. Never one for self-pity, she squared her shoulders and looked about for inspiration.

But her mind did not easily stray from her troubles. How could James say he loved her and kiss her like that, then tell her they needed a chaperone? Was she just another woman in his long string of castoffs? Is that how he got rid of some of his tagalongs? She exhaled shakily and sniffed.

From the onset, she had known what she was getting into with James. He must have confused his emotions on Lunga and their subsequent rescue with love. Now that he was back on terra firma, he had obviously come to himself.

A red squirrel dashed across the paved drive and darted up a tree. He flipped his bushy tail and let off a stream of abuse from the safety of his limb. The lane curved through a dense wood and then opened to meadows and a vast array of fenced pastures.

Digger lagged behind, so she slowed her steps. An enormous stable stood on a slight rise ahead of her at the base of a Munro along with a racetrack and covered stands. Green pastures in the foreground were dotted with arch-necked horses who pranced and tossed their manes. In the midst of a pasture, a lone Highland cow thundered about, bobbing its head, looking for all the world like a bull walrus among a herd of gazelles.

The ludicrous cow did much to calm her inner angst. She let out a sigh and expelled the last of her frustrations. Her eyes lifted to the soaring hills above the tree line, where the crofter's cottage was barely discernible. No smoke rose from its chimney today. Perhaps her photo had captured an illusion.

Her eyes continued to drift across the fenced pastures. Mist hovered in depressions, and a hush hung over the land. Enchanted with the beauty before her, Paisley barely registered the clop of hooves.

Digger barked sharply and pulled on the lead. Paisley spun about just in time to stare up the nostrils of a horse with white, flashing eyes. She let out a cry and jumped out of its path, dropping Digger's lead. The Palomino reared, pawing the air and tumbling its young rider onto the drive's grassy shoulder.

Paisley's heart seized. She rushed to the young rider's side and knelt on the spongy peat as the horse galloped off with a thunder of hooves and dangling reins.

The child lay prone on the grass, his long, thick lashes the envy of any girl. Digger gamboled over and bathed the boy's olive skin with puppy slobber, but an old brindle-haired dog pushed up against the lad's side and growled. Digger wet himself and hid behind Paisley.

"Are you hurt?" Paisley asked, her eyes examining the boy for any hint of injury.

"I dinnae think so."

The boy's accent was slight but most definitely Scots. She judged him to be about ten or older. He rolled to a sitting position and winced as he straightened his right leg.

"Don't move; you might be injured. Let me call for help." Paisley reached for her phone.

"Please, don't call the castle." The boy touched her arm. "I don't want any bother. Just give me a moment." Dark brown eyes met hers.

Digger made another foray toward the child's side, but the older dog bared its teeth and sent him scurrying back to Paisley for protection.

"Sit, Fraggle," the boy said. Fraggle lowered onto his haunches, his eyes on his young master. "You're Paisley. Are you not?"

Paisley's heart skipped a beat, and she nodded slowly. No one called her Paisley here except James and her father. No one dared. An inner quiet filled her. This sweet child with mud-spattered clothes and shy, dark eyes could be no other than her brother.

"You're Torquil."

"Aye." Torquil fairly shimmered with suppressed excitement, then his eyes shuttered, and his expression became guarded as though he expected a rebuff.

She, too, had experienced that two-way pull of emotion and recognized it for what it was. Her inner barriers crumbled, and she smiled at him with real liking. Of all the ways she had envisaged meeting her brother, sitting in wet grass spattered with mud hadn't entered her wildest imaginings.

Torquil smiled tentatively, and then quite suddenly, they both grinned at each other like demented idiots.

"Nice to meet you, brother mine." She reached out and hugged him.

Without hesitation, he leaned into her embrace and returned the favor. The Pressley-Coombes boys wouldn't have hugged a girl at this age to save their lives. Could Torquil, despite his title and inheritance, be as lonely as she? The idea seemed fantastic. When he pulled back, his eyes appeared eager, not sullen as though he had done something distasteful.

"Be honest. Are you hurt?" She sat back on her heels.

"Bruised is all," he muttered with color-stained cheeks.

"I didn't know you had arrived."

"Everyone was busy when Hamish dropped me off, so I went to the stables to see my horse and get Fraggle."

Her heart melted. She and her brother were not so different. She knew only too well what it was like to arrive home after an absence and find no one there to greet her.

"Well, I, for one, am glad you're here." She stood and held out an arm.

A swift glance at her through dark lashes, then he took her proffered hand.

She might have been an only child, but the Pressley-Coombes family had looked in on her. Who looked after Torquil? Granny was too crippled, and their father was often away on business. Did Munira spend time with him? Somehow, she doubted it. Fierce protectiveness overwhelmed Paisley for this small brother.

"We should probably find your horse."

"Boaz has gone back to the stable," Torquil said, unconcerned.

"You're sure?" Paisley asked.

"Aye. Boaz usually isn't verra naughty, but I took him for a ride before he finished his oats. He kept fighting the reins the whole time. No one's ridden him since I left for term."

"Why?" Even Paisley knew horses lost muscle if they weren't exercised.

"He's a Palomino they use for sheep herding and parades. They only let me ride him because I outgrew my pony and wasn't big enough for one of Dad's hunters."

"If you teach me the basics, I'll exercise him for you while I'm here."

"You will?" Torquil's eyes rounded.

"Absolutely."

"Boaz isn't much fun on the flats, but he's sure-footed in the hills as long as you don't mind going slow." Torquil tapped his crop against his boot.

The Highland cow tossed her head in the adjoining pasture and thundered up to the fence.

"That's an unusual cow," Paisley said.

"Buttercup? Aye. She thinks she's a racehorse. We can't keep her out of the pasture with Dad's thoroughbreds. She's forever breaking down the fences."

Paisley blinked. A cow that thought she was a racehorse? Now she'd heard everything. She opened her mouth to ask Torquil more about the dysfunctional cow when a lone rider thundered across the open meadow on a magnificent dappled gray.

The equestrian bent low over the horse's neck, clinging like a barnacle to a ship's hull, while the steed's flying hooves and mane moved in a fierce melody of motion. Without conscious thought, Paisley's camera was in her hand. She adjusted the shutter speed and zoomed her lens to capture the majesty of man and beast.

She heard Torquil's swift intake of breath as the rider caught sight of them and wheeled his mount in their direction. Paisley lowered her camera and caught Torquil's sullen expression before the rider hauled his massive beast to a halt.

The stallion stomped in protest and blew out its nose. Rahim's eyes glittered above her, and she had the distinct impression that he, like his magnificent steed, was barely held in check.

"Lady Margaret." Rahim nodded to her, then turned to his much younger brother. "Torquil, did I see Boaz running free just now?"

Torquil's cheeks darkened, and he flicked a resentful glance up at his brother.

"How many times have I told you? If you expect to receive a decent mount, you must—"

"It was my fault. I startled Torquil's horse," Paisley interrupted his reprimand. Torquil was at an awkward age; no longer a child, but not yet a man. He didn't deserve his brother's attack, not when she was partly to blame.

Not a muscle moved in Rahim's face as he looked from Torquil to her and back again, but the air was rife with undercurrents. Her skin tingled, and the hair on the back of her neck rose.

"No harm done. Doubtless Boaz has returned to his stall." Rahim's lips curled as he took in Torquil's muddied appearance. "I sincerely hope you plan to shower before Mother's ball."

And as quickly as that, the brewing storm between the brothers dissipated, and Rahim turned appreciative eyes on her. "Lady Margaret, I would be honored if you would save a dance for me this evening."

Taken off guard, all Paisley could do was nod.

With a flick of his riding crop, Rahim and his horse moved off, breaking from a walk to a trot, then flowing seamlessly into a rhythmic canter.

She and Torquil watched him go. Without conscious thought, Paisley slipped an arm around her brother's shoulders and squeezed. "I suppose we had better get back to the castle, or Munira will wonder what has happened to us."

Torquil didn't utter a word, but the stiffness in his body slackened. Paisley picked up Digger's lead, and together, they turned toward the castle and the looming festivities that apparently neither of them wanted.

Chapter 28

Paisley sat in front of Granny's dressing table in stunned silence. Esme McMurdie had outdone herself. Sophisticated and smart, Esme's updated sleeves and bodice of handmade lace and crystals were a brilliant addition to the pale-gold A-line Dior ballgown.

Nora, Granny's maid, held out a tartan sash to Paisley.

"What's this?" Paisley asked.

"The finishing touch to your attire," Granny replied as if she should know.

Paisley eyed the Douglas sett, a tartan pattern primarily of forest green and dark blue, accented with checks of black, royal blue, and white. Did Granny really expect her to wear this across her chest?

"Nora, help her put it on, and be careful of her hair," Granny commanded.

Unused to formal Scottish events, Paisley bowed to her grandmother's knowledge of such things. At times Paisley forgot she was in a foreign country; then something like this sash reminded her.

She had been uncomfortable when the hairdresser and makeup artist had arrived earlier that evening, but after their ministrations, she was a convert. Her eyes looked mysterious above her pouty, made-up lips, and her intricately coiled tresses on top of her head lent a certain regality to her diminutive stature.

Granny assessed her appearance. "You need gems in your hair, lass." She turned to Nora. "Add a few brilliants to her updo. They're in my silver case. I think they'll do nicely with the diamond and pearl choker and matching earbobs."

"Yes, Your Grace." Nora opened a case on the dressing table and placed a handful of brilliant hairpins strategically in Paisley's hair.

A furrow formed between Granny's eyes as she examined the overall effect. "It's too bad you aren't married, Paisley. One of my tiaras would look smashing with that gown."

"I have to be married to wear a tiara?"

Granny raised a brow. "How did you get to be so old and not know the basics of proper etiquette? No unmarried female should ever wear a tiara. You've been watching too much Disney."

Paisley ducked her head and tried to hold back a snicker. Only Granny could insult her and the Disney corporation all in one breath.

"Are you sniggering at me?" Granny asked.

"Nooo." But Paisley couldn't hold back a tooth-baring grin.

Granny's wrinkled lips curled in response. "Keep that smile on your face tonight no matter what Munira says to you."

How did Granny know about her issues with Munira?

"You think I don't hear what goes on in this house? That woman is a disgrace, even if she did provide Cameron with an heir. How she ever managed to marry my son, I'll never know. Granted, Cam didn't know she was a terrorist's widow when he married her. That came out much later, of course. That woman never shared that information before they were married. She isn't stupid; I'll grant her that.

"Cameron has always gone his own way. A shame really. I had picked one of Sutherland's daughters for him, a pretty girl with a love for horses. But Cam ran off to America instead and married your mother while at university. Disastrous."

Paisley tuned Granny out. She meant well but rarely realized how often her biases hurt those around her. Perhaps at her age, Granny simply didn't care. Paisley chose not to be offended, though, because what Granny said was true. Her parents' marriage had been a disaster.

She leaned over and kissed Granny's soft cheek.

"You're leaving?" Granny asked.

"I still have a few things to do before the receiving line forms."

"Verra well, but I expect a full accounting tomorrow."

"I promise. And thank you, Granny." Paisley touched the crystals on her bodice that sparkled in the incandescent lighting. "You really are my fairy grandmother."

***

Fifteen minutes was not enough time to settle Paisley's nerves. The Thistle Charity Gala Ball was her first formal event as a duke's daughter. Tonight, every move she made would be scrutinized—every word examined. Her father had insisted she join the family in the reception line to "provide a united front to society."

In the few minutes remaining before she went downstairs, Paisley turned to the only thing that calmed her—photography. She set her laptop on her bedroom dresser so she wouldn't wrinkle her gown by sitting and opened her photo file, clicking on the last one she had viewed, the one with the semi-ruined cottage.

The gray and white pebbles in the foreground beside the water were smooth and rounded, a study in gray-and-white veining. The sky's reflection on the loch took in the variation of fall colors and added a unique depth of field. Tingles of excitement rippled through her. The contrast in this picture would make a perfect black-and-white image.

She clicked grayscale, switching the photo from color to the varying gray monochromatic hues, then enlarged the shot and made sure no blurred areas marred the borders.

Her focus landed on the crofter's cottage on the low saddle of the hill. She leaned forward. Smoke did rise from the broken chimney.

The forestry service did not have permission to traverse Kinross's estate above the tree line. So who was using the cottage? Paisley worked the computer keys and further enlarged the image.

Even with the telephoto lens, the picture was too grainy from that distance to make out clear images. Down the hillside, near the track leading through the woods, a man's face peered around the trunk of a conifer with binoculars pinned on . . . her.

Paisley jerked upright as though someone had dumped ice water down her dress. Two partially obscured men stood beside a dark SUV with automatic weapons slung across their backs.

Her hand flew to her mouth. Men with guns had watched her that morning down by the loch. They had observed her taking pictures of the cottage . . . and not long after, her other camera had been stolen and destroyed. Goosebumps erupted, crawling across her skin.

How many men wandered the Highlands with automatic weapons? Had she inadvertently captured illegal activity during her photoshoot? Had they meant to take her professional camera and not the one her father had given her? No one but James was even aware that the old camera existed. What if they realized she still had the pictures?

Terrorists.

The word erupted inside her mind. Her knees locked, and she was suddenly lightheaded. Were terrorists here on her father's estate? No. Paisley shook her head. Impossible.

With her own eyes, she had seen what had happened in the Treshnish Isles. MI6 said they were monitoring a few suspected radicals in the Copenhagen bombing. Paisley had no idea if the two groups were connected, but she strongly doubted the Highlands were crawling with illegally armed Scots.

Images of her and James's doomed excursion filtered through her mind's eye, the explosion, the dying seals, the unmarked helicopter. Were these men in her pictures the same ones who had killed Captain Robertson and Rod?

She clicked through the rest of the file for additional pictures of the cottage and hillside. There were four photos altogether. She enlarged them to allay her growing suspicions.

In the last photo, four men conversed beside an SUV. Her heartbeat slowed and prickles of dread clawed up her back. Five men had been on Lunga, including the helicopter pilot. Was there a fifth man in her photos? She checked the other images but again counted only four.

She needed to get these photos into the right hands. Selecting a flash drive from her drawer, she downloaded the pictures and printed them off for good measure. Both MI6 agents had invitations to the charity gala ball and would be in attendance tonight, working undercover. Her father had beefed up security to protect several dignitaries and the numerous jewels that adorned his guests.

Paisley folded, then slipped the printed evidence inside her left elbow-length glove, and dropped the flash drive in after them, letting the small metal case slide into the palm of her hand. Tonight, when she met Agents Taylor and Benson, she would pass them the information.

Two men had died, and an entire colony of seals had been destroyed. If these men on her father's estate were the ones she and James had witnessed on Lunga, they were dangerous and must be stopped.

Her hands trembled as she shut down her computer. First, Kinross's resort-build funds had gone missing, and now men with guns were roaming his estate. Nothing like this had ever happened to her when she'd lived in the States.

Paisley gave her reflection one last glance to make sure everything was as it should be. She flexed her hand, and the folded images inside her glove crackled, reminding her what was at stake. Her once-anticipated evening had turned to cinders before it had even begun. And even her fairy grandmother's offerings could not put a smile on her artfully painted lips.

A rapid knock on her door sounded. "Lady Margaret. Are you in there? His Grace sent me to find you. You're late."

Chapter 29

Paisley was late. The grandfather clock struck the quarter hour as she hurried down the corridor. She chewed the inside of her bottom lip. Time had slipped away from her while she had examined her pictures.

The reception line had dispersed by the time she reached the ballroom stairs. Paisley had let her father down. She chewed on her lip some more and worried about how Kinross would take her cavalier treatment of his request to present a united family front to their guests.

At the top of the stairs, she stood in line, what Kinross called a *queue*, waiting her turn to be announced. Below, men in full kilts swaggered across the ballroom floor, sporrans swinging and family tartans swaying with their every step. Married women in long, colorful gowns and glittering tiaras sported tartan sashes like a convention of beauty queens.

Finally, it was her turn. Henderson gave her a steely glare from his station on the staircase landing where he proclaimed her father's guests as the official herald for the evening.

"Lady Margaret Douglas," Henderson announced loud enough for those in the ballroom to hear.

All eyes rose to where she stood on the landing, and a murmur went through the crowd. Paisley could do nothing but watch it happen. Evidently, her absence from the receiving line had caused quite a stir.

Her fingers curled around the flash drive inside the palm of her glove. It didn't matter how badly her father's associates regarded her tardy arrival. Her information might save lives—that had to count for something.

She took a deep breath and started down the flight of stairs, praying she wouldn't catch her heel in the hem of her gown. Guests clustered around the edges of the dance floor in small groups while they examined the glass-encased items up for bid.

Kinross looked her way across the room, his face devoid of expression. Lord Chatto, a man Paisley had met at her father's business supper, continued with his story, apparently unaware of her father's distraction.

Munira had positioned herself at Kinross's side, elegant as always in pale green. Her hand rested on Torquil's shoulder, her expression one of triumph—until her eyes fell on Paisley's gown. Munira's brows snapped together, and Paisley had the definite impression the woman was taken aback.

Oh dear.

Though grateful for her sensational dress, Paisley hadn't meant to rouse Munira's ire. By wearing such a flattering gown, she had one-upped her father's duchess, just as Granny had intended. Unfortunately, women like Munira did not take kindly to being upstaged. Paisley realized that with some people, no matter how hard you tried, they would never like you. Munira clearly fell into that camp.

Rahim, resplendent in a black Gucci tux, disengaged from a knot of guests. He gave her a dazzling smile and started across the ballroom in her direction, but James beat him to the foot of the stairs. He placed an elbow on the bottom post and gave her a lopsided grin as she descended the last few steps.

"There you are. I was beginning to wonder if you were going to make an appearance. You missed the—" James stopped mid-sentence, his dark eyes sweeping over her person. "You're beautiful, Paise. I like that dress. Very chic. It suits you."

She warmed to his praise. "Thank you. It was one of Granny's."

"It's definitely an improvement from that giant bath puff I saw you in. Where did you find someone to alter the dress in time?"

"Granny called one of her friends out of retirement." Paisley touched a satiny fold.

"She's got talent. You should thank Munira for her lapse of memory. May we hope she has many more." James's eyes twinkled mischievously.

He crooked an elbow, and then Paisley placed her hand on his arm and accompanied him away from the base of the stairs. She glanced about for Agents Taylor and Benson but came up empty.

"James, have you seen Taylor or Benson?" she whispered.

"I did. They're monitoring the corridors outside the powder room right now and will be back in half an hour."

Half an hour? Okay. She could do this. The dancing hadn't started yet. She looked up at James and blurted, "I found something—"

A woman in a pale-blue dress backed into Paisley, her heel smashing her toe.

"Umph." Pain shot up Paisley's foot.

"Sorry." The woman turned about, gave her the once-over, and moved off.

"You were saying?" James asked.

"It can wait." Too many people surrounded them for a private conversation. "So, you're talking to me again?"

"We were never not talking." James's dark eyes looked puzzled.

"You said we needed a chaperone, and I didn't see you, so I assumed . . ."

"And you assumed I'd dumped you?" He glanced around. "If we weren't in such a public place, I'd show you how un-dumped you are, Lady Margaret."

And with those unloverlike words, Paisley was thoroughly satisfied that nothing had changed between them that mattered. When James had mentioned they needed a chaperone, he must have been as shocked at the chemistry between them as she was.

Across the room, Torquil peeked at her from his mother's side, looking like a miniature version of Kinross in his Prince Charlie jacket, kilt, sporran, stockings, and ghillie brogues. He also looked about as bored as an eleven-year-old boy could be at a grown-up ball.

Paisley wiggled her fingers in acknowledgment. Torquil, ever the duke's heir, bowed slightly in response and glanced up at Kinross. Their father still appeared deeply engrossed in conversation with Lord Chatto.

Torquil excused himself and made his way around the dance floor, stopping twice to bow to several of his mother's friends. A small glow of pride at his behavior warmed Paisley's heart. Her brother truly had beautiful manners.

Rahim joined her and James, his eyes boldly raking over her person. "I must say, you are simply ravishing this evening, Lady Margaret."

James's arm stiffened under her hand.

"Thank you." Paisley shifted uncomfortably.

Rahim's marked attention would flatter most women, but it was kind of uncomfortable considering they were stepsiblings. With little provocation, she sensed James would take Rahim down for his overly familiar examination of her. And it was obvious that Rahim had enjoyed tweaking James's nose. Into this hothouse of brewing emotions, Torquil arrived, diverting everyone's attention.

"How's it going, brother mine? You look quite the duke's heir." Paisley nodded toward Torquil's attire.

"You look verra bonnie in Granny's dress." Torquil eyed her gown somewhat differently than his older brother had. "Do you still want to dance?"

"I'd love to, but I don't know the steps to your Scottish reels."

"I would be happy to teach you," Torquil offered.

"If you will excuse me, I must speak to one of the donors about tonight's auction," Rahim interjected, then touched her arm. "I'll claim my dance when you are not so occupied."

Paisley heaved a sigh of relief as Rahim turned his attention toward a group surrounding a glass-encased pair of men's eighteenth-century, diamond-studded shoe buckles.

"Torquil, do you know someplace private to teach me? I don't want to make a fool of myself in front of everyone while I learn it. I only have twenty minutes though," she said, marking the time Agents Benson and Taylor would return to the ballroom.

"We could try the red salon. Mummy had it cordoned off to keep people from wandering through the castle." Torquil's voice filled with purpose. "Or we could use the scullery. It has a large open space. Mrs. Grant wouldn't mind."

Torquil's voice filled with warmth when he spoke of Mrs. Grant. First James, now her brother. It appeared the household revolved around the big-hearted woman.

"If you're sure she won't mind, I think the scullery is our best bet."

With a sly glance in both directions, Torquil slipped behind a bank of potted ferns and stealthily opened one of the exits wide enough for his body to slip through. Paisley followed, and James brought up the rear.

Several guests had gathered in the corridor to examine Kinross's ancient artifacts. Torquil spun about and headed in the direction of the servants' staircase.

"Hurry, before someone tries to talk to us." Torquil scurried down the hall.

Paisley gathered her skirts to keep them from brushing up against the walls inside the old turret staircase. Circular and narrow, the stone risers had worn down in the middle from centuries of use. Paisley grasped the metal railing, grateful for the modernized update, and followed Torquil down the cylindrical space.

They reached the kitchen just as Mrs. Grant was putting out the hearth fire. "Och, Master Torquil. I'd given up seeing you this night."

There on the worktop sat a plate of shortbread and a glass of milk.

Instead of rushing to the platter, Torquil plowed into Mrs. Grant and hugged her tight. The woman's face softened, and she stroked his silky hair.

"There, there, Master Torquil."

In Mrs. Grant's kitchen, it appeared Torquil received the uncomplicated affection most small boys craved, and Paisley's heart warmed for Mrs. Grant all over again.

"Paisley, have you met Mrs. Grant?" Torquil asked, his manners quickly asserting themselves.

"I have. Mrs. Grant takes care of Digger when I can't bring him upstairs," Paisley said.

"Kinross will be upset when he finds out that the three of you have gone missing from the ball." Mrs. Grant tsked.

"I'm going to teach Paisley a reel," Torquil explained to the cook.

"Best be on with it then." The woman nodded, bouncing her triple chins.

Torquil escorted Paisley into the scullery, stopping only to flip on the electric switch. The room flooded with light and woke Digger. When he saw her, he set up a ruckus inside his crate.

"*Shhh*, Digger." Careful of her gown, Paisley petted him through the metal cage.

"Och. He'll raise the dead, that pup." Mrs. Grant had followed them inside the scullery and gave the puppy a treat, effectively shutting him up.

"'The Duke of Perth' is Dad's favorite reel. He'll insist the band plays it tonight." Torquil stood before her.

"Why?" Paisley straightened, and her gown billowed out around her.

"Because he's the Duke of Perth and Kinross." Torquil laughed as though she had said something incredibly silly.

"I thought he was the Duke of Kinross?" James asked.

"Dad's duke of both, though he doesn't insist on it here at home. In London, things are much more proper," Torquil assured him.

Paisley fingered the rough texture of her tartan sash and wondered how she would ever keep the intricacies of aristocratic titles straight.

"Four couples form a set," Torquil said, taking charge of her education. "Men stand on one side and ladies on the other. Most of the dancing is done on the balls of your feet."

"Do you think I could get away with taking these off in the ballroom?" Paisley lifted her hem so he could see her heels.

"Remove your shoes? At a ball?" Torquil's eyes bugged.

"Yes."

"Don't you have Highland ghillies?" Torquil thrust out one of his ghillie brogues for her examination. The soft-soled, leather footwear resembled a pair of men's dress shoes with laces that tied above the ankle.

"I didn't think I'd need special shoes."

"You'll break an ankle hopping about in those," Mrs. Grant said, referring to her heels.

"If I can't take them off, I promise to be careful." Paisley dropped the hem of her dress.

"She'll do fine. She's used to them," James said from the doorway. He had helped himself to a piece of Mrs. Grant's shortbread.

"So, how do I dance this 'Duke of Perth' reel?" Paisley asked, turning back to her brother.

"Stand like this." Torquil raised on the balls of his feet and demonstrated a double-step ball change.

"The dance is verra simple once you've seen it done." Mrs. Grant pronounced *done* as *doon* in her quaint Highland accent. "I'm sure the reel is online. Just aboot everything is on there these days." Mrs. Grant removed her mobile device from her apron pocket and did a quick online search. "Here it is." She passed her mobile to Paisley.

Paisley and Torquil bent over the video feed. Men lined up on one side of the set—women on the other. The lead couple met in the center and performed the steps Torquil had exhibited. The head couple rotated through the set until they eventually worked their way to the bottom of the line.

"That's it?" Paisley asked.

"Easy peasy." Torquil nodded.

She and Torquil went through the steps together a few times on the flagstone floor with Torquil shouting directions and Mrs. Grant chiming in from time to time. When they finished, James came up alongside Paisley, draped an arm around her shoulders, and took another bite of shortbread.

"Is that your second piece?" Paisley asked him.

"I think it's my third," James said, polishing it off. "Mrs. Grant, I might try to hire you when I get my own place. Would you be willing to cook for me instead of the duke?" James winked.

"Och, Jamie lad, quit yer teasing," Mrs. Grant said, her voice inflecting her pleasure.

He gave Mrs. Grant a lopsided grin and squeezed Paisley's shoulder. There was no sense of rejection in his behavior toward her. Paisley needed to stop reading into James's words; he and his brothers had always been straight shooters. It was time she remembered that.

"Let's see," James said, motioning for her to dance.

Paisley executed the simple steps and stopped.

"That's it?" The corner of James's mouth inched up.

"Pretty much."

"You're sure Torquil isn't pulling a fast one on you?"

"Positive." Paisley looked at her brother for affirmation.

"No tricks. Promise." Torquil crossed his hand over his heart. "Mrs. Grant, may I have a slice of shortbread now?" Torquil asked the motherly cook.

"Aye, lad, if Jamie hasn't eaten them all."

Torquil ran through the doorway into the kitchen with Mrs. Grant bustling after him.

James placed his hand on the small of Paisley's back. With one eye on the doorway, he dipped his head and pressed a firm kiss on her mouth, leaving her in no doubt that his feelings toward her remained unchanged. "What was it you wanted to tell me earlier?"

"Remember the pictures I took at the loch?"

"Yeah. What about them?"

"I accidentally photographed four men with automatic weapons in the pines."

His pupil's dilated, but he gave no further sign of surprise. Considering the events they had experienced the last few days, she doubted much would shock him.

James rubbed his jaw. "MI6 is here tonight. You need to let them know what you've found."

"I plan to as soon as they return to the ballroom."

"Good." His voice was filled with deep satisfaction. "Well, my little sleuth, do you have any more surprises up your sleeve?"

"Nope, I'm done." She kept her words light, but she could see the worry furrowing between his brows.

James dipped his head and kissed her again. "Then I think we'd better grab Torquil and skedaddle back upstairs. The sooner you find Taylor and Benson, the better."

Chapter 30

ACHMED CREPT DOWN THE HALL and stopped outside Kinross's home office. He wiped his sweaty palms on his trousers, then glanced over his shoulder. All clear. The security guards were on their rounds.

He punched the code into the number pad. A green light flashed. He slipped inside and stood against the wall until the door eased shut behind him on its soft-close hinges.

His blackmailer had demanded he steal the charity ball donations from Kinross's safe. Without Kinross's knowledge, Achmed was to assist MI6 in catching the mastermind behind this by exchanging the packets with the two agents on the second floor. Easy—if he didn't get caught. If he bungled the job, MI6 would refuse to acknowledge their part in the operation, and Achmed would face the consequences of his thievery.

Though prison loomed, Achmed was grateful his sister was safe. At least he had done something to protect her from further harm. If he had gone to the duke in the beginning and taken his punishment, she would not have sustained long-term injuries. But prison was better than the alternative—certain death at the hands of his tormenter.

Achmed glanced about the high-tech office. The space smelled of cleanser, and pictures of Kinross's children were everywhere. According to his extortionist, Kinross had converted the fireplace mantel into a safe with three interlocking hurdles, the first obstacle being the mantel itself.

He crossed to the fireplace and ran his fingers slowly over the ornately carved wood, then locating the spring mechanism inside the hind's ear, he pressed the lock. *Snick*. Achmed expelled a shaky breath and stepped back as the mantel opened outward.

Inside the alcove was a smooth piece of steel with another touchpad. This one triggered a silent alarm if he didn't touch the pad dead center. He took a deep breath, then entered the nine-digit code.

Snap. The second lock opened. Achmed shut his eyes and exhaled, his body weak with relief. Just one more to go.

Bending, he opened the hinged metal casing to find a large lead box with a combination dial.

According to his source, this last lock was the most treacherous of all, diabolical in its simplicity with a timer and a hair-trigger alarm. If he made the slightest mistake when he tumbled the numbers, the office door and the shatterproof windows would bolt shut. Alarms would sound throughout the castle, and police would descend to haul him off to prison.

Being arrested was one thing, but being arrested in front of a crowd of Kinross's fancy friends was another. Achmed couldn't imagine a more humiliating experience.

He flexed his hands to stop their shaking before he spun the dial to the first number in the sequence.

Click.

"Two more, just two more," Achmed whispered to himself.

He moved on to the next number in the combination, careful not to rotate the dial past the stop.

Click.

Sweat beaded on his forehead and ran down his face as he slowly spun to the final number.

Click.

Tension drained from his body. He couldn't stay there for long. The guards would return in only a few minutes, but he took a second to calm his racing heart before he opened the safe door.

Inside the lead box, neatly stacked envelopes alphabetized by surname and donation amounts awaited an armored courier escort to the bank. Kinross's benefactors did not trust large wire transfers. Too many had gone missing recently to cybercrimes.

Achmed loaded the envelopes inside the lining of his tux and closed the mantel safes. After his rendezvous with MI6 on the next floor, he would wash his hands of crime.

He checked his watch. He had thirty-six seconds to reach the stairs before the security team returned to this corridor. His heart clanged like crashing symbols as he let himself out of Kinross's office and made for the stairs.

Voices. His heart skittered. The guards were coming.

Stepping up his pace, he gained the stairs just as the security team rounded the corner and started down the corridor toward the duke's office. Weak with relief, Achmed leaned against the balustrade before he hurried up the stairs, passing the duchess and her butler on their way down.

He turned his face away, praying to Allah the duchess would not recognize him. A snippet of her conversation drifted back.

"He's not in his rooms?"

"No, Your Grace. Master Torquil is not in any of his usual places."

Achmed passed the life-size oils of the duke's son and daughter, rounded the landing, then raced up to the next floor. Without rapping on the heavy wood panel, he opened the first door on the right and slid inside, breathing hard.

Agent Taylor whirled, gun in hand. When she saw it was him, she lowered her weapon.

Agent Benson lounged against the fireplace. "What's the matter, Taylor? Spooked?"

Benson's double entendre was not lost on Achmed.

"Nonsense." Agent Taylor straightened, her poise restored. "You're late, Mr. Razool."

"By ten seconds." Agent Benson's eyes glinted.

Taylor ignored her partner. "Take off your jacket, Mr. Razool."

Benson removed the envelopes from the tux coat and handed them to Taylor.

Agent Taylor inserted false packets of similar weight inside the lining of his tux and handed it back. Achmed slipped back into his jacket, the new packets brushing against his body through the lining.

"Let's go over your instructions one last time," Taylor said. "Go to the main hall and ask the footman at the coat check for Mr. Hanif's overcoat. Hand him this claimant."

Achmed grasped the coat check ticket she handed him and tucked it inside his pocket.

"On the way out," Taylor continued with a slight gleam in her pale blue eyes, "ask the footman for the nearest toilet. Switch these packets into your overcoat. When you leave the toilet, go back to the footman and tell him that you've decided to stay. He will recheck your coat, and you can slip outside the castle the way you entered. Nigel Thatcher will be waiting for you."

"Very good." Achmed noticed Agent Taylor had tactfully excluded the fact that Officer Thatcher would arrest him the moment he exited the castle.

Chapter 31

While Paisley was in the ladies' restroom fixing a few loose strands of hair that had slipped their pins, the deejay announced over the sound system, "On behalf of the Duke and Duchess of Perth and Kinross, we would like to thank those who contributed tonight to the auction. Almost £400,000 was raised for Scottish charities: the Glasgow School for the Blind, and Head and Mind, a mental health initiative for young people."

Clapping and cheers ensued from the adjoining ballroom.

Warmth spread through Paisley's heart at the open generosity of her father's associates. So many lives would be touched by the contributions her father had obtained.

The ball was in full swing when Paisley returned from the ladies' restroom. She had looked everywhere for Agents Taylor and Benson during the charity auction, but they had been conspicuously absent for the whole of it. If Taylor and Benson weren't part of the extra security her father had requested, what were they doing on the premises?

Again, her eyes swept the ballroom for the missing agents and came up empty. Where were they? She needed to pass them the flash drive and photos before someone asked her to dance.

That was when her artistic eye truly took in the repurposed ballroom for the first time. Her father kept this room closed, and Munira had refused her help with the decorations. Paisley had been so nervous when she had come downstairs tonight that she hadn't fully taken it all in.

Only the minstrels' gallery and hammerbeam ceiling hearkened back to medieval times. Robert Adam, a Scottish architect and interior designer, had refurbished the once-massive hearth in the 1760s. The plank floors had been sanded and lacquered until they shone. Even the paneling had been removed and stored in the attics a century ago to be replaced by white plaster. It was a delightful, airy space that met her father's needs.

Paisley finally spotted Agent Benson on the dance floor; his height made him hard to miss. Benson chatted amiably with his middle-aged companion, his head bent so he could hear her over the music. Now and then, his eyes lifted and scanned the room.

On one of his sweeps, Benson's eyes passed over Paisley. She motioned for him to come over at the end of the dance. He turned slightly and tilted his head toward his partner, Agent Taylor, standing on the far side of the room talking to Kinross. Was he trying to tell her to speak with Taylor?

When Benson swung about in the dance, his eyes met Paisley's. She shook her head slowly. No, she would not do as Benson urged, to seek out his companion. That would mean talking to her father. Before Paisley dealt with Kinross, she intended to deliver her information to MI6, then, and only then, would she speak to her father.

She was fairly certain Kinross was furious with her.

Unused to strong parental emotion, Paisley had no idea how to navigate the rapids of such behavior. An angry father was virgin territory for her. With her own fears swirling at high tide, Paisley didn't feel equal to the confrontation.

Instead, she motioned to Benson with more vigor.

He excused himself from his dance partner and came up alongside her, facing the ballroom. "You needed to speak with me, Lady Margaret?"

"I might have found out where the terrorists we saw on Lunga are staying."

He turned his head sharply, his gray eyes probing. "I'll get Agent Taylor." Benson's eyes scanned the room. "Meet us by the fountain. It looks devoid of guests."

Paisley entered an alcove created by potted greenery supplied from the conservatory. In this sheltered corner away from listening ears, a small fountain trickled into a pool.

The information inside her glove had practically branded her forearm all evening. She prayed something on those photos would help MI6 identify the terrorists. While she waited, the trickling sound of the splashing fountain helped soothe her growing agitation.

It had occurred to her that the armed men on her father's land might have accessed the stable block's corporate offices. If they had, could they access the castle as well? And if that was the case, the field of suspects had narrowed to only those people with entrée to both. Paisley went through the list of those who met the criteria: James, Ward MacKenzie, Rahim, Kinross, and Munira.

Automatically, Paisley removed James from the list. Despite the way she felt about him, James was a peaceable man. He would never attach himself to individuals or groups associated with violent acts. It went against his core values.

Ward MacKenzie, Kinross's CEO, was the dark horse in this roundup. He had an office in the stable block and often met with Kinross in the castle. Kinross paid him a generous salary. Unless he was a jihad convert, sending money to the Middle East didn't make sense.

Rahim, Munira's oldest son, was only a small child when he and his mother fled Uzkahzikstan—too young to form extremist associations. Even if he had, his excellent education would have dispelled any such leanings, and he seemed to enjoy the wealth and luxuries his current life provided. If Kinross suffered, Rahim would as well.

Kinross? The idea was absurd. Kinross stood to lose the most. Still, he could have easily manipulated the money transfer, her wicked mind countered. *No.* Paisley would never believe it. He couldn't be the guilty party. She couldn't prove Kinross wasn't aware of the armed men on his land, but it was highly doubtful he was involved. Her father had nothing to gain from it.

That left Munira. To Paisley, the duchess was the only one with a foot in both camps. The woman was at odds with Kinross and did little to interact with his friends. She had been married previously to a known terrorist and kept an office in the stable block where she served refugees—a perfect cover to aid a terrorist cell. On the other hand, Munira would likely lose custody of Torquil if she left Kinross. Torquil was the duke's heir. Despite the woman's coldness, Paisley sensed a deep possessiveness in Munira for her son.

Each of the individuals on her list stood to lose if the resort failed, but one of them must be guilty. The question was who?

A click of heels. Paisley looked up from her musings. She didn't know how Benson had signaled his partner. But here she was.

Agent Taylor, looking resplendent in a forest-green gown of crushed velvet and the obligatory tartan sash, converged on Paisley's corner. She stopped on the opposite side of the fountain, pulled out a compact from her clutch, and powdered her nose.

A little perplexed, Paisley said, "Agent Taylor, I have proof I'd like to—"

"Don't look at me directly. You do not know us. Is that clear?"

"Yes." Paisley turned away. Wow. Agent Taylor could sure bark out orders.

Benson joined Taylor. He leaned down and whispered into her neck.

If Paisley hadn't known better, she would have sworn they were a couple. A wrought-iron bench stood three feet from Paisley. Benson led his "girlfriend" to it, and they took a seat.

Taylor gazed adoringly into her partner's eyes and said, "What proof?"

Paisley startled. So, this was the game? All right. If they could play at subterfuge, so could she. Paisley drifted closer to the pool and looked down into the water.

"I photographed four men on the estate with automatic weapons. They might be some of the men James and I witnessed on Lunga." Paisley paused as Ward MacKenzie walked past her along the edge of the dance floor.

"Why do you believe that?" Benson toyed with one of Agent Taylor's red curls.

"I don't think there are too many people running around the Highlands and islands with weapons like that. If terrorists are on my father's land, what are they doing here? Could they have accessed information from the estate's corporate offices as well as the castle's? If they did, they would know schedules and codes and . . ." Her voice trailed off.

Who was she to tell MI6 agents her wild theories? Once started, she determined it was better to share it all.

"Look, I know it's a long shot, and I'm probably way off track and don't have any business telling you how to do your job, but my father told James he believes an employee on the estate delayed his reaching the bank on time for that money transfer. If that's true, the only people who have access to both the corporate offices and the castle are my father, the duchess, Ward MacKenzie, Rahim, and James Pressley-Coombes."

Agent Taylor leaned against Agent Benson. "Those are definitely some interesting theories, Lady Margaret."

Paisley burned with embarrassment for sharing her wild ideas. "Do you still want my flash drive and pictures?" she asked in a tight little voice.

Benson nuzzled Taylor's ear, his face hidden from the ballroom. "Drop them on the floor. I'll pick them up."

That was easier said than done. The things were in her glove. Paisley chewed her bottom lip for a second until inspiration struck.

She bent to touch a lily pad and "accidentally" dampened her fingers. Making a face, she lifted her dripping glove from the water and shifted so her back was to the dance floor. Quickly, she removed her glove, and the flash drive and pictures fell to the floor.

A group of guests started her way. Paisley froze for two heartbeats before her brain cells kicked into gear. She stepped over her pictures, letting her long skirts hide them from view until the guests passed. Agent Benson rose from his seat, messing with an inner pocket of his tux. A few pound notes fluttered to the floor.

He lowered to his knees, hunting for his dropped money. Paisley stepped back a pace and returned her attention to the lily pads. In one swoop, Benson slipped the flash drive, photos, and pound notes into his pocket, then reclaimed his former position on the garden seat beside Taylor.

"Where did you come by these pictures?" Taylor asked, smiling up into Benson's face.

"I did a photoshoot one morning by the loch," Paisley answered.

"We'll be in touch." Benson pulled Taylor up beside him. It appeared that she was about to move off, but Benson slipped his arm around her waist and planted a kiss on her mouth.

With her back turned to the room, Agent Taylor's eyes shot angry sparks up at her partner. "Unnecessary, Benson."

Benson chuckled before they moved off. "I assure you, Lady Elise, that it was."

Chapter 32

Paisley tugged on her damp glove and glanced around the ballroom for James.

"I believe you owe me a dance," Rahim's voice purred from behind her.

Her heart dropped to her toes. She spun about and found Rahim standing beside the potted ferns. How long had he been there?

"Rahim. It's good to see a friendly face. If you were back here, why didn't you keep me company?" Paisley silently prayed Rahim had not seen her pass the information to Benson.

"I did not believe you were alone," he answered softly.

Her mouth went dry. "Why do you say that? I don't know anyone except family and a few of my father's friends."

"My mistake," Rahim acknowledged with a bow of the head.

Paisley glanced about for James. Her eyes landed on him out on the dance floor with Munira.

Rahim followed her gaze. "I see our resident guest has rather better manners than I gave him credit for."

"James's family is well connected and highly thought of in the States. Was that your horse I saw you riding this morning?" Paisley asked, abruptly changing the subject.

"Yes, one of them. I have several Arabians and an Irish hunter as well. I enjoy horses that give me a challenge." Rahim's eyes raked over her, and Paisley had the distinct impression he wasn't just referring to horses.

She frowned slightly. Rahim must have realized that she and James were mutually attracted. Unfortunately, some men thrived on competition. Was Rahim one of them?

The music ended.

The deejay spoke into the mic. "An Englishman, an Irishman, and a Scotsman went into a bar. They had just started drinking their first round when a fly landed in each of their drinks. The Englishman refused to drink his and ordered another. The Irishman blew his away in a cloud of froth and carried on drinking. But the Scotsman, well, he carefully lifted the fly out of his drink by the wings and held it over his glass. 'Go on,' he said. 'Spit it oot, ya wee pockle.'"

The audience roared with laughter, and the music started again. Rahim turned toward her and cocked his head expectantly. Paisley took a step in his direction, but James came up behind her and slipped his arms around her waist.

"Here you are. I've come to claim my reward for fulfilling my obligatory dance to my hostess."

Rahim cleared his throat.

James flushed and let go of her like she was a hot potato. "Sorry, Rahim. I didn't see you there."

"Obviously. It appears I am intruding. Perhaps another time, Lady Margaret?" Rahim asked.

"Of course." Paisley watched Rahim walk away.

"If my mom were still alive, she would beat me with a wooden spoon for that comment about his mother." James's voice was filled with self-derision.

Paisley didn't argue. Mrs. Pressley-Coombes had been death on her children for their bad manners.

"Actually," Paisley said as Rahim disappeared into the crowd. "I think she would have grounded you from baseball *and* beaten you with a wooden spoon."

"Probably. Shall we? I've been dying to dance with you all night." James led her onto the dance floor and pulled her closer than necessary. He nuzzled the side of her hair. "Ouch."

"What's wrong?" Paisley leaned back and looked up at him.

"Your hair stabbed me in the mouth. What's in that skyscraper of yours?"

"I thought you liked the way I look." James, Paisley realized, did not have a romantic bone in his body.

"I did until I got close to you. What stabbed me?"

"They're called bobby pins." Paisley rolled her eyes.

"I can't get near you with your hair piled up that way."

"Are you saying you don't like me to dress up?"

"You're beautiful all the time, Paise, but if your hair keeps me away from you, then no, definitely not."

"I think there was a compliment disguised in there somewhere," she murmured, well pleased with his unromantic dialogue.

"Yeah?"

She met his warm gaze, and her heartbeat increased, throbbing in the hollow of her throat.

"I love you, Paisley, even if your hair reminds me of Marge Simpson."

Laughter burst from her at his unexpected remark. She sobered immediately. "No woman enjoys being compared to a cartoon character."

"I'll remember that."

"See that you do." She diffused the severity of her words with a sassy smile and flutter of lashes.

He pulled her close and squeezed her hand. In perfect harmony, they danced, happiness flowing around her like a newly uncorked bottle of champagne.

The song ended, and the deejay, who was growing loquacious after several rounds of drinks, said, "We'd like to thank our host, the Duke of Perth and Kinross, for lightening our pockets tonight."

Polite chuckles emanated from the crowd.

"The next two songs are for every true Scot and Scot at heart," the deejay said.

The lively tune of "The Duke of Perth" began. Paisley's father took Munira by the hand and led her into a set on the dance floor. Paisley glanced about for Torquil, not seeing him among the gathering.

"Where's your brother?" James asked. "Isn't this the song you were practicing in the kitchen?"

"Yes. I don't know where he is. He must have gone to bed." A sharp pang of regret pricked her heart. She had looked forward to their dance.

Since James didn't know the steps, they stood to the side of the floor while kilted couples danced to the catchy tune. James interlaced their fingers, and a deep pool of contentment filled her. Not once had he gazed at her friends like this. This was new territory for James.

She sighed, and every cheesy, canned expression she had read or watched on TV flitted through her mind. Still amazed at the turn of events that had brought them to this place, she let the fizzy, bubbly emotions bottled inside froth to the surface. Underneath the giddy joy lay a deep-seated rightness to it all.

Kinross caught her eye several times, and Paisley gave him a tentative smile.

The reel segued neatly into "The Skye Boat Song," a Gaelic favorite. The slow, mournful tune soaked into Paisley's soul and made her want to weep for those who had fallen on Culloden's moor for following the bonnie prince. Their loss was her loss. This land was her land, her heritage. And despite the mixed welcome she had received in her father's household, she had grown to love this country.

"Kinross is coming this way," James whispered into her ear and dropped her hand.

"Paisley, may I have this dance?" Kinross's face still held that firm expression she had noticed when she had first entered the ballroom.

"Excuse us," Paisley said to James and took her father's arm.

"You missed the receiving line," Kinross said without preamble.

"I was unavoidably delayed." Paisley couldn't tell him why. Too many people would overhear.

"Delayed? I was to introduce you to society, and you all but absconded the event."

"Dad, I'm sorry. I never meant to embarrass you."

"Smile," her father commanded in a low undertone.

"What?"

"Smile. The Duke of Norfolk is looking this way."

She dutifully flashed her teeth while she inwardly seethed.

"I told everyone you were horribly shy and had a case of sick nerves."

Paisley glanced around the dance floor, trying to keep the asperity inside her shoved deep. Numerous dancers hastily looked elsewhere when she glanced their way.

"Norfolk is the premier duke in Britain."

"What does that mean?" Paisley asked more out of duty than interest.

"His is the oldest dukedom, and through his earldom, he is the Hereditary Marshal of England which controls all arrangements for state functions. He also regulates all armorial bearings and standards."

She shook her head. Her father might as well have been speaking to her in a foreign tongue. "I'll never understand it all."

"You are my daughter and need to make an effort." Kinross's voice was firm. "Whether you like it or not, you are an aristocrat by birth. We are expected to uphold the royal family and its traditions, honor the titles we carry, and support our country."

"But I'm only going to be here three months. Remember our agreement?" She couldn't extend her stay indefinitely, not with Munira treating her the way she did.

"I have high hopes that you will grow accustomed to life in the UK and determine to stay. If you leave, you are not the woman I thought you were."

His words held it all: the displeasure, jury, verdict, and sentencing. Paisley could not speak if she tried. They danced on in silence.

"I've meant to tell you . . ." Kinross cleared his throat. "I had hoped there was another way."

"Tell me what?"

"I set up a trust fund for you when Torquil was born. With his inheriting the title and entailed estates, you deserved something for yourself."

Trust fund? Her father had cared enough about her, even though she had never been part of his life, to provide for her future. Warmth permeated her body. He hadn't forgotten her.

"The trust was to go to you on your thirtieth birthday. It's been somewhat of a bone of contention between Munira and me. She believes everything should go to Torquil, as it would in her country."

Ah. The missing key to Munira's dislike of her. She believed Paisley was siphoning from her son's wealth.

Kinross cleared his throat again and looked uncomfortable. "To meet the financial deadline for the resort build, I, *er* . . . It became necessary to . . ." Kinross couldn't meet her eyes. "Liquidate your assets."

His words sank into Paisley's consciousness. For a second, her emotions were completely detached from his words. She felt nothing. Then, pain sliced through her like a bayonet and impaled her on its spiked tip.

Her father had betrayed her. Spots danced before her eyes.

"Say something."

She couldn't. Words refused to form. She just stared at Kinross while her heart bled out.

"I'll make it up to you, Paisley. I promise. In fact, I—"

"I don't care about the money, Dad." Money had never mattered to Paisley, not this way. "For once in my life, I'd like to be treated fairly or at least with respect. I'm not a second-class citizen, even though you and Mom treat me like I am."

"Will you just listen? Your assets were the easiest to liquidate. You will get back every pound. To make up the difference, I—"

His excuses sounded weak. She tried to step away, but her father held on tight.

She lifted her chin and said with as much dignity as she could muster, "All my life, I have yearned for a parent who loved and treated me like I mattered. When you etched those words on my camera, I believed them. So I came to Scotland to see if you were that parent. I never expected a trust fund, but I did expect to be treated with consideration. That you could so quickly give away my inheritance is indicative of how you perceive me as a person. Even though I am your daughter, I am to be easily dismissed. It was silly for me to have come. I realize that now."

"It's not what it seems, lass. I—"

The music ended. Paisley bowed her neck in dismissal, then stepped away from Kinross. Blindly, she skirted the edge of the ballroom, looking for an exit. She refused to allow her father's fancy guests to see her cry.

Chapter 33

PAISLEY MADE FOR THE GRAND staircase, but several couples milled about the main hall, examining her father's collection of Grecian urns and Ming porcelain, blocking her escape. She changed direction and started for the servants' stairs near the conservatory.

Finding the way clear of guests, she approached the red salon and scooted around the cordoned-off blockade, then picked up her skirts and ran, her heels silent on the Turkish runners.

Outside the conservatory, Paisley stopped to catch her breath, her chest heaving with exertion. Each door looked exactly alike—camouflaged by the paneling. She could never remember which one led to the servants' stairs.

"Where are you off to in such a hurry, Lady Margaret?" Rahim exited the red salon.

He must have seen her rush past. Paisley closed her eyes and prayed for a calm she didn't possess.

"I say, you look rather pale. Are you unwell?"

"I'll be fine, just a little shaky." Her father's betrayal, on top of her recent discovery and the experiences on Lunga, was almost more than she could handle.

"I need to change my heels. They are too high for dancing." Not used to telling fibs, it was the best Paisley could come up with on such short notice.

Rahim raised an expressive brow but didn't contradict her. "The main staircase is in the opposite direction."

"I was going to use the servants' staircase, but I can't remember which door it is."

He went to the opposite wall and opened a door, revealing the narrow, dimly lit stairs.

"Thank you."

"I didn't get the chance to ask you the other day where you went on your tour of the Western Isles."

"I-I," Paisley stammered. Considering her recent procurement of possible suspects and MI6's request to not mention specifics about her and James's outing, Paisley prevaricated. "We visited several islands. I don't know all their names." It wasn't a lie exactly. She had no idea what the small skerries around Lunga were called.

"Did you encounter many tourists?"

"A few." The few being herself and James, but Rahim didn't need to know that. "I was in a bit of a snit, so we didn't interact with them much."

"Why is that?" He had been looking down the corridor in the direction of the main hall, but her comment caught his attention.

Ward MacKenzie, Kinross's CEO, appeared to be coming their way.

"I upset the pilot when I climbed out onto the ladder while he was taxiing."

"I can't imagine why." Rahim's white teeth flashed against his swarthy skin, and his dark eyes gleamed. "You were late coming back. My mother was quite distressed. Gossip in the glen travels fast."

Paisley expelled a heavy breath. "We had a little trouble with our transportation."

"Oh, run out of petrol?" Rahim appeared more polite than curious, his attention on Ward.

Paisley shuddered when she remembered the excursion boat's explosion. "Something like that."

"After you," Rahim said.

Paisley entered the stairwell, appreciative of his holding the door for her. She lifted her skirts above her ankles and started the long climb to her floor. The stairs were slow going in the dim interior, and she stepped on her hem more than once.

Halfway to her floor, a rustle behind her made her pause. Someone was coming up the stairs fast. Thinking it was one of the maids, Paisley smooshed her dress closer to her body so they could pass and not snag her skirts against the stone walls.

She turned to see who it was just as Rahim closed the distance between them. His handsome features were twisted with hate. In that second, she knew: Rahim was the thief. The fifth man—the inside man—the one not shown in her pictures.

The daily mask he wore had vanished, and a fanatical gleam shone from his eyes. He lifted his arm high above his head, his hand holding a hypodermic needle, and quoted, "'God says, *Indeed, they were about to drive you from the land to evict you.*'"

Ice filled Paisley's veins. She froze, her mind refusing to accept that this charming man had destroyed, killed, and robbed.

"Daughter of Kinross, you are the infidel. The earth shall be cleansed." Rahim charged up the last few steps.

Paisley flung her arms out to ward him off as his hand swung forward. The sharp sting of a needle jabbed her neck.

She gasped and scrabbled backward in an attempt to put distance between them, but her heel tangled in her gown. Rahim's face swam in front of her, distorted and unfocused. Her knees buckled, and she grabbed for the rail.

Everything went black.

***

Where is Paisley?

James jangled the change inside his trouser pocket and scanned the ballroom where he had last seen her dancing with her father. "The Skye Boat Song" had ended some time ago. Had she and Kinross wandered off together?

Kinross had better not have upset her for coming down late. Maybe she and her dad had worked it out and Paisley had gone off with him to meet some of his associates.

As the minutes ticked by, James paced the small area around him that wasn't overrun with guests. Growing impatient, he circled the ballroom. Kinross stood inside a cluster of men James recognized from the business supper, but Paisley was nowhere around.

He was about to turn away when he saw Munira hastily motion to her husband. Her quick movements bordered on frantic. James wasn't close enough to hear her, but he read her lips.

"Torquil isn't in his room or any of his usual places," Munira said.

Kinross's brow furrowed. "You're sure Henderson checked the secret passage? You know how he loves to hide there."

"Positive."

James joined the mix. "Have either of you seen Paisley? She promised me this dance."

Kinross looked uncomfortable. "She left the ballroom."

The man knew something and wasn't telling. "Did you upset her?" James asked.

"Do you think she's with Torquil?" Munira clenched and unclenched her hands.

"No," Kinross told her.

"Torquil has been gone for a while," James said, taking pity on Munira. "He was supposed to dance 'The Duke of Perth' with Paisley. They practiced in the scullery earlier to make sure Paisley knew the steps. When the music started, Torquil never showed up."

Kinross and Munira shared an alarmed glance.

"Care to tell me what's going on?" James asked, their agitation starting to rub off on him.

Munira clasped her hands. "Kinross, you don't think . . . ?"

"I'm sure we'll find him." Kinross patted his wife's arm, but he didn't look as though he believed his own words.

"I feel like two different conversations are going at the same time." James kept his eyes on Munira. She appeared the most likely to unburden herself.

"Sutherland's son went missing a few months ago. His father received a ransom note he could not meet." Munira's musical voice throbbed with emotion.

"And?" James was fairly sure he didn't want to hear the rest.

"He hasn't returned," Munira said.

"How old was he?" James asked.

"Ten. He was ten years old." Munira raised her eyes.

"We have heightened security tonight. Someone can go through the footage tapes and see if Torquil left the estate, can't they?" James suggested when both parents appeared to be frozen with worry.

"Yes." Kinross nodded in agreement.

"And what about Paisley?" James asked when their attention seemed focused on Torquil.

"I'll send Henderson up to check on her while I speak to David Hume, the head of security," Kinross said and started for the ballroom exit.

James watched him go and prayed they were wrong about Torquil.

Chapter 34

THEY WEREN'T WRONG ABOUT TORQUIL. Both of Kinross's children were missing!

Tightness squeezed James's chest, warning him of an approaching attack if he didn't get himself under control. He had to hand it to Kinross; the man periodically entered the ballroom to keep rumors from circulating among his guests. Kinross had refused to place his children's names on the tongue of every gossip, especially when doing so might put them in further danger.

Munira had gone to her rooms, out of her mind with grief. In the time James had resided at Castle Rannoch, he had not seen her behave in such a way—mourning as though someone had died. She was always so calm and aloof.

Kinross had tried to console her, but she had refused even a gentle embrace. They had an odd relationship. The duke's eyes followed his wife, but Munira deliberately kept the man at a distance. From time to time, James had even caught an expression of contempt in her almond-shaped eyes.

He understood Kinross had met his wife in a refugee camp when Rahim was little more than six. Her husband had been killed when a terrorist regime had taken over the region in which she lived. James supposed it wouldn't be the first time people married for gain. In Munira's case, Kinross had probably offered her freedom from the life she had known. And in her desperation, she had accepted him.

James turned away and paced the salon, his anxiety mounting. As worried as he was for Torquil, he'd never forgive himself if something happened to Paisley.

With both of the duke's children missing within an hour of each other, the police had warned Kinross there would likely be a ransom. Kinross rubbed his temples.

James's steps took him to the man's chair.

"I can't lose Paisley like this. Not until I tell her—" Kinross didn't finish.

"Tell her what?"

"Tell her I love her. I hurt her tonight. Badly. I told her I'd emptied her trust fund. She left before I had time to tell her I'd placed the equivalent of the amount into resort build shares in her name. With MacKenzie's latest projections, she'll more than double her drained account in the next three years."

Was the man so caught up in making money that it occupied his mind even during an emergency?

"I've been such a fool. I let the things that mattered most take a back seat."

***

Reviewing security footage was not what James had envisioned when he offered to help search for Paisley and Torquil. But here he sat, inside Kinross's security room, facing sixteen monitors and waiting for instructions from David Hume, Kinross's head of security.

Agent Taylor took the chair beside James. She had offered her services when she heard Kinross's children were missing. Her partner, Agent Benson, had assembled with the local police outside the castle. All searchers were equipped with NVGs (night-vision goggles) and a com set synced to the same station and tied to the wireless feed that would play simultaneously on the castle's monitors.

The cops had split into three groups: one to comb the formal grounds, another to search the castle itself, and a third, Benson's group, to pursue any guests who had left the ball early.

Stomach bile lodged halfway up James's throat. He should never have taken his eyes off Paisley. When Paisley's dance had ended with her father, he should have gone to her.

"Quit beating yourself up," Taylor said.

How had she known? James marveled at her perception.

Taylor's pale-blue eyes shone with sympathy. "Kidnappers are opportunists. They lie in wait for the perfect moment. Trust me. Lady Margaret and Lord Crieffmore could not have avoided this situation for long. The good news is Kinross has a huge task force at his disposal. We will find them." She pulled the pins out of her hair and let the red mane tumble down her back. "Due to the information Lady Margaret gave us this evening, a special forces unit is en route to Castle Rannoch as we speak. They arrive before dawn," Taylor said, running her fingers through her hair to smooth the tangles.

James took heart. With the veritable army of police, military, and MI6 agents on hand, along with the beefed-up security Kinross had hired for the evening, Paisley and Torquil had to be somewhere close by.

The sixteen screens above the horseshoe-shaped desk blinked to life. David Hume emerged from the control room and took a seat on the far side of Agent Taylor, placing the spare NVGs and com sets on the counter beside his keyboard.

"Since Master Torquil disappeared a little over an hour past, I've gone back ninety minutes on our feed. There's a wee bit to go through," Hume said, scratching his bald head. "The castle has a good deal of exits."

"There are three of us. We should be able to plow through that fairly quickly," James assured him.

They would find Paisley and Torquil. Kinross had bribed the local precinct with new technology for their police station if they found his children.

"Mr. Hume, we can cut the search to a minimum if you place three of these monitors on manual. I assume the castle security is on separate quadrants due to its size?" Agent Taylor asked.

Hume nodded, opened the control-room door, and flipped several buttons on a stack of black power boxes.

"Our kidnapper will try to leave quickly. Which exits allow easy access to a closely parked car?" Taylor asked, her eyes on the monitors.

"There are four main exits and three secondary ones that meet that criteria." Hume retook his chair.

"We know our kidnapper is bold. He has abducted two individuals within an hour. The front-door exit might appeal to him if Lady Margaret or Lord Crieffmore was drugged," Taylor said.

Drugged? James whipped his head in Taylor's direction. She met his gaze. Her face was set, her eyes hard. She did not offer false hope; she dealt with facts. Some of his earlier confidence slipped away.

"The west side of the castle is out. No vehicles other than a motorbike could get close enough to primary or secondary exits there," Hume informed her.

"Excellent." Taylor nodded.

Hume went out into the hall and recruited a member of his security team to monitor the ongoing feed and that of the search parties while he, Taylor, and James pored over the last ninety minutes of footage.

A member of the security team entered and took the chair on the far side of Hume.

"The rear of the castle has two exits: one for servants, the other for family. Both are close to the car park." Hume flipped a few more switches, the clicks sounding above the hum of electronics.

"We'll check both rear exits." Taylor looked expectantly at Hume.

"The east side of the castle has one exit, but a car could access any of the long salon windows closer to the front."

Agent Taylor drummed the counter absently, reminding James of his brother Jack's obnoxious habit. The temptation to smack her fingers tugged at him.

"How close to the main entrance are those windows?" Taylor asked.

"Too close to handle a successful kidnapping. The footman and maids working the coatroom would notice if a car parked there, even momentarily."

"And the exit?" Taylor asked.

"It's a good place to smuggle someone out," Hume admitted. "Large rhododendrons, a covered porch, and steps that lead directly onto the drive."

"I'll take that side exit," Agent Taylor said decisively. "Mr. Hume, you take the back of the castle, and Mr. Pressley-Coombes will handle the main entrance. If we don't find anything, we will widen our search."

The room quieted as the three of them pored over the feed. Only the occasional click of computer keys broke the silence.

"It's been a while since I've worked on a wired feed," Agent Taylor said after ten minutes.

"Trust me," Hume said, zooming through a stream of blank footage. "Kinross looked into wireless security, but with intermittent internet service due to our gale-force winds, His Grace made sure the castle was protected at all times."

"I assume you have generator backup for power outages?" James kept his eyes on the screen, interested, despite the worry singing through his soul, on how Kinross worked around Scotland's unpredictable weather.

"Aye. His Grace doesn't miss a beat. Four generators, one for every quadrant of the castle. He does things top-notch, our duke." A great deal of pride threaded through Hume's voice.

James was over halfway through his feed when the castle front door opened on his monitor. Ward MacKenzie exited, his arm supporting a dark-haired woman who appeared a little worse for wear. James backed up the feed and hit replay, his focus on the woman.

She was short with her hair piled on top of her head, but she stood in shadow on the far side of Ward, away from the camera. James exhaled sharply and squinted at the feed. The darkness didn't help with visuals after Ward and his companion left the porch.

A man's overcoat hung about the woman's shoulders, which camouflaged her dress and build, but the shiny gold material below MacKenzie's coat was exposed when he opened the right side of the car and helped his wobbly passenger into her seat. James's heart whooshed like a bilge pump.

Could it be Paisley? James wasn't sure. He checked the time stamp: forty-five minutes ago. If this was Paisley, that monster had three-quarters of an hour head start.

"I think I found something," James said, but doubts niggled at him. If this was Paisley, where was Torquil? Was he already inside Ward's car?

"Let's see." Taylor leaned over, her eyes on his screen.

Hume got up from his chair and stood behind James for a clear shot of the footage.

James replayed what he had found. "What do you think?"

"I was hoping for better imagery. Her face is hidden," Taylor said, her shoulders rising, then falling. "It's the only lead we've got." Taylor clicked her nails on the countertop. "I'll call Benson—"

The security-room door opened, and Kinross stuck his head around the edge. "Anything?" Lines were etched deeply between his brows.

David Hume glanced at James, his blue eyes anxious, then he said, "Ward MacKenzie left with a small brunette in a gold dress over forty minutes ago."

"Have the police been informed?" Kinross asked, his voice abrupt. He reached for one of the spare com sets on the counter and slapped it on, adjusting to the correct channel, then grabbed an action cam.

"Not yet. We just found—" Hume said, but Kinross had gone.

Chapter 35

James found the live-feed monitor in the castle's security office and switched to Kinross's video. Of the duke's person, only his arms and legs were visible as he followed the local detectives and Agent Benson to Ward MacKenzie's house.

Kinross's action-cam and com set were tuned to the castle's transmission tower so those viewing the feed could call in backup if needed.

Watching Kinross drive reminded James of a video game without controls.

Kinross smacked the steering wheel and colored the air with expletives as his car's fog lamps cut a swath through the swirling mist. The rear lights of Detective Inspector Skene's car were barely visible on the loch road ahead of him.

"Can you hear me, Hume?" Kinross asked.

"Aye, Your Grace," Hume answered from his seat on the far side of Agent Taylor.

"Any sign of Torquil?" Kinross asked.

"No, sir, only Lady Margaret," Hume responded.

"Wait till I get my hands on that scunner. Och, the man deserves a pummeling, betraying my friendship . . ." Kinross's voice trailed off.

James didn't ask what a scunner was; he had a fairly good idea.

After several minutes of complete silence, filled only with the noise of the engine, Kinross turned off the B846 onto a residential street and parked behind the DI's sedan. Kinross flipped off his headlamps. The detectives and Agent Benson were in the drive holding a confab.

Benson disengaged from the group and approached Kinross's window.

"Is that MacKenzie's only vehicle?" Benson asked with a chin jerk toward the car parked in the drive.

"Aye." Kinross climbed out from behind the wheel and slammed his car door.

Benson clicked on his torch and ran it over the number plate. "The plate matches the security footage, but the engine's cold. If MacKenzie snatched her, she's inside. He hasn't had time to take her elsewhere and return."

"Is there more than one exit in the back garden?" Benson shifted to take in the house's front elevation.

"No, just the one off the kitchen." Kinross transferred his weight from one foot to the other.

"Thanks."

Why didn't they just get on with it? James made an impatient movement with his hand.

Benson went soft-footed up the drive and spoke in a low tone to the DS. A minute later, the DS skulked around the side of the house and disappeared into the back garden. Benson and DI Skene continued to the front door, leaving Kinross on the drive.

"Your Grace, we've lost visual," Hume said softly into the speaker. "We can't see what is happening. Can you move closer?"

"Och. I forgot you were there, Hume." Kinross stepped toward the entrance, and the images brightened.

Loud pounding.

"Ward MacKenzie, open up. Police Scotland," DI Skene's voice rang out.

Silence.

Skene banged again, this time even louder. "Ward MacKenzie, open up. We know you're inside."

No response.

Skene went to his car, removed a short battering ram from the trunk, and then trudged up the driveway.

"Know how tae use the Enforcer?" Skene asked Benson, who stood a good head taller.

"I've had some practice." Benson took the Enforcer, swung it three times against the panel, and breached the entrance.

"Police Scotland," Skene called from the doorway.

The men moved inside, leaving Kinross on the walkway. A few seconds later, the DS came around the side of the house and entered the door.

No noise reached the street.

"If Ward's home, he would have launched himself at the first person through his door," Kinross said into his com set. "He's probably hammered. The man is dead to the world when he has a few pints."

After several minutes, Kinross made his way to the door and poked his head inside the splintered frame. Lights were on in every room. Men's voices carried from the end of the hall.

Kinross stopped in the bedroom doorway. MacKenzie lay sprawled across the rumpled bed, fully dressed. Benson checked MacKenzie's pulse, then lifted the man by the shoulder and rolled him onto his back. He shone his torch directly into the man's face.

If James had been there, he would have popped MacKenzie. Instead, he clamped his molars to keep it together. Giving in to his rage helped no one.

"Where is she?" Benson demanded.

MacKenzie opened his bloodshot eyes, then scrunched them shut and covered his face with his arm.

Benson flung MacKenzie's arm away, lifted one of his eyelids, and shone the flashlight directly into his eye. "I asked you a question. Where is she?"

"Stop that." MacKenzie batted the flashlight away and squinted up at Benson. "Turn that off. My brain's going to hemorrhage."

"Tell me where she is first."

"Who are you?" MacKenzie raised up on his elbow. "What are you doing in my house?"

"Agent Benson, SIS." The flashlight clicked off.

The detective sergeant entered the room, a gold dress in his hands. "I found this upstairs inside the bath."

"Where is she?" Benson demanded a second time, his tone brooking no nonsense.

"Who?" MacKenzie asked, beginning to sound like a broken LP.

"The woman who wore this dress," DI Skene said.

Kinross took in the brassy gold fabric. "That's not Lady Margaret's gown."

"That's my sister's dress." MacKenzie's head flopped backward and smacked the metal headboard. "Agh." He rubbed his head, then rolled to a sitting position on the mattress and peered at the men inside his room, his gaze resting on the duke. "What are you doing here, Kinross?"

"Lady Margaret and Torquil have gone missing," Kinross said flatly.

James leaned forward in his chair. If he hadn't had so much riding on finding Paisley, he would have been sorry for MacKenzie. The detectives and Benson wore impassive expressions, but fury burned in their eyes.

"And you thought they were here?" MacKenzie's voice cracked.

"Security footage showed you leaving the castle with a woman in a gold dress. That was our only lead." Benson stepped back from the bed.

MacKenzie closed his eyes. "My sister is upstairs in the solarium if you need to check. Kinross gave me an extra invitation. I brought Maureen to the ball. She had one dram too many, so I brought her home."

James's heart sank. Their only lead was a dead end. He twisted his chair to face Taylor and Hume. "If MacKenzie doesn't have Paisley or Torquil, who does?"

***

She was cold. So cold.

Paisley shivered and tried to burrow under her blankets, but there weren't any. Slowly, she came awake. Her hair had tumbled into her face, and she pushed it back but still couldn't see. Everything was black.

Her fingers pressed into a thin layer of straw beneath her and touched stone. Groggily, she raised onto her forearms and groaned, the straw poking her skin through the thin satin of her gown. Her shoulder ached, and her ribs were sore.

Where was she?

She sat and brushed up against a solid surface behind her. Reaching out, she touched frigid rock. Goosebumps broke out on her exposed skin, and she rubbed her arms to warm herself. Why was it so cold? And why was she here?

Something moved beside her—something alive. A rat? She recoiled, scooting as far away as possible, a mere six inches, before she bumped into more rock. Her ears strained for the squeak of rodents, but only breathing filled the space.

Who else was here? Curiously, she stretched out a tentative hand and groped in the dark. Not a rat—a body.

The last vestiges of sleep fled. If the body moved, it was alive. If it was alive, it was warm. Shivering, she inched her way toward the person, her hand settling on the head. The hair was cropped short. She continued her exploration, her hands running over the lapels of a man's jacket, pleated wool skirt, sporran, long socks, and shoes that tied around the ankles.

A Scottish male. Whoever he was, he was small, even smaller than she. Paisley checked the person for possible injuries. No blood. That was a good thing because her nursing skills extended no further than the first aid certification she had learned each summer at camp.

She sat back on her heels and pushed at her disheveled hair. Hairpins dangled from what remained of an elaborate updo. She finger-combed the mess and secured a few strands back from either side of her face.

Hairpins.

Memories of Granny and the hairdresser stirred. The ball. She had been at a ball.

Paisley touched the front of her clothing, her fingers encountering beading and satin. The person beside her groaned in his sleep. Unless her father had invited a leprechaun to the ball, Paisley assumed the child beside her was Torquil.

The temptation to wake him was strong, but she refused to give in to it. The less time he was conscious in this horrible place, the better. Paisley wrapped her arms around herself to keep her teeth from chattering. If this was Torquil, why were the two of them here?

Then she remembered—Rahim running up the stairs behind her, his face twisted with hatred as he plunged the needle into her neck.

Of all the suspects on her list, Paisley had almost removed Rahim from the group. Why had he done this to her and Torquil? Torquil was his half brother.

Paisley strained to make out any movement by anything other than the person beside her. That's when she noticed the soft red glow under the straw a few feet away. Paisley crawled toward it. Her hand closed over the small, hard device with wires. She flipped it over and gasped at the red numbers: 59:00.

A bomb.

Shockwaves crashed over her body as she stared at the device. The number changed. Fifty-eight minutes and fifty-nine seconds.

Chapter 36

THE MINUTES WERE TICKING—AND they were right back to square one. James's hands clenched into fists. He wanted to punch something. His only lead, the search of Ward MacKenzie's house, had turned up zilch. He reentered the red salon where half the members of the room resembled a sci-fi comic convention with their headsets and GoPros clipped to their chests.

The local police had converted the space into an on-site headquarters and had ordered a task force to search the racing stables and all derelict buildings on the estate.

Technically, DI Skene was in charge of the operation, but Kinross was doing his level best to usurp his authority. Too close to the situation, Kinross and James were denied the ability to take part in the physical search with the police, but that didn't stop Kinross from ordering two officers at all estate exits to examine each car's interior and trunk.

Unable to sit, James paced one end of the over-civilized room while Kinross held a council of war with David Hume, DI Skene, and both MI6 agents.

Taylor's watch pinged. She held up an arm to pause the conversation while she read the communication, then said, "Earlier this evening, Lady Margaret passed us vital information on a case we are currently working on."

"Is that why my daughter is missing?" Kinross demanded.

"It's possible her photographs incited her abduction." Taylor didn't candy-coat her response.

Her watch pinged again, and she stopped once more to read the incoming text.

"Lady Margaret's pictures were forwarded to SIS headquarters. A special forces unit mobilized immediately and is on their final approach by helicopter. The chopper needs a level field to land on. Where would that be?" Her pale-blue eyes flashed to Kinross.

"The most level bit on the estate is the east pasture near the racing stables," Kinross supplied. "Why are they coming? What's this about?"

"Your daughter photographed armed men on your estate. Two are suspected in the Copenhagen bombing."

Kinross paused as she relayed the information, then said, "We'll need to direct a group to the field and lay out flares so they can land."

"I can't spare any men, Your Grace," DI Skene said.

Munira entered the room, and DI Skene lowered his voice. "The likelihood of a ransom is high, Your Grace. Don't be surprised if we receive a phone call or ransom note in short order."

"Is there a way to trace the call if one comes through?" Kinross's manner was collected, but his face had paled.

"Yes, if they stay on the line long enough. Try to keep them talking. My DS is setting up a trace in Hume's security office as we speak. When—if you should receive a call, place it on speaker when you pick up," Skene counseled.

The DI's mobile rang. He moved to the doorway to answer.

From the outer perimeter, James watched the room like a spectator, as near to panicking as he had ever known.

Agent Taylor's brow had furrowed while her partner, Agent Benson, lounged near the doorway, observing the room in general, much like James. Munira took a seat in one of the overstuffed chairs, her eyes swollen. Without her heavy makeup, she looked fragile, as though she might splinter into a million pieces.

"The Perth Control Room is searching CCTV feed on all motorways surrounding the castle from the time of Lord Crieffmore's disappearance onward," DI Skene announced when he hung up his mobile.

Another phone went off. This time it was Kinross's, its ring sending an electric volt through the room's residents. Utter silence reigned as all eyes stared at the duke. Kinross flicked a glance to DI Skene before he answered and hit the speaker icon as instructed.

"Kinross here," he answered, then motioned toward his phone.

James crossed the room and crowded behind the duke, while Taylor and Skene leaned in from both sides to view Kinross's mobile screen. A dark stone room appeared showing Paisley and Torquil, both lying unconscious on a thin bed of straw. Not far from Paisley, a small mechanism with red lighted numbers lay on the ground.

"I have your children." A computer-generated device disguised the kidnapper's voice. "A timed bomb will detonate if you do not explicitly follow these instructions.

"If you want to see your children again, deliver £350,000.00 to the west gatehouse in fifty-five minutes. Don't be late." The line went dead.

Kinross stared at the phone, his face blank. "How am I to raise that money? The banks don't open for another five hours. I don't keep that much cash on hand."

Munira burst into tears.

Nearby, Agent Taylor held a whispered conversation with DI Skene. James overheard part of it.

"Did you get a make on that device?" Skene asked.

"It's a scatter bomb. Homemade. Lots of shrapnel," Taylor said.

James rolled his shoulders and tugged on his tie as a cold sweat broke out on his body. This wasn't happening. In no possible way could Kinross access that much currency before the bomb went off. Charitable donations had poured in tonight at the auction, but the checks were written directly to the organization of the donor's choice. The kidnapper must be aware of that and had used this "ransom" as a metaphorical way to twist his knife.

No ransom could save Paisley and Torquil. They would die if the search parties didn't locate them before that timer went off. James's stomach roiled, and deep, searing pain, animalistic in its intensity, spread throughout his body.

Into this quagmire of emotion, Ward MacKenzie and Rahim entered the room. MacKenzie carried a map under one arm.

"I brought the estate map. I thought it might prove useful." MacKenzie unrolled the layout on top of the coffee table.

Kinross joined him.

Rahim lit up a cigarette and puffed out a cloud of smoke, his eyes roaming the occupants of the room as though noticing the tension for the first time. He came to a halt behind Munira's chair and rested a hand lightly on her shoulder.

Munira gave Rahim a furtive glance, then dropped her eyes to her lap, her nails digging into the fine silk upholstery.

"How old is Lord Crieffmore?" Agent Taylor asked suddenly.

"Eleven." A tear coursed down Munira's cheek.

"And who might you be?" Rahim asked Taylor, his eyes filled with interest.

"These are Agents Taylor and Benson with Secret Intelligence Service," Kinross said absently, his eyes poring over the map.

Agent Taylor flashed a brief smile that resembled more of a grimace. Benson, who stood in the doorway, nodded.

"You never let on that we had special guests this evening." Rahim stubbed out the cigarette he'd been smoking and glanced at Kinross.

"There's rather a lot I don't share." Kinross reached for the liqueur decanter, poured himself a shot of whiskey, and tossed it back.

Taylor rose to her full height from the upholstered chair, her crushed green velvet gown clinging to her figure, and joined Kinross and MacKenzie where they scoured the map.

"Your Grace, this is an old Scottish castle. Are there hidden tunnels or passages?" Agent Taylor asked.

"A secret passage might appeal to a child, especially if he was bored at an adult party and didn't want to be found. Could the kidnapper have used one to lure Torquil away?"

"Castle Rannoch has two secret passages," Rahim said.

"Three actually," Kinross corrected. "You're forgetting the one in the servants' staircase that leads to the cellars."

"I did, rather," Rahim agreed pleasantly.

"Would someone be willing to show us those passages?" Taylor asked, her gaze focusing on the castle's three chief residents.

David Hume, Kinross's chief of security, interrupted, "The police have just returned from searching the grounds. We can enlist their aid if someone will show them the way. That will provide more than enough people to divide into three parties."

"I'd be happy to show you," Rahim offered.

"Very good." Hume nodded.

Benson straightened to his impressive height. "I would be delighted to join you as well."

"Send six men to the red salon at once." Hume spoke into the mouthpiece attached to his headset as he exited the salon and followed Benson and Rahim into the corridor to await the rest of his team.

Only MacKenzie, Kinross, Munira, Taylor, and James remained. Kinross and MacKenzie discussed possible places left out of the previous search, then conferred with Agent Taylor.

"In the video call, I noticed the walls appeared rounded. Is there an old well on the estate, one in disuse?" Agent Taylor asked.

"None of the wells are dry. The water table is too high," Kinross said.

While Kinross, MacKenzie, and Taylor discussed possible hostage locations, James's eyes strayed to Munira.

Tears continued to seep down her face, but her jerky movements and inability to meet anyone's eyes spoke of something else too—something was preying on her mind. James decided it was time to put the thumbscrews to her and find out what she was holding back. He took a seat beside her in a matching chair.

"Your Grace?"

"Yes?" Munira turned to face him.

"I hope you'll forgive me, but we Americans cut to the chase when time is of the essence." James met Munira's eyes. "I know you don't like Paisley, but if you want Torquil back in one piece, we could use your assistance. Paisley isn't a bored little boy who wandered off and ran into a kidnapper. She knew how much this evening meant to Kinross."

"I beg to differ. Lady Margaret missed the reception line."

"She had a good reason, a reason that appears to have gotten her kidnapped."

Munira stiffened in her chair, her eyes like a hunted bird's.

"You know something." James narrowed his eyes.

"I know nothing." Munira shook her head vehemently.

"Yes, you do, and it has you frightened. Let me ask you this, Your Grace: if Torquil never returns, can you live with it?"

The duchess's chin quivered.

"Without a living heir to inherit, what will become of you if Kinross precedes you in death? Will his cousin let you stay at Castle Rannoch? Or will Rahim take care of you?"

Munira's hand jerked as though stung. "I would never live with Rahim."

"You live with him now."

"Not of my own—" Munira's words ended mid-sentence.

Progress. It wasn't just Paisley who Munira disliked. "Why won't you live with Rahim?"

Munira clamped her lips shut and refused to answer.

James was done. If semi-polite didn't work, it was time for mean. "My mother would have risked her life to save any of her children from harm. But *you*, you say nothing when you know it might help Torquil."

"How dare you." The duchess's eyes blazed. "You know nothing of what I have done to protect my family. For years I have—"

"Yes?"

Kinross, MacKenzie, and Taylor lifted their heads from the map and openly listened to his and Munira's exchange.

"My first husband was a terrorist. He took Rahim everywhere with him. Spoiled him. Indoctrinated him. When he died, I saw a chance to raise my son away from jihad and took it. Kinross knew I did not love him when we married. I was Muslim, but I 'converted' to Kinross's faith to put distance between those who would make my son become like . . ."

"Like?" James prodded softly.

"His father." Tears coursed down her cheeks, but the dam had burst within her and continued to pour, rushing at an ever-increasing tide. "Rahim was so young. I believed that if he grew up a proper gentleman, he would be safe from that life. Kinross treated him well, sent him to the best schools, gave him horses, cars, and a job. But he was not the heir, and Rahim resented it. Resented Kinross—grew to hate him and everything he cared for.

"During university, Rahim fell in with radicals." Munira's nails dug into the silk fabric. "Rahim resents Torquil—resents what will be his one day. He wishes to destroy his brother's birthright and to fund his own beliefs."

Kinross moved suddenly, but MacKenzie placed a hand on his arm and shook his head.

"Are you saying that Rahim is behind Kinross's financial loss?" James asked.

"I do not know. I only suspect. Who else has access to the proper codes? Who else would know when Kinross had scheduled that money transfer?"

Four of the five people in the room could have, but James refrained from saying so.

"I was relieved when Torquil went away to school. I thought it would be easier for him without Rahim, but the students bully Torquil because he is quiet and has a learning disability." Munira bowed her head and wept great wracking sobs that distorted her features.

"Forgive me, Duchess. You have tried to protect both your sons." James's heart went out to her.

Agent Taylor spoke quietly into her sports watch. "Benson, which passageways are you searching?" She waited a minute before her watch pinged with a text. "They are at the top of the castle," Taylor informed Kinross, her voice carrying so all in the room could hear. "May I suggest we search the passage that leads to the cellars before Benson returns with Mr. Zamar?"

"Yes, of course," Kinross agreed and started for the door.

"Is anyone lighting the pasture for our special forces unit?" Agent Taylor asked.

Kinross slowly turned to face her and expelled a heavy sigh. "This is ridiculous."

"I can't light the pasture. I have no idea where it is," Taylor said. "Nor does Mr. Pressley-Coombes."

"Ward, you light the pasture." Kinross deflected his assignment. "I'm searching the cellars for my children."

"Merry Way needs to be tethered or she'll spook, and Buttercup is in the field."

"That crazy cow?" Kinross clamped his jaw. "You catch her. I'll take care of the flares. Munira, please show Agent Taylor and Mr. Pressley-Coombes to the cellars. The rest of you examine that passageway. I'll see if I can convince the SF unit to help hunt for my children before it's too late."

Chapter 37

It was almost too late. James checked his watch. He stood shoulder to shoulder with Munira and Agent Taylor in front of a tall narrow cupboard on the servants' staircase.

"I think the catch is on the bumblebee's stinger, or it could be the middle of that daisy." Munira's fingers poked frantically at the wooden carvings, hunting for the camouflaged mechanism.

Click.

James stepped forward and pushed at the shelving unit. The cupboard rotated soundlessly on its center, revolving like a circular door and exposing a dark hole beyond.

"Put the stopper underneath the door," Munira said. "We have to make it secure. There isn't a mechanism inside to let us out if the door swings shut."

Taylor picked a wooden chock out of the basket on one of the shelves and wedged it in place.

"How do you normally reach the dungeon?" James asked, curious if there was a separate entrance from within the castle.

"From outside. The castle was originally built so supplies could be unloaded from carts and stored within the cellars," Munira said.

Dank, musty air filled the corridor. Agent Taylor started down the secret passage, her weapon drawn. James followed, and Munira brought up the rear. Braces for torches hung at intervals along the wall. The corridor hadn't seen a remodel since the late Middle Ages.

Agent Taylor sneezed.

Two sets of footprints showed clearly on the darkened plank floor—coming and going. Both appeared the same size and shape.

"Someone entered the passage recently. Those footprints are fresh." James pointed to a set of prints just inside the doorway.

"Where does this lead?" Agent Taylor asked, shining her flashlight into the dark passage.

"Down to the cellars," Munira answered, her voice not quite steady. "Torquil never plays there. It used to be a dungeon and is haunted by the white lady."

"With such an atmosphere, I would have stayed away myself," Taylor said.

"Who's the white lady?" James asked.

"The second Duke of Perth and Kinross's youngest daughter." Munira's voice shook more noticeably. "She met her lover in the cellars. Her father found them and locked her sweetheart down here to die. The white lady walks the cellars on stormy nights, calling for her lover."

"I'll have to tell my sister-in-law. She's a sucker for ghost stories," James said.

At the end of the passage, Munira pressed an iron lever. A camouflaged door slid open onto a wooden stairwell and descended into the cellars.

Agent Taylor started down the steps, one hand on the rail, the other holding her gun.

Munira's eyes were so wide that James could see the whites around her irises with his flashlight. Her fear was palpable. But he didn't have time to soothe her. If they didn't locate Paisley and Torquil soon, that bomb would finish them off.

"I will wait for you—" Munira's words were cut off by the slam of the cupboard door at the far end of the passage. "The white lady has locked us in here to die," Munira cried out and rushed back to pound with both fists on the backside of the cupboard.

Taylor raced up the stairs from the cellar floor, gun in hand. "What's happened?"

James motioned toward the closed cupboard door. "We're going to be down here for a little while." He didn't add that if Paisley and Torquil were down here, even if they found them in time, the bomb was likely to go off before they got out.

Agent Taylor holstered her gun.

"Duchess, calm yourself. When Kinross realizes we are missing, he will have the castle searched. Benson will do the same." Taylor texted a message to her partner and hit send. Her brow furrowed, and she hit send again.

Agent Taylor's pale-blue eyes were filled with worry when she turned to James. "Do you have mobile reception?"

James checked his cell phone bars. "No."

"May I suggest that we search the cellars while we wait? The time is ticking away," Taylor said, focusing on the business at hand.

"I will not go down there," Munira said. "I will wait for you on the stairs."

"Suit yourself," James said and followed Agent Taylor down to the cellar floor.

Oddly enough, the gloom didn't bother James. With Gothic arches soaring overhead supported by massive Medieval pillars, the space did not trigger his phobia.

"If Paisley and Torquil are down here, where would someone keep them?" Taylor called to Munira from the base of the stairs.

"I do not know. Kinross cleared the cellars years ago."

James started along one side of the vast area while Taylor took the other, their flashlights sweeping methodically over the space, searching for a place two small people could be secreted.

Growing impatient, James cupped both hands around his mouth and called, "Paisley? Are you down here?" His voice echoed throughout the chamber.

James reached the far end of the cellar. It was empty, just like Munira had said. Not even a leftover manacle remained attached to the wall. He scrubbed his face with both hands. Where was Paisley? They were running out of time.

A grating sound across the dungeon caught his attention. He glanced to the far side of the space. Agent Taylor appeared to be inspecting the floor.

"I think I found something," she said.

***

Achmed exited Castle Rannoch and took a deep breath of fresh air before he started down the steps to the drive.

Nigel Thatcher came out from the shadows, a pair of night-vision goggles wrapped about his forehead. He brandished a pair of handcuffs. Cold metal slapped around Achmed's wrist, then attached to Thatcher's.

"Achmed Razool, I am arresting you for collusion and extortion of William Bancroft. You do not have to say anything that may harm your defense . . ."

Achmed had heard the *Right to Silence* numerous times on the telly, just never in person. His shoulders slouched, and shame filled his body. He was a criminal, no better than any of those arrested on his favorite shows. No better than the anarchists of his homeland.

But Padma would live. Achmed had assured her safety by turning himself in—he wasn't all bad.

Instead of leading him to a waiting sedan, Officer Thatcher put on his NVG helmet and grasped him by the upper arm. "This way. I've a transport to meet."

They started down the lane. A hundred yards ahead, two dark figures stood out on the drive, making for the gatehouse, going the same direction as Officer Thatcher.

The moon had set, and the stars had hidden behind clouds. Despite the darkness, Thatcher pressed forward with the assurance of a man who knew the area well. The road dipped. Achmed stumbled and lunged forward onto one knee.

He grunted.

"Sorry about that," Thatcher said, his voice containing zero emotion.

"We can't all have NVGs to see where we're going." Achmed couldn't quite contain the bitterness from his tone.

He needn't have worried; Officer Thatcher wasn't attending. He had started forward, pushing to keep pace with the figures ahead.

"Slow down, Cam."

Achmed recognized Ward MacKenzie's voice.

"My head's pounding something fierce."

"You should have left off the booze tonight." Kinross's relentless pace didn't slow one iota.

"I only had two pints," MacKenzie defended.

A sharp breeze ruffled Achmed's hair, and he was glad for his coat. Why was Thatcher following Kinross?

"Och. Save your breath to cool your porridge." Kinross veered off the lane toward the shortcut through the woods. "You should never touch the stuff, and you know it; you don't have the head for it."

"You owe me a new door when this is over," MacKenzie grumbled.

"Aye. But you can't blame us for following our only lead, not with a bomb ticking," Kinross retorted.

"No, I suppose not. We'll find your children."

Achmed stiffened and turned toward Thatcher. "A bomb? I take it the duke's children are being held hostage?"

"They've been kidnapped, and time is running out." Thatcher yanked Achmed's arm when the figures ahead widened the gap between them.

"Why don't we let them know we're here?" Achmed asked.

"Because I'm not altogether sure MacKenzie isn't part of this," Thatcher hissed. "I want to see what he does."

Achmed didn't believe it of MacKenzie. The man and Kinross had been fast friends since early childhood.

Achmed's foot stepped on a branch. *Snap.*

One of the figures ahead of them turned back. "What was that?"

"Probably a deer," Kinross grunted. The killer pace he set was now close to a jog.

"Think we'll beat that transport to the pasture?" MacKenzie's voice floated back.

"It will be close. I wish I hadn't let the stable lads off for the night. They would have been a help with Buttercup."

"Aye. She's a rare beastie, that one," MacKenzie agreed darkly.

"Take her into the barn with Merry Way while I lay out the flares for our helipad," Kinross said, turning on his torch.

"Aye." MacKenzie clicked on his torch as well. "I was planning on it."

"Think they'll find my children?" Kinross's worry carried in the night air.

"I do. You've a lot of help, Cam. I doubt Lady Margaret and Lord Crieffmore have left the estate. Heaven help the kidnappers if they did." MacKenzie rubbed the back of his head. "They'll have a fair rousing if they do."

"Paisley and I had a row earlier this evening. I told her about emptying her trust fund." Kinross shone his torch onto one of the trees, turning the gold-colored leaves white in its glare.

"Didn't she understand about the resort shares you gave her?"

"I didn't get the chance to explain. She cut me off and left the ball."

"That doesn't sound good."

"It wasn't, but I can hardly blame the lass. She accused me of treating her like a second-class citizen. Fair broke my heart to see her so cut up."

The crunch of rocks underfoot and the occasional hoot of an owl were the only sounds to break the stillness.

MacKenzie slapped Kinross's back. "We'll find her. Don't you worry. She and Master Torquil can't be far. When you have the chance to tell her, the wee lassie will thank you for changing her inheritance. Our corporate bookings have exceeded all my projections. That lad of Richard's is a marketing genius. His online website is smoother than cream."

Kinross grunted. "Right now, I don't care about the resort build and its projections, not when my children are in danger."

"Sorry. I was trying to take your mind off things."

At length, Achmed and Thatcher emerged from the trees. The pasture lay before them with the mist hovering in low-lying depressions. In the middle of it, Achmed made out the shaggy-haired Highland bovine Lord Crieffmore had dubbed Buttercup. The notorious animal knocked down fences to frolic with Kinross's thoroughbred mares.

"Cheers." MacKenzie headed for the adjoining pasture to coral Buttercup.

Turning, Kinross let himself through the kissing gate and cut across the first field to reach the east pasture. The breeze picked up, tossing his kilt with it.

Achmed shivered. His cuffed hand was fairly frozen from the chill air.

"Now that MacKenzie's gone, we can catch up with Kinross," Thatcher said, heading toward the kissing gate.

"I'd rather not," Achmed said. Kinross was sure to recognize him. "I lost his million pounds." And had associated, no doubt, with those who had snatched the duke's children.

"Too bad." Thatcher yanked his arm and propelled him forward.

"Lord, you know I'm not much of a praying man," Kinross addressed the heavens.

Achmed's eyes bugged. Kinross was praying? In a field?

"It's been a while since we last had a chat. You ken I'm not one to burden others, even you, with my troubles, but things aren't good. My children have gone missing." Kinross spoke aloud, obviously not worried about being overheard. "I've made a terrible muddle of things as a parent. You ken I'm telling the truth when I say I would give up my title and estates just so I could tell Paisley and Torquil how much they are loved. Och. Dear God, I dinnae ken I can handle it if something happens to them. Please help us find them in time."

Achmed's heart ached for the proud man. By the look of things, Thatcher was not unmoved.

In the distance, the deep throb of a helicopter engine coming up the glen reached Achmed's ears.

"Hurry, Mr. Razool. Time is wasting." Thatcher tugged on his arm and started to jog. "We've got to reach that transport."

Kinross rushed across the field and climbed the last fence, landing squarely in the east pasture. Holding the torch with his chin, he dumped the contents of his bag on the ground and lit the flares, creating a makeshift helipad.

He turned on a second torch and waved both above his head to attract the chopper's attention. Within seconds, the helicopter circled, then began its descent, the wind from the blades whipping and tossing his kilt.

Achmed and Thatcher climbed the last fence together. The chopper landed about thirty yards south of Kinross. Achmed covered his eyes from the flying grass particles and sneezed. The helicopter was so loud that he doubted Kinross could hear their approach.

The duke backed to the fence line, well clear of the army transport. The noise was deafening. The engine cut, and the chopper blades slowly wound down and stilled. Men dressed in camo and loaded with gear hopped out the side door.

Their leader stepped forward. "Captain Sitwell, UKSF."

"Kinross."

"Your Grace." Sitwell turned back to his men. "This is the Duke of Perth and Kinross. Look smart."

Eight men stood at attention.

"We received orders to rendezvous with Officer Nigel Thatcher, SIS," Captain Sitwell said.

"We've another spook running free about my estate?" Kinross's tone held surprise.

"That would be me, Captain," Thatcher called and started forward, practically dragging Achmed with him.

Kinross turned, his eyes sweeping over Thatcher, then coming to rest on Achmed's manacled wrist.

The captain saluted Officer Thatcher.

"I have a man here in need of transport back to SIS," Thatcher said with a head tilt toward Achmed.

Captain Sitwell's eyes swept over Achmed, then swiveled back to Kinross. "Is there somewhere we can chain him until we wrap things here?"

Kinross's eyes hardened. "I have just the place."

With such a malevolent look in Kinross's eyes, Achmed prayed the duke did not find out about his role in the lost million.

"Brilliant. Johnson, escort this man to the castle and secure him until liftoff," Captain Sitwell ordered.

One of the SF men detached from the unit. Thatcher unlocked the handcuffs, drew on his gloves, and gave Jackson the key. Jackson cuffed both Achmed's wrists behind him.

"We need a map of the estate. Can we borrow one, Your Grace?" Thatcher asked.

"I'll have it sent out immediately."

Evidently, Thatcher outranked the captain. Achmed glanced up and found Kinross's eyes on him. He shuffled his feet, growing more uncomfortable by the minute.

"Your Grace, I strongly recommend everyone stays indoors until these militants are immobilized and rounded up."

"I will pass the word along. Do any of your men have bomb training?" Kinross folded his arms across his chest.

"Aye. Do you have a bomb on your hands?" Captain Sitwell asked.

"We do. My children were kidnapped tonight. A ransom video was sent twenty minutes ago showing my son and daughter lying imprisoned beside a bomb."

A gust of wind swirled about Achmed's legs accompanied by a spatter of rain.

Thatcher turned to Captain Sitwell. "Do your orders allow for a bomb search?"

"I'll call it in. I'm fairly certain a bomb applies." Captain Sitwell removed a military-issue SAT phone from one of his cargo pockets and placed a call.

"We'll rendezvous at the castle," Thatcher said.

"We're in." Sitwell's teeth flashed in the helicopter's landing lights as he repocketed his SAT phone.

"Excellent." Thatcher's eyes swept over the SF unit. "These men have automatic weapons and know how to use them. Stay alert. I'd prefer we avoid a twenty-first-century gunfight if at all possible. Dead men don't give up their secrets."

Jackson grabbed Achmed's upper arm, but Kinross blocked Achmed's way, forcing him to meet the duke's eyes.

"I intend to find out what you've done, Mr. Razool. You can count on it."

Chapter 38

A BOMB.

A thin sheen of sweat broke out on Paisley's body. She was stuck in the dark with a bomb. Paisley shifted, and the straw rustled beneath her. She couldn't see anything but the movement of those red numbers.

The person beside her stirred.

"Torquil? Is that you?"

"Aye." Torquil's voice sounded small and thin and scared. "Paisley?"

"Yes, it's me." Paisley put as much heartiness into her tone as she could muster. No sense letting him know about the bomb.

"Where are we? I can't see anything."

"We're in some type of enclosed space." *About to be blown to bits if we can't figure a way out of here.*

The straw rustled, and Torquil slid up alongside her.

Sensing his need for comfort, she wrapped her arm around him. "How did you get here? Do you remember what happened?"

"No."

"What was the last thing you remember?" Paisley asked.

"I got tired of waiting for the band to play 'The Duke of Perth,' so I went upstairs."

"Did you go to bed?"

"I don't think so. I didn't want anyone to see me leave the ball. Dad wouldn't have liked it, so I took the servants' stairs, the one in the turret. They have a secret passage behind the cupboard. I don't remember anything after that."

"The last thing I remember was being on those stairs too." She didn't tell him that his brother had jabbed her with a hypodermic needle. "Do you have any idea where we are, Torquil?"

"No."

"I'm not sure how we got in here," Paisley said. "There aren't any doors or windows." She rose to her feet and whacked her head. "Ouch."

"Are you quite all right?" Torquil asked, his voice concerned.

"I'm fine. The ceiling's too low to stand." Praying they hadn't been entombed, Paisley's fingers splayed across the rough stones overhead. She located an opening, like a vertical shaft, that was little more than three feet wide. A draft stirred her hair.

"I've found an opening above us. It feels like a shaft."

"We might be in the oubliette," Torquil said, his voice the merest whisper.

"An oubliette? What's that?"

"It's a hole they kept prisoners in a long time ago. For the last few centuries, we've used it as an ice house. There's a grate in the dungeon floor so no one will fall in," Torquil said.

"How deep is it?"

"Ah dinnae ken," Torquil responded in Scots.

"What?" Paisley had heard a few Scottish expressions since her arrival, but her father's impeccable English, and that of his staff, had kept her insulated from more common phrases.

"I don't know. Dad used a short ladder to get down there once."

"Oh." If Rahim had dropped them into the oubliette, no wonder her side hurt.

"Torquil?" Paisley took his hands in hers. "Do you think you could shimmy up that stack with your back on one side and your legs on the other?"

A pause. "Maybe." Torquil's voice sounded uncertain.

"You know what? I'd like to climb that funnel. You don't mind if I try, do you?" Paisley asked, realizing her brother must have a fear of heights.

"Och, no." The relief in Torquil's voice was almost comical.

It had been years since Paisley had last climbed, but once upon a time, she had been the neighborhood streetlight-climbing champion.

"I need to stand on your back to get a boost into the funnel. I probably don't weigh much more than you do. Do you think you can support me?"

"Aye."

Paisley removed her heels and nylons.

"Here, help me get this silly dress unbuttoned. I can't climb up to that grate if it keeps tangling against my legs."

Torquil complied, and the dress slithered off her shoulders onto the floor of their cell, leaving her clad in her slip. Fresh goosebumps broke out across her skin.

"Okay. I'm ready."

He knelt beside her, directly under the chimney. She climbed onto his back, her head immediately entering the narrow funnel. He shifted under her feet, and she promptly lost her balance and fell heavily onto her bruised side.

"Agh." Paisley sucked in.

"Sorry. Are you hurt?"

"I'm good." Paisley gritted her teeth and waited a second for the pain to subside, her eyes on the ever-changing timer. "Let's try that again. This time, I'll use your back to spring into the chimney."

Tentatively, she placed a foot on Torquil's back and lifted off, her head immediately entering the funnel. With her forearms braced on either side of the stack, she swung one leg up, her bare toes gripping stone on the far side.

Torquil sneezed and jostled her. Her hold wasn't firm enough, and she slipped and landed on top of him.

"Ow," Torquil cried out. "You weigh a lot."

"I do not." Paisley sat up and rubbed her hip, realizing suddenly that she needed a way to pull Torquil out once she reached the top. Gathering up her gown, she double looped it around her neck to keep her arms free.

"I'm going to stand on your shoulders, then I want you to get up."

Carefully, Paisley climbed onto Torquil's shoulders, then as her brother rose to his feet, she grasped the rocks for a handhold to help take the weight off her brother.

"Hold steady."

Torquil swayed, but he managed to keep on his feet. She placed a bare foot on the far side of the chimney wall, her toes digging into the cracks between the stones. Simultaneously, she pressed her back against the opposite wall, her hands splaying on the surface behind her, using the crevices between the stones for leverage.

Bent almost double, Paisley used her legs and back like a spring tension rod between two windows and inched her way up the wall, pushing with her hands and forearms, then thrusting up with her feet.

Over and over, like a crazy relay, she went up the narrow funnel until her limbs shook with fatigue and sweat dripped down her face.

When she reached the grate, Paisley was too exhausted to lift her arms over her head and remove it. So she stayed where she was, scrunched in half, suspended in the air, trying to breathe. The only thing keeping her from falling was the pressure between her back, forearms, and feet.

Her body trembled from the cramped position, and a sharp pain started in her right calf muscle, then escalated, radiating up her entire leg. She gasped.

"Paisley," two voices called in tandem—one from below and one from above.

The pain was too intense. Her fingers loosened their hold, and she started to slip.

Above her, a light flashed. The grate lifted, and years of dirt and metal shavings dropped into her eyes. But it was too late. She couldn't hold on and slipped further, her one leg entirely useless. A strong pair of hands grabbed her under the arms and lifted her clear of the chimney.

When her toes touched the floor, she crumpled into a ball on the cold stones and gripped her calf, stretching the cramped muscle until the charley horse subsided.

James crouched beside her and hugged her close, his lips grazing her temple. She clutched him tightly while tears slid down her cheeks. He had come for her. He always came for her.

"Paise, are you okay?" James held her back, his flashlight skimming over her body.

"Yes. Torquil's down there." Urgency filled her. "Use my dress to pull him out." Paisley loosened the gown from around her neck.

"Good thinking." Agent Taylor took Paisley's gown while James draped his tuxedo jacket around her shoulders.

"Please hurry," Paisley said. "There's a bomb."

***

Achmed's humiliation knew no bounds. Jackson frog-marched him back to the castle and cuffed him to the iron fender beside the fireplace, leaving him on full display to the room's occupants like an animal in a cage.

"Stay put," Kinross warned him.

The search parties had regrouped in the red salon and hallway to report their findings. Kinross's wife, her son, Agent Taylor, and James Pressley-Coombes were missing.

"You are saying my wife hasn't returned from searching the hidden passage to the cellars?" Kinross asked DI Skene, his eyebrows raised.

"No, Your Grace." Skene adjusted his helmet strap. "Agent Benson texted, then called Agent Taylor's mobile, but there was no response. Mr. Zamar left his search party to help them."

"Munira would never stay down there of her own free will. She's terrified of the place—so is Torquil." Kinross spun on his heel and started toward the hallway where Captain Sitwell's unit had congregated to await orders.

Achmed's eyes widened at the duke's behavior. Kinross appeared to have forgotten who was in charge.

"When all else fails, ask the military. They know how to get a job done," Kinross muttered, stopping in the doorway to the salon. "Captain, is your unit ready to search the cellars?"

"Ready and willing, Your Grace." The hall light glinted off Captain Sitwell's helmet.

"Good. Follow me," Kinross said.

"Out of the way." Agent Benson jostled past the special forces men as he propelled himself to Captain Sitwell's side.

"You're a civilian, Your Grace," Skene said to Kinross. "You need to stay above stairs so we can do our job."

"This is my home, and they are my children. I have a right to be there," Kinross argued.

"You will only be in the way," DI Skene said, reasserting his command. "Stay put, Your Grace, or I'll have you arrested."

***

Paisley knelt on the cellar floor beside the hole to the oubliette. "Torquil, there's a clock down there with red numbers. Tell me what it says," she called.

Shuffling sounds rose up the stack from below.

"Eight minutes," Torquil hollered.

Paisley sat back on her bare heels and deflated. It had taken her nine to climb the chimney. She clenched her hands, and her breath came in short gasps. Eight minutes until the bomb exploded. Eight minutes to get Torquil out of that hole. And eight minutes to tell James how much she loved him.

It isn't enough time!

Paisley's mouth went dry, and she swallowed convulsively. "If we anchor James so he can hang from his waist into the chimney and extend my gown to Torquil, he could drape the knotted sleeves under his arms, and James could pull him up, couldn't he?" Paisley asked Agent Taylor.

"It's worth a try," Taylor said.

With Paisley holding the flashlight, James knotted her gown's sleeves together, then tore the skirt, knotted it tightly, and draped it around his neck. Paisley and Agent Taylor each held one of his legs to make sure he didn't slip farther into the chimney. It was a tight squeeze, but James was able to lower his torso into the funnel.

"Torquil, I'm above you in the chimney." James's voice was muffled. "I've lowered Paisley's dress. Loop the sleeves over your shoulders and under your arms. I'm going to pull you out. We need to do this quickly. Let me know when you're ready."

"I've got the dress," Torquil said. "Wait."

Paisley chewed the inside of her lip, her arms stabilizing James's weight.

"Ready?" James asked, his tone as calm as though they had all the time in the world.

"Aye."

"Up we go," James grunted.

"Walk backward," Taylor instructed Paisley. "It's easier to pull them out that way."

Paisley complied, her frozen feet scrabbling numbly against the smooth stones, straining with everything she had.

James's torso and head came out of the hole, then the top of Torquil's head emerged immediately after. James had pulled Torquil up by the dress until he had the boy's forearms clasped firmly in his own.

"Step it up, we're almost out of time," Taylor said. "Run to the far side of the cellar. Cover your head. Now!" Agent Taylor commanded.

Taylor took Torquil's hand in hers and pulled him to his feet. Paisley turned to run and stumbled over her frozen toes, her bare feet refusing to cooperate. James clasped her free hand in his and propelled her forward.

"Go, James. You can run faster than me. Go." Paisley tried to pry her hand free.

"I love you. We go together," James said matter-of-factly, then almost yanked her arm from its socket in his effort to speed her along.

Torquil and Taylor soon outdistanced them.

Paisley tripped and fell to one knee, but James kept her upright and half dragged her. When she couldn't regain her footing fast enough, he picked her up like a sack of potatoes and slung her over his shoulder, his shoes pounding on the cobbles in the direction of the stairs.

Boom.

The floor rocked. Debris shot into the air, and something hard hit Paisley in the shoulder and side. Pain lanced through her.

One minute they were running, and the next, she and James were tumbling across the stone floor.

Chapter 39

Paisley tumbled in a dark sea, her ears ringing. Pain. She swam up from the deep. Muffled shouts came from a long way off. Her body shook, and her shoulder was like ice on the outside and burned like hot embers under her skin.

"Stay with me, Paise. Oh, baby, please stay with me. I need you to stay with me." James's voice broke.

Why was James upset?

"Sweetheart, listen to me. Don't leave me. You're the most important—"

Important. Paisley opened her mouth to tell James. It was important. "Rahim," her voice croaked.

"What is it, baby?" James leaned closer and kissed her forehead, his hands holding hers.

"It was Rahim. Rahim did this," her voice croaked. Her mouth was dry, like she had swallowed sand.

Darkness edged her vision, and she was swimming again, struggling to stay afloat in the sea of blackness. "James . . ."

But it was too hard to speak, and she floated away.

***

Due to Castle Rannoch's remote location, Captain Sitwell's military transport flew them to the Golden Jubilee National Hospital in Clydebank. Paisley had regained consciousness before takeoff, answering the unit medic's questions coherently enough to dispel his immediate concern. Though favoring her arm, she and James had entered the helicopter on their own steam, as had Torquil. Munira and Agent Taylor had followed on stretchers.

The pilot had called ahead and the A&E staff was waiting for them when they arrived. Agent Taylor had rebroken her pelvis. Munira had suffered a concussion and tinnitus due to the eruption in an enclosed space. Other than a slight concussion, James had gotten off with a few stitches. Torquil had a ruptured eardrum and a cut that required nothing more than what the Brits referred to as a sticking plaster—what looked like a simple Band-Aid.

The doctor had set Paisley's collarbone and stitched some lacerations on her back from flying debris. Her vitals had continued to drop. That's when medical personnel whisked her away for exploratory surgery.

Internal injuries.

James had been walking for what seemed like hours along the River Clyde and praying harder than he had done in years. He clenched and unclenched his fists, his body rigid. Would the medical personnel find the issue in time? His mind looped back to the doctor's words.

Exploratory surgery.

That was just another way of saying they had no freaking clue what was wrong with Paisley.

James's tattered tux garnered a few stares when he passed people on the pavement outside the hospital. Finding a bench, he faced the river and buried his face in his hands. That's when he started to shake, the fear twisting his guts into knots.

Paisley had always been part of his life—the best part.

Memories of their shared childhood washed over him, of the time that jerk kid in her fifth-grade class had teased her about her glasses. James had found Paisley crying in his backyard. He had pried the information out of her in very small increments before he figured out what had happened.

The next day, he and Ben had cut middle school to pay Paisley's bully a visit on the elementary school playground. They hadn't touched the kid, but that little twerp and his nasty friends had never bothered Paisley again. No one made Paisley cry, not on his watch.

Whitecaps danced on the River Clyde, and an icy wind stirred his hair and cut through his tux. James pushed the heels of his palms into his eyes and groaned. Why had it taken him so long to figure out that he loved her?

It was so obvious now that he was aware. How many guys abandoned a hot date to help a girl fix her garbage disposal? And that wasn't the only occasion he had bailed on a date for Paisley. Throughout high school and after, he'd mocked Jack for his girl-stupid ways. But James had been every bit as thick. God had placed his own girl half a mile from Edgehill House, and he had been too blind to notice.

Now, just days after he had come to his senses, Paisley was hemorrhaging from internal injuries. James raked a hand through his hair and considered going back inside the hospital to pace its claustrophobic halls.

Before he could, his cell phone rang. Too miserable to respond, he let it go to voice mail. A few seconds later, it rang again. He scowled and considered chucking the annoying contraption into the Clyde.

"Leave a freaking message already," he muttered, pulling the phone from his pocket to hang up.

Ben's face lit up his caller ID screen. Why was Ben calling? It was the middle of the night in the States.

"Hey," James answered.

"I swear if you didn't pick up, I was going to fly over there and pop you one," greeted his twin.

"What are you doing awake?"

"I don't know. Why don't you tell me? That twin vibe of yours woke me out of a dead sleep. What's going on?" Ben asked, sounding crankier than a cow in need of milking.

Their intuitive link was not uncommon among twins. Over the years, James had come to realize other identical twins shared similar connections. He attributed it to the whole wombmate thing.

"Paisley's hurt," James said.

"I'm sorry to hear that. Is she going to be okay?" Ben sounded a little more awake.

"I don't know. Her vitals keep dropping. They took her in for exploratory surgery."

"What happened?" Real concern filled Ben's voice.

"She and her brother were kidnapped and held for ransom—with a bomb. We barely got them out in time before it went off."

"A bomb? As in things that go boom?"

"You heard me."

"Are you okay?"

"Yeah. Just a few scratches." James had refused treatment when the doctor had diagnosed him with a slight concussion. "I've been such an idiot. She's the one, Ben."

"I figured that out in middle school."

"You knew?" James couldn't believe Ben had never mentioned it.

"Of course I knew. The whole family knew. Strike that. Jack didn't; but he doesn't count."

James gazed unseeing across the river as the rain clouds darkened to deep gray.

"Will you call me when she comes out of surgery?" Ben yawned on the question.

"Yeah, I will. Night." James disconnected.

A droplet of water hit James on the head, then a few more spattered his clothes. Without warning, the heavens opened, pelting the pavement, himself, and the bench. James sprinted for the hospital. By the time the sliding glass doors parted, sleet had set in.

In silence, he rode the elevator up to the surgical waiting room, sharing the compartment with a nurse just coming on shift and an intern with a meal cart that smelled of overcooked vegetables.

James got off at Paisley's floor, turned the corner, and halted outside the waiting room doors. He hated everything about the clinical ambiance and worried eyes of those around him as they waited for news. But if he didn't go inside, he wouldn't find out what was happening with Paisley. And not knowing was killing him.

***

"Any news?" James asked Agent Benson, the only other occupant of the waiting room except a well-to-do couple sitting by the windows.

"Lady Margaret's still in surgery," Benson informed him. "The duchess was just wheeled to her room. The doctor is hopeful she will have a full recovery. Kinross and Crieffmore are helping her get situated."

Benson rocked back on his dust-coated heels. His tux wasn't in much better shape than James's, having entered the cellars shortly after the explosion with Sitwell's men to search for survivors.

"Agent Taylor has a broken pelvis, her second in as many years." Benson cleared his throat, his eyes sober. "I doubt SIS will keep her in the field after this."

"I'm sorry to hear that," James said. Taylor was an exceptional agent.

"Riding a desk isn't Taylor's style. This won't go over well."

"That's too bad. Any news on Captain Sitwell's unit?"

"They rounded up four men outside a crofter's cottage above the castle." Benson flashed his crooked incisor. "That's not all they found."

"What do you mean?"

"The cottage was a kitted-out lab. Our forensics team is collecting samples as we speak. It appears this cell created a toxic powder that is untraceable when wetted. One of the terrorists confessed to wildlife experiments in the Treshnish Isles, Pitlochry, and the Cairngorms."

"They were connected to the murders on Lunga." James exhaled loudly. Up until now, it had only been supposition.

"No one has confessed to the Robertson murders. Ballistic testing on the firearms retrieved from the cottage, along with wreckage recovered by our divers, will confirm it soon enough."

Agent Taylor was wheeled past just then by two orderlies.

"Well, I'm off," Benson said and headed for the door.

"Where are you going?"

"Agent Taylor's room. Rahim Zamar is still at large. I'll be playing watchdog until he's found."

"You're a very conscientious partner."

"Taylor and I go way back." Benson shoved his hands inside his pockets.

Sensing a whirlpool of emotions swirling beneath Benson's surface, James switched topics. "What's being done to find Rahim?"

"We've put an APW on Rahim Zamar to all airports, railway stations, and ports. He can't leave the country unless it's by private boat. With the North Sea and Atlantic so rough this time of year, it would be foolhardy to try. We'll find him. It's only a matter of time."

***

Rhythmic beeps. Rolling carts. The smell of disinfectant with an overlay of roses. "Dr. Holland, call the nurses' station. Dr. Holland," a female voice announced over a PA system.

The tight squeezing of Paisley's upper arm pulled her from a state of semi-consciousness. She opened her eyes and stared at the nurse beside her hospital bed.

"Good morning, Lady Margaret." The nurse removed a blood-pressure cuff from Paisley's arm and jotted something on her tablet. She had short-cropped hair, and her nametag read Carole. "Your vitals are much better today."

"Today?" Paisley's voice was faint, the merest whisper.

"You've been sleeping around the clock. Are you still a little woozy from your surgery?"

Paisley shrugged, and pain jolted her shoulder.

"Sorry. Try not to wiggle that shoulder too much."

Paisley glanced at her arm; it was encased in a blue sling. "What's wrong with it?"

"You've cracked your collarbone, lass. You gave us all quite a scare, but Dr. Holland found your torn liver and patched you up." Carole held a digital thermometer a few inches from her forehead and pulled the trigger.

Beep.

"Your friend here's got a broken pelvis."

Friend? Paisley turned her head and noticed the second bed. Agent Taylor smiled faintly. Her skin was as pale as parchment. Her eyes were dull, and she appeared faintly put out, despite the wireless earbuds and e-reader in her hands.

"We were short on rooms. I hope you don't mind sharing." Carole recorded Paisley's temperature on her tablet.

"Not at all." Paisley closed her eyes as a wave of dizziness crashed over her. "Where is James?"

"He stepped out a wee bit ago to shower and change. Your father told him he smelled and needed to see to his personal hygiene," Taylor said.

Paisley tried not to laugh and jiggle her shoulder. When it came to hygiene, James was fastidious. By the sound of things, her father and James had a male standoff in the works.

James didn't care about titles. To him, people proved who they were by their behavior. Despite Kinross's hardworking ways, he was a duke, and preferential treatment had been given him all his life, whether he demanded it or not.

Agent Taylor removed her earbuds. "Kinross and your brother went down the hall to check on the duchess."

"What's wrong with Munira?" Paisley asked.

"She's concussed. So is James, but he refuses to stay in bed."

Paisley rolled her eyes. That sounded like James. "What about Torquil?"

"He has some inner-ear damage the doctor said would heal. We were lucky it was a scatter bomb."

"How so? I'm not well versed in bombs," Paisley said. Agent Taylor had obviously forgotten she was speaking to a civilian.

"They're usually homemade devices that are partially filled with nails and metal. The shrapnel is deadly, but they don't destroy buildings. Because the bomb exploded inside the oubliette, the shrapnel was largely contained below the cellar floor. Our injuries were largely due to its detonation in an enclosed space."

Tension drained from Paisley's body and left her exhausted. "Is the castle damaged?"

"One of the pillars needs reinforcing. James's father and brother are on their way to oversee the repairs."

"That's a long way to come just to fix a pillar."

"James muttered something about babysitting." Agent Taylor's eyes twinkled.

Agent Benson poked his head inside the doorway. "I'm going down the hall to get some coffee. I'll be back in a few minutes. Do you ladies want anything?"

"Could you ask the nurses' station to keep an eye on our room until you return?" Taylor asked.

"On it," Benson said.

"Did anything come of the photos I gave you?" Paisley asked after Benson left the room.

Paisley doubted Taylor could give her much information—it was probably classified—but she wanted to know if her pictures had triggered interest up the MI6 chain.

"I passed your photos to my boss. He made some calls, and a special forces unit arrived at the castle shortly before the bomb detonated. Thanks to you, our SF unit flushed out a terrorist cell in the hills above Castle Rannoch. They had fitted up a lab in that crofter's cottage."

"A lab?" That was the last thing Paisley had expected to hear.

"Yes. Evidently, they had manufactured a toxic powder that dissolves with moisture."

The seals. Paisley's heart jumped.

The seals had died of a toxic powdery substance. When the armed men had appeared in the background of her photos, she had strongly suspected they were part of the group she and James had witnessed on Lunga—the ones who had murdered the captain and Rod.

Paisley offered a silent prayer of gratitude that her pictures had led to their arrests.

"Several of those apprehended were suspects in the Copenhagen bombing last year."

"What about the Robertsons, the men who were murdered on that excursion boat?" Paisley fingered the thin blanket on her bed.

"They've sent divers to recover wreckage. They'll run ballistics to see if anything matches the weapons recovered from the cottage." Taylor put down her e-reader. She popped in her earbuds and closed her eyes.

Paisley followed suit, but she couldn't rest, her mind considering everything that had occurred. How many lives would have been lost if that powder had been used on a population base? She shivered at the thought.

An orderly entered the room and checked Agent Taylor's IV fluid. Paisley could hear him moving a few things around before he pulled the privacy curtain partially closed between her and Agent Taylor's beds.

Paisley opened her eyes to tell him to keep the partition open. Rahim stood at her bedside dressed in scrubs, a large pillow in his hands. While the police watched the UK borders, he must have doubled back and raided a hospital storage closet. His dark eyes were filled with fury.

She sucked in. "Aa—"

Rahim slammed the pillow over her face.

She kicked out, fighting to get Taylor's attention while her good hand clawed at Rahim's arm to dislodge the pillow.

"Lady Margaret?" Agent Taylor's voice came from a long way off.

Paisley's lungs burned like fire. Everything was red. Her heart raced, and her chest was crushing her.

Rahim pressed harder.

Paisley's strength failed, and her legs stilled. Sounds faded into the distance, and a great whooshing filled her ears.

She was dying.

James . . .

Chapter 40

James walked past the nurses' station, a massive bouquet of helium balloons in one hand and a large stuffed Highland cow in the other. He smelled a little more human after his shower and quick trip across the street for new clothes.

Paisley was going to be all right. The surgeon had located the liver tear and had patched her up. All she had to do now was stay down and heal. And he was going to make sure that she did, because they had things to discuss. Big things. Things her father wasn't going to like one little bit. A smile tugged at the corner of James's mouth.

The empty chair outside Paisley's room had him stepping up his pace. Where was Benson? He was supposed to guard Paisley's room. Unease slithered across James's skin.

Rahim was still at large. Security footage had shown Munira's son leaving Castle Rannoch in a sedan. Scotland police had located his abandoned car in a layby just past Tempar a few hours later.

Metal crashed inside Paisley's room. Footsteps slapped in the corridor, coming fast from the coffee station. James sprinted to Paisley's door. Agent Taylor was on the floor beside her bed, an IV stand on the floor. A man in scrubs stood over Paisley's bed, a pillow pressed to her face.

James let go of the balloons and stuffed cow, took three running steps, and launched himself into the air.

Pop. Pop. Pop.

Two different guns fired in quick succession from two different angles.

James tackled Rahim's body as it crumpled to the floor and slammed Paisley's bedside cart into the wall. Three red-singed holes showed high on Rahim's chest. James recoiled, scrabbling backward like a crab, his stomach writhing with revulsion.

Sulfur. Blood. Smoke.

James vomited on the floor beside Paisley's bed.

Benson vaulted over him and yanked the pillow from Paisley's face. She gasped and made a huge sucking noise. Agent Taylor lay prone on the linoleum, panting, a gun still in her hand. Benson, too, smelled of gunpowder.

James's stomach lurched again. Some hero. He wiped his mouth with the back of his hand and got to his feet.

Medical personnel rushed in and one of the nurses screamed.

"We need a stretcher in here," Agent Benson barked out orders, then leaned over Paisley. "Are you all right, Lady Margaret?"

What a stupid question. James stepped over Rahim's body and came around the opposite side of Paisley's bed.

"James." Paisley's voice was no more than a whisper.

James grasped her good hand, careful of the IV.

"What happened?" Paisley croaked.

"You mean besides Rahim trying to suffocate you?" James's bouquet of helium balloons hovered near the ceiling. Their colorful ribbons dangled and bobbed in an irreverent display of cheerfulness. James shoved the balloon strings out of his face.

"Is he . . . ?" Paisley kept her eyes averted from the floor beside her bed.

"Yes," Benson said, his voice grim. "I don't know how he got past the nurses' station."

"He was dressed like an orderly. Even I didn't give him a second glance," Taylor gritted out in obvious pain.

"Where's that stretcher?" Benson demanded of two nurses who stood in the doorway, gaping like newly caught fish. "She's got a broken pelvis. We need to lift her onto the bed." Benson behaved like a man used to command. "And while you're at it, one of you call the local DI and send him over here."

Benson squatted on the floor beside Taylor. "I'm terribly sorry. I should never have left, but I must say, that was a nice piece of shooting."

"I was almost too late," Taylor said. "He moved my call button out of reach. Good thing he didn't find my gun in that bedside cart."

"How did you end up on the floor?" Benson asked.

"I couldn't shoot from the bed. Mr. Zamar had pulled the curtain." Agent Taylor grimaced and closed her eyes.

Two orderlies arrived and lifted Taylor onto a gurney, then carefully deposited her back onto her bed.

Dr. Holland, a short man with a paunch, entered with a retinue of medical personnel chattering over the top of one another.

"Ms. Taylor fell out of bed."

"He tried to suffocate Lady Margaret."

"Shots."

Dr. Holland knelt beside Rahim and checked his vitals. "Dead." He glanced at the clock and called the time. "Anyone know this fellow's name?"

"Rahim Zamar," James supplied. "His mother is the Duchess of Perth and Kinross."

"Thank you," Dr. Holland said, jotting a note on his tablet. "Wheel Miss Taylor to X-ray. I need to see if that fall has worsened her injury."

Two of his retinue detached themselves and wheeled Agent Taylor down the hall on her bed. Benson hovered in the doorway observing his partner before he turned back to the room.

"Can you open your mouth and stick out your tongue, Lady Margaret?" Dr. Holland stepped over Rahim's body to reach Paisley's bedside and brandished a small light.

Paisley did as she was told.

"Mr. Pressley-Coombes, get back from this bed while I am with my patient. You are already in my black books for refusing treatment after my prognosis."

James turned to the sink to wash Rahim's blood from his hands and rinse out his mouth.

"I'm going to listen to your lungs and heart. Let me warm up my stethoscope. There. That's not so bad, is it?" The doctor was all sweetness and bedside manner with Paisley.

Paisley started to laugh, and tears poured unheeded down her face.

"Hmmm. Patient is exhibiting signs of mild hysteria." Dr. Holland entered something on his electronic pad. "Perhaps a diazepam."

"I think she's entitled," James defended, tired of the doctor's flip-flopping behavior. "She was almost murdered, and a dead body is lying five feet from her bed."

"Yes. Yes. No doubt. Perhaps not such an uncommon reaction in a situation such as this." Dr. Holland turned to Carole, Paisley's nurse. "Wheel Lady Margaret's bed into the corridor so she doesn't have to look at this corpse."

Carole removed the stops on Paisley's bed wheels.

Benson stirred in the doorway. "After Lady Margaret leaves, make sure no one enters this room or tampers with anything in here until the DI releases the body to the coroner. This is a crime scene."

"I want my balloons." Paisley motioned toward the balloons bobbing about the ceiling.

"What?" Benson looked as though she had lost her mind.

"James always brings me balloons when I'm sick. Those are mine." Paisley pointed to the helium balloons.

"I'm sorry, Lady Margaret. They're evidence," Benson said.

"I agree," Paisley rasped. "They're evidence of James's concern, and I'm not giving them up." She turned her head. "James, can you tie them to my bed?" Paisley ignored Benson's request.

James gathered the bouquet of balloons and followed Paisley's procession into the corridor. Agent Benson brought up the rear and resumed his seat outside the hospital room.

"I don't think you need to guard the room anymore," James said.

"I need to safeguard the crime scene and provide a statement when the local DI arrives." Benson planted his feet shoulder-width apart. "Then I've got to inform the duchess that her son is dead."

***

One week later.

Paisley reclined on the chaise lounge in her bedroom, a tartan rug over her legs.

Kinross rapped on her open door and poked his head around the frame.

"Come in. I'm awake."

The duke hesitated. This was the first time he had sought Paisley's individual company since their falling out at the charity ball gala. More silver showed at his temples, and he wore his glasses full-time, as though his eyes were too tired to do their job properly.

Munira had only left her suite once—for Rahim's funeral the day after his death, as befitting those of his faith.

"How are you feeling?" Kinross's gaze bounced around the room, never settling on any object for long.

"Better every day."

"Are you? Truly?"

"Yes. In fact, I've been editing my portfolio. James is helping me create an online gallery for my website."

"That's verra good." Kinross placed his hands behind his back and paced in front of the chaise lounge before he stopped to look at her. "I need your help."

Paisley's brows rose. "I'd be happy to help in any way I can."

"Munira is still concussed and in deep mourning. Could you meet with Mrs. Grant and select menus for the next few weeks? Two business dinners are scheduled, and I have absolutely no idea how to go about planning the domestic side of things."

"And you think I do?" Paisley hid a smile.

"You would certainly be much better at it than I," Kinross said. "I've never so much as made tea."

"You do have a point."

"Also, you might be happy to know that we are expecting guests. Richard and Benjamin Pressley-Coombes are due tomorrow afternoon. Would it be possible to meet with the housekeeper and select their rooms so she can prepare for their arrival?"

"Of course." Paisley bit the inside of her bottom lip. Organizing menus in a foreign country with foreign food wasn't intimidating in the least . . . Who was she kidding? Scots didn't even call eggplants *eggplants*. They were aubergines.

While Paisley didn't mind haggis, it wasn't her first, second, or third choice at a restaurant. And though she adored fish and chips, especially with homemade tartar sauce, it wasn't exactly something her father would serve at one of his business dinners.

Panic bubbled inside, frothing higher and higher as she considered the possible issues that could arise from poor supper decisions. Granny would know what to do. She had run the castle for many years. Surely she could give Paisley pointers about what to serve for a business dinner.

Kinross wandered to the window, then toyed with a brass peacock on top of the desk that served as a paperweight. "I am deeply sorry for the distress I caused you at the charity ball."

She rolled the fringe on the edge of the plaid blanket between her fingers and refused to look up. Paisley didn't want to have this discussion, but she had expected it. Eventually, she knew she had to address what lay between them, the issue that had kept them stationed in their emotionally polite corners for the last week.

All her life Paisley had been polite, grateful for whatever crumbs of affection her mother had tossed in her direction. She had dreamed that her father was different, that if he knew her, she would matter to him—a dream she had consoled herself with during hard times. She had beat herself up over the years hoping her mom would change and blaming herself when she didn't. Since her arrival in Scotland, her father hadn't been much better.

Now she had the chance for real happiness with the love of a good man. A loyal man. A man she had leaned on throughout her entire life and had refused to see their relationship for what it was. Timing was everything, she supposed. A year ago, she wouldn't have looked twice at James. Now he was her world.

"Please hear me out, Paisley," Kinross said.

She glanced up, her hands stilling in her lap.

"I am guilty of emptying your trust fund. It was the only thing I could liquidate in time to finance the resort build, or dozens of Highlanders would have lost their jobs. They counted on me to help them provide for their families. Some of them had already relocated to the area from Aberdeen and Inverness when we were awarded subcontracts.

"But lass, I didn't take your money without your best interest at heart. I put your name on my shares in the resort build to the equivalent amount of your trust. Due to James's early online marketing strategies, we have almost doubled our initial investment, and our doors aren't due to open for another eighteen months."

Paisley looked up at him. He still didn't understand why she had been so hurt. "Dad, I wasn't upset about the money. That was the last thing on my mind. I was crushed because I always come dead last with you and Mom. Neither of you consider my feelings before you act. That's what hurt so deeply."

"For what it's worth, I do understand and beg your pardon. I'm sorry for causing you such distress."

Kinross removed his glasses and cleaned them on the end of his button-down shirt. "When you and Torquil went missing, many things were made clear to me. I realized that if the castle had blown up, it wouldn't have mattered to me, not if I had lost you and Torquil. I got off-course from the things that mattered most. I'm here to ask you for a second chance—a chance to prove that you matter, that you aren't a second-class citizen. I want to show you how I feel with a gift of my time. Do you think you can bear it?"

"Bear it?" Paisley sniffed, and her watery eyes spilled over. "That's why I came to Scotland, Dad. I came to spend time with you. To get to know you. To see if I belonged."

Careful of her shoulder, her father knelt on the floor beside the chaise lounge and gathered her close. "You belong, little one. Never doubt that for an instant. Please don't cry."

Paisley sobbed even harder because for the first time since she could remember, her dad held her like he really loved her.

Chapter 41

James glued the final piece of Paisley's camera housing in place and sat back in his desk chair to admire his handiwork. A few chinks were glaringly absent, but it was the best he could do. He had even cleaned the camera strap and reattached it to the housing.

Every night for the last week, instead of going downstairs to snuggle with Paisley on the sofa and binge watch *Doctor Who* reruns, he had labored to reconstruct her casing. He rolled his shoulders and rose stiffly to his feet, determined to see if she was still awake.

He wandered the ground floor of the castle, poking his head into various salons before he found her in Kinross's office. Kinross had an open laptop on his thighs. He and Paisley sat close together on a sofa with Digger sprawled fast asleep on her lap.

James rapped on the doorframe to announce his presence, then sauntered into the room, giving the coal fire a wide berth.

He pointed at the pup. "Smuggling contraband into forbidden territory while the duchess is incapacitated?"

Digger raised his head from Paisley's lap when he heard James's voice, gave a sleepy yawn, and thumped his tail.

"He was making a racket in the kitchen, so Dad brought him upstairs," Paisley said. "Dad's showing me family pictures. Come and join us." She patted the open spot beside her on the couch.

He complied, scooting close, his hand ruffling Digger's soft fur.

"This is Torquil on his first pony. The lad loves horses and spends an excessive amount of time at the stables. The stablemaster has high hopes he will keep our racing program in top form after I'm gone." Kinross's voice was filled with pride.

A picture of Paisley popped up on the screen.

"I'm surprised you have so many pictures of me," Paisley said.

"I told you I hired a private investigator to take them. After Richard and I met by sheer accident, I asked if he would send me photos from time to time as well." Kinross bobbed his head from side to side. "He and Dana made sure I was well supplied."

"That was kind of them," Paisley said.

"If you think the Pressley-Coombeses attended your 'milestone' activities due to obligation, think again. Dana adored you, and Richard still does." Kinross looked away. "I was grateful for the photos, especially of indoor events I could never attend, but I envied them the part they played in your life."

"I'm here now." Paisley patted her father's arm. "Why did you wait all this time to reach out to me after I was of age?"

Her father's ears turned red, a sign Paisley had witnessed once before.

"Sheer pride and uncertainty. I had no idea how you would respond to my invitation after your mother's poisoning."

James decided it was time to ratchet down the heavy emotion blanketing the room.

"I remember this picture." James pointed to the computer screen.

Catherine and Paisley were seated side by side driving a riding mower across Edgehill House's extensive lawns. Ben was waving his arms, obviously giving instructions. James had jumped onto the back of the mower and was making Paisley laugh. Jack had Betsy and Bramble, their two German Shepherds, hooked to a double leash, ready to take them for a walk. Mrs. Pressley-Coombes stood on the white-pillared porch, an indulgent smile on her face, her eyes on the three kids riding the mower.

Paisley touched Mrs. Pressley-Coombes's image on the screen. "I miss your mom."

"Yeah." James's throat tightened. Talking about her was still hard.

Paisley squeezed his hand. He flipped his palm and interlocked their fingers. She understood how much a part of their lives his mother had been.

Out of the corner of his eye, he saw Kinross's jaw harden. The man would have to get used to his and Paisley's attachment. If things went as James planned, he would become a permanent fixture in Paisley's life.

"I received verra good news this evening from DI Skene," Kinross said, closing down his computer. "Ballistics from the wreckage on Lunga match one of the automatic weapons recovered from the crofter's cottage."

"We were right." Paisley leaned back on the sofa and rested her head against the cushions.

“That’s not all. When I visited Agent Taylor in the hospital yesterday, she confirmed MI6’s cyber unit had breached Rahim’s firewall. Rahim had accessed our mainframe and had downloaded spyware on all corporate and personal electronic devices on the estate. That was how he found out about Mr. Razool’s embezzlement and was able to blackmail him into threatening a middle manager at WFB. An ugly business.”

James whistled. “Wow.”

“How’s Munira taking the news?” Paisley’s eyes searched her father’s face.

“Better than I expected. For the last several years, she has feared the worst about Rahim. To have them confirmed has not been easy. She loved her son. But you must remember Munira grew up in a war-torn country. Her husband killed many innocent people. Her son, despite Munira’s best efforts to remove Rahim from that life, was the same. Munira, of course, is saddened but somewhat relieved to no longer worry what her son might do. I expect her attention now will turn fully on Torquil and her humanitarian projects.”

“What about you, Dad? Are you going to be all right?”

“I’m pure dead brilliant.” Kinross grinned and chucked Paisley under the chin. “I’ve you and Torquil and my businesses. And if I’m lucky, perhaps one day, Munira might come ’round.”

***

James paced the yellow salon, an intimate room that faced the front drive, and checked the wall clock for the hundredth time. Early afternoon sunlight filtered through the sheers covering the windows. A fire crackled merrily inside the hearth.

“You’re going to wear a hole in that rug,” Paisley commented from the sofa.

He turned and caught the twinkle in her eyes. “What’s so amusing? Dad and Ben should have been here hours ago.”

“I’ve never seen you like this before; you’re always so laid back.”

“I am?”

She nodded. “Come here, Mr. Pressley-Coombes. I need to tell you something.” A little smile hovered on her lips.

“You do, do you?”

“Aye,” she said, using her father’s Scots.

He came to the sofa and sat carefully beside her so he didn’t jostle her shoulder. He picked up her hand. “What do you need to tell me?”

“That I love you,” she said softly. “I don’t think I’ve said it today.”

He leaned forward and pressed his lips to hers, running a hand over her long, dark hair. "That's something I'll never get tired of hearing, Lady Margaret." He kissed her again, but this time, he savored the feel of her lips and the currents that sizzled inside him whenever he held her close.

A commotion in the main hall reached them. James shot off the sofa and started for the door.

"I'll give you a few minutes before I join you," she called after him.

James returned to her and gave her one last kiss. "Thanks."

"Hey, does anyone live in this museum?" Ben Pressley-Coombes's voice rang from the entrance.

Henderson shut the front door with a slam. "His Grace will be with you momentarily."

James jogged to the entrance hall and found Richard and Ben, their eyes glued to the array of medieval weaponry displayed on the walls.

"Hey." James grabbed his father in a bear hug and thumped his back one-handed.

He faced his twin, and his own smile lit Ben's face, flashing white teeth in a tanned complexion. Ben had never been much for hugs, but James didn't care. He grabbed his brother and pounded his back with enough enthusiasm for both of them.

"Okay. Okay. Enough of the girly stuff," Ben said, stepping out of hugging range. "Don't knock these over." He indicated the wrapped packages propped against the wall.

"You brought me a present?" James teased, his mouth rising in a lopsided grin.

The size and shape of Ben's packages could only mean one thing: his twin had stopped at an art gallery on the way to the Highlands.

"Why would I do that?" Ben asked.

"Ben visited the National Art Museum before we left Edinburgh." Richard shook his head at his oldest son.

Ben had a great eye for new talent and often "discovered" up-and-coming artists before they hit it big, meaning he purchased their artwork before they hit it big.

"How are you going to get them home?" James asked.

"I have no idea, but I'll figure it out. You have to see these." Ben removed the wrapping from the first painting. "The artist is a Scottish recluse. No one knows if they're a man or a woman."

"'The Old Man of Storr,'" James read out loud.

The watercolor palette in blues and grays, with a vivid splash of green on the hillside, held the eye. Gray clouds billowed, almost visibly moving.

"Are you sure it's a watercolor?" James bent forward to have a closer look.

"Yeah. Pretty great, huh? The other is of the Fairy Pools. Both were painted on Skye."

James untied the second package. Dramatic peaks rose in the background, and turquoise water glistened in a series of pools so clear that the rocks under the surface were visible.

A soft tread sounded on the Turkish runner. Paisley approached, her face alight with joy at the sight of Richard and Ben.

"There's my girl." Careful of her sling, Richard pulled Paisley to his side and kissed her forehead. "How's the shoulder?"

"It's good. I only have a few weeks left before I'm sling-free. Let's get your things upstairs before I give you the grand tour."

"That would be nice," Richard said.

"Henderson, could you send someone up with their luggage?" she asked her father's butler, who stood beside the front door staring straight ahead.

"Yes, Lady Margaret." Henderson moved off to see to her request.

"Lady Margaret?" Ben whispered the question in James's ear.

"They use their first names with formal titles over here. You remember that British king who abdicated, the one who married an American?"

Ben nodded.

"The family called him David, but he was King Edward XIII."

Paisley caught sight of Ben's paintings. "Those are stunning. Who's the artist?" Paisley glanced at the signature. "IKM."

"No one knows. They work through an agent."

"A mystery. Well, let's have those paintings moved upstairs too. They make me nervous being propped up like that." Paisley took Richard's arm and proceeded toward the grand staircase. "I hope you'll like the rooms I selected."

James started after them, and Ben followed with his paintings.

"You're going to love the resort site. It's the best one I've seen in the last five years," James said.

"I'm looking forward to it. The video you sent was impressive. How's that presentation for Amsterdam coming along?"

"Great. I have some ideas I think will win over the European corporations. We're crossing our fingers that Paisley gets a clean bill of health from the doctor so she can go with me."

Ben glanced up the stairs and lowered his voice. “Have you popped the question yet?”

“Shhh. Keep it down.”

“Dude, you practically salivated when she walked into the room.”

“She’s amazing.” James couldn’t keep the grin off his face.

“Yeah, yeah, yeah. I’m not interested in the gooey stuff. But just so you know, Jack would have proposed by now.”

“Don’t bring Jack into it. This is a different set of circumstances.”

“Doesn’t it bother you that Jack’s record beats yours?”

“Maybe. But I have something great planned.” James gave him a smug look. “And I need your help.”

“Aha. I knew it!”

“Jack practically eloped after he proposed. My planning takes more than a few days’ notice. If I went all Wild West on Kinross, he’d have me shipped off in an unmarked container to the Antarctic.”

Chapter 42

Paisley leaned against the wall outside Granny's room the next day while James shuffled and dealt the UNO cards. She had been camped outside Granny's suite all afternoon reading while she waited for Granny to wake up. James had found her there after he returned from the resort site with Richard and Ben.

She fanned out her cards and organized them by color, noting two draw fours and several skips. "What did Richard and Ben think of the site?"

"They were totally impressed, Ben in particular. He's very forward thinking. Dad's a little concerned about the bottom line after he saw how much granite covers that terrain. He's used to bulldozing everything flat. Ben and I had to talk him into working with the terrain by drilling into the bedrock to stabilize the foundations instead of dynamiting out the rock before he poured the foundations. In the long run, if we drill into the granite, the buildings will be much more stable." James placed the remaining UNO cards in the middle, flipped the top card over, and laid it next to the stack.

"You should have been an architect." Paisley laid her yellow five on top of the yellow two beside the stack.

"Why?"

"You see possibilities. Nothing is a stumbling block; you simply readjust, then move forward."

"Not a bad thing for a guy in marketing though, is it?" James placed a yellow draw two on top of her card.

"No. I love that about you. And from what I hear, my father and Ward MacKenzie couldn't be happier with your work. In fact, and I quote, 'That lad's a boy wonder.'" She drew two cards from the pile, a wild and a green five.

"Thanks. That means a lot." James laid down a yellow skip, then a green skip, and then a blue skip. "Can I ask you something totally unrelated to this conversation?"

"Sure." Paisley smiled at him sweetly, then laid the first draw-four on top of the stack. "Blue," she said, calling out a color.

"Why are you in the hall instead of in there with your grandmother?" James drew four cards.

"She isn't well. At first, I thought she had a cold, but I think her arthritis is acting up." Paisley laid down her second draw-four card. "Red."

"I forgot what an UNO shark you are." James groaned and picked up four more cards. "If the dowager duchess isn't well, why are you still hanging around outside her room?"

"Because I haven't seen Granny since the night of the charity gala ball. I'm staying here until that nurse lets me in. Torquil had to go back to school without saying goodbye to her."

"Paisley, has it occurred to you that your grandmother is seriously ill?"

"Granny has rheumatoid arthritis, and she's in her seventies." Paisley laid down a red nine.

"She's also sleeping a lot more than others her age would normally do," James told her, putting down a green nine.

"Are they giving her meds for the pain?" Paisley dithered between a green reverse and her yellow nine.

"I think it's more than that. I asked around. That nurse only came on full-time right before you arrived."

Paisley lifted her eyes to his. "What are you saying?"

"I think something else is wrong with her. My mom slept a lot right before she passed."

A chill went through Paisley, and she set down her cards. James wouldn't bring this up if he wasn't trying to prepare her for something. Her mind went back to Kinross's strict orders that Granny visits were to be kept to a minimum.

"You think she has cancer?" A sudden coldness settled in her core.

"I overheard the servants discussing it when I visited Mrs. Grant. It's pancreatic cancer, Paise. I'm so sorry."

"Why didn't anyone tell me?"

"That might have been on your grandmother's orders." James patted her hand.

"Why would she do that?"

"I can think of a few reasons, can't you? She probably wanted to get to know you without sympathy. She's a proud old lady, a former duchess." His thumb rubbed circles on the back of her hand.

"She's still a duchess, a dowager duchess."

"Yes, but she's not the lady of the house. That's Munira's title."

Paisley rose to her feet and paced to Granny's door. She didn't want to believe James. But all the signs of Granny's illness were there: her sleeping almost around the clock, the nurse playing watchdog at her door, her father's orders for visits not to exceed a set time, and Torquil's having to leave for school without saying goodbye.

Would Nora turn her away too without letting her see Granny? Paisley tapped softly on the door.

Nora opened the wooden panel a crack. "Lady Margaret, is there something you need?"

"Nora, I'm going to be in the hall until Granny wakes. I need to talk to her, even if it's just for a minute. I know you're protecting her, but if she's ill, I want to . . ." Paisley's voice faltered, and she bit the inside of her bottom lip to keep it from trembling. Clearing her throat, she continued, "I want to tell her I love her. I want to . . ."

The nurse's eyes softened. "She's a wee bit more alert after her bath, and she's due for one in an hour. I'll let you in for a few minutes before I give her the medicine. It's only a few minutes, mind. She's in a good deal of pain."

"I'll be in the hall in case—" Paisley swallowed, the lump in her throat making it difficult. "In case she wakes up sooner."

Nora closed the door.

Paisley placed her hand on the white panels and bowed her head as memories of Granny flooded her. The woman had an acerbic tongue that disguised her kind heart. She had welcomed Paisley into the family and had played fairy grandmother so she could attend the ball.

The ache inside her heart deepened—the pain almost unbearable. James came up behind her and took her gently into his arms, not saying a word.

"How can I be so sad? I hardly know her. But it hurts, James. It hurts so much." Her throat constricted so tight she could hardly swallow. She buried her face in his shoulder while the tears slid down her face.

"Love doesn't understand time. It's like music. It bypasses the reasoning powers of the mind and reaches straight into the soul." He rubbed her back and kissed her temple. "You're fortunate to know her."

Paisley agreed with him wholeheartedly. "You're right. I never expected to have a grandmother. Or a brother." She sniffed, then wiped her eyes. "I'll cry later. I'm going to celebrate the time I have left with Granny."

James let go of her and reshuffled the deck of cards. "Let's start over."

They played four games before the nurse opened the door.

"She's awake."

"Would you like to come in with me?" Paisley asked James.

"I think you need to see her without me. Get in there, Paise; we can talk afterward."

She entered Granny's suite. The curtains were open, letting in the weak afternoon light. The room, as always, was stifling hot.

Paisley peeled off her sweater and pulled up a chair beside Granny.

"You've been crying," Granny stated. It wasn't a question.

"Yes."

"Someone told you." Also not a question.

"Yes."

"Two things we can be certain of in this life: we're all born and we all die." Granny motioned toward her wedding picture on her bureau. "I miss my husband."

Paisley studied the picture of Granny in her wedding finery standing beside a man that looked a great deal like Paisley's father, except for the eyes. Her father had inherited Granny's dark eyes. So had she and Torquil. Paisley brought the picture to Granny.

"He was a good man." Granny touched her husband's image with her twisted fingers before they dropped onto the counterpane. "I would have liked you to wear my wedding gown when the time comes, but moths got to it."

Paisley set Granny's wedding picture back on the dresser. "I'm sure I would have loved your dress, Granny." Paisley bit the inside of her lip. Unlike his brother Jack, James appeared in no hurry to rush to the altar. Not once had he touched on the subject of marriage, not even obliquely.

"Since I can't wear your wedding dress, I think I'd like my mom to help me select or design a gown." Who knew, perhaps she and her mom would bond over the experience. Paisley would like to try anyway.

She came back to the bed and climbed up beside her grandmother, careful not to jostle her. Granny appeared frailer than ever, the veins standing out on her forehead.

"My child, I have something for you."

"I don't need anything, Granny."

"I want you to have it. It isn't part of the estate. It's mine to give to whomever I please. You are to have my jewels and personal effects. My gowns." She gave Paisley a faint smile. "And you and Torquil can fight over my rock collection."

Paisley laughed. "I think that will matter more to us than anything."

"I expect so. But I have a special gift just for you. My father gave it to me when I married." Granny turned her head and said, "Nora, bring me my box."

"Yes, Your Grace." The nurse went to retrieve a box from inside the closet.

"I like your young man," Granny said. "He's just the sort I pictured for you."

"James?"

"Aye."

Nora laid the box beside Granny on the bed.

"Open the lid," Granny encouraged her, a flash of eagerness in her pain-filled eyes.

Paisley untied the ribbons and lifted the lid. Inside was a key and a handwritten note on yellowed paper.

"What's this?" Paisley asked, holding up the key.

"I'm giving you a house. The directions to it are on that paper. My father wrote them out for me when I was a young bride."

Paisley's eyes rounded. "A house?"

"It's nothing so grand as Castle Rannoch. The estate is small and located in the hills above Loch Tay, but it has a commanding view. There's not a lot of land, only a few hundred acres of forest. But it's a bonnie place. A happy place."

"Granny, I don't know what to say. Shouldn't your family home stay with Torquil?"

"Nonsense. You are part of the family too," Granny said, her crotchety personality making its presence known. "My great-great-great-grandfather, the first Earl of Garry, was quite a botanist, if they were called such things back then. He traveled all over Europe collecting seeds, going as far as St. Petersburg. He brought them back and planted them all over the property. Due to the crags, some of the hillsides were too hard to reach. So he, being the canny Scot he was, placed the seeds inside a cannon and shot them onto the hillside. They took hold in the fertile soil and are now part of the Big Tree Country here in Perth and Kinross."

"He shot seeds with a cannon?" Paisley laughed in delight.

"Aye." A smile hovered on Granny's lips, then faded. "Your father loves you, lass. He gets preoccupied, but that doesn't mean he doesn't care. Demand your time. Pull him out of himself. Invite him often to your home. He'll come. He'll put it on his schedule. You've known much of loneliness in your life. So has he. Don't let it continue."

"I won't. I promise."

"Torquil too?"

"Torquil too." The lump had returned to Paisley's throat. This was goodbye. She could feel it.

"Don't lose that key," Granny whispered.

"I won't. I will treasure your home. Thank you."

Granny's eyes hazed with pain. "I know you will, lass."

"I am so happy I was able to know you. Thank you for being my fairy grandmother." Paisley's throat burned and made it difficult to swallow.

"Aye. The fairies will take me home soon, I expect. You be happy, lass," Granny whispered.

Carefully, Paisley eased herself off the bed and kissed the withered cheek. "I love you, Granny. Thank you for the present." Holding tightly to the key, she left the room.

Chapter 43

Paisley read Granny's instructions out loud. "Make a left just past the turnout for the Queen's View and follow the lane as it climbs the hillside."

James hit the blinker and turned the MGB onto the B8019. Soon they were enveloped in forest on the single-track road without one verge to pull into should a car come from the opposite direction. A dozen feet off the road, a red deer lifted its graceful neck and stared, poised for flight.

"I think this is a private drive," James said after a while. No other homes or lanes branched off into the trees.

"My directions say it's the Tay Forest Park."

A minute later, a sign on the left said, "Tressail House." James downshifted and followed an even narrower lane that branched off the national park road. Up ahead, a pair of pillars and wrought-iron gates stood closed.

James put the car in park and let the engine idle while he hopped out to open the gates.

"If you're interested, I bet Nick would replace that gate with an electronic one," James said, hopping back inside.

The lane meandered through leafless trees and acres of rhododendrons for five hundred yards before it stopped in front of a large, white Georgian manor house with a slate roof. The turquoise door was bracketed by two potted evergreens standing sentinel on either side.

Paisley stared at the beautifully proportioned mansion Granny had gifted her.

James parked beside the door and came around the hood to let her out. "Say something."

"I don't know what to say. I have no idea why Granny gifted Tressail House to me. It's too much."

"Considering Torquil inherits the castle and two other estates, I think you can handle it."

Paisley went to the front door and slipped her key in the lock. James pushed it wide and waited for her to enter. Paisley's first impression was of light airiness. No dark wood paneling for this house.

The symmetrical foyer with its semi-circular staircase and wrought-iron railings of elaborately entwined peacocks hearkened back to the neo-classical era with a few touches of Art Deco. The wood floors were in good repair as well.

James took her good hand, and they wandered the public rooms on the ground floor, stopping to admire the sash windows, Adam fireplaces, and ornate plasterwork. It was a magical place. The rooms were spacious but not massive like Castle Rannoch's. This was a family home, a country estate where one could relax and not worry if something irreplaceable would shatter.

"Do you think Catherine would help me decorate?"

"I don't see why not. Send her some pictures with dimensions. If she gives you a few suggestions, I think you've got a good enough eye to handle the rest."

In the dining room, a card table was set up with two folding chairs. A bouquet sat on top of a linen tablecloth.

"You've already been here," Paisley said accusingly.

"Nope. This is my first visit."

"Then how is that there?" she asked, pointing to the beautiful flowers and tablecloth.

"Ben set it up for me."

"Is he still here?"

"No, he and Dad took off for the Isle of Skye. They're going to climb the Cuillins next year."

"What are the Cuillins?"

"A challenging mountain range on Skye." James motioned toward the table.

"Shall we?" He seated her and disappeared, returning with two crystal dessert bowls filled with yellow pudding topped with whipped cream.

"Is that banana pudding?" Her heart fluttered like butterfly wings.

"Yeah. You like it, don't you?"

"I like to eat it, but I'm not so fond of wearing it," Paisley said with a sassy smirk.

He grinned back at her, one side of his mouth rising higher than the other. Her insides trembled as though she stood on the edge of a precipice. Before she made a fool of herself, she leaned forward to admire the pink lilies, white roses, and pale pink daisies.

"The flowers are beautiful."

"I'm glad you like them." James raked a hand through his hair and glanced around. "I wasn't sure which were your favorite, but I did remember your favorite color."

"Pink's my favorite color?" That was news to her.

"Yeah. You used to wear it all the time."

"When I was like seven years old."

"You don't like pink?" The happy animation drained from his face.

"Relax. I'm giving you a bad time. I love pink. And these are stunning."

James jumped up from his chair. "I have something for you." He left the room, and she could hear him rummaging in the kitchen.

He was acting weird, and it was making her nervous.

The pudding in front of her smelled delicious. With one eye on the door, she picked up her spoon and scooped up a bite, then set it down just as James returned to the dining room and set a small bag in front of her.

"What's the giftbag for?" She eyed the colorful present container suspiciously.

"Just open it already."

Tentatively, she lifted the tissue covering from the top and looked inside. The first thing she saw was the strap to her old camera. Her heart gave a great thump. She lifted it from the bag, and her shattered camera rose with it.

The camera was pasted together like a crazy 3D puzzle with a few missing pieces.

"My camera," she whispered, blinking fast against the burning sensation in her eyes.

"It's only the housing. I couldn't fix the internal guts."

"You glued my camera back together!" Paisley flipped it over, exposing the back. Sure enough, *To Paisley. Love, Dad* was still intact.

"I knew how much that thing meant to you, but I didn't have a clue why until I started putting it back together and found that etching on the back."

Something rattled inside the plastic housing.

"You might want to open it," James encouraged her.

With the greatest care, Paisley undid the latch. Inside was a sparkling, princess-cut diamond solitaire. Her good hand covered her mouth.

James took the ring and knelt before her, his eyes filled with hope.

"Paisley, you know everything there is to know about me: the good, the bad, and the stupid. The stupidest thing I've ever done was not realize how much I loved you. I know it's sudden, but I love you so much. Will you marry me? I can't imagine a forever without you in it."

Less than two weeks ago, the thought of marriage had terrified her when she realized she was in love with James. But in the days since, she couldn't imagine existing without him at her side.

"Yes." She couldn't restrain the giddiness that bubbled like a natural spring, building, growing, then rocketing to the sky.

He slid the ring onto her finger. She caught his smile of deep satisfaction.

"I have a confession to make too. I've tried all my life *not* to love you. It was hard," she said, dismissing the years of females pounding on her door, confessing their adoration for James in the hope she could fix things for them.

Careful of her sling, James pulled her from her chair and into his arms. His lips settled on hers tenderly for a brief kiss before he pulled back and said, "Somebody sneaked a bite of banana pudding when my back was turned."

She blushed. "I like banana pudding."

He let go of her relatively quickly for someone who had just proposed. "There's something else inside your bag."

She peeked inside, then withdrew two envelopes. One was a manilla envelope, its sides bulging. The second was a monogrammed gray invitation with her father's crest.

"Open that one first." James touched the expensive pale-gray stationary. "And read it out loud."

The sling made it difficult, and she fumbled with the envelope until James took pity on her and opened it. She took the thick cardstock from him and read,

"The Duke of Perth and Kinross and Mr. James Pressley-Coombes
invite you to attend the private photography exhibition of
Lady Margaret Douglas Pressley-Coombes
National Art Gallery ~ Edinburgh.
January 12th ~ 7–9:00 p.m.
Cocktails and appetizers
Black tie."

Lady Margaret Douglas Pressley-Coombes. Her fingers ran over the embossed surname.

"Say something, Paise."

"I can't." Then she burst into tears. "It's too much, James. You've done so much for me," she sobbed, not caring if her mascara ran.

He chuckled and once more wrapped her in his arms, then whispered into her ear, "Open the other envelope."

"I don't know if I can handle any more of this."

"Let me help you, then." James slit the envelope.

Inside were several brochures. One was to the Greek Isles, another to the Cayman Islands, and the third was to the Sahara Desert. Paisley raised her eyebrows at that one.

"Please pick someplace warm for our honeymoon. Scotland's beautiful, but I need to thaw out."

"The Sahara Desert?" she asked, examining the brochure.

"It was the warmest place I could think of." James sat on her chair and lifted her onto his lap. "Don't you like the Sahara Desert? Nomads. Spitting camels. Hot burning sand?"

"If spitting camels and burning sand are your idea of a romantic honeymoon, we're in trouble," Paisley said dryly.

He laughed, then picked up her hand, moving the one-karat solitaire to catch the light.

"That's a gorgeous ring, James. How did you know it would fit?"

"I didn't. I've been staring at your fingers for weeks trying to figure out the right size. Your dad insisted I repurpose one of the Douglas family heirlooms, but I wanted your ring to be from me, something that I purchased."

"Was he okay with that?" Kinross, as she had learned, was used to having his way.

"Yeah." James shrugged and made a face. "After a while."

"So you talked to my dad, huh?" She poked him in the ribs.

"Of course. He wasn't happy about losing you so soon, but this house isn't too far away. Since I'll be stationed in Europe the next few years to expand Coombes Enterprises and promote the resort, I thought we could use Tressail House for our home base."

"You won't have to headquarter out of Virginia?"

"No. Marketing is different. I have monthly meetings, and I'm sure we'll hop the pond regularly, but I kind of thought you would like to stay here and get to know your dad and Torquil."

She swallowed, pushing past the sudden knot in her throat. James was offering her every dream her heart desired, but she worried he was coming up short by marrying her.

"What do you get out of all this?" Paisley asked, almost afraid of the answer.

James tucked a strand of hair behind her ear, his eyes warm. "You really don't get it, Paise?" He kissed her, his lips firm and insistent as though driving home a point. He drew back and murmured in her ear, "You. I get you."

Chapter 1

February 1940

Karl Lang kept his back ramrod straight as his father bid Herr Sauermann farewell from the gravel drive in front of their two-hundred-year-old manor. Part of the posture was upbringing—boys from families like his didn't slouch when seeing visitors off. Part of it was a desire to close the gap in height. Sauermann loomed over all of them like a statue of a Hapsburg war hero.

Sauermann shook Karl's hand. "You look just like your father did when I met him. That blond hair and straight nose. Fine Aryan specimens." The warmth of the compliment lessened the effect of the bitter winter wind slicing through their coats. Sauermann turned to Papa. "Give it some thought, Leopold. You're needed."

"I'm a widower with three children to care for." Papa kept a polite expression, but his blue eyes contained a hardness that Karl wasn't accustomed to seeing from his father, especially not around old family friends.

With a wave of his hand, Sauermann directed his driver to open the door of his black Gräf & Stift automobile. "You've the means to hire help for the children. And your son will soon be in uniform, just like you."

The muscles along Papa's jaw hardened. "Karl is only seventeen. He's too young to fight."

"For now." Sauermann slipped into the car. "I'll see you in a few days, Leopold. Be ready."

At a nod from Sauermann, the driver closed the door and walked around to the driver's seat.

Karl held his tongue until the man climbed in and started the engine. "I'm not afraid to be a soldier."

Papa folded his arms. "But for whom will you fight?"

"For Austria. Just like you, in the last war."

Papa watched Sauermann's car pull away. "Austria no longer exists. Do you wish to fight for Herr Hitler, Karl?"

Karl didn't answer immediately. He'd found little to like in the newsreels of the führer, and he'd picked up on his father's less-than-enthusiastic response to the Anschluss of two years before, but Karl couldn't very well change the course of history. Herr Kaufmann, the literature teacher at his boarding school, was quick to point out the economic benefits of union with Germany. Most people agreed with him, but now Karl wasn't sure. "I just want to be brave like my father."

"Courage isn't always about fighting."

"Herr Sauermann seems to think you should fight again." Karl watched Sauermann's automobile disappear around the stone lions that marked the estate's entrance. "I would think you too old to fight."

"He's not asking me to pick up a rifle again." Papa chuckled. "Too old? Is forty-four so old?"

Karl straightened his back again, trying to stretch the inch of height he had over his father into something more impressive. "No, I don't suppose you're that old or that short. But I imagine they'll give the rifles to strapping recruits like me."

"Well then, my strapping son, run to the top of that hill to make sure Sauermann really leaves. Then meet me in the study and bring your sisters."

"You think he might not really leave?"

Papa shrugged. "I need to know for sure. Plan the first has failed, and I don't expect plan the second to work out either. Which brings us to plan the third."

"What's plan the third?" Papa always had multiple plans, but this was the first Karl had heard about anything related to Sauermann. "And what was plan the first and plan the second?"

"Later, Karl. I'll tell you later." Papa pointed to the hill. "You brought your field glasses, as I asked?"

Karl nodded and ran off. He wore his best suit and dress coat in honor of Herr Sauermann's visit, not his normal choice for taking a shortcut through the damp woods that encircled the manor. But none of the staff would reprimand him if he abused the clothing just a bit, and his father certainly wouldn't, not after being the one to send him on this errand.

Thick growth of spruce, pine, and larch surrounded the snowy lawns and gardens of the estate. Karl ran awhile, then trudged the rest of the way over the brambles and uneven roots. The top of the hill cleared just enough to offer a view of the entire estate. Schloss die Punkt Falke stretched out to the north and the west. Falcon Point. The turrets of the limestone manor house peeked above a thick curtain of tree branches, and flashes of light reflected off the surface of the lake to the east. Most of Kristall Lake was still frozen, but parts had thawed over the last week. Karl turned to the village and caught sight of the black automobile making its way down the slope. He pulled the small field glasses from his pocket and verified there was still a passenger in the back seat.

Wilhelm Sauermann had been his father's friend for years, and he'd stayed at Falcon Point time after time. Karl didn't buy the excuse that there was less staff now, so the Lang family wasn't in a position to host. They still had a maid, a gardener, and a cook, who doubled as a housekeeper. Welcoming Herr Sauermann into one of the dozens of empty rooms would have been a simple enough affair. Something had changed. Now Sauermann was staying in the village and making what sounded like threats if Papa didn't agree to whatever Sauermann had asked. And Karl had been sent to make sure their guest had really left Falcon Point—it felt a lot like spying.

Karl watched until the car passed the kirche, with its pointed spire, and disappeared between the steep-roofed buildings of the village. The small inn on the settlement's eastern end hadn't anything so grand as one of the rooms at Falcon Point. Would Sauermann resent not being asked to stay?

Karl was at the wrong angle to see the rest of Sauermann's progress, so he trekked back to the manor. Going downhill was far easier than going uphill, but he didn't rush. He avoided the roots that seemed determined to trip him and did his best to ignore the way the cold mud clung to his shoes, making them ever heavier. What was his father planning? And which two plans had already failed? Karl could keep a secret—his father should have confided in him.

When he reached the manor, he left his muddy shoes by the kitchen entrance and grabbed a slice of gugelhupf while the cook's back was turned.

"I know what you've taken, young man." Frau Pichler scrubbed out a pot from the early supper they'd shared with Herr Sauermann.

"But you don't mind, do you?"

She chuckled. "No, I remember what an appetite teenage boys can have. But don't track dirt across my kitchen, or Gerta will put green wood in with your coal. She just cleaned the floor." Frau Pichler turned around and nodded when she noticed Karl's stockinged feet.

"Have you seen Ingrid and Anna?"

"I believe I heard Miss Anna making some sort of noise on the piano."

Karl climbed the flight of stairs to the foyer, then took the grand staircase to the next level, and went through the hall to the music room. Anna's simple tune drifted out to meet him. She played the notes with precision but without feeling. Maybe that would come with time. She was only seven years old, and as Karl walked around the piano to get a view of her wheat-colored curls and furrowed concentration, he held his tongue rather than commenting on her unemotional style.

Anna finished her line with a flourish and smiled up at him. "Did you hear that? No mistakes."

"Well done, Anna. Are you finished? Papa wants us in his study."

Anna stood and scurried toward the hall.

"Have you seen Ingrid?" he asked as Anna dashed through the door.

"I'm over here."

Karl followed his sister's voice to a wingback chair turned toward the window. Ingrid sat with her feet pulled up and tucked at her side. A novel lay in her lap.

"You'll strain your eyes reading in the dark."

Ingrid pulled a ribbon into her book to mark her place. "It wasn't dark when I sat down."

Karl turned the chair—with Ingrid still in it—to its proper position. "Papa asked to see us in his study."

"I heard you tell Anna."

"Let's not keep him waiting."

Ingrid ran her finger along the spine of her book. "I can't very well stand up while you're moving the furniture."

"It would have been a lot easier to move if you weren't still sitting in it. And anyway, I'm not moving it now. Come on."

Ingrid took her time putting her book away and heading for the hallway. Sisters. Brothers would have been easier. If Ingrid were a boy, Karl could have used a little more force, but Papa would scold him if he didn't treat Ingrid like a lady, regardless of how she acted.

Papa was crouched by the hearth when they arrived, coaxing a fire from the day's embers. He stood and pulled the curtains shut against the fading daylight and gestured to a table overflowing with piles of paper. "Ingrid, I need you to burn these. Anna can help, but make sure she doesn't get singed."

"Burn them?" Ingrid's mouth pulled into a frown. "Why?"

Papa put one hand on Ingrid's shoulder and his other on the table. "Just trust me. Don't go too fast, or you'll smother the fire. And don't read them;

just destroy them. Only the ones here." He tapped the table again, then pointed to his massive Victorian-era desk. "Those aren't to be touched."

"Yes, Papa." Ingrid picked up a folder and held it. Anna picked up a pile too, but she didn't hesitate. She went right to the hearth and began feeding the fire, one paper at a time.

"Good, Anna. Just like I told you. Not too fast."

Anna grinned. Karl would have, too, at her age, had their father granted permission to play with fire.

"Come, Karl. I need your help."

Karl followed Papa from the room. "What papers are those? And why are you burning them?"

His father held a finger to his lips. "Not now."

Karl grunted his irritation, but he obeyed. Curiosity as much as discipline kept him from rebelling.

"You'll need shoes."

"Mine were muddy, so I left them by the kitchen."

"Fine, we'll go that way." But Papa didn't head toward the kitchen. He led Karl upstairs to the manor's top floor, toward the suite where Karl's parents had once slept. Since Mama died, Papa had slept in one of the other suites—one that was still comfortable but not quite so grand.

They passed through the main room, with its enormous four-poster bed, and went into a dressing chamber off to the side. Papa bent to pick up one end of a trunk. "Grab the other end."

The trunk was about the size of a wine crate, so Karl was surprised by how much it weighed when he lifted his end. "What's inside?"

"Some of your mother's things."

The dressing room still held most of Mama's gowns. At fifteen, Ingrid wasn't quite old enough for them to be reworked to fit her, and some were no longer in fashion. The trunk had to have more than clothing inside, unless the clothing was made of chain mail. "Why is it so heavy if it's full of satin and velvet?"

Papa's eyes flashed with memory, something sweet and sad at the same time. "Not her clothes. Her jewelry."

Karl glanced at the trunk. "She had that much?"

Papa nodded. "And a little more. I asked Gerta to sew a few pieces into all your coats."

"Why?"

"Wait until we're outside. Gerta is trustworthy enough, but it's best she stay ignorant about most of it."

"And Herr and Frau Pichler?

"I've given them the evening off. Frau Pichler might be tinkering in the kitchen still, but I imagine Herr Pichler has gone down to the village."

"You don't trust them?"

Papa shrugged the shoulder that wasn't involved in hefting the trunk. "I prefer to keep as much as I can a secret. Only those who must know the truth should have to bear its burden."

Was truth a burden? "I don't understand."

Papa motioned for them to set the trunk down before descending the stairs. They switched sides, then lifted it again. "I'll explain once we're outside."

Karl held his tongue. The trunk seemed to grow heavier as they made their way down two long flights of stairs, then a shorter set to the kitchen and back entrance, but Karl wouldn't complain about the weight, not after the conversation they'd had when they'd said farewell to Herr Sauermann. If Karl wanted to be treated like a man, he couldn't very well complain that a trunk full of his mother's jewelry was too heavy. But he was relieved when they set the trunk down long enough for him to put on his boots. He followed his father's example and pulled on wool mittens and a coat.

The sun had sunk beyond the western horizon when they left the manor, turning the sky a dim gray that matched the shadowed snow.

"Do you remember the gamekeeper's home?" Papa asked.

Karl changed his hold on the trunk. The mittens helped with the cold, but they didn't help with his grip. "No. I remember hearing about it, but I've never seen it."

Papa nodded. "It burned down when you were a baby. Most of it, anyway. I've repaired the root cellar, and we're putting a few things there."

Karl eyed the trunk. "A few rather valuable things."

Papa shuffled past one of the ice-covered hedges marking the boundary of the garden. "They'll be safe until we return."

"Are we leaving?" Karl tried to keep his voice down in case one of the servants was still around, but he couldn't remove the surprise that crept into his words. Falcon Point had been his home his entire life. It had been in the family for generations. They were tied to the land almost as deeply as they were tied to each other.

"That's plan the third."

"And the other plans? What were they?"

Papa was silent for a while, leading Karl up a slope and into the trees. "After the Anschluss, I held out hope that Hitler's bluster would blow over, that we'd still have some autonomy. But I've watched what's happening—here and in Czechoslovakia and in Poland. Herr Hitler is leading us to ruin. If it were only our ruin, I might not feel the need to protest. We can weather economic downturn, and we can even weather a drawn-out war. But I've heard things. He won't just destroy Germany and Austria. He'll ravage all of Europe. He's evil, Karl. I can't support him. I certainly can't work for him and help him with his plans."

"Is that why Sauermann was here? To get you to work for Hitler?"

"Yes."

"Doing what?"

Papa hesitated, then seemed to come to a decision. "Let's switch sides again on the trunk." They paused at a bulbous rock formation that jutted from the hillside, traded places, and continued. "Not a word to anyone. Do you understand, Karl? I'm putting my life in your hands."

Karl swallowed hard. "You can trust me."

Papa pulled them on, up the slope that was gradually growing steeper and steeper. "Codes. That's what I did in the last war. That's what I do most of the time when we go to Vienna."

Karl shook his head. "I thought you worked with the university. You're a professor, aren't you?"

"Yes, but that's mostly a cover." Papa sighed. "I don't want to make better codes for the Reich or try to break the codes of their enemies."

"But Germany is our country now, isn't it? If you're asked and if you refuse, isn't that . . ." Karl couldn't say the word, couldn't accuse his father of anything so dishonorable.

"Dangerous? Treasonous?"

Karl nodded.

Papa began lowering their burden. "It's time to switch sides."

Karl set the trunk down with relief. He went to pick up the other side, but Papa held his shoulder. "I can betray my country, or I can betray my conscience. Which would you have me do?"

Karl stared into his father's eyes. They were blue, like Karl's, though it was hard to see the color in the twilight. Maybe Karl wasn't ready to be a man, not if being a man meant facing choices like this. "You have to do what is right, Papa. That's what you've always taught me."

Papa nodded and motioned to the trunk. They marched on with only the crunch of snow and their heavy breaths to accompany them. "What is right is plan the third."

"What were plan the first and plan the second?"

"Plan the first was that we'd all stay at Falcon Point and wait out the conflict. We'd ignore the war and let it ignore us."

"And Herr Sauermann isn't letting that happen?"

"No. Nor will he allow plan the second—me taking up a respectable position at a university. Teaching young people—that wouldn't be wrong, wouldn't weigh on my conscience."

"So what will you do?" Karl's words came out with a puff of cold, opaque breath.

"I'll take my family and leave."

"Where will we go?"

"I have friends. I met Jean-Yves Poncet when I worked in Paris, back when Ingrid was a baby. He's with the Deuxième Bureau. And the Defense Attaché at the British Consulate in Zurich is an acquaintance. If we get to either of them, I have useful information, and I expect they will help me in exchange."

A chill not related to the weather crept into Karl's chest. "That sounds . . . dangerous. And treasonous."

Papa rested the trunk on a fallen tree. "Are you with me, Karl?"

Karl nodded. It might be dangerous, and it might be treasonous, but he trusted his father to do the right thing. "Yes, Papa."

Papa walked a few steps forward, then bent and hefted what looked like a trap door. Karl rushed to help him, first with a wooden door, then with a pair of metal ones.

"Is this the root cellar?"

Papa nodded and handed Karl a flashlight. Karl switched it on and pointed the beam down narrow wooden stairs. "I'll go first," Papa said. "Watch the third step. It wiggles."

They hauled the jewelry down and placed it on the floor. A metal door roughly Karl's height dominated the far wall. A keyhole and a padlock protected whatever was inside. Papa took a key from his pocket and pressed it into the keyhole, then twisted the brass tumblers of the padlock into a series of five letters. He removed the padlock and pulled open the door to reveal a small room. Karl turned the flashlight on the contents: trunks of various sizes and three large wooden crates. "You've been planning this for a while."

"Yes. I didn't want to involve you if I didn't have to. It's a burden, what I've told you. But Sauermann's visit means we're out of time. We leave tomorrow."

That was sooner than Karl had expected. "Will we ever come back?"

"I certainly hope so. And if you and I and both your sisters return to reclaim all we've left behind, we'll have the greatest treasure of all."

The greatest treasure of all. Karl scanned the trunks and crates, then focused on his father.

Papa patted a wooden crate. "I'd like to add a few more paintings to the collection. Will you help?"

"Yes. Is that where Anna's favorite painting went?" Karl pointed to the crate.

Papa smiled. "All the most valuable, including Anna's favorite. I think it will snow before morning, so let's get a few more, and then the fresh snow will cover our footprints. I think everything will be safe here, for years, if needed."

They stowed the trunk of jewelry, locked the metal door, and left the cellar, closing it behind them.

"There's something else, Karl."

"Yes?"

"Plan the fourth. If for any reason I can't go with you, I need you to keep your sisters safe. And I need you to take the papers to my contact in Paris or Zurich. I hope it won't come to that."

Karl nodded, accepting the new weight of responsibility that pressed on his shoulders. "But you always have another plan."

"Not always." Papa's voice grew wistful. "I never planned on meeting your mother. It was the best thing that ever happened to me, and it was an accident. Nor did I plan to bury her. Life is full of surprises and hardships, Karl. Plan for what you can, and do your best to get back up when you're knocked over by something unexpected."

About the Author

Born and raised in Southern California, Paige Edwards is an award-winning author who thinks the color turquoise is almost as great, but not quite, as See's Candy. A BYU–I alumna, she went back to school and graduated summa cum laude from NOVA with a degree in interior design. Her husband's job transferred their family to the mid-Atlantic states where they have lived ever since. When she needs a break from writing, you can find her shooing deer out of her garden, biking battlefields, or kayaking on the lake.

You can find and follow Paige at:

Bookbub: Author Paige Edwards
Website: authorpaigeedwards.com
Goodreads: Paige_Edwards
Facebook: facebook.com/authorpaigeedwards
Instagram: Instagram.com/authorpaigeedwards
Linkedin: paige-edwards